Praise for BROCK'S AGENT

"BRAVO! In the great tradition of master storytellers
Bernard Cornwell and C.S. Forester, Taylor takes you
to another world until you don't want to leave! One
of the most thrilling stories I've read in years!"

— Lory Kaufman, author of *The Lens and the Looker*

"THE WAR OF 1812 is wonderfully represented
and brought to life in this fast paced exciting story that
I could not put down until it raced to its conclusion."

— Tom Fournier, Captain and Officer Commanding
41st Regiment of Foot MLHG

"In BROCK'S AGENT, Tom Taylor writes with
a passion, power and pace that will leave you breathless
and thirsty for more. A born storyteller, Taylor weaves
a gripping yarn with the very strands of own history."

— Terry Fallis, winner of Canada Reads
and the Stephen Leacock Award for his book
The Best Laid Plans, and author of *The High Road*

Tom Taylor is a Canadian writer who graduated from York University with a B.A. majoring in history. He once served in the militia with the Toronto 7th Artillery. He resides in the Greater Toronto Area.

BROCK'S
AGENT

BROCK'S AGENT

TOM TAYLOR

Enjoy the story!

Tom Taylor

Hancock and Dean

Hancock and Dean
6 – 80 Citizen Court
Markham, Ontario
Canada L6G 1A7

Published by Hancock and Dean

A Division of GIFTFORCE INC.

Brock's Agent is distributed by Auralim Gift. For information about
special discounts for wholesale purchases, call 1-800-265-9898.

Cover and text designed by Tania Craan
Cover photography of soldiers by Elizabeth Woodley-Hall

Manufactured in Canada

ISBN: 978-0-9868961-0-1

3rd Printing in 2013

For Mum and Dad
who took me to the library all those years ago

ACKNOWLEDGMENTS

Every novel takes a team of interested people to bring it to fruition so I would like to thank the members of the *Brock's Agent* team: Geri Das Gupta, who believed from the beginning I could write this thing; my family, who sacrificed their time to allow me to write; Natalie Taylor, who helped me with this damn computer; Fred Ford and the Pickering Writers Circle; the Humber School for Writers; my great humanities teacher, Brayton Polka; Rick Olsen; John Stewart; Frances and Bill Hanna; Tom Fournier; David Brunelle; Terry Fallis; Tania Craan; Elizabeth Woodley-Hall; Barbara Kyle; Dr. J.J. Rosenberg; Ray Argyle; Bob Coffey; the gang at Open Mic in Newmarket; Bernard Cornwell for showing the way; and my patient editors, Peter Lavery and Heather Sangster. Lastly, thank you to two special writers who nudged me to be better at my writing craft, Lory Kaufman and Sally Moore. Please accept a heartfelt thanks to all of you, without whom it would not have been.

One last mention: Certainly, there would be no novel, and perhaps no Canada, without the extraordinary efforts of both Tecumseh and Sir Isaac Brock. To them, we will forever owe our deepest gratitude.

BROCK'S
AGENT

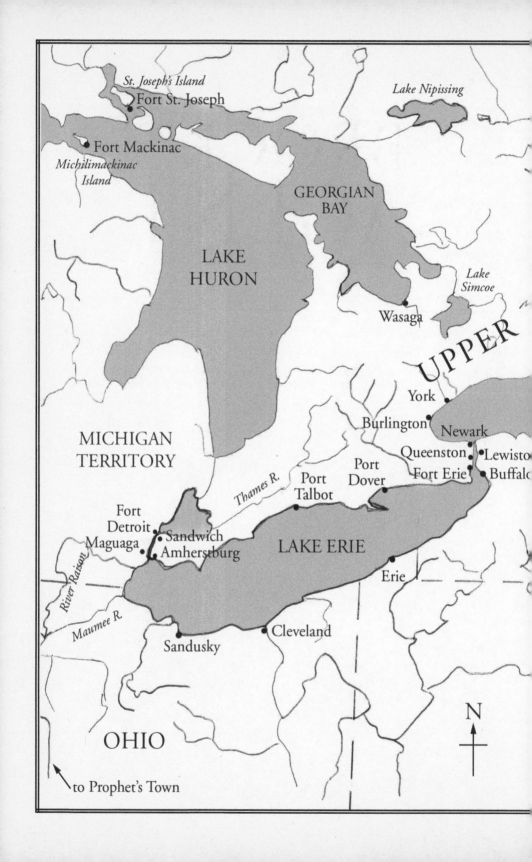

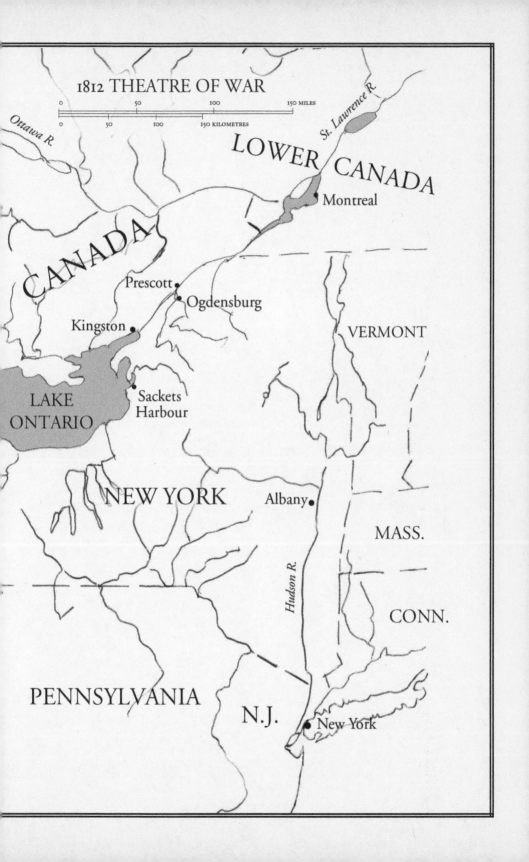

1

. . . . . .

UPPER CANADA

March 1811

Jonathan Westlake stood on the snow-covered path and wondered. It shouldn't have come to this. He stared back at his school door. On the other side of it, his schoolmates continued their lesson, minus the "troublemaker." That's what Reverend Strachan had called him before ushering him out by the collar.

It didn't matter that Westlake was in the right: three-time offenders got expelled, no exceptions. Just one punch to blacken the eye of the class bully and Westlake was going home, leaving the town of Cornwall and his friends forever, never to graduate, at least not from this school. *And so close to the finish line.*

As he inhaled the sharp morning air to calm himself, he smelled smoke from the schoolhouse fire, which reminded him of home, of his father, and the hell to come after this kind of news. And he'd have to watch the disappointment and sadness in his mother's face. She held such faith in him.

"This is going to be awful," he said out loud to no one. He'd have to think of the right words to explain to her what had happened and why.

The sky had clouded over gray and a light snow began to fall. Westlake rubbed his palms over both ears and tugged down the rim of the knitted hat that covered his blond hair. He stamped his feet to keep them warm, then in anger kicked hard against the snow on the partly shoveled path. Some broken rocks appeared. He glanced back at the school door again, twenty-five paces away, and picked up a handful of stones. An inner voice told him not to do it. He hesitated yet still leaned back to throw, but instead of the door, he aimed for a tree beside the schoolhouse. The stone struck its target.

He clenched his other fist in victory: "Dead center." He laughed as an idea came to him, something to make amends for the bad news. The family fur-trading business needed a special type of help from someone able to write. A proposition to his father now formed in his mind, one that also offered independence and perhaps adventure. He could work out the details on his long ride home to York.

The next stone, bigger than the first, smacked the same spot but ricocheted aside to hammer the school's external wall. Seconds later the door burst open. In his black garb, Reverend Strachan stood there with legs planted well apart, gripping a cane ready for battle. That chiseled face, large and round with sunken cheeks, was set hard to project his authority. The gusting wind rippled the hem of his gown.

"God doesn't suffer troublemakers, laddie," the clergyman announced in his harsh Scottish accent. "Heaving rocks at my school will only make matters worse for you in the eyes of the Lord."

"I was just aiming at the tree, sir." Westlake pointed. "If I wanted to hit that door, it would be too easy." He tossed a stone in the air, caught it again, and grinned.

Strachan glanced back at the open door where he stood and frowned. A few students had gathered just inside and Westlake's friend, Danny Lapointe, waved to him from behind the teacher's back. Strachan shut the door.

"Was that a threat, young man?" Twice, he slapped the cane against his palm and one black boot began tapping. "You're finished here, so go home. Trouble follows some characters around all their lives, and you're one of those characters."

Strachan had said much worse on other occasions to different students. Anyone deemed the least bit out of order—his order—was labeled "God's enemy" or "Satan's imp." What such intimidation had to do with teaching, Westlake couldn't understand. In the contemptuous curve of Strachan's lip, there was a nastiness that reminded Westlake of another reason he had come to hate this school. Reverend Strachan was a prick.

Westlake reared back to throw his missile and yelled, "Your problem is that you have no sense of humor." The snow blew harder and he felt some flakes melting on his cheek.

"Don't you dare!" Strachan shook the cane in the air, but he didn't budge from the doorway, as if the fate of the world depended on how rigid he stood.

Westlake tested the smooth stone between his fingers, his arm poised behind his head. They couldn't do any worse than expel him, and Strachan was right: there was no reason to linger. Besides, he had that proposal to offer his father. He would never enter the Cornwall school again, and in this moment he realized that was fine with him.

Westlake let the stone fly. It bounced off the tree and shot right between Strachan's boots.

"Just like I told you," he shouted. "Dead center." Then, laughing quietly to himself, Jonathan Westlake took one last look, through the falling snow, at the black figure of Reverend Strachan and his school-house. He gave a broad smile, saluted goodbye, and turned his back. He was free.

2

· · · · · ·

TIPPECANOE

THE FIRST TIME young Paxinos tried burning down a settler's log cabin, the beams wouldn't catch flame. The settlers had by then vanished, leaving their wooden bed frames bare and even the windows stripped of their curtains. Paxinos scanned the interior of the cabin, happy the family had gone but wishing they had left something easier to burn.

In one corner of the room, his friend Kawika helped him rebuild the flagging embers by adding dead grass and small sticks, soon throwing on entire branches. As the fire hissed to life and filled the cabin with smoke, Paxinos coughed and rubbed his eyes. He finally broke apart a crude table and threw its narrow legs into the flames before running out the door, his eyes watering but with a face lit up in a wide grin. After the fire stretched its way through the roof, black smoke billowed up against a blue morning sky. In their triumph, Paxinos and Kawika locked arms and sang.

Later that same year, in early September 1811, across an elbow bend in a narrow stream, Paxinos crept toward another cabin. It sat twenty paces from the water, and to the rear of it stood a gray board outhouse. The place appeared deserted. This time he had brought fire with him: burning embers cradled in a small hollowed-out log.

Accompanied by six other Shawnee warriors, Paxinos and Kawika circled the house for signs of movement. The front door was ajar, leading Paxinos to expect that at any moment the settlers might lunge out with muskets blasting. His mouth was so dry he could barely swallow as he stopped, then crouched, and waited. The cabin and the acres of cornfields around it were still.

Paxinos and his circle of painted warriors closed on the cabin like a noose tightening around a neck. Since no smoke swirled from the chimney to indicate a breakfast fire, he hoped the place was abandoned. A warrior peered through the only window but reported nothing.

Musket in hand, Kawika was first through the door. He poked his head in quickly, then jumped back, but there was no welcoming blast so he stepped farther inside, waving on Paxinos to follow quickly. Kawika howled a cry of victory and smashed out the window with the butt of his musket.

As Paxinos entered the cabin, he realized the occupants had disappeared in a hurry because in their race to escape, they had abandoned the gray blankets on an unmade bed. This house would be easier to burn. He heard a warrior hollering and ran back to the door in time to see a skinny white man bolt from the outhouse, pulling up a loose suspender. The man stumbled and ran on again, but by now a warrior was tackling him from behind. Paxinos could hear the man whimpering in terror.

The warriors gathered around the kneeling captive, shouting at him to be silent, but the frightened man couldn't stay calm. "Mercy, please. Oh God, have mercy," he cried, rhythmically rocking back and forth, his hands praying in front of him. A warrior threatened him with a club, but the prisoner only wailed louder.

Paxinos cupped his hands to his mouth and yelled in English from the doorway, "Be quiet, white man. You make them angry by showing your weakness. They must put an end to your shame."

"Please, I'm sorry, please," the thin man pleaded.

Kawika ran out from the cabin and joined the shouting circle, calling him a coward and a thief for stealing Shawnee land. The white man stumbled to his feet, turned to his left, then lurched right, falling to his knees. Tears trickled from great bulging eyes over his scrawny cheeks.

Paxinos shook his head; there was no hope for this foolish white man who couldn't control his emotions. Although the prisoner knelt in surrender, the warriors would not continue to endure his whining. "You take our land," Kawika yelled, "so our people starve."

The thin man stood suddenly and drew out a knife, whereupon Kawika charged at him with his tomahawk raised. Paxinos winced. The captive threw his hands in the air, the knife useless, and cried, "No!" Kawika darted behind him and slashed the tomahawk down through the man's neck, severing the back of his head from the spine. The head lolled forward, arterial blood arcing out of the hideous gash in his neck. He was dead by the time his limp body crumpled to the ground. In the silence that followed, Paxinos sighed, hung his head, and looked away.

One hundred yards away, a white man and a boy lay hidden among the cedars at the forest edge, their muskets pointed at their farmhouse.

"Oh, Christ. No, for God's sake." The man suppressed a moan, his forehead dropping to the ground as he drove his fist into the grass. "That was plain murder, your Uncle Victor wasn't given a chance. I told him he didn't have time, but he wouldn't listen." He tried to quiet his whimpering son with a gentle pat on the shoulders.

"If we fired together, we'd kill at least one of them," the boy suggested, his eyes full of tears.

"And then what? Your mother and sister are still running not a mile down that path. They'd only catch and kill us all." He spit. "Those are goddamn British muskets they're carrying. Look how they paint themselves, the savages."

The warriors were dressed only in breechcloth with black and red streaks covering their faces and bare chests; one man's head was completely shaved and painted blood-red. Two of them appeared in the cabin's doorway, peering south, as if they knew they had observers.

"Uncle Victor always said this was Shawnee land." With the back of his hand, the boy wiped his damp cheeks while his father watched the Indians in the doorway, remembering their faces.

"We've got to get out of here, now. Back away slowly. I can't watch the place burn." Never taking his eyes off the Indians in the doorway, the man edged backward on his stomach after tugging at the boy's collar. He stood up and turned round only when he knew for sure they were well out of sight. "I'm not building another house, not without the army cleaning out these bastards first. Let's go, quick. They could still come this way." He started to run, and his son ran along beside him.

"But is it Indian land?" the son persisted.

"Governor Harrison will decide. The Indians say it's their land, but I say it's mine. We need the army to settle it."

A glance over his shoulder and the man saw yellow flames already licking out through the shattered window. "Your mother forgot the goddamn blankets."

Their campfire slumped and a birch log rolled to one side. It could have escaped the flames, but the warrior kicked it back into the center of the red coals. The bark flamed and filled the air with the smell of burning birch.

"My brother cannot make the sun disappear, so what did you see?" the warrior asked. "Explain it to me."

The young man, Paxinos, listened. There were just the two of them at the fire, under the night sky. Paxinos wanted to believe in the legend. He had witnessed it, yet here in front of him stood this great warrior chief who claimed that the story of the Prophet's dark sun was false. But if Paxinos could not believe in the Prophet, then all his beliefs would have to be questioned. White smoke curled up from the fire, changed direction, and blew toward him. Paxinos jerked his head away and pushed out both his hands to block its path.

"The Prophet stretched out his arm to the sun and shouted, 'Behold, the earth grows dark.'" Paxinos stood and pointed upward with a straight right arm. Thick nighttime clouds drifted across the sky, blocking out the sweep of stars. With the smell of fresh air, an October breeze gusted down Tippecanoe River and over the breastworks protecting the scattered wigwams of the Shawnee village.

"All the world went cold as a black ball rolled across the sun—and it stayed dark. The great chiefs crouched down, so the Prophet said, 'Do not be afraid.' He looked up at the sky, raised both his hands: 'Great Spirit, bring light back to the world.' The Great Spirit heard him, and the light slowly returned to warm the earth. I saw this with my own eyes." Paxinos raised his eyebrows with the excitement of his

7

tale and sat down again, satisfied that he had proved the Prophet held great power.

Close to the fire, the warrior leaned back on his elbows and glanced up as the last few stars visible in the eastern night sky disappeared behind drifting black clouds. Paxinos watched the warrior, who was perhaps thinking how to accept defeat and admit that the legend was true. He thought back to the precise moment the sun went black.

Tenskwatawa, known as the Prophet, had been challenged by Governor William Harrison of Indiana Territory to perform a miracle as proof he commanded a power greater than other men. If he was truly a prophet, then he could perform miracles, Harrison taunted. Now, the miracles were complete and it was reported that, on hearing the news, Governor Harrison's entire head turned different shades of red.

The warrior chief jabbed a branch into the glowing coals. He stared into the fire and then pulled out his burning staff that now lit up the young Shawnee face of Paxinos. His round brown eyes showed no sign of concern at the stresses he would soon face. If this young man were to become a chief, or a leader, the warrior knew that Paxinos would need to distinguish between a description of the world and an explanation of it. One day soon, Paxinos would have to think for himself.

"We need the tribes to believe in my brother so they will follow the Shawnee and refuse the ways of other chiefs who would give away their land for nothing. This belief in the Prophet is in our interest," the warrior declared. "Many tribes are now coming to the Shawnee because they believe in his power. Do you understand why we need this miracle?" After a pause, giving Paxinos time to reflect on what he had just heard, the warrior continued, "But you have given me only a description of the legend. I asked you to explain it."

Paxinos gazed at him with an expressionless face, so the warrior decided to show him the difference between description and explanation. He stood up as a first light sprinkle of rain struck his cheek, then swept out his arm toward the blackened sky and shouted, "Rain!" A few more drops fell, and Paxinos held out his palms also. "Rain!" the warrior repeated. He then waited, and as the drops fell heavier he shouted again, only in a deeper voice, "Cover the earth with rain!" The rain descended and he asked Paxinos, "How did it come to rain?" He crossed both fists over his chest. "Did I make it rain or did the clouds make it rain?" Then he stretched both his arms skyward, as the Prophet had done when the sun darkened.

The young man laughed. "You waited until the rain clouds came, then shouted and pointed at the sky. You cannot fool me with such a simple trick." Paxinos uncrossed his legs and stood up again as raindrops caused the fire's red coals to hiss. The rain fell even harder and the two men hurried toward their wigwam. The warrior peered around from the under entrance to watch other villagers scattering for cover.

"Do you understand how my brother made the sun go away? Your description was no explanation. Can you *explain* it to me?"

"There was no magic," Paxinos replied. "The Prophet figured out exactly the right time to shout up at the sky, when he already knew the sun would soon go dark. Am I right—is that what he did?"

The warrior nodded. "You must learn to see truth and not believe in magic or miracles. Have faith in yourself or your friends, or even in your enemies, but do not believe in tricks or those who claim to perform them." The warrior glanced back at the fire as the rain continued its assault on the coals. "Do not be satisfied with simple descriptions of the world, or those who offer them. Instead, seek out the explanations. No one can make the sun vanish and, my good friend, no one can make it rain." He laughed loudly and slapped the young man on the back.

Paxinos dipped his head to enter through the low door of a small hut that kept out most of the weather. Outside, a sudden wind hammered the wigwam, flapping the roof of birch-bark shingles, and he glanced up at the sound of banging, his eyes wide. The Shawnee camp was in for a storm.

"I have told my brother that he must not attack the Long Knives while I am away," the warrior said. "Never can he do this without me, and I am telling you the same. Soon I travel south to persuade the other tribes to join us in stopping the white man from taking Indian land."

He spoke with a forceful urgency that Paxinos had never seen in other men. It was always as if he was almost out of time. This warrior saw deeper into the world than did other chiefs, and all men agreed that he had a commanding presence: some unique attraction that Paxinos could not quite describe or understand. He could even read and understand English books. Paxinos remembered listening as he read "to be or not to be" and then explained it to his English teacher, a white woman who once loved him.

"If the warriors force my brother to fight, then you must save the little ones when the enemy comes against our village. This is a promise you must keep for me." The temperature was dropping, and as the warrior lay down, he snatched a bearskin to cover himself and then propped up his head on one elbow. Physically, he was a big man, almost six feet tall, with a striking oval face, clear eyes, and a copper complexion.

The rain continued tapping steadily on the wigwam's roof. "But why would the other tribes believe what you have to say?" Paxinos asked him. "Why will they follow you?"

"They will know I have journeyed far so that we may stand together, and they already know my brother as the one who can darken the earth."

But Paxinos understood differently. The tribes knew of this chief as a fierce warrior, and it would be enough for him to mention his name, "Tecumseh."

They marched in two parallel columns but far apart, close to a thousand men in four battalions, two battalions in each column, all kicking up their separate trails of mud. In their blue jackets, the U.S. 4th Infantry hastened at the front of each column, followed by the dawdling militiamen of Kentucky and Indiana dressed in their gray and brown homespun. Scouts galloped ahead to give ample warning should they spot a force of Indians. Intermittently, the ground rumbled under three companies of mounted Indiana riflemen patrolling one hundred and fifty yards out on either side of these marching columns.

When the front of his column wavered, Sergeant Frank Harris winced, knowing he was in for bother. Lieutenant Daniel Jackson spurred on his horse, only to haul up the animal until it dance-stepped beside the mud-stained sergeant.

"Sergeant Harris, bring these men back into line. You have the privilege of leading the entire battalion. For God's sake, do it right and show some pride." Jackson had spent hours drilling these same men in basic maneuvers, so Harris knew there would be trouble if he let them flounder now.

"You took the words right out of my mouth, sir. I was just telling the boys here how lucky we's is to be the first to get to kill Injuns when they attack. Straighten out your line, lads. Keep the lieutenant happy," Harris shouted. "That's better already. Privates Haggard and Mack, march to your left."

Harris had been given his orders from the outset of the march. If they were attacked from one side or the other, one column was to turn and close with the side under attack, so as to support their fire. Attacked from both sides at the same time, each column was to turn outward and battle back to back with the other column as they retreated together. The most difficult drill came if they faced a frontal attack, and then it could be performed only on open ground. The columns were to pivot at their centers so that the regulars of the 4th Infantry would form a single solid line at the front. The militia would do the same and form a similar line behind.

After Harris had caught sight of Indians among the trees earlier that day, each man kept a keen lookout. For the most part, their path gave way to bare dirt or short grass on either side, so it was easy to keep watch, but every few hundred paces the path narrowed amid bulrushes growing past shoulder height. When the waving reeds closed in thick on the path ahead, Harris was unnerved to find himself prevented from seeing anything at a distance. Though he could see his own breath, he became aware of sweat trickling down over his thumping heartbeat.

Luke Haggard tugged hard at Malcolm Mack's arm, forcing him to the left, and gradually the blue column straightened, the men marching again in good order.

"See for yourself, sir, as good a bunch of soldiers as exists anywhere on God's green earth," Harris replied once the column was straight again. In truth, he cared less about maintaining straight lines than about angering his lieutenant.

"Do you understand why we must keep the columns straight, Harris?" Jackson again pulled his horse to the sergeant's side.

Despite his aching feet, Harris managed a smile while he thought about his answer. On a narrow path, as they marched up a small incline, he skidded in the mud but caught himself before he fell and then straightened up to give his reply, "'Course I do. 'Cause you said so, that's why, sir." Harris felt proud of himself and stood to a sloppy form of attention while leaning slightly to the left, trying to salute without fumbling his musket. Except for young Ensign Poole—whom he had managed to convince that old Sergeant Harris knew more about soldiering than anyone else on earth—Harris had never known of any good coming out of too much talk with a probing officer. He was determined not to let this officer cause him any grief.

"We can only maneuver out of straight columns," Jackson barked. "How could we pivot our columns if there is no column? We would just have a bunch of stragglers wandering all over the place, getting scalped by the Indians."

Jackson held up his finger like a schoolteacher giving a lesson. "Stay in column, though, and it will save your life." Before Harris could respond, Jackson spurred his horse and wheeled away.

Harris had survived the interrogation, but he gritted his six remaining teeth, fuming inside. He watched Jackson gallop away, with a light-blue knitted scarf bouncing off his back. To make up for the distance lost while prattling with Jackson, Harris now had to march at double time, his broad shoulders and barrel chest heaving until he fell in again beside his men.

"I'll cuff you two hard and piss on your boots if I've any more fuss with him. Maybe I'll even take a round with that new pretty wife of yours." Harris spit the last words out close to Mack's unshaven face. The man did not look him in the eyes, for it was safer to stare down at his worn boots as they marched along. "Did you get those brainless militiamen to ditch the bloody shovels and axes like I asked you to?" Harris was still panting.

"They were happy to, Sergeant," Mack replied with a grin.

"At least you did something right then. We've been digging trenches every night for nothing, and I ain't seen one Injun drop dead just 'cause we dug a trench." Harris cleared his throat and spit. "We're all sick of bloody digging."

Lieutenant Jackson had galloped off to where a group of officers with field glasses were surveying an Indian camp at the base of a ridge. At seven hundred yards' distance, precise details were difficult to see. A gust of wind forced one officer to turn his head away from the swirling leaves. Lieutenant Colonel James Miller of the U.S. 4th Infantry beckoned Jackson over and offered him the field glass. "You've always had good eyes, Jackson, so tell me what you can see."

Jackson studied the camp, which was a village of wigwams placed haphazardly in a clearing. Hundreds of men and women scurried about, scooping up children who cried under the tight grip of their elders' arms. Jackson closed the glass with a snap and handed it back to Miller.

"They certainly know we're here. The ground sloping up to that village appears to be some kind of marsh, sir. There's also a solid breastwork of logs surrounding the village, at least on this side." Without the glass, Jackson squinted. "Fires are still burning, but it appears they're getting ready to leave … or perhaps attack us, hard to tell for certain."

A large man wearing a beaver fur hat, topped by a waving ostrich feather, wheeled his tall gray mare out of the pack of officers who were all watching through glasses of their own. After his horse had taken a few steps forward, the man peered down at Jackson with a frown on a face so gaunt he looked ill.

Governor William Harrison didn't take kindly to negative messengers. "Nonsense, man, you're looking at Prophet's Town, and those Indians are scared to death. Tecumseh is away inciting riot elsewhere so they know they have to vacate that village or get wiped out." Harrison urged his mare forward and leaned over to speak into Miller's ear. He then turned and shouted, "Major Daviess, you're with me." Clad in a white blanket coat, another large man pulled on the reins of his horse and with a slight spur was off at a gallop. Although Harrison looked thin and breakable to Jackson, this other ruddy-faced individual appeared to be made of iron. The enormous white plumes in his hat floated on the breeze as he galloped alongside Harrison.

Miller's horse stepped up beside Jackson's. "Don't worry, Daniel. He's a little sensitive these days. I've always admired you for telling me the truth, and not just what I wanted to hear."

Lieutenant Jackson had served in the regular army his entire adult life and he judged Miller a fair man, but how much of the truth did Miller want to hear? Jackson considered how far he should push. For these few moments they were alone, he decided to speak his mind. "That village is obviously on Indian land, and I should add, sir, so are we. Are we trying to provoke a conflict?"

Jackson took off his brown leather glove and with his bare hand patted the smooth neck of his horse, then looked Miller in the eyes for an answer. It was November 6, 1811, and Prophet's Town, Indiana, was in frightened chaos.

"Our job is to protect white settlers from getting killed by the Indians living in that village." Miller gestured. "If we have to fight them to achieve that, so be it." There was a hard edge to his voice, his breath emerging in white puffs.

"But those settlers are trespassing on Indian land, sir, as are we," Jackson pressed.

Miller made no comment, preferring to stare up at some rolling gray clouds. "Did you notice anything unusual in the village?"

"The young white man playing with the child," Jackson replied. "Difficult to speculate on what he's up to."

"No matter, for our purposes. Now, these are your orders." Miller then explained how Harrison wanted them to halt near Prophet's Town. Scouts had earlier reported a flat clearing just beyond the village, and Jackson was to camp his men there.

At least it was above the marsh, Jackson reflected, beyond the thick smell of swamp vapor that made his clothes sodden. But from Miller he had received no answer to his question about provoking the Indians.

Lieutenant Jackson galloped back to the front of the column just as it started to rain. "Ensign Poole, march the men a thousand yards farther to a ten-acre clearing just northwest of Prophet's Town. We camp there for the night. That Indian village will still be within a mile's jog so keep your wits about you tonight."

Ensign John Poole, recently promoted, stood sharply to attention and snapped an impressive salute. Jackson returned it from the saddle. Like everyone, including young Poole, he was tired and cold, in need of a good night's sleep, and wishing he could stay dry. Only another thousand yards would do fine for him.

Jackson jerked the reins, turning his horse to face his men. "Everyone sleeps with muskets loaded." He tapped Poole on the shoulder. "In this bloody drizzle, make sure your men keep their muskets dry and ready to fire. Wrap rags around the locks if you have to, but be ready."

"Sir." Poole saluted again as murmurs passed through the ranks about their new camp ahead.

Haggard whispered to Mack, "At least we won't be digging bloody trenches again tonight." They both laughed.

Paxinos watched the one-eyed man as he listened to the chiefs of the other tribes. Tenskwatawa—the name meaning "the open door" in Shawnee—was the famous Prophet, brother of Tecumseh. Assembled around the grand fire, all dressed in feathered head garb, this nighttime council of chiefs would follow the Prophet anywhere. The Prophet pointed to a Shawnee chief called White Horse to speak.

"Tecumseh has ordered that we must not fight while he is away. This is a command, not a request. The army of white men is more than one thousand and we are five hundred. We will die if we force battle on them. We must do as we have been commanded."

The Potawatomi chief stood up next, a tomahawk in one hand, punching the air with the other fist. "But Tecumseh is not here, and we must defend ourselves. My scouts have counted more than one thousand Long Knives marching against our land. They have not come for a visit between friends but to kill us and destroy our village. Therefore, we must attack tonight." The chief glared at others around the campfire as they bobbed their heads in agreement.

A burnt branch collapsed at the base of the fire, sending up a blaze of vanishing red sparks. Paxinos saw the Prophet's face grow concerned. There was tension in the air as he pointed to yet another man.

The chief of the Winnebago was a small man with a soft voice who wore buckskin breeches and an oversized deerskin poncho to keep the cold off his thin frame. Each chief in the circle leaned forward, straining to hear. "Despite Tecumseh's command, he would not have us die for nothing in our beds. Can we just stand aside and let them destroy our village? Even if we run, they may pursue us and we will still have to fight. They have come here to kill, so we must attack first to show them how we will fight to protect our land."

Paxinos sat up straighter from the damp ground. Except for Chief White Horse, each warrior in turn made an argument to attack that same night. The enthusiasm for battle was so strong, even the Prophet had to accept the consensus of the council. Since Paxinos had received Tecumseh's direct order, he could take no part in any battle. After the Prophet announced that they would attack that night, but be gone the next day, Paxinos jumped to his feet, thinking of his task ahead. Along with his white friend, he would arrange a safe journey for all the children.

Malcolm Mack was sure he'd heard something, yet in this darkness he could barely see the steel bayonet at the end of his musket. The rain maintained a steady drizzle, and he wiped his forehead with his shirtsleeve. Noises, again, and he turned his head to listen. Every few minutes he thought he heard footsteps, but this time he raised the charged musket, his nervous finger on the trigger, and held his breath, waiting to sight a target.

"Christ, Luke, you scared the hell out of me. I almost shot you!"

Private Luke Haggard of the U.S. 4th Infantry stumbled out of the bushes and put a shaking hand on Mack's shoulder. Mack shivered as he felt a cold dribble trickling down his neck.

"I think I saw something moving through the bushes, but I can't be sure of a bloody thing in this darkness. What d'you reckon the time is?" Mack whispered.

"Must be four. First light won't be for a while yet."

Perhaps the wind tossed branches made the noise. Mack squinted, exhaled slowly, and watched the frost from his breath dissipate amid the light rain. The wind in his ears made it hard to distinguish sounds, and for another moment he stared questioningly at Haggard, listening hard.

"If the damn Injuns are out there, then why haven't the other pickets fired yet?" Haggard asked.

Before sundown, Mack had counted at least a dozen pickets scattered around him, and while a couple may have dozed off, surely one of them would have spotted any Indians on the move.

"Just the leaves, I reckon. Sergeant Harris will kill us if we set off a false alarm. You know how the bastard likes his sleep … and my new wife. What was that?" Mack interrupted himself. A shape flitted by, only a few feet away. He studied the surrounding dark, praying for nothing to be there. But instead he glimpsed a vague shape, then something more definite: the silhouette of a man's head, with the hair plastered straight up on end. It could only be an Indian, and when it disappeared, Mack sat motionless, hoping to remain unseen. He saw another shape and another, and again heard the rustle of leaves. Oh God, his stomach clenched, they were all around him.

"Haggard, did you see it?" he hissed.

The sound of an arrow whizzed passed before it slapped the tree he was crouching beside.

"I'm not waiting to see anything. Let's get the hell out of here," Haggard gasped.

Half a step taken too late: an arrow pierced Mack's left shoulder and in agony he cried out as Haggard turned and fired. So close to Mack's left ear, the musket sounded more like a cannon. His foot skidded and he fell to the ground, his ears ringing and his hands covered in slippery wet leaves. A dozen pickets then fired, shots exploding in sparks and flame. Their musket blasts lit up the forest, illuminating painted demons running through flashes of light.

The sounds of hell shrieked and hooted all around him. Where the arrow stuck in his shoulder, the pain now seared him unbearably, and Mack began to faint. He groaned, "Oh Christ," and felt blood oozing down his chest, wondering briefly if he would live to see his newly wed wife again. With one hand resting against a tree, he staggered to stand upright.

Two white eyes appeared out of the darkness; too late Mack saw the axe. He clutched his throat, where the blade sliced through, and he fell to his knees, pain still burning in his shoulder and now his neck too. Through his fingers gushed his own warm blood. He rocked backward, then slumped forward, face down. Malcolm Mack was dead.

Ensign Poole bolted upright at the sound of the first shot. He peered through a gap in his tent door to see that the soldiers who slept around the campfires were sitting up. More muskets exploded near his tent, lighting up human shadows on its sides. As he glanced out through the door again, the first soldier standing up tumbled backward, shot as he rose from beside the fire. Poole struggled to jam a foot into his boot, seeing a second man shot as he also tried to stand. More shots cracked and a soldier wailed while another fell, clubbed by a musket butt. A screaming red-painted Indian was now inside the camp perimeter. Then two more of them lunged out of the darkness, firing point-blank at a fourth soldier who had barely got to his feet.

His heart pounding, Poole realized how the fire was silhouetting all who stood close to the flames. He needed to warn everyone to stay down for it would be the same throughout the camp. His hand thrashed about under his cot until he found the second boot and rammed in his foot. Poole grabbed his loaded musket, but even as he charged out of his tent, three Indians, with chests and faces painted white, came running for him.

"My God, they're everywhere."

The Indians fired together, and Poole's chest took the full blast, lifting him off his feet and throwing him back inside. He didn't even have time to fire the musket but collapsed still holding it by his side. Above him he caught the glint of a knife as a smiling white-striped face came into view. Poole felt blood seep from the side of his mouth and knew he was about to be scalped.

"Not yet," he whispered. He jerked the musket up and fired just as his life left him. The bullet penetrated one eye and erupted out the back of the Indian's skull. The attacker fell forward, on top of Poole. Face to face, they died.

"Sergeant Harris, where's Ensign Poole?" Lieutenant Jackson shouted.

"Dead, sir. I saw him get blasted back into his tent. Bastards have a lot of muskets. They've pulled back to reload."

"They broke through our northern perimeter easy enough, and there's hundreds of them. Stay away from the light of those bloody fires and you'll live longer." Jackson gestured his men away from the flames. "Those damn muskets they have are British, I'll stake my life on it." He dismounted and unsheathed his sword.

"We's ready for their return, sir. Ain't we, lads?" Harris declared, putting the best face on their predicament.

"No, we are not—no trenches dug, no breastworks, nothing. Pathetic, if you ask me. Make three lines of twenty, well behind this fire. Now, move yourselves!" Jackson ordered. "All these men died needlessly," he added bitterly.

Haggard winced as he shuffled into line with the others, remembering the discarded shovels and axes. *Poor Malcolm.*

"Sergeant Harris, straighten out the lines," Jackson hollered.

He heard scattered musket fire from the south end of the camp. The Indians were obviously attacking at both ends, and Jackson only hoped the south would fair better.

"The front rank will kneel and fire only on my command. The second rank will fire over the heads of the first rank, and then kneel. The third rank will fire on command, as the other two ranks reload." Jackson had positioned his three ranks safely in the shadows, twenty-five yards behind the blazing fire. "Remember, you fire only on my command, just like we practice in those drills you love. Make ready, here they come."

The Indians charged toward the fire, and this time it was they who were lit by the flames. They stopped, fired, then resumed their charge. The man standing beside Jackson slumped to the ground without a sound. Jackson sheathed his sword, picked up the man's musket, and took the dead soldier's place in the line. The musket slid within his sweaty palms, and his heart was beating so hard it felt like it would burst through his chest.

"Front rank, present arms!" The soldiers brought their muskets to shoulder level, pointing at the Indians, who, packed together, were now clear targets.

"Fire!" The muskets crashed out in a solid line of sparks and smoke. Through ringing eardrums, Jackson couldn't hear himself shouting his commands. The first volley dropped a half-dozen natives, yet it seemed to have no effect on their charge.

"Second rank, present, fire! … Third rank, present, fire! … All ranks, make ready and present."

For a few seconds the gun smoke blinded everyone so Jackson could not see more than a couple of feet in front of him. When it cleared, there were bodies scattered on the ground near the campfire. The remaining Indians had checked their charge and now stepped onward cautiously. A flying spear appeared out of nowhere and lanced through the neck of a kneeling soldier. He strained to call out but could make no sound as he tumbled sideways, clutching at the shaft.

"All ranks, fire." A sheet of flame erupted beside Jackson. "Fix bayonets!" he shouted as his heartbeat pounded in his ears. *Now this fight's going to get nasty.*

The Indians were several steps past the fire now, and this last volley exploded at point-blank range. The center of the native line collapsed into the darkness of the ground as bullets ripped into their flesh and bones. Directly in front of Jackson, one Indian with red stripes painted on his chest groaned and thrashed at the earth until he suddenly stopped. The volley fire proved too much, and the Indian flanks skirted to either side of the camp. Jackson squinted through the dense smoke to see the last of his enemy flee. Beyond the light of the fading embers there was soon only blackness.

For a few moments there was silence, each man looking for signs of further movement by the fire. There, a single Indian lifted and began carrying off one of their wounded.

"There's one," a soldier shouted.

"Can we fire, sir?" Harris asked.

Jackson held up his hand. "Hold your fire. We'll not waste another volley on just one Indian." The men obeyed, waiting in line for another charge.

With Jackson's hand raised, minutes passed, but it seemed like hours before a soldier proclaimed, "The Injuns have gone." Jackson unconsciously lowered his arm.

"We've won, then," Harris cheered.

Three lines of grinning soldiers, faces dripping with the sweat of fear and drizzle, yelled, "Huzzah! Huzzah! Huzzah!" Now out of the smoke and the battle, with a slightly dizzy head, Jackson started to breathe again. It felt like he had held his breath for the entire bloody skirmish. He cheered and pumped his musket overhead, thrilled to be still alive. Many of his men were shaking hands with comrades and some even embraced.

He spit out the taste of gunpowder and marched to the front of the lines, his ears still ringing. The acrid smell of burnt powder filled his nostrils while, about him, isolated pockets of gun smoke hung thick in the air.

"We've held them off for now, but they may be back," he declared. "Move up six paces behind the fire, toward our new perimeter, till morning."

Jackson scanned an overcast sky for the first hints of light, thinking dawn could not come too soon.

"Spread out and stay close to the ground. Don't let me catch any of you lit up by that fire, and for God's sake keep your firing pans dry in this drizzle."

From behind their lines, a young boy darted out of the darkness.

"Lieutenant Jackson, sir, Major Daviess has got himself killed. Colonel Miller requests you to personally take over on your right. Thank you, sir." With that, the boy scurried back into the night.

Jackson imagined that, in his white coat and plumed hat, Daviess must have made a pretty target. "Sergeant Harris, you're in charge here until an officer arrives." Jackson took a deep breath, turned sharply, and strode off.

"You heard the lieutenant, spread out and stay down," Harris ordered. "Haggard, you come with me."

They crept out from the front line toward the campfire. Harris guessed that the natives had meanwhile carried away their wounded, for there were very few dead Indians to count. A slight movement on the ground, just past the smoldering fire, caught his attention and told Harris he had found what he was looking for. He ran straight toward the figure holding up a hand as he approached.

The Indian, whose face was lined with charcoal from his nose to his ear and then down to his chin, had taken two musket balls in the left side of his chest. He was coughing up goblets of blood and it was clear he was going to die. The warrior's head was completely shaved except for a three-inch-wide lock of greasy black hair that ran from the center of his forehead, over his skull, straight back to his neck.

Harris drew his knife as he lunged forward to yank at the hair on the man's head. "This is for what you bastards did to my friend Mr. Poole," he growled.

A right arm thrashed out in panic as the wounded prisoner used up his final strength even as Harris ran his knife hard just under the man's hairline and slit it round from front to back. A little groan that became a gurgle was all the Indian could manage as more blood spurted out of his mouth. Stepping quickly to one side, Harris puffed his chest out as he held the bloody scalp above his head.

Haggard, who had been watching, twisted away and stared at the ground.

"Stomach a little queasy this morning, Luke?" Harris grinned and shook the dripping scalp toward him.

"That's disgusting," said Haggard, waving him away with both hands.

"It's what they do to us."

"I haven't seen it, but anyways, they're savages," Haggard protested.

A discharge of muskets sounded from the southern end of the camp. Then came another as the Indians shifted the direction of their main attack. The man on the ground moaned and closed his eyes. Harris gazed down briefly at the pathetic figure with no scalp before running the sharp edge of his knife across the man's throat.

Paxinos followed his orders from Tecumseh obediently; he and his white friend did no more than watch as the attack was made on the northern perimeter of the white soldiers camp. Even before dawn, he had ushered the children along with their mothers deep into the safety of their forest-hiding place. Their trip through the marsh terrain of bulrushes and tall grass had been arduous in the dark, each individual closely trailing the one who proceeded directly in front. Feeling sick in his stomach about deserting his home at Prophet's Town, he knew there was no choice but to flee for safety. Children clung fearfully to their blankets and their mothers wept. On their backs the women lugged younger children, or tools, clothing, and food, as they wound in silent procession through the swamp. His sad face expressed the thought that much of the winter's food supply had to be left behind.

By first light Prophet's Town was empty, and returning warriors had a long run to catch up with this exodus. They guarded their rear against a constantly expected counterattack, but curiously the Long Knives never appeared.

Not until late that evening, the night following the battle, and when half their new camp was already asleep, did Paxinos realize that two people were missing. He went round to ask if anyone had seen them: an old woman with a young boy no more than four years old.

"That crazy woman, Wapana, has always done just what she wants. She has taken her grandson and she listens to nobody," Chief White Horse complained tiredly. He'd been awake for more than thirty-six hours, having spent much of the day escaping after the fighting the previous night.

"But Tecumseh told me to bring *all* the children," Paxinos insisted.

"I can no longer stay awake," the chief said, closing his eyes. "Now I sleep."

Paxinos took a deep breath and glanced silently at his white friend. He could face death if they returned, but there was no hesitation.

"I'll come with you, let's go, and I won't need this." His friend downed his musket, and the two young men headed off in the dark, back to Prophet's Town. With little light to guide them, their progress was more like a series of continuous stumbles, but by first light they reached the edge of the village. There they halted, out of breath, before creeping on through the northern breastworks. The quiet of the empty wigwams seemed strange and unnerving, as if the entire village was already dead. In the center of the camp a few leaves tumbled with the wind, but otherwise there was silence. Convinced the place was empty, Paxinos hurried along to the home of elderly Wapana while his companion jogged to the southern breastworks to watch for soldiers.

In her hut, Wapana slept, her grandson lying by her side. Paxinos nudged the old woman's shoulder to wake her, and she opened her eyes with a start.

"The soldiers are coming. We must go now."

Wapana groaned, trying to wake up. "Paxinos, you are young and full of energy, but I am too old to run away." She sat up, heavy on the cot, and rubbed her eyes.

"They will kill your grandson."

"This is my home, and I am not leaving." As she tried to stand, Paxinos reached under her arm to give her support.

"Tecumseh has ordered to take all the children to safety, so I must take your grandson as well."

Awakened by the sound of their voices, the little boy had rolled off the end of the bed. Now he stood waiting near the door. Just then a young white man stuck his head through the wigwam door and said, "Horses approaching the south end of the village. We must leave immediately."

Paxinos jumped between the old woman and her grandson. "Pick him up," he instructed his friend.

He nodded to Wapana. "We will return him when it is safe."

The two men raced to the north end of the village, the child bouncing and giggling on the white man's back. At the breastworks, Paxinos stopped and put a finger to his lips, urging the child to keep silent. He peered into the dim light and saw a mist rising off the long grass, then nothing beyond the first few feet of a footpath that lead into a labyrinth of similar trails that would take them through the marsh. The long grass waved and rustled in the wind, but Paxinos heard no hint of soldiers ahead. He inhaled slowly, waiting for the scent of horses, but only the thick smell of the marsh reached his nostrils. As they launched their way through the breastworks to escape the silent village, at the same moment, the soldiers were entering it at the other end.

"Movement at the far end, sir. Was that a white man I saw?" Sergeant Harris pointed. "He'll know too much, sir. Maybe we should go after them."

"We're here to burn a town, Sergeant, and I'm not particularly proud of it either. Tend to your duties and fire the damn torches." Lieutenant Jackson guessed that Tecumseh would never forgive what they were about to do to his home, but he was pleased that at least the village was empty. In the previous night's battle, the U.S. 4th Infantry and accompanying militia had taken one hundred and eighty-eight casualties, of which sixty-two were dead, but he had so far counted only forty Indian fatalities. Tired and dirty, he did not feel like killing anyone today.

"But, sir."

"I didn't see a thing, Sergeant," Jackson lied, for he'd be damned if he was going to start killing children. But he did wonder again what a white man was doing here in Prophet's Town, on the banks of the Tippecanoe River.

3

. . . . . .

YORK

Where the snow lay flat and hard, exactly at the shoreline, a solitary figure pushed his snowshoes east along the northern edge of Lake Ontario. Certainly one could no longer call him a boy; he was past that now. Jonathan Westlake was considered a young man ready to make his mark.

Intended to last only three months, his trek to the great middle of the continent had taken more than twice that time. He reached down to rub his aching thigh, aware of the strain in his frozen shoulder. *Keep your feet moving—almost home.* He leaned forward into the cutting winter wind that stung his face as he peered up at the wooden palisade surrounding the barracks of York's garrison. Long barrel cannons watched him, ready to pound any intruders approaching from the south.

Westlake turned north up Yonge Street, glancing back over his shoulder to the lake's ice and slate-gray waves that rolled to an indistinct horizon. Low-scudding clouds made it too dark to see clearly across to the south side. However, America was there. Everyone sensed it. Always.

A few paces farther up the street he stumbled and put a steadying hand against a cabin wall. Not quite midday, most residents were indoors, preparing to eat. In the strange quiet of a busy town with deserted streets, he paused in the stillness to relax his muscles.

A scream, seemingly from nowhere, made him crouch slightly, like a man about to receive another blow. He untied his fur cap, tilted his head and listened, his eyes searching from house to house. A woman sobbed and something crashed against the interior wall of the log cabin beside him. As she wailed, her moan sent his heart thumping.

He released the straps on his snowshoes, stepped backward, and pressed down on the wooden latch, but the small door would not open. *Good.* Westlake knew enough to mind his own business, and he was tired. Nevertheless, he hesitated to leave.

"You nosy little bitch, I'll kill you." From inside the cabin, he heard a man's slurred voice. Westlake looked up and down the row of houses covered in ice and snow. There was no one in sight, no one he could ask for assistance. *Why do I have to be here, now?* He just wanted to go home, but the more he listened to the woman's sobbing, he knew had to intervene. The man inside had threatened to kill her.

Westlake unharnessed his pack and lowered his fur overcoat on to the snow. He blew a white shaky breath, and as his shoulder struck the door, the wooden latch exploded into slivers. His headfirst charge pitched him to the middle of an oven-hot room, illuminated by a blazing fire. To a man accustomed to months of winter chill, the heat overwhelmed him. He staggered but checked himself enough to turn back to the fresh air and deeply inhale. A stiff blow to the back of his skull sent him sprawling forward, his jaw striking the dirt floor and jarring his neck. He felt a dull head pain and the cold air gusting across the floor from the outside was all that kept him conscious.

A gruff voice snarled, "Get the hell out of here. Who d'you think you are, breaking into my home?"

Westlake rolled over to stare up at large man with a birch log raised above his head, ready to strike again. The younger man spun to his left just as the log hit the floor where his head had been resting a half-second before. He rolled back to his right, grabbing for the log, and kicked up hard at the groin of his attacker. The groaning man stumbled backward three paces toward the fireplace, clasping his crotch. Westlake shot to his feet, the log now held firmly in both hands.

Always keep moving in a fight, his Indian friends had taught him, but he was distracted when a trembling female voice from the darkness pleaded, "He doesn't mean real harm. It's just the drink."

Puzzled, Westlake squinted into the shadows for the source of the voice.

"He's my stepfather. Just leave us."

The big man charged again, only this time he jabbed at him with a red-hot iron poker. In the confined room, Westlake twisted aside enough to save his chest, but his left arm was not so lucky as the poker stabbed and seared its way through his buckskin jacket. His sleeve caught fire and he dropped the log to smother the flames with his other sleeve.

The stepfather then spun the poker round in a wild slash at his head. Westlake ducked to the floor again still gripping the log as the poker hissed overhead. For an instant he caught sight of glaring blood-shot eyes above low-hanging jowls: a face more suited to a bulldog than any human.

The birch log struck home, and the bridge of the man's nose collapsed as his lower forehead took the full blow. Blood spurted from his nose, and the skin just above his eyebrows parted into a thin red line. His legs gave way and he crumpled to the floor.

Westlake stared at him in disbelief and then at the girl. From the shadows she emerged, a slight figure with dark eyes and a round trembling chin. She stepped warily at first, keeping well clear of him, and then darted over to her unconscious stepfather's side. This was the first white female he'd seen in months of travel, and her skin was like ivory in contrast to her straight black hair. Her blouse had been torn, and Westlake caught a glimpse of one bare shoulder before she reached for a woolen wrap.

"There's hot water and a cloth by the fire—please bring them to me." Her voice was unsteady from crying but the fear seemed gone. "And close the door."

Two passersby had halted and were straining their necks to investigate the commotion before Westlake shut them out. He winced as the girl limped to a table for another clean cloth and then returned to her stepfather.

"It's nothing," she explained, noticing his reaction. "The log caught me in the thigh and I fell against the wall, but I'm alright now." On the injured man's forehead, she worked to clean away the blood and shreds of bark.

"Nothing you say, but you must have been wailing for a reason. What's your name?"

She turned her head slightly and studied his face. "Mary ... Mary Collins."

"Pleased to meet you, Miss Collins. I'm Jonathan Westlake. So he struck you with a log?"

"I'm afraid this time he got carried away." She put a hand to her forehead and covered her eyes, but not before Westlake caught the stress in her plain round face.

"Normally he just gets drunk, and he's not hurtful," she sobbed, "but I brought this on myself. I overheard things I shouldn't have when he was talking with his friends. He warned me to stay out of the house, but it was so cold I crept in through the outside cellar door and hid below." She pointed to a trapdoor in the floor and let out brief whimper.

As she dabbed away a trickle of blood from the man's broken nose, Westlake stepped forward, wanting to hold her. "But why would that be enough for him to strike you?"

He peered round at the rough log walls and felt the heat from the fire warm his face and hands. Forks of black soot fanned out around the top of the fireplace where at some point the fire had grown too large.

"I must have made a sound because one of the men came down and found me. He even threatened to kill me if I spoke a word of what I'd heard. He gripped me by the neck so hard, I was choking."

"Who was this man?"

"Don't ask me that. It's too dangerous." She closed her eyes and bowed her head.

"Miss Collins, if he comes back, I need to know what he looks like. I've gone this far, so you know I'll help you. Now what did he look like?" He rubbed his arm where the poker had seared its way through and for the first time realized just how seriously it had burned him. Rubbing only made the pain worse and he grimaced.

"It's dark down in the cellar, but I know he was very tall and he wore a sword underneath his army great coat because I could feel it pressing against me. Then my stepfather moved between us and said he would solve the problem in his own way. I think that's the only reason the other man let me go."

"What did you hear them talking about?"

"I was too cold to care. Not very much … just a bit about furs. I shouldn't say."

"But your life was in danger." He pressed her for an answer. There was something in her manner, that plain face, her white skin, that attracted him.

"My stepfather gave them some money for the information they were to gather and the tall man promised to kill anyone who got in his way. The others, I think he had three or four with him, kept quiet except to laugh."

By now the girl had wiped away the blood, so for the first time Westlake could properly see the bulldog face, grotesquely swollen and cut. He propped the man's head on a cushion and stood holding his own left arm. "What's your stepfather's name?"

"I'm afraid he's not breathing very well. His name's Bill Wagg and I think he's dying." She sobbed and started to cry again. Westlake moved closer, and for a moment she gazed up at him.

"I'm very sorry," he said. "I didn't try to kill him, believe me. I'll get someone to fetch a doctor. It will only take me a minute."

"Wait, don't go." Mary reached for his right hand with both of hers. Her small hands were soft and warm, and he felt a kindness in the way she touched him.

"Thank you," she whispered. "It was brave of you, to risk your life in saving mine."

Locked in her stare, Westlake couldn't think clearly. He felt his heart racing again, and he wanted desperately to embrace her. Instead, he froze but managed to blurt out, "It seemed the right thing to do."

She too stood still and did not let go of his hand. Instead, she raised it slowly to her cheek and then kissed it. Confused, Westlake thrilled at the warmth of her lips against the back of his hand.

"Mr. Westlake, you should go now." She motioned with her head toward the door.

"There'll be trouble for this and my stepfather has powerful friends in business. If he's really dying, it will look very bad for you with the law."

"What will you do?" He considered the cabin, smaller than he had first thought, and made darker by the absence of a window. Rolled-up rags plugged a few gaps between the logs, and there was a thin layer of straw scattered on the dirt floor to soak up the dampness.

"I don't know what I'll do, I've no family. I'll have someone else fetch a doctor, it'll be safer."

"Promise me that if you ever find yourself in danger again, you'll go straight to the stone house on the ridge, Maple Hill, and mention my name. Just say I sent you. Promise me that."

"Go now before someone comes," she insisted. "Yes, I promise. I'll say your name." She reached out with both hands to urge him along.

Westlake let himself be prodded toward the door. With one last glance at the man lying on the floor, he stepped out into the cold, already shivering.

Maple Hill crowned a crest of rock and woodland overlooking the lakeside village of York. The settlement had begun its life as an Indian trading post, but with the arrival of British troops to man a garrison, it had gradually turned into a small town. Its natural harbor made an excellent port for company ships serving the lucrative fur trade, and now it was the seat of government for Upper Canada's legislature. From Maple Hill the entire town was visible below; its numerous dwellings sketched the foreground for the wide expanse of Lake Ontario beyond which itself merged with a giant sky.

Maple Hill was Jonathan Westlake's home. Built from granite, finely cut and chiseled, it ranked as the most impressive farmhouse in all of York. Imagining the smell of baking bread as his mother cooked the midday meal, he trudged steadily upward lifting his snowshoes and once again felt the wind's teeth biting into his stinging cheeks.

Every bone and muscle in his frozen body ached except inside his boots, where he wriggled his toes and felt nothing. He had surprised himself, at being able to move so quickly in his fight with Bill Wagg. Apart from the painful cold, Westlake had but one thought: in less than a mile he would be home, and that meant food. But most importantly, right now, home also meant warmth.

In the heat of her spacious kitchen, Elizabeth Westlake pressed hard, kneading the dough for dinner's bread, stopping only to tuck a strand of blonde hair into the tightly wound bun at the back of her head. Possessed of blue eyes and a somewhat angular face, these fine features were combined with a trim yet full body that had always caused men to stare. Hers was a face and figure more suited to appear at a royal court than in the stone-house kitchen on Maple Hill. Today, she wore a white apron over a basic black dress, with short white-lace cuffs and a white-lace collar buttoned up at the neck. Elizabeth moved with a natural grace, and even with flour-white hands and a powder smudge on her cheek, she looked like the queen herself was baking bread.

Yet her forehead was set in an agitated frown and her full lips pinched together. For too many days, every few moments, she would unconsciously glance out the window and down the hill. Her son was at least three months' late in returning home, and with her husband still in Europe on business, it had been a lonely vigil.

When Jonathan missed Christmas Day and then New Year's, Elizabeth requested a favor of her army friend. "Please send someone to find my son."

"Consider it done," her friend replied without hesitation.

Even if she had asked for the whole garrison to be sent out, she knew the reply would have been the same.

Since she had still received no news, Elizabeth wondered if further efforts were now required. She cursed herself for letting her son go: he was too young and rebellious. She went along with her husband only to keep the peace with Jonathan. The acrimony in her own home had to end, and after being thrown out of his Cornwall school, she knew in her heart that Jonathan would have gone anyway, regardless of her opinion. He needed most of all to prove his worth to his father and perhaps to himself. He wanted out.

Elizabeth wiped her hands on a towel and walked into the front room to look out the window. Patches of bright blue appeared between the racing clouds; so another weather front was blowing in. Down the roadway lined on each side with bare maple trees, a figure at the bottom of the hill headed straight up to the house. Elizabeth gasped and then exhaled deeply. Whoever it was, he moved like her son, yet somehow this boy looked too tall. Then the sight of a single lock of blond hair jutting out from under his fur hat was all the proof she needed. She eased her clenched fists; there were preparations to finish, everything would be perfect when her son entered the house.

Westlake paused to study the snow-covered stone house from whose roof's edge hung enormous jagged icicles. The outer wall of the fire-place chimney shone with an ice-clear coating over shades of gray and pink granite beneath. Untouched by winter, the oak entrance door loomed as massive as ever. For the last few paces he jogged from side to side, then stepped out of his snowshoes and gave the door a nudge with his shoulder while pressing hard on the handle.

Just as he had imagined, the warmth of the home fire flowed over him. That special cedar-wood smell of Maple Hill's interior mingled with the aroma of baking bread to suggest goodness itself. He pushed the door closed and knelt down to feel the fur of the entranceway's bearskin carpet. The great fireplace crackled and burst with new light from the gust of outdoor air sweeping across the floor. His heavy pack slipped from his shoulders as he turned to flop backward on to the giant bearskin. He took a deep breath, squeezed his hand on the fur, and closed his eyes.

He was home.

A minute later he rolled over to see his mother emerge from the kitchen. Her eyes went straight to his scorched arm but still she remained in her place. In all his lifetime, he had never seen his mother display open emotion, and this would be no exception.

"Have you completed your chores for the day or have I caught you lying down on the job?"

"Mum!" Westlake jumped to his feet and with a bound he swept her into the air.

"It's so good to be home and see your face again. I've so many things to tell you and you won't believe what I've seen. There's been some trouble though, some serious trouble."

"Put me down, Jonathan. I'm relieved to have you home, but I'm not to handle like one of your Indian wrestling friends."

He lowered her gently as his injured arm started to burn again.

His mother gave him an extra hug and a kiss on one cold cheek. "My goodness, young man, when I said goodbye over six months ago, we were still the same height. Now look, I swear you're half a head taller. You've shot up faster than a young pine tree." Elizabeth tugged her dress back into place and patted it down.

Westlake took a step back. His mother was strikingly beautiful, and it was easy to see why men curried her favor and women viewed her with envy. He thought his father foolish for being away from home so often, yet here he himself was returning after so many months.

"How is everything, Mum? Have you been well?" He touched his arm where it was stinging.

"We have flour and feed enough for the winter, and anything else we need, we can purchase. What have you done to your arm?"

"How about our extra hands?"

"You should go and say hello."

"And the horses … how's Warman?" Westlake pictured his personal steed and wondered if the great horse would remember him.

"Your arm, Jonathan, what's happened to it? Are you not hungry?"

"First I must tell you that something terrible happened to me in town, just now. I may have killed someone."

His mother paused in silence. "Take your coat off. We'll see to that arm while you tell me all. Then you'll eat your dinner."

Westlake was too tired and hungry to protest. Seated at the kitchen table, relieved to be home, he pulled away the charred shirtsleeve and raised his arm. He told the story of his confrontation with Wagg while his mother cleaned and bandaged the wound.

She remained silent as he stuffed himself with steaming pea soup, rabbit stew, and apple crisp, then reached across the table for another slice of warm bread. Direct from the oven, the loaf was still hot and reminded him of the burn. If not for his buckskin jacket the poker would have pierced his arm. His knife slid through the butter, and he shuddered; this time he'd been fortunate.

They moved into the living room to sit by the fire and finally his mother spoke again. "Do you think the man's dead?"

"If not, he's close to it. His stepdaughter said he was barely breathing and couldn't wake him up. She claimed he has powerful friends." Westlake sat down by the hearth and leaned back, exhausted. Flames flickered as he stared at the changing pattern of the red coals.

"We're not without our own well-placed friends, but dead or not, there is room enough here for trouble. And the law must still take its course. What of this girl, will she go against you?"

"Never." Westlake thought of Mary Collins's grateful embrace, her warm eyes and his excitement at her lips touching the back of his hand. "That man said he was going to kill her. I couldn't just stand there. How can I have committed a crime by saving her life?" The fire sparked and he kicked a stray ember back into the coals.

"A man can say whatever he pleases inside his own home. Fairly or unfairly, he was disciplining his daughter." Elizabeth spoke without emotion. "And whether it's just or unjust is beside the point to the authorities." She pursed her lips and sighed. "You broke down the door to enter his house without invitation. When he demanded you leave, your response was to strike him with a log. He lies unconscious, dead or dying. These are crimes for which prison or worse is the punishment."

Westlake shook his head but said nothing.

"Did anyone else see you?"

"Two people poked their heads through the door, but they didn't recognize me nor I them."

"They can cause problems though so you had better stay indoors."

"That will be a pleasure. You think I'm fighting again, don't you, that I should've minded my own business?"

His mother's blue eyes seemed to look right through him. "That thought had occurred to me, but the answer is no. You did the right thing I think—you usually do." She smiled sarcastically.

"A young girl is still alive who, but for your intervention, might be dead. The problem is that you may have murdered her stepfather in the process."

Westlake thought about revealing that he had volunteered Maple

Hill to the girl, but he decided that should the time arrive, his mother would also do the right thing anyway. He was tired, feeling the aches and stresses of a long trek, and his arm continued to sting. "I've not told you anything yet of my trip, or the remarkable people I've met. I watched a whole Indian village being destroyed by the U.S. Army. I've seen Indians scalp white men and white men scalp Indians. I can tell Father more than he may wish to know. Since the Americans are flooding into the Old Northwest and trapping more furs, the Canadian traders are outraged. They'll even kill to protect their livelihood."

The warmth of the fire in the cozy drawing room was too comfortable for him to stay awake. Another spark cracked, his head rocked forward, and with a start he opened his eyes realizing he'd dozed. He struggled to stand. "I'll tell you the rest later. Excuse me, but I'm going to bed. If Father cares to see it, I've written a report for him, as he asked." From his travel pack he drew a thick journal and handed it to his mother. "There's a summary at the front. Thanks for a great dinner. Goodnight."

Westlake left the parlor and spread wide both his arms, letting his fingertips touch the smooth logs that paneled the hallway to his room. He opened the bedroom door, flopped on the bed, and let his head sink into the old down pillow. His fingers traced the pattern on the quilt he'd had from boyhood while he breathed in the welcome smell of clean blankets. He was home.

The distance he had traveled and the events he had witnessed made him feel older; but he was indeed older.

He dozed into sleep along with images of Mary Collins, her terror, her dark eyes, her bare shoulder, and the softness of her cheek. She appeared to him so ... alone.

Elizabeth finished the summary prefacing Jonathan's report and then sat staring at the fire. For such a young man, both the writing and the insights were remarkable. His report exceeded even her expectations and her husband's directions were followed to the letter. Jonathan had proceeded to the Old Northwest, and there made contact with a network of fur traders who had introduced him to the Indian tribes. He had inspected furs and surveyed trap lines in Michigan, Ohio, and Illinois, but his report went much further than a simple summation and forecast of the year's catch. It would pass for a political assessment as much as for any business summary.

Elizabeth leaned her head back in the chair, contented. Her insistence on Reverend Strachan's tutelage at his school in Cornwall, in spite of Jonathan's expulsion for fighting, had not been wasted. She thought of her army friend, and how he might use this report's information. If Mary's stepfather had powerful friends, Elizabeth's influence reached right to the top level of power in Upper Canada.

She had not planned to attend tonight's dinner and dance at the officers' mess hall but now decided it would provide ample opportunity to raise her concern. She had just enough time to roll her hair, and jewelry she would think about later. Her blue gown would suffice, low cut but not too revealing; after all, she would be attending unescorted. On second thought, arriving in an open sleigh with her friend might cause less chatter among the women than if she arrived alone but departed with him. She would send word to him that she needed an escort, feeling positive that he would come in person.

She hurried to the back door of the house, where she beckoned to one of the stable hands.

"Joseph, I need you to carry a message to the garrison."

"My pleasure, ma'am."

"I want you to report that I'm in need of an escort. I've decided to attend tonight's ball. Saddle up Warman and be careful, the paths are slick."

"Very good, ma'am, but who should I ask for?"

"Say that you are from Maple Hill and ask for Major General Isaac Brock." Her objective was to arrange an interview for Jonathan with no less than the great man himself.

4

. . . . . .

ON A MID-FEBRUARY afternoon in the year 1812, General Brock, recently turned forty-two, sat staring out the window of his study. What a strange country, this: one day mild and muddy and the next deathly cold and sparkling, a difficult land in which to wage war, if only on account of the weather.

A warm nighttime breeze had crept over the land and melted the top snow into a cover of heavy moisture, but now a stinging north wind was charging through the town, turning every wet tree and bush into glistening chandeliers of ice. The clouds, bulky and gray, were pushed away so that under a blue sky and the morning sun, the rooftops of York appeared to be made of glass.

In his black leather chair, Brock shifted his generous six-foot frame, his thoughts drifting to his compatriots serving with Wellington in Spain. A thousand times he had asked himself how he managed to get stuck in Upper Canada, while all the real fighting was an ocean away. Finally the Prince Regent, through Governor General Prevost in Montreal, had given him leave to depart for England, yet how could he desert the colony just as war was about to find him? His frustration was doubled; his sense of duty made leaving now impossible.

But was war in fact likely? he wondered. By seizing U.S. seamen from their ships, the British Navy was antagonizing the American Congress. Britain claimed that too many of His Majesty's sailors were hiding as deserters in America's navy and in that she had a point. Many enterprising sailors were jumping ship to join the new American navy for better pay and easier working conditions.

The wind hammered at Brock's window, a reminder of how warm and comfortable it was, here in his office. Scattered about on the hardwood floors were three large black bearskins, shelves of books lined one wall from floor to ceiling, and in the hearth a fire crackled with dry wood.

Brock turned to his two advisers, who knew enough to keep silent whenever they saw him lost in thought. "You're the politician, John, so what's your judgment?"

Lieutenant Colonel John Macdonell, Brock's twenty-eight-year-old aide and Acting Attorney General of Upper Canada, was known for his keen mind. He leaned forward in his chair, reaching out with one hand to take hold of the edge of Brock's desk.

"The news of the day is the 'war hawks' in Congress are pressing President Madison for action." Macdonell sat back in his chair and vigorously patted the palms of his hands on the armrests. "They're allied with France, but it's doubtful that they would declare war on Britain and invade us here. Are you with me on this, Major?"

Brock's military aide, Major J.B. Clegg, was warming his hands over the fire, and he turned on hearing his name. "Not sure, difficult decision really, but these war hawks have more in mind than the theft of a few sailors. They're dead set against an Indian buffer state between the U.S. and the Canadas. And it would please the hell out of them to kick our fur traders out of the Old Northwest."

Brock had little patience with these minor North American squabbles while most of Europe suffered under Napoleon's boot. Everyone had an opinion, but no one could tell him for sure if war was imminent for the Canadas. If war did come, there were three hundred thousand inhabitants in the north against eight million in the south. He had only twelve hundred regulars here to defend an area larger than England. At the top of his study window the dipping sun pierced great daggers of hanging icicles. One of them suddenly snapped in the wind and he watched it fall, stabbing into the snow. He nodded to himself, no Wellington for him just yet; he was still wanted here and he needed to devise a plan.

A knock at the door interrupted his thoughts. "Enter," Brock called out.

His personal aide-de-camp, Captain Nelles, opened the door just wide enough to squeeze his head past the door frame. "Sorry to break in, sir, but there's a messenger here who insists on speaking with you. He appears to be a stable hand from Maple Hill."

The muscles in Brock's chest tightened. "That'll be all, gentlemen. We'll continue tomorrow. Show the man in, Captain, and let's see how we can help the fellow."

"Of course, sir," Nelles replied.

Brock watched Clegg and Macdonell frown at the intruder as they passed him on their way out. The stable hand was ushered to the center of the room and stood watching.

Captain Nelles made the introduction, "Joseph, from Maple Hill, sir."

Cap in hand, Joseph stammered, "Sir, beggin' your pardon, sir, but I've been asked by Mistress Westlake to tell you that her son, Jonathan, has come home and if you would be kind enough to send an escort for her to attend tonight's festivities." His mouth gone dry, he cleared his throat.

Brock grinned; he should have guessed. The illustrious Elizabeth Westlake wanted to attend a social gathering, so whom else would she ask for an escort? He would go with her himself, of course.

"Captain Nelles, see this man is given something to warm his stomach for the return journey." He turned back to Joseph. "You may tell Mistress Westlake that a sleigh will arrive at four. Go with Captain Nelles, and he'll see that you're taken care of."

The two men excused themselves, leaving Brock alone. What good fortune. The lovely Elizabeth Westlake openly approaching him. But, of course not, that would be too good to be true; there had to be another reason for her request. One thing was for sure, this was not simply about hitching a ride to dinner.

With two sharp knocks, Captain Nelles re-entered. "Shall I ready a sleigh and escort, sir?"

"Yes, ready the sleigh, but I will be going alone."

Brock went over to the window. Already the blue sky was giving way to a new bank of dark clouds, and he thought he could see snow falling to the south.

Edward Nelles, a tall and wiry captain who had grown into a friend, inquired gently, "Perhaps, with the changing weather, you'd enjoy a chaperon, sir. It might be safer and would give the local hens less to squawk about, especially if the driver was myself and we picked up my friend Melissa on the way to Maple Hill."

There was no reply from Brock, so Nelles continued, "She could sit up front with me while Mrs. Westlake sat with you in the rear. I could have extra blankets laid out on both seats." He had pushed far enough.

Brock hadn't moved from the window, nor yet said a word. He was aware that for the sake of appearance, Nelles was correct. While he didn't give a damn about his own reputation, Elizabeth's was another matter. "You know, Edward, this is a very strange country. Yesterday was quite warm, but last night so cold it couldn't snow. Now look, here it comes. This must be the only place on earth where it has to warm up in order to snow."

They both laughed and as Nelles made to leave, he gave it one last try. "Sir, the arrangements for the sleigh?"

"Yes, order it so. You're exactly right and, Edward, thank you."

Drawn by four large mares, the green sleigh with front and rear high-backed seats carried a warmly wrapped party of three to Maple Hill's front door. Behind it, a guard of four dragoons reined to a halt, their horses snorting frost. General Brock leapt with ease from the sleigh and knocked twice on the large oak door.

"No need to disembark, Edward. I shan't be more than a minute." He'd secure at least one private moment.

Although it had warmed since the morning, Nelles replied, "We await you eagerly, sir."

The door opened and Brock stepped inside. He was still stamping the snow from his boots when he heard Elizabeth's voice, "You may leave us, Joseph. That will be all for tonight unless my son awakens."

Brock raised his head and decided that Elizabeth Westlake was even more striking than he remembered. The blue gown, with ruffled cuffs, bunched shoulders, and a revealing front was actually rather plain, but she had added a single pearl necklace, with earrings to match. The simplicity of both gown and jewelry served only to contrast and heighten the woman's beauty, her blonde hair curled to perfection. To suppress any desire, a less seasoned veteran might have bitten down on his own hand; Brock had different ideas, however.

He took two steps forward and kissed her on the cheek. "You look stunning, Mrs. Westlake."

"Major General, how kind of you to come yourself. This is an unexpected honor, indeed." She seemed to ignore his kiss.

"There's no need for the 'Major General,' and you knew well enough the moment I heard your request, I'd come myself."

She smiled, her blue eyes flashing.

Brock continued, "We only have a minute. I've Captain Nelles and his lady companion waiting in the sleigh to drive us. You obviously wanted me for something more than an escort to a dance. I'm happy to hear that your son has reached home safely, so how can I help?"

"Mr. Brock, you see right through my little plans." She stared at him in admiration. "Are there no mysteries in the world you can't unravel?"

Brock spread his hands wide and grinned. "You're the only mystery remaining, Mrs. Westlake."

"Thank goodness there's something left to intrigue you." She smiled. "However, what I have to say will take more than a minute and must remain secret."

"Then you must tell me on the way. We can fully trust Captain Nelles, and Miss Kent is more interested in listening to herself talk. But to be safe we'll cover ourselves with blankets and sit extra close," Brock finished with a laugh.

Elizabeth handed him her son's journal. "Scan the summary while I get my cloak. I'm afraid what I have to tell you then will end your laughter."

In the sleigh, Brock listened to Elizabeth struggle with her admission that her son was perhaps a murderer. She fidgeted with the blankets and kept her eyes away from his while she requested her son's protection from the law. That was just as well for him because, if he had caught her gaze, he would give her anything she wanted. He put his arm around her as support when she slumped down in the seat, clearly distraught at her predicament.

Brock's heart quickened. He was cheek to cheek with York's most beautiful woman, even if they were discussing murder. From her story, it appeared that a British soldier wearing an army greatcoat and sword had visited a father and daughter in York. The soldier was earning extra pay for obtaining information, and he even threatened to kill civilians, but for what purpose and who he was, Brock had no idea.

The summary pages of the journal provided intelligence of the first order, and confirmed his worst suppositions: the potential for war with neighboring America was growing. Brock's head was spinning with military plans, yet the very closeness of the woman's face to his intoxicated him. Even the smell of her perfume made it difficult for him to concentrate.

And what should he do about a young man who could turn out to be a murderer and yet, next to himself, possessed more valuable military intelligence than anyone else in Upper Canada? Elizabeth Westlake's son had witnessed events of historical proportions, so surely this young fellow couldn't be allowed to hang. The military provosts would be informed at any moment. They'd begin searching for him in the morning, and if they found Jonathan Westlake it would be too late. Action was needed this very night.

The horses puffed white steam from their flaring nostrils as the iron sleigh runners glided to a halt. Brock jumped down first and felt Elizabeth's gloved hand clutch his own as she stepped carefully from the sleigh. He waved a thank-you to their escort and the horses trotted into the growing darkness.

When Brock entered the officers' hall, it was as if lightning struck. In one thunderous movement every officer shot up, stamping to attention. Some of the women let out startled squeals, to which Brock announced quietly, "Ladies, gentlemen, this is to be an evening of eating, dancing, and merriment. Please continue at ease."

Most of the room was now standing, staring not at him but at his companion.

"And let us have a special welcome for Captain Nelles's guest, Miss

Melissa Kent, and also for Mrs. Elizabeth Westlake, who has come all the way from Maple Hill to be with us this evening."

Murmurs of "Hear, hear" and "Good show" were heard throughout the room. At the back of the hall, Ensign Robert Simpson's enthusiastic shout of "Welcome, Mrs. Westlake," uttered just as the noise subsided, earned him a gentle punch to the shoulder from a friend. The women locked their gaze on Elizabeth, greeting her with pretend smiles and icy stares. She gave a small nod. Captain Nelles pointed to the musicians and they resumed their play.

Brock viewed the room as it settled back into conversation. Long tables, covered in white linen, were decorated with green wreaths of cedar branches and interspersed with pinecones. Adding friendly warmth to the austere military hall was a difficult task, so white candles flickered at the center of each wreath. The chandeliers overhead completed the illumination of the big room.

A waiter arrived with glasses of wine for the newcomers. After a round of toasts and a few sips, Brock announced to his guests that he would join them later but for now he had duties to attend.

Elizabeth whispered in his ear, "In their red and gold uniforms, your officers look even more opulent than the women. Hurry back."

He grinned and departed, with Jonathan Westlake's journal tucked under his arm.

Back in his study, Brock again scanned the journal's summary. A battle had taken place on the banks of the Tippecanoe; the killing had begun. And after being kicked out, Canadian fur traders were now pushing back into the Old Northwest. The more he read, the more certain Brock became of a plan taking shape in his head. To act hastily now, during the evening festivities, would reveal his agitation and call attention to what he had in mind. He'd wait until the dancing was over before he set his plan in motion.

Dinner was eaten amid the usual conversation about the changing weather. A toast was proposed to Wellington's latest exploits in Spain and a few comments exchanged about an incident with the Americans some time ago in Chesapeake Bay. To the boisterous Ensign Simpson, a few mongrel sailors seized off Yankee ships by the British were not worth all the American fuss. "Talk of war is just a lot of chatter. Killing Frogs is one thing, but shooting Americans? I have a cousin there!"

"I wonder if General Brock thinks there'll be war?" Young Simpson had inquired a little too loudly so that Brock had no choice but to respond. The room went silent, and inwardly he winced.

Seeing all eyes upon him, Simpson revised his last words quietly: "I mean, does he think we'll have to fight the Americans?" Simpson slumped down into his chair as friends urged him to shut up. The room shifted in their seats, which had suddenly become uncomfortable.

Except for Brock, who had now collected himself well enough. "Our Mr. ..."

"Simpson," Nelles whispered.

"Mr. Simpson seems to use his boots for more than just marching; one of them always seems to be in his mouth." The entire room laughed, and Simpson took a few more punches to the shoulder.

But Brock didn't leave the young man hanging once the laughter eased.

"Mr. Simpson, you seem to have a knack of saying out loud what everyone else is thinking but afraid to say."

Simpson smirked at his friends sitting nearby.

Brock continued, "The Americans have their own legitimate self-interest, and while they may be our friends for now, they will always do what is best for themselves. There is nothing wrong with that, but we here, in British North America, must be prepared to do the same, and act in our own interest, always. We must expect the worst and train accordingly. You are prepared to fight, are you not, Mr. Simpson?"

Simpson sprang to attention. "Yes, sir!" he said and saluted sharply.

Brock stood up, and with a reverberant rumble of the moving chairs, all the other officers jumped up with him. The room's light shimmered from the vibrating candles. There was an edge to Brock's voice as he stabbed the table in front of him with a finger. "War is serious business, gentlemen. I stand along with Ensign Simpson and the rest of you when I say that we will do our duty to our King and the Canadas and fight if called upon." Brock raised his glass and toasted, "To the King."

All in unison joined, "To the King."

He was not finished. "To the Canadas and the soldiers and volunteers who are prepared to fight for her." The men replied with the same, their voices rising to sound more like a cheer. Brock held his glass in front of him and looked each officer in the eyes, holding their gaze, for a moment. It was to them he was drinking, and they knew it. Finally, he set his glass down. There was silence. They would fight, and perhaps even die, together, with him. Then he smiled and nodded, "At ease, gentlemen, be seated."

Captain Nelles sat down, grinning, and leaned close to Elizabeth's ear. "That's something you don't see every day, Mrs. Westlake, a major general joining ranks with an ensign. It's supposed to be the other way round, but that's why the men love him. Just look at Simpson and his friends: they'd follow their general through the gates of hell."

Brock was pleased by the reaction. Everyone who could reach Simpson was shaking his hand. The young man's face beamed, his chest was thrust out, and his shoulders straight.

During the evening, all eyes lingered on Elizabeth. Brock's single dance with her, strangely distant, was almost unnerving. He understood why they held each other apart, but she seemed remote, certainly changed from the woman who had greeted him only hours before. Perhaps she had in the meanwhile guessed his plan for her son.

Nelles went to call their escort. With the sleigh back at the front door, Brock and his party were set to leave. Ensign Simpson approached him warily. "I was just wondering, sir. With all the wine, I'm not sure if I heard you say whether war was likely or not?"

"I didn't, Mr. Simpson." Brock gripped the young man's shoulder. "However, if you prove as persistent on the battlefield as you are in conversation, then those Americans had better think twice about invading Upper Canada."

Brock turned away from him. "Ladies, the sleigh awaits us." He held out his arms, elbows raised, and each woman took hold. Once they were seated in the sleigh, he turned around to see the parallel lines it cut in the fresh snow, leading back to the lights of the veranda. Simpson was still standing in the doorway and had raised both arms in a gesture of triumph. Brock smiled and waved to him, his spirits lifting. If every man could be so inspired, there was a chance, though a slim one, that he could defend Upper Canada with some success.

Brock used the time during the ride home to explain his plan to Elizabeth. Her son, Jonathan, dressed in the major general's own overcoat, was to return that night to Government House, the military headquarters. His head completely covered, he was to stagger slightly, as if drunk, and be escorted by Captain Nelles directly to Brock's private apartments. The captain would then post a guard outside the door to prevent anyone entering. Brock himself would return before dawn to explain to the young man his plans for an escape, which would take place a few days later.

Brock studied the expression on Elizabeth's face, so tense at the thought of losing her son again after only a few hours together. Yet the choice now was either to send him away or perhaps lose him to prison or worse.

Finally, she spoke. "It seems the only safe way out … let's get on with it." She tucked a blanket in tighter and patted it down, in a gesture seeming to say the conversation was over.

With her husband still away, Brock understood that her son's departure was an additional punishment enforced on her. The constant worrying would return and so would the loneliness; yet she now made the sacrifice with no argument. Such selflessness was yet another quality of this woman that made his admiration grow.

Westlake was struggling to open his eyes, and his stiff limbs wouldn't move. He heard his mother's voice close by and felt her hand touch his shoulder.

"Jonathan, you must wake up. Someone's here to see you."

He stretched until his toes touched the tucked-in ends of the blankets. The aches of his long journey home reminded him of the cold, and his bed felt far too warm to leave. Again came his mother's voice. "Jonathan, wake up. You must prepare to leave."

Suddenly he was conscious and remembering the previous day's events, Mary Collins's face again clear in his mind. "I'm awake," he groaned. "Just let me get dressed."

As he entered the parlor he found two men and his mum seated in front of the fire, talking. His mother jumped up to give him a hug, holding him longer than usual. The men stood up more slowly, and she introduced them.

"This is Major General Isaac Brock, Upper Canada's chief administrator. He is our friend, here to help you, and this is Captain Nelles, his aide-de-camp."

In his dress uniform, Brock was an imposing sight, and there was something in his face and manner that instantly commanded respect.

Without delay, Brock explained the evening's plan.

"I've been away from home a long time," Westlake interrupted. "And I'd rather stay here. As chief administrator, why can't you just ensure that I'm not charged with any crime?"

"Young man, we're discussing murder. You broke into another man's home and attacked him. The residents of York would be outraged if you weren't charged with a crime. They'd fear their own homes wouldn't be safe." Brock's tone was calm and firm. "So there's only one solution, and that's the one I've outlined. Now, please step with me to the front door."

Westlake rose, shaking his head, but noticed his mother nod to him in acceptance.

After leaving the room, Brock fetched his greatcoat and handed it to Westlake. "Put this on, and let's see how you look."

"Why do you bother helping me?"

"Because your mother has asked me to. And because, after reading your journal, I know you can probably assist me beyond your imagination."

"That journal was for my father's eyes only, and why are you so keen to rush to my mother's aid?"

The two men confronted each other only an arm's length apart. Westlake could feel Brock's intense stare as the older man replied in an even tone.

"Be careful when you push the limits of good fortune, Mr. Westlake. Your mother handed me your journal because she felt it could help our cause. I choose to help her because she is a person of noble character and high intelligence. You will find in life that such qualities in a woman motivate men to do all sorts of deeds."

Mary Collins's face suddenly appeared in Westlake's mind and he imagined Brock's meaning. Without further protest he slid into the greatcoat. Although too bulky, it fit well enough for a nighttime sleigh ride and a brief impersonation.

"Why is my journal so important to you, anyways?"

"We'll discuss that later. For now it's enough that I'm willing to bend several laws to save your neck."

Wearing Brock's overcoat, Westlake returned to join the others. "Don't you think I'd make a fine general," he joked.

"There is nothing light-hearted about this, Jonathan," his mother reproached him. "You'll not be so cocky if our plan fails and you face a hanging. Time for you to be off now, I've already prepared a bag."

Westlake gave his mother a goodbye kiss and Captain Nelles reassured her. "I'll get him there safely, ma'am. Have no concerns about that."

"I'll see you both before dawn," Brock added.

"The sooner the better," muttered Westlake as he closed the door.

Their sleigh ride to Government House was uneventful and no one challenged the staggering general as Captain Nelles aided the imposter toward Brock's rooms. Private Fred Burns, infamous for his own drinking and slack attention to his duties, had been wakened from his slumbers to post guard outside the door. At first light, it was a *real* major general who nudged the dozing private.

Burns leaped to his feet, desperately trying to focus his eyes. "Sorry, sir. I was not asleep, sir. Just didn't hear you return."

"Did I ask you to speak, Private?" Brock demanded.

"No, sir." Burns clenched his hands, standing to attention.

"If I want to hear from you, I'll tell you."

"Yes, sir." He had started to sweat, knowing he could be flogged or even shot for sleeping on duty.

"Were you asleep when I went out an hour ago?"

For a moment, Private Burns thought carefully. For his life he could not remember Brock leaving, but he realized he was probably asleep. "Er, of course not, sir. Wide awake, I was, sir. 'Bout an hour ago, as I remember, sir." He thus convinced himself that he truly had seen his commander depart and then return an hour later in the early hours of that cold February morning.

"Very good, Private. You'll remain outside this door for the rest of day so keep an eye. Carry on."

"Yes, sir. Thank you, sir."

Brock entered his quarters to find his fugitive still asleep. The young man was so obviously Elizabeth's son. The fine facial features, athletic build, and confident posture all defined him as a fellow to be reckoned with. Brock had made thousands of judgments on new men coming under his command and for a first impression, he always found that looking into a man's eyes was most revealing of the character that lay behind them. In Westlake's, he'd seen a concentration and wisdom beyond his years. For Elizabeth's sake, he hoped this would translate into good judgment too.

Physically and mentally the young man was obviously ready, but would he accept the proposed mission? Brock nodded to himself, recognizing that their meeting in a few hours' time would shape the rest of Westlake's entire life, one way or another.

5

......

THROUGH BROCK'S study window, Westlake watched Lake Ontario glitter in the morning sun. When he squinted, the blurred northern shores of the United States came into view. A feeling of unease crept into his mind, and he turned away to glance back at the fireplace, the bearskin rugs on the floor, and the bookshelves that lined one wall.

He had arrived at York full of good feelings and ended up fighting for his life in a struggle to rescue a girl. He touched the spot on his hand where her lips had kissed him. Closing his eyes so that the vision of her bare shoulder was before him again, his heart quickened. Westlake now wanted some answers—answers that he hoped would come with breakfast.

A soldier entered the room with a breakfast tray, laid it on the table, and exited without speaking. General Brock followed behind, unwrapping a hot shaving towel from around his chin. "Good morning, Mr. Westlake. Let's eat," he gestured to the table.

Seating himself opposite, Westlake picked up the silver lid covering his breakfast plate. Before he could reply, Brock was ahead of him. "In case you're wondering, Miss Collins is fine."

The lid jerked in his hand, clanging against the tray's bottom.

"Come, young man, you must learn to hide your emotions better or people will read you like an open book. I was young myself once, hard as it might be for you to imagine." Brock took a quick sip from a steaming cup of coffee. "We needed to know the present condition of her father and I had Captain Nelles check on her too. Still walks with a limp, which will heal, but unfortunately Bill Wagg is in far worse shape."

Westlake winced on the news about Wagg and shifted the silver cover gingerly to one side, relieved to know about Mary. *Did Brock anticipate everything?*

"All his bleeding has stopped, but the swelling is apparently grotesque. He's not yet woken from the slumbers you induced." Brock took a sharp bite of his bacon.

"Thank you for inquiring, sir, and I'm sorry about her father." Steam simmered off Westlake's porridge, so he blew on a spoonful. "Can the doctor yet tell if he'll live?"

Brock shook his head slowly.

"Those men that came to see him the night Wagg pushed her outside, did Captain Nelles find out who they were?" Westlake asked. "I explained to the captain everything Miss Collins told me about the meeting held at her house, and that at least one of those men was probably a soldier. But he said that was ridiculous because—"

"Be more careful to whom you tell such stories," Brock interrupted. Westlake began to protest, but Brock raised his hand. "Yes, I'm sure you thought Captain Nelles could be trusted, and in this case you're correct, but not everything in this world is as it seems. It's difficult to guess who those men were and what they were being paid for, unless Wagg wakes up and talks … no thanks to you there." Brock raised an eyebrow and Westlake was quick to reply.

"I had to hit him with that log since he was going to kill me and probably the girl too. I've no regrets. I traveled from here to the Tippecanoe and far beyond without any trouble. I don't ask for fights so don't try to scold me." If Westlake were going to be pushed, then he'd push back. "If we don't know who the men were, then who exactly is this Bill Wagg and what's his business? Miss Collins could tell us that, surely?"

Brock replied quietly, "Miss Collins has told us her stepfather keeps his cards close to the vest, but she knows he's connected to the fur trade. Who he works for she doesn't know, but he's some kind of business agent." The fire sparked suddenly and he turned his head to look. "As for one of my soldier's involvement with Mr. Wagg in something clandestine, I wouldn't like to think so, but it's entirely possible. We're told only that the soldier was very tall, and unfortunately we have a great many tall soldiers at York garrison."

"Well, where do we go from here, sir?" Westlake asked. "That journal you now carry everywhere belongs to my father."

Brock lifted a last forkful of egg and ignored his comment. "You're a young man, Westlake. Have you thought what you want to do with your life?"

"Make a difference." He had thought about this question many times during his travels alone. "Do something worthwhile and try my best. What else is there?"

"If you had the chance to fight for your King and for Upper Canada against her enemies—"

"I don't know the King." Westlake knew he was being confrontational but couldn't help himself.

"—to protect your home and perhaps save your own skin from this mess you're in, would you take it?"

"Of course."

"Even if there was a good possibility that you could be killed? This isn't like a scrap in the schoolyard."

"I like the part you mention about saving my own skin and protecting my home. As to the fighting, well, I think we know the answer, but ..."

"But what? What exactly were your plans? Maple syrup season is almost on us, so I suppose you could make syrup. Or else you could work with me and secretly prepare this place for war."

"I was going to ask, but what is it you want me to do?"

"To begin, you can tell me all you remember about the battle at the Tippecanoe River. Your journal already gives an overview of this encounter, but would the Indians be prepared to fight with us against the Americans? I need to know more about the Canadian fur traders and if they too would fight. Those are vital questions that you can help answer."

"You talk as if we're already at war with the United States. In fact, the Shawnee were instructed not to fight by one of their chiefs. Have you heard of Tecumseh?"

Brock nodded.

"He left his village in the hands of his brother, the Prophet, and urged him not to fight while he was away," Westlake continued.

"How do you know this? And if it's true, why did they fight?"

Westlake pushed his chair back and stood. "They tried to avoid a conflict, but General Harrison had too many soldiers, at least a thousand encroaching on Indian land. If the Prophet hadn't given the order to attack, then the village would have been wiped out anyway. The Indians attacked at night and gave Harrison a bloody nose."

"You witnessed this?"

"A full day later, Harrison attacked Prophet's Town and burnt down Tecumseh's own home. He will never forgive them. Every inch of Indian land that the Americans steal, Tecumseh will make them pay for with their own blood." Westlake felt his face flush in anger and he glanced down at his hands bunched into two fists.

Brock eyed Westlake closely, for it was like seeing himself at that same age, full of questions, answers, and energy. He would need lots of such energy to keep Upper Canada secure in the future, and he was now convinced that Jonathan Westlake could play a key role in the struggle ahead. Brock had heard other interesting rumors about the Tippecanoe battle, so he questioned Westlake further about Indian tactics and American defenses during the battle. Each time he asked a question, the answer came back clear and succinct. His respect for the young man was growing.

"You were living among the fur traders for quite a long time and your journal speaks to tension growing between traders so tell me more about that."

"Everyone knows the Americans want the Canadians out of the Ohio Valley and the Old Northwest, but the Canadians have nowhere else to go, so it's only a matter of time before fighting breaks out everywhere. The voyageurs may or may not fight for England, but they'll surely fight to protect their own livelihood—just as the Americans will."

Brock considered each word the young man said, particularly thinking over the phrase "everyone knows." Everyone knew, it seemed, except the politicians on the other side of the ocean who wouldn't believe they were drifting to war in the Americas. This war would not come about over stealing a few Yankee seamen or injured American pride. It would be fought over land and furs, and when it finished, nothing would ever be the same again. Of this, Brock was sure.

He had heard Thomas Jefferson's comment that seizing Canada "would be a mere matter of marching." Perhaps Jefferson was right: three out of five Upper Canadians had recently arrived from the United States, mostly on the lure of free land to farm. Yet if Brock could seize the initiative with his twelve hundred British regulars, and bring the Indians and fur traders on side, he had a fighting chance. This was his key to the successful defense of Upper Canada.

Breakfast finished, with a white napkin Brock wiped the corners of his mouth before rising and stepping over behind his desk. He sat on the edge of his leather chair and leaned forward.

"Mr. Westlake, I have an urgent task for you, a difficult and dangerous one. Should you fail, it's doubtful you will return home alive."

Westlake listened as Brock outlined the mission. The choice between the confines of jail or acting as an agent for Upper Canada, albeit a secret one, was an easy decision to make. Besides, he hated small spaces; to be locked up in a tiny jail cell terrified him even more than the thought of hanging. And he had no real concern for the mission's danger. Like most young people, he felt he was immortal, but Brock had made two comments that kept his mind focused: "urgent" and "return home." They meant he must be leaving and soon and, if that was true then he realized there was one person he had to see before his departure.

Over the next week, Westlake silently pushed aside all the maps and routes drawn up for his mission. The paths he would take, the places he would stop, they were all in his head. At first, he resisted Captain Nelles's attempts to commit them to paper, but as Brock's detailed plan unfolded, Westlake developed a heightened respect for the deadly game he was about to play. He had previously rejected discipline at home and at school, but here his very life depended upon the precise execution of their plan.

The week ended with a reward.

"Mr. Westlake, pull your things together. You're off to Maple Hill for twenty-four hours," Captain Nelles explained, "and you'll be traveling in a canvas-covered wagon. I'll give the provosts something else to distract them. You're not to leave your house for a moment and stay well away from the windows, understood?"

"Yes, sir." Westlake finally saw his chance.

Nelles smiled and reached out to shake his hand. "And one more thing, I'll be there myself to pick you up late tomorrow afternoon, so be ready."

"Absolutely."

"Pardon, Mr. Westlake?"

"Absolutely, sir."

Nelles slapped him on the shoulder and laughed. "That's better."

The wagon trip to Maple Hill was cold and bumpy, but it gave Westlake time to work out what he would tell his mother. On arrival, he slid out from under the canvas and entered through a side door. Excited at the prospect of telling her his story, he rushed through the house to find his mother standing by the fire in the living room.

From the battle at Prophet's Town to the scuffles between French Canadian and American fur traders, he retold the account of his trek. But this time his report was not of battle tactics but rather a tale of personal adventure, of bitter cold, and of the good friends he had made among the Indians, especially mentioning Paxinos, a Shawnee roughly the same age as himself. He told his mother about tomahawk games and how he excelled in a knife-throwing competition. It was a tale of expeditions, fur traders, and of seeing his old school friend Danny Lapointe. Finally, he came to the topic of Mary Collins.

"I'm still very concerned about her, Mum. Once it gets dark I'm going to see her," Westlake said.

"That's not possible," Elizabeth replied sharply. "I've given my word to Captain Nelles that you won't leave the house."

"You don't speak for me, and I'm not a child anymore. If I'm supposed to risk my life for this country, then I'll decide who I see before I go." He suddenly felt like he was back in school, angry, miserable, and thwarted. "Whatever you say, I'm going, excuse me."

Elizabeth remained sitting in her chair, stunned and silent. Only a short time ago, she was the only woman in the world that her son cared about, but something had happened to him with this Mary Collins, something was drawing him away. He was growing up and Elizabeth was sure she didn't like it.

She had listened attentively to his story, feeling her pride in him grow with each of his successive accomplishments. She wished he could stay here in York, but there was no choice in that. All Brock would tell her was that her son's mission was vital, which was cause for worry enough, but this business with Mary Collins was another matter, something else to take him away.

On the north shore of Lake Ontario, the mid-February light faded quickly. By six o'clock, Westlake was guiding Warman toward the cabin residence of Bill Wagg and his stepdaughter. He diverted his route somewhat to the west so as to approach Yonge Street from the back side. In the warmer midday air, the ice-covered snow had softened so that Warman punctured the top layer with each careful step. Some time ago the sun had edged below the treetops, and the air grew sharply cooler.

Westlake stopped a few cabins back with both himself and Warman exhaling a frost. There was no one to be seen anywhere around the house. Any military investigators had probably quit days ago, and for civilians the night was too dark and too cold. Nevertheless Westlake perspired, his mouth gone dry and his throat unable to swallow.

Many times he had rehearsed in his mind his opening words, presented with a casual demeanor. Yet when Mary Collins opened the door, and he saw her face again, he could think of nothing to say other than, "It's me, Jonathan … Jonathan Westlake."

In obvious surprise, she stood staring at him and then glanced at the fur hat clasped in his hand. "Of course, I know who you are. Just come in before we freeze to death."

Inside, he felt the same dense heat as on his first visit. The fire blazed from a gust of outside air, and the interior of the cabin brightened. Westlake instinctively scratched under his hair for the bump left by the birch log. For the first time he noticed how the back of the cabin was divided by a plank wall running from floor to ceiling, Mary's smaller room on one side of it and Wagg's domain on the other. Although curtains strung across the front concealed the occupant beyond, privacy was at a minimum here. Westlake frowned, imagining her lying in bed while Wagg's cronies drank and guffawed around the dinner table. Little wonder that Wagg had sent her outside during his ever so secret meeting.

"I'm sorry if I scared you by turning up like this, but I have to leave York soon and I wanted to say goodbye." He stared at the floor. "I just wanted to make sure you were alright before I leave. Are you well, I mean?" Westlake shifted his weight from one foot to the other and brushed back the stray hair emerging from under his toque.

She threw back her head and laughed, then spun around in a dance. "I'm better than alright, I'm almost perfect."

"You *are* perfect," he said. His heart was beating faster.

"Let me see your arm. No more heroics, I hope."

Westlake took off his coat and bared his left arm, not feeling at all like a hero. Then Mary took his hand in hers, and he understood why he had come back.

"You're not fully healed. I can feel it under the bandage," she said with concern.

"With you holding my hand, I feel better than new."

"Don't get cheeky with me, Mr. Westlake, or you might feel that hot poker again." He took her other hand, and as she looked up into his face, he kissed her full on the lips. She pulled away abruptly.

"I'm sorry, I shouldn't have, but I've been thinking about you a great deal." He felt his face flush red. "I'm going away now, but if I make it back, you must come to Maple Hill to meet my family."

Mary touched her lips with her fingers, remembering the kiss. "What do you mean, make it back? Will you be doing something dangerous?"

"I can't say, but I'll be back to see you, for sure. That's if you want to see me?"

He stood just inches away from her, unsure how to proceed. The girl took a step forward and put her arms around his shoulders. He reached for her waist, embracing her tightly, feeling the curves of her body against his.

"I've been thinking of you also, Jonathan, but you must leave now." She stepped back. "The provosts have already been here several times, looking for you." Mary emphasized the urgency with the wave of her hands. "They asked all sorts of questions about you, and what you did to Bill."

"How is he? I should've asked."

"The cuts are healing and he's able to take liquids, but he's not really moved or spoken at all. He hardly breathes. If he dies, I have no one else."

"I regret what I did, Mary, but you can go to Maple Hill for help anytime, remember." Westlake slipped back into his coat.

"You had no choice," she said firmly. "You saved my life and I'll never forget it."

The soft sound of her voice was making it more difficult for him to leave.

"One more thing occurred to me, how everyone addressed that big soldier who grabbed me as 'sir.' Could that be important?"

"Perhaps he's an officer then, I don't know." He shrugged. "I should go now, Mary. One last kiss before I go?" He grinned. "It's freezing outside."

She stepped into his embrace and they kissed, and kissed again. Then, with both her arms outstretched, she pushed him away.

"You're spoiled enough already, Mr. Westlake."

He reached for the door without looking back. "I'll not forget you either, Mary Collins." He pulled his fur hat over his toque and closed the door behind him, his heart pounding with exhilaration and a feeling that he could almost fly. He now had another reason to return home alive.

6

· · · · · ·

RUMORS TRAVELED QUICKLY in the small garrison town of York. A stranger wearing a wide-brimmed hat was reported traveling east on the Danforth Road, toward Montreal. Perhaps it was Bill Wagg's attacker. No one knew for certain, but it was best to have the man out of town. Although someone reported he was on horseback, another felt sure he was on foot. A provost decided that any man with a wounded arm would not make it to Kingston, let alone Montreal, in the dead of winter. The criminal would soon perish in the snow.

Besides, Bill Wagg had made a miraculous recovery. For weeks after the incident he had lain semi-conscious, then one afternoon his eyes opened fully. "I'm hungry," was the first thing he said.

His recovery was slow, and he even found walking was difficult on legs that had been inactive for too long. When Wagg learned that his assailant had escaped arrest and probably fled to Montreal, he swore to everyone that if he ever caught the intruder, he would kill him with his bare hands.

It was on hearing of his recovery that a six-man military patrol of Redcoats, with Captain Nelles in charge, paid a visit to the Wagg residence, where they questioned him thoroughly for more than two hours. For an entire patrol to be thus sent, Wagg must have some important friends, or so the townsfolk thought. When the same patrol returned the following morning, the tinsmith shouted out, "Go get 'em, Bill" as he was driven away by sleigh toward the garrison. Some paused to wonder why Wagg did not respond or even look too pleased.

Late that afternoon, Wagg returned home with neither a nod to his driver nor a wave to any onlookers. He struggled his way down from the sleigh, lifted his new wooden door-latch, and closed out the curious behind him.

Several days later Bill Wagg again emerged from his cabin.

Townsfolk laughingly said he must have gone back to sleep. Gone now was his customary boasting, and instead he barely spoke. Supplies, rations, and two sturdy horses were purchased. Of his military carriage ride, and what transpired at the garrison, Wagg would say nothing; all was confidential, he claimed.

Several days later, on a cool dawn with the sun just over the tree-tops, Wagg and his pale stepdaughter departed York on horseback, heading eastward after his rumored attacker. But later someone said they had seen two riders traveling far to the north. Why north? No one knew for sure, but a few joked that it was probably confidential.

Westlake was waiting for the complaining to begin. From a distance, the three of them approaching on horseback from the east must have looked barely alive. They were all hunched over their mounts' necks, leaning forward as far as they dared clearly to take pressure off their rumps and ease the pain from their saddle sores.

Westlake himself had pulled his fur hat down over his toque and his chin was tucked into his coat so that only his eyes felt the full sting of the wind. He brushed snow off his fur coat and glimpsed some icicles dangling from the saddle that swayed with each tired step. It appeared that at any moment some part of him was sure to fall off.

The crest of a small knoll now allowed him to peer down on the rooftops of Amherstburg, a town huddled beside the ice-covered Detroit River. They had ridden all day, just like on the other days, and Westlake knew it was time.

"Please can we walk the horses, sir? Me arse can't take it anymore," Ned said. "I think me cheekbones have rubbed clean through to the saddle."

"Shut up your whining. We's almost in Amherstburg, ain't we— just like the ensign promised," said his twin brother, Walt.

Newly appointed Ensign Jonathan Westlake, recent recruit to the York Volunteer Militia, viewed his two companions without sympathy. "Dismount, gentlemen." He thought to himself that three less likely looking soldiers could hardly be found, but whether they would pass as fur traders either was another matter.

With Westlake, the Parrish twins had crept out of York during the night. Brock had introduced them merely as a couple of insubordinate ruffians with a whisper that they were the toughest pair of soldiers in Upper Canada. They were both half a head taller than Westlake, and half as wide again. Their bulk was a surprise since, for the last few weeks, they had been subsisting on a military prison diet.

Brock's words to them had been concise and brutal. "Don't say a word, either of you. Just listen. For your misconduct, Captain Nelles tells me you deserve the lash, but I'm going to give you a chance to redeem yourselves. You're the shoddiest pair of soldiers we have, but that suits our purpose. Just bring this young gentleman back alive and all will be forgiven. On the other hand, if anything should happen to him, then I will make damn sure that worse happens to you. If you agree to the rules of your parole, simply nod but do not speak."

The Parrish brothers grinned wide-eyed at each other and shrugged.

Brock grabbed each man by the lapel and pushed his face up against theirs. "And if either of you attempts to run, know that for sure I will hunt you down and hang you."

The brothers dropped their grins, stared at the floor, and nodded slowly.

"Right then, be off with you. And, Mr. Westlake, do come back in one piece or I fear your mother will have *my* life." Brock shook his hand and strode out of the room.

Earlier in the day, Westlake had drawn rations, supplies, and horses for three men so he knew that Brock's performance with the Parrish pair was just a formality. They were going from the moment Brock had determined Westlake needed protection. Westlake had protested earlier that he required no protection, having journeyed the same trails before. But when Brock reminded him of the deteriorating situation as described in his own journal, he couldn't argue further.

All quartermasters are naturally inquisitive about dispensing their closely guarded supplies, and Sergeant George Puffer proved no exception. Westlake guessed that he was a tough man beneath his ill-fitting uniform, for he had a fat round face that might have appeared friendly except for the savage scar just above his right eye. Puffer stood behind his counter and inquired about the use of his precious supplies. After he spoke, the scarred eye gave an unconscious wink.

Westlake replied that he was simply traveling. "But to where?" Puffer pressed as he eyed him up and down and winked again.

"Places you can only imagine." Westlake sheathed a foot-long hunting knife outside his right boot so that it reached just below his knee.

"You must be a friend of the captain's, I reckons, and what a fine knife that looks to be. Lord, it's halfway long as a sword!" Puffer winked a third time. "Where might you have got hold of that treasure?"

Westlake gritted his teeth. "This knife belongs to me and it is no business of yours. If you must know, it was a gift from a friend, and he showed me how to pluck out a man's eye at one hundred feet, whether it was winking or not."

"Ouch! A man that knows how to use his words as well as his weapons, that's an unusual combination." Puffer winked yet again.

Captain Nelles marched into the room. "Too much chattering, Puffer. Go and get on with your duties."

The man snapped to attention. "Yes, sir," came the reply, followed by the inevitable wink.

Nelles put a firm arm around Westlake's shoulder and walked him away. "You must learn to give orders and expect them to be instantly obeyed, without argument or discussion. Especially from a man like Winky there." He laughed. "I think it's an involuntary habit."

"Of course, sir," Westlake agreed.

"I'm sure you'll catch on soon. General Brock is rarely mistaken in judging character and it seems he has high hopes of you."

"Do you consider yourself his friend, sir?"

"I was once his second in a duel on a beach in Barbados. The other officer, an insolent cad, was an excellent marksman, yet Mr. Brock let him choose pistols, so long as he himself could decide on the distance. The fellow laughed at that and appeared on the chosen morning with pistols, thinking Mr. Brock would lengthen the distance to increase his chances of survival." Nelles sighed, peering out the window at a blue sky. "Instead, Mr. Brock produced his handkerchief to cover the distance from which they would fire, and of course this would ensure both their deaths. The expert marksman went running off the sand, resigned his commission, and has never to my knowledge resurfaced."

"A bold gamble." Westlake could see the pride in Nelles's face.

"Like I said, the general understands character and sees more in the world than I ever will. He's fair to his men but has responsibilities that don't always allow for friendship." Nelles gave his pointed chin a rub as Westlake watched him consider his next words. "He complains about not fighting with Wellington, but he will still do his duty to protect Canada's inhabitants. If that means putting himself, you, or me in harm's way, then he will do so."

Brock had appointed Westlake as a junior officer, a militia ensign, explaining that in order to be in command of his small escort, a gentleman should be an officer.

"I'll do my best to live up to everyone's high hopes, sir."

"Don't do your best, Westlake. Just do your duty and return alive. He's counting on you," Nelles advised.

But that was twelve days ago and Westlake could hardly believe they had traveled over ground so fast. The weather had held stable and he used every minute of it to cover the required three hundred and seventy-five miles. In heavy snow, the three men had ridden and snowshoed their way west-southwest from dawn until dusk every day. They paused only to eat or sleep in the cabins of Westlake's friends from his former trip, or they sheltered alone in whatever was available at dusk. The previous night, while their fire blazed, one of them remained on watch at all times. The other two slept like dead men in a semi-collapsed, abandoned farm.

Outside Amherstburg, the horses were about ready to give in. With Captain Nelles's authorization to the commissary in Fort Amherstburg, Westlake was to receive fresh horses there and start out again. He joked with the Parrish brothers that they were losing weight as they walked themselves into better shape.

"How can you tell with all these furs wrapped around us," Walt asked.

"Because you're leaving shallower dents in the snow," Westlake laughed.

Ned pushed Walt on the shoulder from behind. "God strike me down if he doesn't miss anything." Walt peered at his footprints to find if it was true.

Situated on the eastern bank of the Detroit River, Fort Amherstburg was Upper Canada's most southwesterly military post, a collection of two dozen buildings, of which the largest was the blockhouse where the soldiers slept. Surrounded by a sixteen-foot-high parapet, it looked to Westlake like a small fortress.

"We've had our look, gentlemen, so now veer away from the fort on to the road leading right. Our destination is the town of Sandwich, farther upriver."

"But you promised us a decent rest and three new horses, sir, before we crossed to Fort Detroit," Ned protested.

Westlake suspected Ned was angrier at the thought of missing some rest than going without a fresh horse. "Are you suggesting that I'm practicing some deception, Mr. Parrish?" Westlake's own horse could barely lift its hooves as he urged it down the road to Sandwich.

Ned looked to his brother and Walt shook his head slowly. "No, sir," Ned replied. "It's just that we need rest, and these horses can't take much more."

Westlake remembered the lesson learned from Captain Nelles. "I'll be the judge of that, Ned Parrish. Keep moving."

At the end of the day, with the light fading, they finally arrived in the small town of Sandwich. Many of its two hundred houses hugged the river's edge and so peered directly across at Detroit. Other than some lightly armed militia, the place was undefended. Westlake told the brothers that most of its one thousand inhabitants were United Empire Loyalists.

"What's a Loyalist?" Ned asked.

Westlake explained what he knew about them, which was considerable since his uncle was one.

After the American Revolution, thousands of immigrants escaped to take up residence in Upper Canada. Many claimed they simply wished to live under British rule, but it was common knowledge that most came for the free two-hundred-acre land grants. And as was the custom in North America, they were all familiar with serving in the local militia.

"Like my uncle," Westlake said.

Fortunately for the local government a great number of these fleeing loyalists were British ex-officers. With free land and receiving half-pay from the army, they became relatively affluent, building homes to match their prosperity. Westlake pointed to one and a few minutes later knocked on the door. A man jerked it open a notch, cautious to be receiving callers at dusk. Even before he could speak, Westlake blurted, "Uncle George, it's me, Jonathan."

"My God, we just got rid of you and here you are back again." The man laughed.

Westlake's uncle ushered the three of them into a large area that served as kitchen and living room. A head shorter than Westlake, and in his early fifties, he had the same angular features, his bearing was distinguished, perhaps even authoritative. He obligingly helped his new guests out of their winter garments.

Westlake inhaled deeply, relieved to be rubbing his colds hands before a blazing fire that warmed his cheeks. A steaming pot hung from two black S hooks above the fire, and the aroma of simmering stew soon made his mouth water. As such, the comforting memories of home filled his thoughts and he wondered what his mother might be doing at this moment. His Uncle George led him by the arm toward the table where three men, who were already seated, had obviously just finished dinner.

"Before my guests here depart, I would like you to meet Lieutenant Frederic Rolette of the Provincial Marine, and my young friends Privates James Hancock and John Dean of the 41st Regiment. This is my nephew Jonathan Westlake, and two friends I've not yet had the pleasure of meeting properly."

Rolette was in his late twenties with a weather-beaten face while Hancock and Dean looked like they should still be in school.

"Sorry, Uncle, this is Ned and Walt Parrish." The men shook hands.

"You two look the same," Hancock remarked innocently.

"We's twins, brothers like." Ned smiled back.

"And what brings you all to Sandwich, Mr. Westlake?" Rolette asked.

"These men are my escort. My father didn't want me traveling alone into Michigan Territory. We have a fur-trading company, Westlake Trading."

"Your father is wise ... a little tense across the river now. When are you going over?"

"I thought I'd visit my uncle here before crossing tomorrow."

"The ice is thickest directly in front of the Baby house. This year you can walk clear across."

"That's good news, thank you," Westlake replied.

"Let's go now, Messers Hancock and Dean. You have to return to the Babys' and I to my command." Rolette turned back to Westlake. "Follow the river about a mile up the road toward the Baby place until you see the big wharf, and you cross there."

"Goodnight, John, and thanks for bringing my wagon back. Remember to keep your head down," George Moore advised.

"My pleasure, Captain, and goodnight." John Dean tied on his fur hat, picked up his musket, and closed the door behind him.

"That fellow Rolette is from Lower Canada. Imagine ... he fought with Nelson at the Nile and Trafalgar. You met someone very special here tonight." Moore rubbed his hands together. "I guess you and your friends are hungry."

"Now that you ask, Uncle George, can you spare a little?" Westlake headed straight for the stone fireplace with his hands stretched out in front of him.

"Your Aunt Iris has gone off to nurse the Baby family for a few days, and that young fellow Dean was good enough to bring me back my wagon," Moore said. "Anyways, before leaving she made me that big pot of stew that would last me a month if I didn't die of monotony first. Help yourselves, everybody. Did your friends say their last name was Parrish? My hearing's not so good, cannon fire, you know."

Westlake interjected before either of the brothers could speak. "Actually, Uncle, now that your guests have gone, I can tell you that these are Privates Walt and Ned Parrish of the 41st Foot." Both men stepped forward to extend their hands and Westlake continued proudly, "Gentlemen, meet Captain George Moore, recently retired from His Majesty's Army, originally from Sussex and then New England and still known in these parts as the Captain."

"Honor to meet you, sir," Walt said.

"Same said for me, sir," Ned echoed. "And may I say this is the nicest wooden floor that me and my brother have ever seen."

The hardwood floor was nicely flat, scrubbed clean, and set the standard for the entire interior of the house. Westlake scanned the kitchen and living room that were both as tidy as a doll's house. He remembered his Aunt Iris always saying, "A place for everything and everything in its place." Even the floor around the fireplace showed no sign of wood chips or ash.

Moore started laughing. "Give me a couple days and I'll change all that. It's sure good to have company. I'm not as mobile as I used to be, what with this gimpy leg, but I can still ride as good as ever." He tilted his head toward Westlake. "Could you tell me why on earth you're out traveling in the dead of winter because I hope it's not another falling-out at home?"

Westlake ignored the question and handed out some plates. He used a black-iron soup ladle to extract the bubbling stew for each of the other's plates, finally filling his own plate. He reached for the bread pan and, after the thumbs-up from his uncle, broke off three large chunks and dropped one piece on each plate.

"This must be what heaven is like." Walt sighed.

"This is what we's has to do too, Walt, retire and grab us some free land for a farm." Ned grinned. "Then we could be proper gentlemen farmers, like they have back home. Who'd of thought two yobs from the London docks would end up here and we've young Ensign Westlake to thank for showing us the way."

"Ensign Westlake?" Moore cried out. "What the hell is going on?"

"Ensign Westlake of the York Volunteers at your service, sir." Westlake stood to attention and saluted.

"And we's is escort, to keep him alive, like. The way I see's it, he joined the army and we joined the fur trade." Walt then laughed at his own joke, as usual.

"Does my sister know what you are doing ... Ensign?"

"It was Mum who encouraged me. General Brock saw he needed my help and I agreed."

With his elbow on the table and his chin resting in the palm of one hand, George Moore sat drumming his fingers with the other hand. His years of experience told him something was wrong here and he began with the obvious question.

"Where are your uniforms, then?"

"We have to journey through Michigan Territory, Uncle," Westlake replied quietly, "and because I'm known among the fur trade, it's best we go dressed as traders."

Moore rose from the table, one hand leaning on it for support, the other clenched in a fist. "Let me give you some advice, my boy. First, you must never repeat this story to another soul. Second, if you're working for Brock, you can bet that what you're doing is deadly serious. And lastly it's doubtful you'll all come back alive, so stay very sharp and at least one of you might make it."

"I only told you because I know I can trust you."

"Well, don't—not even me. Don't trust anyone."

"We reckoned this whole business was a bit dodgy, didn't we, Walt?" Ned said.

"Shut up, you two," Westlake snapped. "We need your three horses, Uncle."

"That's all the horses I've got except for the old one to pull the wagon. No." He stared at his nephew as if the boy was crazy.

"I've a written requisition from Brock's aide-de-camp to the commissary at Fort Amherstburg instructing him to release three fine horses to the bearer of this note. You can use it in my place." Westlake handed the document to his uncle.

"So why didn't you go there?"

"Because too many people would have seen us, and some might have guessed what we're about. If I get the horses from you, we'll be long gone by the time you fetch the replacements, and no one will know any better."

"I congratulate you. That's the type of thinking that might keep you alive. In that case, of course, you can have my horses. I'll use the wagon to pick up my replacements in a couple of days. I suppose you want to stay the night."

Westlake nodded, relieved after the scolding that his uncle thought he had done something right.

"Jonathan, you take the couch and you two get the bearskins here by the fire. Throw another log on, but whatever you do, don't let the damn thing go out. I suppose it's good to see you again, Jonathan, but I'm not so sure. Tomorrow you're into danger the second you cross that river, so better get some sleep. As for me, my day is done, so I wish you goodnight, gentlemen."

7

· · · · · ·

WESTLAKE STEPPED OUTSIDE into the early dawn to relieve himself and check the weather. His cheeks tingled under a light breeze, but it was not snowing and the first rays of the morning sun lit up a sky streaked with thin white cloud. No one had showed themselves around the farmhouse ... so a good time to travel.

A breakfast of eggs and bacon, thick toast, and tea encouraged the Parrish brothers to chatter again about the dream of owning their own farm. Moore meanwhile probed his nephew quietly about why his mother had encouraged him to join the York Volunteers, but minding the man's advice from the previous evening, Westlake only conceded that he'd reveal everything the next time they met. With breakfast over, he tied up his coat, thanked his uncle for the hospitality and the horses, and said goodbye.

Moore waved them off with the final warning: "Keep your heads down."

The trail veered left along the Detroit River until they came to the wharf. There, Westlake paused the lead horse while the two behind shifted from side to side. His eyes studied the opposite bank of the snow-covered river for any signs of life but spotted no one. Michigan Territory appeared agreeably peaceable, but he felt a nervous twinge in his stomach. Not that he disliked the new American republic, for many of his friends lived there. He just felt different about it and was unsure why. His horse edged forward again, and the three travelers descended, alongside the wharf, on to the ice, and proceeded across the river easily into Michigan.

Reaching the other side, the trio ascended a bare rise and rested again in the saddle to give Westlake time to survey the scene. The landscape on the American side mirrored that of Upper Canada. The flat ground by the river gradually rose into snow-covered hills wooded with pine, oak, and maple, separated by trails and streams.

"Before heading on to Indiana Territory, we have to make a visit," he announced. "It's just a few steps north, to another farm beside the river."

"Another uncle with food, no doubt?" Walt smiled.

"Not an uncle but a friend from my school days in Cornwall. He traveled most of Illinois Territory with me. Name's Danny Lapointe."

"A Frog in Detroit? A long ways from home, ain't he?" Walt said.

"Mr. Parrish, three-quarters of the inhabitants hereabouts have French ancestry. The French were settled in this area long before you were born."

"Don't mean we can trust them, though, do it? Remember what your uncle said, sir. I don't want to talk to anyone," Ned said.

"It means I can trust Danny Lapointe, that's all. His family home's not far. Keep moving."

The horses moved in a slow trot along a hardened snow path leading away from the river. They stayed close together, heading downhill toward a small fast-moving stream that stood out black between two white banks covered in snow. As the horses crossed the water to jump up on the opposite side, Ned commented, "We got company, looks like a dozen American soldiers. If you like, we could kill a few of them from here, then ride like hell back the way we came, sir."

"Fur traders do not kill soldiers and we don't run. Forget the 'sir,' I'm plain Jonathan Westlake to you now. Let me do the talking, so you two keep quiet unless you're directly asked a question. You know our story. Just stick to it and we're safe."

The two groups met partway up the rise, the soldiers gathering in a circle around the threesome. A gust of wind whipped up the snow so that all were forced to turn their heads away. When it subsided, a rider edged closer. "Where d'you think yer going?"

The man had only two visible teeth biting down on an oversized lower lip.

"We've just crossed the river ... thought we'd check in at the fort. Who are you, may I ask?" Westlake replied.

"I'll ask the questions here. What's your name and purpose in these parts?"

"We're traders working for Westlake Trading Company, passing through on our way to Illinois Territory. My name's Jonathan Westlake." So far, he felt things were going along fine.

"Have you not heard of the Non-Importation Act? It means no bringing stuff across the border to trade in exchange for furs with the Injuns … you bloody Canadians should keep your filthy hands off our furs. Now I'd say with the load you're carrying, you're smugglers."

"That's a lie!" Westlake burst out. "These supplies are all for our own use."

"Whoo, a temper on this one. It's going to be fun dealing with you lot." He twisted round, grinning at his group of soldiers. "If you don't have any trading goods, then why should I believe yer fur traders? See what I mean? I think it's you who's been doing all the lying."

He spit to one side. "Now you three have a choice. You can run for it, which would please me and my boys to no end, 'cause we'd shoot you down like the stinking dogs you are. Or you can hand over those muskets, come along peaceful-like, and make me a hero with Captain Jackson by telling him all you know. What will it be gents—do I get to kill you right here?"

"We've nothing at all to hide. And by the same token, sir, we have nothing to tell your captain."

"You don't have to call me sir, though I like the sound. Sergeant Harris will do."

Harris then bowed to his own men in an overcourteous manner. "Mr. Trimble and Mr. Haggard, kindly take their weapons and move this bunch out in front of us. Let's get going before I freeze to death." The others laughed, snatched the muskets, and shoved their captives to move forward.

Harris stuck out a hand to halt them. "We'll be taking any knives you might be hiding also."

Westlake drew his knife from the sheath outside his boot and handed it to the sergeant, who tossed it to Haggard. With a quick lunge, Harris then drove his musket hard into Westlake's belly.

A blinding pain seared under his ribcage, and he felt himself on the edge of passing out. He doubled over in the saddle, reaching for the pommel to prevent him from falling off his horse, and only recovered his breath after the pain subsided.

"That's for raising your voice to me," snarled Harris. "Next time I'll smash in all those pretty teeth."

Westlake grimaced, looking away, and promised himself there would be another time to deal with Sergeant Harris.

The troop sauntered up the hill, attaching itself to a narrow trail hedged in on each side by high drifts of snow so that Westlake felt like he was riding through a tiny canyon. At a signpost with the name *Lapointe*, he glanced down to a road that curved toward the river. Smoke from the farmhouse chimney and a half-open barn door told him that the Lapointe family was in residence. If he'd arrived moments sooner, all of them would be now warming themselves in front of the Lapointe hearth. Thoroughly discouraged, he shook his head at his bad luck.

At the crest of the hill, the settlement of Detroit came into view, consisting of some three hundred houses packed inside a wooden stockade of fourteen-foot-high pickets. The little troop continued in a semi-circle, south to north, where Westlake noticed two massive gates allowing entry to the town. He assumed another gate would give access on the extreme north side. They continued climbing to higher ground until they reached the fort itself.

A smaller outbound patrol paused at the fort's gate so they could pass. Westlake guessed the parapet to be twelve feet high and equally as thick. The ramp through the main entrance crossed a six-foot-deep ditch, twelve feet across. It was surrounded by a double row of twelve-foot-high pickets.

"I got mine," Sergeant Harris bragged to the outbound patrol.

Inside the fort itself, Westlake counted six cannons spaced at intervals around the walls, with two of them on guard at the gate. He was assessing the fort's impregnability when the gates slammed shut behind him and a terse order ended his observations.

"Boggs, Haggard, lock 'em up in there. I ain't going in myself ... hate the vile smell of that place. Put 'em all in together. We may need the other cell. I'll go tell the captain so the rest of you can stand down."

Their prison was a small stand-alone building with two windows of iron bars. A sharp breeze swirled through the two adjoining cells, each just nine feet wide and about the same as long. Westlake clenched his stomach and his breathing quickened at the sight of the cramped cells. He thanked God for the wind that shifted the pervasive stench of stale urine. After Ned had entered the closest cell, Westlake stepped over to the next, but Private Rufus Boggs shoved him back into the same one. A club to the back of head brought Walt stumbling in and he swore at Boggs, "Bugger off."

"You heard what the sergeant said. We'll need this other cell for more garbage like yourselves. Enjoy the stink." Boggs clanked the metal door shut.

Westlake kicked at the straw covering on the floor, then noticed three bales more stacked in a corner. In the opposite corner, a wooden bucket served as a toilet. There wasn't even a bed so the three of them slid down to the straw with their backs to the wall. Westlake put one finger to his lips, gestured to the barred window, and whispered, "Remember, you are simply my escort working for my father's trading company. If they should ask, you can claim you hate everything British, including the army." His palms were sweating, his heart racing. *I have to get out of here*, he thought.

"That will be a pleasure, sir. I mean, Mr. Westlake, Jonathan, if you like." Walt grinned.

"If you use the word *sir* again, I'll strangle you myself," Ned jumped in. "You'll have us all hanged, if you don't mind your mouth. Are you okay, Jonathan? You've gone right pale."

Again Westlake put a finger to his lips, only this time he closed his eyes and shook his head. "I hate confined places," he confessed. The brothers nodded and remained silent.

Westlake sat with his eyes closed and his arms folded across his chest, imagining the interrogation he knew was bound to come. He sweated despite the cold, praying for a release from this tiny cell. The interrogation couldn't come too soon for him.

Captain Daniel Jackson stood only five feet tall, a neat man, closely shaven. Unusual for that time, he kept his brown hair cut short to his head, for he had the novel idea that long hair collected dirt, and he despised filth in all its forms. His modest office reflected its immaculate occupant; the chairs to the dining table tucked neatly beneath a shining tabletop. At the knock on his door, he called out, "Enter."

Sergeant Harris stepped in and closed the door behind him. His clothes had not been washed in months, so that he smelled like he slept with the horses. Harris unwrapped the scarf from around his head and removed his fur cap. His sweating bald head shone with the reflection from the fireplace. Jackson viewed him with disgust and Harris knew it as he stood at his sloppy version of attention, the snow from his boots melting on Jackson's clean floor. The scarred, cherubic face with fat lips broke into a two-tooth smile. "Sergeant Harris reporting, sir."

Jackson pointed to a wooden chair close by the door as a puddle continued to expand around Harris's feet.

"Sit down, Sergeant Harris. You can ... well ... whatever you're doing, settle by the door. What have you got to say for yourself?"

"I should say, on behalf of the boys and meself, congratulations on your promotion to captain, sir. After that Tippecanoe business, you deserve it." Harris sat down.

"Thank you, Harris. What's your report?"

"It's like this: I took the boys out as directed and patrolled for a couple of hours early this morning and found nothing. Then, just as we was beginning to get real cold, we spots three riders at the bottom of a hill on the Sandwich trail. We put the grab on them and brought 'em here, under arrest, for smuggling. That's my report, sir."

"Are they smugglers, Harris?"

"Yes, sir. Maybe, sir."

"Did they run when they saw you?"

"No, sir."

"Did they have anything to say?"

"Very little. They claims to be fur traders working for the Westlake Fur Trading Company, but they've little to trade, which may not be surprising with our new law on trading goods. It's hard to make out, sir. They could be those sneaking couriers you're looking for or they might not."

"Examine their packs. Go through everything twice. Look for a message of some kind, and anything written bring to me. When you're finished, put the packs back together exactly the way you found them, with not one thing missing. No stealing, Sergeant, is that understood?"

"Yes, sir."

"What would happen to you if I caught you stealing, Harris?"

"Why, you'd want to hang me, sir."

"Sometimes you're very perceptive, Sergeant."

"Thank you, sir. Would you like me to soften them up a little before you talk to them—a nice and friendly how d'ya do?"

"The American army is not a bunch of thugs and we're not at war, remember. Not yet anyway." Jackson turned away and stared out his window. "A night in the cell should cool them off. Commencing at eight in the morning, escort them here, one at a time. They should be hungry by then. You're dismissed, Sergeant. But tell me what you find inside those packs before the day is out."

"Yes, sir." Harris came to attention with a small splash. "And sorry about my mess, sir."

"Dismissed, Sergeant Harris."

"Yes, sir."

Westlake sat crossed-legged on the floor, the initial panic at confinement in the cell receding. Several hours had passed with no one else coming for them. It was dark and although mid-March didn't have the bone-numbing cold of January, today the temperature in the jail cell hovered just above freezing. Apparently their interrogator was using the cold as a weapon against them. Although Westlake had entertained his own ideas about fighting back, first he had a small detail to take care of, so he ordered the Parrish brothers to face the barred door while he moved over to where the bucket lay tipped on its side.

Walt heard the rustling of clothes and the crinkling of paper. "You're a bashful fellow, John," he said, grinning at Ned. "Your willy a wee bit short, then?" He laughed out loud, elbowing Ned in the ribs.

Westlake slid back into his heavy fur coat, "Just for that, Walt, I think I'll turn around now and pee on your head."

Both brothers abruptly stopped chuckling and twisted around to see Westlake standing there fully dressed and the bucket upside-down. He had merely used it as a chair. Ned frowned and opened his mouth to speak, but again, Westlake put a finger across his lips and whispered, "I will explain another time. Right now we have to stay as warm as possible, so let's sit in tight together, the three of us side by side. The one in the middle—that's you, Walt—will first pack that straw thickly around and across the two of us." He indicated the extra bales. "When you sit down between us, drag as much straw as you can across yourself, and we'll squeeze in tight on each side to keep you warm."

"Can we eat first?" Walt produced a loaf of bread from under his coat.

"Where did you get that from?" Westlake demanded. "I'm starving."

"I sort of borrowed it from your uncle," Walt said softly, looking away.

"Nelles warned me you were thieves, but that better be all you stole. Give some over and you can start on the straw."

When Walt had finished the arrangements, the two men on the either side of him couldn't be seen at all and only Walt's fur-capped head and shoulders remained without a covering of straw. "Ooh, ain't this nice 'n' cozy like," he said. "I could come to appreciate you two fellas."

"Very funny, but I suggest we get some sleep. Tomorrow will be a really unpleasant day," Westlake said.

The next morning, just after dawn, he stood up, shivering from his cocoon. The straw had done its job so that only Walt's face showed a tinge of frostbite. Not much later, twelve soldiers with fixed bayonets, under the command of Sergeant Harris, turned up to march the three prisoners through the snow toward a large single-storey building that acted as headquarters of Fort Detroit.

With his musket butt, Boggs smacked Westlake and Ned into separate rooms while Walt was taken through the next door for the first interrogation. The three men had the same thoughts: at least they were warmer here and the longer they stayed indoors the warmer they would remain.

One half-hour later Walt and Ned changed places, with Walt's face betraying absolutely no emotion. When Westlake's turn arrived, Harris and three of the guards thrust him through the office door and motioned to a chair. Westlake didn't make a move, but a musket butt to his ribs convinced him that he should sit. Still bruised from the day before, he grimaced and swore to himself again that Harris would pay.

"There is no need of that." A man behind a desk dropped his papers and glared.

"My apologies, Mr. Westlake." Harris made an exaggerated bow to the prisoner.

A tray with steaming porridge, some toast, and hot coffee was placed on a table. Westlake stared at it hungrily.

"My name is Captain Daniel Jackson." The man behind the desk stood up. "Your two men have been well fed, and they've answered my questions completely. Would you care to join us for breakfast and some questions too, Mr. Westlake?" He pointed to the table where the breakfast continued to steam.

Westlake made for the tray and began gulping down the porridge and slurping the coffee. As he broke off a piece of toast, he finally looked up at the interrogator. "Pleasure to meet you, Captain Jackson, but if my men have already answered all your questions, then how can I help you?"

"You have no need to act clever. Just explain why you are traveling in these parts."

"You know very well that we're traders, so why are we being held against our will?"

"If you are genuinely traders, then where are your goods to trade? What other purposes are you hiding?"

"Captain Jackson, I work for my father." Westlake finally put down his spoon. "He wants to know how the current trouble in the territories may damage his trade. We're merely here on a scouting trip." He shrugged as if it was of no importance. "So why detain us?"

Westlake returned to eating, confident that he had made a plausible case.

"Our two countries are edging toward war—if you can call Upper Canada a country. We are stopping everyone passing this way, so don't feel like you're receiving special treatment."

The porridge had warmed Westlake's stomach and for an instant he thought of the breakfast he had eaten at Maple Hill before his departure. He sipped some more coffee and smiled.

"Why would a simple fur trader need an escort of two armed men?" Jackson continued.

"You've just answered your own question, Captain. Rumor has it that American traders have attacked our people and stolen Indian furs destined for Canada. Whether that's true, you cannot deny that a certain hostility exists between American and Canadian fur traders." Westlake grinned, holding out his hands to make an obvious point. "If there was any threat to your own son would you not him give some protection? My father thought it best to be careful. So, when can we leave?"

"When you tell me the truth. I don't have a son, but if I did I wouldn't send him into harm's way. You're not being helpful, Mr. Westlake, so I can only assume you're a possible threat to us. Take him back to his cell, Sergeant Harris."

"We're a threat to nobody, and you must charge us with some crime or release us. Is it now common practice for the U.S. Army to seize Canadian fur traders?" Westlake scooped up the uneaten toast and swallowed a last mouthful of coffee, dreading a return to his little cell.

"Take them all away, Sergeant Harris, and strip-search them back in their cell."

"Sir, could we not do that here?" Harris pleaded.

"No you may not. Just get on with it, man."

On the short trek back to the lock-up, a warm wet snow started to fall. Once incarcerated again, the other men confirmed to Westlake that they had kept strictly to the story; Jackson knew no more now than he did before the interrogation began. They had just settled down when Rufus Boggs burst through the outer door, yelling, "Off with all your clothes, and get outside for the sergeant's inspection."

"We will not do that. Our feet will freeze in the snow," Westlake said firmly.

Boggs had not expected confrontation, so he did not know what to do. He stared from one face to another.

Westlake assisted him. "The sergeant will either have to come in here himself or leave us with our boots on."

"It stinks of piss in here, and the sergeant can't abide it." Boggs paused to think. "Leave your boots on and get outside now! The sergeant won't want to be kept waiting."

He turned his back and left.

The three men disrobed quickly and headed out into the icy weather, where Harris and his patrol were already waiting for them. Boggs and Haggard took a deep breath and darted into the cell, frantically searching all the discarded garments.

"I protest, Sergeant Harris," Westlake yelled. "This is outrageous!"

"You wouldn't be hiding anything up your arses, would ye?" Harris snickered. His patrol had now formed a circle around the prisoners, and Harris motioned for Trimble to go and take a look. The entire patrol started to chuckle as Westlake felt the point of Trimble's bayonet poking his bare behind. Meanwhile, Boggs and Haggard raced out from the stinking cells to report that nothing had been found.

"Well, you've passed the test—for now, at least." There was evident disappointment in Harris's voice. "Get back in the cell before your willies shrink completely, and maybe you'll survive till the morning." Harris grinned, happy again. "That's when the real interrogation begins."

The captives marched back inside, whereupon Trimble locked them up and left immediately. Just the clang of the door closing and click of the lock had Westlake's heart pounding again. Ned sneezed loudly and Westlake wondered how long they could hold out there against the cold before they became too sick to travel. After he'd dressed again, he peered through the bars toward Jackson's headquarters, though the snow was falling so thick he could barely see a few feet beyond the bars. "C'mon, gentlemen, back under the straw. Ned, you take the middle this time. Cover us up good and warm, as I have a feeling we may not see anyone for a while."

Disappearing under a blanket of straw, Walt asked, "Why is that?"

"Do you know what they do in Detroit when it snows hard?" Westlake grinned.

Walt shook his head, and Ned shrugged his shoulders.

"Nothing, they stay inside." Westlake started laughing.

"Is that your idea of a joke?" Walt asked him.

"A poor one, but it means we will be on our own for now. Let's stay close and rest." By now, Westlake was completely covered in straw.

Ned shifted up to Westlake's ear and whispered, "Can I ask one question? Where did you hide that note from the boss?"

"You are too inquisitive, Ned Parrish, but if you must know I stood on it. After I asked you two to turn away, I sat on the bucket and hid it in my boot."

"My God, you're brilliant, Jonathan."

"Shut up and go to sleep."

The snow fell unabated, past dusk. The men finished off Westlake's few pieces of cold toast and for moisture sucked on the snow from between the bars of their cell window. Apart from Ned's sneezing and coughing, they could hear only the sound of a quiet wind as they huddled together and slept.

Well past dawn, the routine of the previous day was repeated except this time Westlake woke in a miserable mood. He was tired of freezing, and the stench of urine had him thinking he could even taste it. When Walt said, "Good morning," Westlake pretended not to hear him, instead thinking only of his hunger. His ribs ached too, and this reminded him of his loathing for Sergeant Harris. If the man had been in the cell at that moment, he'd have strangled him.

Outside in the winter weather, he heard Harris swear bitterly as his men dug out the snow for a path by which to escort his captives to Captain Jackson. Overnight, the snowfall had added another ten inches, making it difficult to shovel. Where the wind had created giant drifts, the new heavy snow lay more than two feet deep on top of its previous level. When the deep path was finished, the three men marched single file back to Jackson's office.

By the time Westlake saw the steaming breakfast tray, his stomach was groaning. Harris motioned him, with the musket butt, to a different chair, assuming he could force Westlake to wait a little longer. But Westlake seized the musket with both hands, jerking it up hard so it struck under Harris's chin. The sergeant collapsed on the floor, with the bayonet's point to his throat.

"Stop!" Jackson shouted in alarm.

"I should kill you here and now and save the world a lot of trouble," Westlake growled between clenched teeth. He glanced over at Jackson and then back to Harris's bulging eyes. "I would like to eat my breakfast in peace—a small bargain for this man's life?"

"If you killed him, you wouldn't make it out of here alive, but I think you know that already. So be it then, let him up," Jackson ordered.

"I have a right to protect myself." Westlake laid the musket across a chair before he went to his breakfast. Then he gulped down porridge while Captain Jackson began his questioning.

"Tell me again why those two fellows are with you," Jackson demanded.

Westlake sat up straight, assessing the captain's uniform so spotlessly clean and sharply pressed.

"I am my father's only son and they're my escort." Westlake took a swig of coffee. "Maybe he wants to make sure I get back home safe. When can we leave?"

"What are you doing here in Michigan Territory?"

"You appear to be an intelligent man." Westlake looked up from his breakfast. "My answers are the same as last time, except this. My father will have serious complaints to your government about our ill treatment here."

Jackson raised his own coffee cup, studying Westlake. It seemed improbable that such a young man would be sent on a secret mission to stir up trouble among the Indians. Nevertheless, if the rumors were true, the British were planning something, therefore he had been warned to watch for anyone the slightest bit suspicious passing through his area.

If Westlake and his friends were telling the truth, then Jackson had done his job. If they were lying, which he thought they may very well be, then what more could he do without proof? Their two countries were not at war and this young man seemed utterly plausible, but there was something … just something.

Jackson strode across to the chair where Harris sat, nursing his bruised chin. He put his hand on Harris's shoulder.

"Mr. Westlake, you may take your coffee with you. No need to gulp like a savage. Sergeant, take him to the waiting room and then come back to me. No trouble on the way."

"Yes, sir."

When Harris returned a few moments later, Jackson gave him his orders.

"I have decided to detain our three friends a little longer, Sergeant. You will escort them to the original barracks building. It has a fireplace."

Harris frowned, and Jackson raised his voice for emphasis. "Get a fire going in there. I don't wish to have British civilians freeze to death in the custody of the American army. And bar the doors too. That way we'll not have to post guard outside in the cold."

"But, sir, we've dug the pathway back to the guardhouse, and now we're supposed to give these bastards use of the old barracks," Harris complained. "We've only just moved into the new ones ourselves, so the men won't like it. Why can't we just shoot them?"

Jackson made an effort to control his voice. "Because we've no evidence at all that they are anything other than what they say they are. As for shooting, they could've done the same to you at twenty yards." Jackson pointed toward the river. "If they're really our enemies, then my guess is that you're only still alive because that young man stopped the other two from killing the lot of you. Shoot them? Try thinking before you open your mouth, Sergeant, and it will improve our relationship immensely."

Jackson guessed that Harris was hoping to lay a beating on the prisoners before the second interrogation, but now he was being ordered to build them a fire. He could sense Harris's frustration when he saw him bite down on his lip, showing those two teeth.

"Listen carefully," Jackson continued. "By holding them, we can make sure that if they were due to rendezvous with someone hostile, they'll be too late or miss their meeting entirely. They'll be with us until I tell you otherwise. You're dismissed and not another word, go."

The captain turned to the window and waited until he heard Harris shut the office door. The next interrogation would need to take a different tack—and one that he did not relish. To work, it had to be brutal. Harris would enjoy the job, but removing the leash from him would be dangerous because one never knew how far his men would go. *How would young Westlake hold up under such punishment?* Jackson wondered.

He watched from the window as the men waded hip-deep through the snow toward the old barracks. Harris annoyed him: he was a brute, and only in the American army would a sergeant dare to question an officer, yet this was the new republic, his and Harris's chosen home. Maybe the British had it right after all. He shook his head at the thought of harsh British discipline, and the beatings with the lash. There had to be a better way then that: he'd stay with America.

8

· · · · · ·

IN OPEN GROUND, in the bowl of a gentle hill, Mary Collins leaned forward, straining against the storm. Straight out of the west blew a wind that drove the snow horizontal, slashing against her face. The sky was a cold gray, and between gaps in the trees the wind seemed to pick up speed. Well inside the next stand of pine, the barest outline of a small cabin was visible through this curtain of white. Whoever built it had wisely known how the forest cover provided shelter against the elements. No smoke rose from the cabin chimney, but she knew they had to reach the place before the storm's grip smothered them.

All the way from York, Wagg had led the way and Mary had followed. Their progress was slow and, as regards their final destination, he wouldn't say. He would not even tell her why they were now traveling north at the end of a long winter. But she didn't really care where they went; there was little choice but to go with him. However, the farther from York she traveled, the farther she'd be separated from Jonathan Westlake. Eventually, he had to come home, and Mary worried about being absent on his return.

Mary thought of him now while pushing her snowshoes against the storm. From the first time she had seen him come charging through their door, she'd known he was special. Who else would risk their life to save her? She had told the investigators how Westlake had no choice but to beat off Wagg for her protection and she prayed it would save him.

When he returned, his blond hair had been matted to his forehead and he didn't know how silly he looked. Mary smiled under her scarf as the wind suddenly whirled around her face. He was someone she could depend on, but he almost forgot to ask about her stepfather. She giggled out loud, the sound lost to the wind. He wanted that kiss—that's why he came back.

Mary paused and glanced up at the sky through the driving snow.

She remembered his eyes and under all her clothes felt herself flushing warmer. Never having been with a man, she wondered what it would be like. Impossible, how would he ever find her? She was marching the wrong way.

The wind had dropped noticeably once they were inside the forest, but its swirling persisted through the trees, whipping into small snowy tornadoes that rose, swirled, and disappeared. She saw Wagg, his musket at the ready, approach the cabin, stop, and call out. She waited but no one replied. He raised his musket to fire at the doorway, took a few more steps to peer inside, then beckoned her forward.

The cabin offered little comfort in its current condition for it had no door, only a four-foot-high opening where the door should have been, and a single room no more than four paces long and about the same in width. Although the place was clearly abandoned, she stepped in to see that except for a spider web in one corner of the ceiling, it was at least empty and clean.

The ceiling was more than five feet high so she could stand upright while Wagg was forced to bend over. Slivers of daylight penetrated the log walls, but otherwise the cabin seemed sturdy enough. On one side of the room there was a small fireplace of rough stones, with a hole directly above to emit smoke through the roof.

Previously, they had stopped at another empty building, a small barn where Mary learned the routine. From inside, she plugged out the daylight between the logs using leaves, twigs, and a few old straps of leather found on the cabin's dirt floor. She darted outside and packed the same gaps with snow, her cheeks burning from the pelting wind.

Wagg hauled in their supplies and stashed them along the west-facing wall where the wind blew the stiffest. Two steel spikes above the doorway allowed Mary to hang a bearskin wrap across the small entrance. Suddenly the wind was locked out.

On the forest floor, the snow falls in uneven drifts depending on where the treetops allow the storm to enter. Thick on top, thin on the ground was the rule, and in the sheltered areas where snow barely covered the ground, Wagg found some wood for their fire. A few roundhouse swings of his axe and the fallen branches were ready for burning. With a few pieces of the dry kindling Wagg always carried with him, the fire started.

Mary had worked quickly, knowing that if she slowed, her body temperature would drop before the fire had a chance to warm their new home. Before long, the dark cabin crackled with flames and light, and she felt the warmth redden her cheeks. With stocks of firewood and their belongings piled high, there was barely enough room for them both to lie down, but she managed to curl up on a bearskin and cover herself in blankets.

They had been lucky this time, Mary figured. Forests of evergreens under pillows of white snow piled high were beautiful to look at, but to be caught without shelter in a blizzard soon turned them into open-air tombs. Wagg lay down beside her and was soon asleep, so she listened as the storm whistled and howled around them, bending the great pines to its will.

From the day her mother had died with the fever, Wagg had supported her, yet she always felt alone; that is, until that day in York. Where was Jonathan Westlake now? Her cheeks flushed and she grinned. The warmth from the fire eventually made her drowsy and in a few minutes she was asleep.

Two weeks had passed since Westlake and his companions were first imprisoned at Fort Detroit, but at least the interrogations had stopped after their release from the stinking jail cell. Now they were lodged in the old barracks, and although there were cracks in the walls, there was no longer an icy breeze through an open window, and here there were blankets, a small fire, and lots of space. Walt talked a little about life back in England, and Westlake in turn told them about growing up near the border of Upper and Lower Canada. Both men were careful with their words, but in the main there was silence and staring at the fire. Then Ned asked his question.

"Why are we here?"

Since Westlake was already half asleep he couldn't quite believe what he'd heard. For a second he just stared at the other man, then the words sunk in. Westlake put his finger to his lips and pointed to the wall. He blamed himself, for he should have told these men about the snow tracks leading to the rear of the barracks, but he had already given them orders not to discuss anything that might give them away. He never anticipated anyone saying something to reveal their identity; after all, their lives were at stake.

"Ned, we're fur traders and the bloody American army is holding us without reason. That's why we're here." Westlake repeatedly pointed a finger at the wall. Understanding the unspoken message, Walt shook a fist at his brother. If someone overheard Ned, all three of them would hang if he continued.

"Of course we are, I know that, but I was thinking, do you ever wonder why we're here … on earth? When you said you went to that Cornwall school, it reminded me of Robbie, a bloke in my Sunday school class."

"Bloody hell! Are you on about that Sunday stuff again? It wasn't real school, I told you to forget it. Wondering about things like that'll make you into a bleeding idiot," Walt yelled.

Westlake was relieved, and the truth was he had thought a good deal about the same question. In the isolation of his travels, he would come over a rise to see a beautiful snow-drifted forest ahead, untraveled and virgin. He'd lose himself and become part of it, feeling himself as part of the scene and yet separate from it at the same time. That's when he would think about himself and his place in the world, and wonder if there was a great purpose to it all. At his school in Cornwall, Reverend Strachan's response of "to serve God" seemed inadequate to him. Westlake now knew that Ned had asked an honest question and he whistled from relief, "What made you think of that, Ned?"

"Robbie was a little fella that I whacked around a bit, y' know, to show him who was boss. One Sunday he comes out with this, 'Why are we here?' The teacher had the same saying for everything, 'To do God's work.' She never said, 'You're doing God's work,' 'cause we was never doing any good. But that's another question: what's God's work supposed to mean? He never told me, since I never met the Top Dog.

S'truth, I don't even know if He exists. Does He? You don't have to worry yourselves because I don't have no other questions—just those three. Not much for a whole life, when you think about it."

Westlake remained seated on the floor, back to the wall and legs crossed. Until that moment, he had thought Ned somewhat of a simpleton; not in an uncharitable way but rather that he would not look to Ned for any insight, if he needed help. All that was now changed.

"To live, Ned—that's why we are here. It sounds too simple, doesn't it, but that's the best I can suggest, to live the fullest life possible. I'm not sure but I think God, if He exists at all, would like us to make a difference. That's His work: to do something good. It doesn't have to be big, but you have to give it all you've got. You know what I mean?"

Ned was quiet for a moment. "Did you learn that in school?"

"In the forest, just listening—after I left school. I'm not sure that I got it all right. Somehow that answer doesn't sound big enough."

"Can we all go back to that—I mean, to the quiet? Between the two of you, I'm getting a headache," Walt said.

Westlake laughed, fell silent, and pointed again to the wall.

One of Sergeant Harris's men was always listening under the window for any clue to their prisoners' treachery. This time it was Luke Haggard who reported his news to Harris, who then conveyed it to Jackson.

"Sergeant Harris reporting, sir." Harris gave his supervisor a half-hearted salute as Jackson looked up from his desk in disgust. It was not just that the man muddied his floor every time he came in; it was more the stringy hair hanging from his mostly bald head and his grimy uneven beard. The man was top-heavy and Jackson, try as he might, could not conceal his distaste.

"What have you got for me today, Harris?"

"Well, sir, we've been snooping outside the walls of the old barracks—and I might say that the boys have done so in some miserable conditions, with the cold and snow and all."

"Get on with it, Harris."

"Yes, sir … as I was saying, outside the wall this morning we heard one of the twin brothers, and we don't know which one cause we can't tell their voices apart, well he asks outright, "Why are we here?"

Captain Jackson uncrossed his legs and sat upright.

"That conniving Westlake lad tells him, 'To live a full life and make a difference by doing good.' A rather strange answer, if you asks me. I knew they was up to something so I came straight to you," Harris finished, smiling as if he had just caught a big fish.

Jackson watched as a new pool of water expanded around Harris's boots. "Harris, I think you have just secured their release. After two weeks of captivity—or let's say as our guests—it's apparent to me that either we've made a mistake or, in any event, that these men are going to tell us nothing. Release them and set them on their way with all their belongings. All their belongings, do I make myself clear?"

"But what did I say that makes you want to let 'em go?" Harris whined. "You said I might have a go at 'em next."

"We've held them a long time, and they've told us nothing. We froze them at first and they told us nothing. We've eavesdropped on them and they told us nothing except that they want to live a full life and do good. So tell me how I can keep British citizens locked up here any longer with no reason to charge them. For God's sake, Harris, I've already told you, we're not kidnappers and thugs in the American army."

"We're not ... sir?"

"No, we are not!" Jackson yelled back. "Release them immediately and bring Westlake to me. The other two can wait next door. Now get out and get off my floor."

Jackson turned his back on him and when Harris left the room, he turned his mind to the interview he would now have with Westlake. He had to admit that he liked the young man, and in different circumstances he was sure they could be friends, but at this point he knew Westlake was angry and there would be protests. A knock at the door signaled the beginning of their final encounter.

"Enter," Jackson called out from behind his desk. "Mr. Westlake, it's good to have you and your friends on your way again. I hope your visit with us has been an agreeable one."

Westlake stood and glowered, the knitted black toque in hand. "We've been deprived of our possessions and held here against our will, without charge, for two weeks. I suppose this may be standard practice for the American army, but when I get back to York, the highest authorities will hear about it."

"Come, Mr. Westlake, apart from being a little cold while we made your quarters ready, there's been no harm done to you. We've every right to investigate strangers passing through our territory. What else would you expect me do in uncertain times?"

Jackson got up and went to perch on the front of his desk, one leg brushing the floor. "You can complain to General Brock if you will, but I doubt very much whether he'll take your protests seriously. Tell him to drop by and see me." Jackson slid off the desk and extended his hand with a grin.

Westlake took hold and held on. "I'm afraid, Captain Jackson, that if you should ever meet General Brock, it'll be at the dangerous end of a cannon. Now, goodbye."

Westlake turned and marched out of the room.

With some parting threats from Sergeant Harris about killing all of them if he ever got the chance, the three travelers on horseback passed through the gates of Fort Detroit and headed to freedom. A short distance along, and ensuring they were not being followed, Westlake turned his party around and headed back to the Sandwich trail. They were still going to make that visit to the Lapointe farm.

"So where did all the Frogs come from around here?" Ned asked.

Westlake explained to his companions how Danny Lapointe's family was like many French settlers who had arrived in the last forty years to farm alongside the river. Most had come through connections with the fur trade, and now the French comprised more than a quarter of the total population in Detroit. The Canadian side of the river boasted former American residents, the United Empire Loyalists, and on the American side of the river were farms held by former Canadian inhabitants. Westlake could not imagine these two groups actually going to war and killing each other.

He approached the Lapointe lane just as the warmth of the first springtime breeze gusted past; it was easy to tell the change in the air and, although no one spoke, Westlake recalled their capture in this same spot two weeks previously. He turned in his saddle to look for signs of American soldiers. With nothing in sight except rolling hills covered in snow, Westlake and his two friends proceeded on down the lane. Ned reached over and slapped Walt's shoulder, hinting to observe four strong and well-groomed mares that stared at them from behind a gray fence of split-cedar logs. As before, the barn was partly open, and they heard the sound of an axe splitting wood. Westlake banged hard on the big door.

Danny Lapointe stepped out from around the barn door, his red woolen shirt showing sweat stains under the arms. He was about the same height as Westlake but with a darker complexion and sturdier build. "Jonathan, where the hell have you been? I've been chopping this damn wood all morning. Look at my shirt, I'm soaking—you should have been here to help." As he yanked off his toque, his curly brown hair sprang to life.

"I guess we could have timed our arrival from York to be two hours earlier. We'll run faster next time, eh lads." Westlake laughed.

"Have you guys been putting up with his lousy humor all the way from York? I'll bet he told you the one about your weight and the dents in the snow. He tells everyone that and it's not even his joke."

Westlake gripped Danny's shoulder. "I would like you to meet my friends here, Ned and Walt Parrish." They shook hands with vigor, and Lapointe said, "Wait, I want to show you guys something I bet Johnny hasn't told you about."

He darted into the barn and returned a minute later with his coat on while in his hand he gripped a foot-long black-handled hunting knife. He led them back along the path and stopped about forty feet away from the barn. A vigorous throw planted his knife in the barn door, with a thud, at eye level. "Okay, Johnny, I want to see your knife land at the same exact level, and no more than six inches to the right."

"I'm here to ask you an important question, not to play games with knives."

"C'mon, throw it," Lapointe demanded. "You did it for the Shawnee, now do it for us. I'll answer your question later."

"I can't do it, it's much too far and what knife are you talking about anyway?" Westlake laughed.

"That knife." Danny pointed to Jonathan's boot. "The one from Paxinos."

In a single motion, Westlake drew the weapon sheathed outside his long boot and, with a sidearm toss, the knife was stuck to the barn door, gently waving, six inches to the right and dead level with Danny's.

"Very good," Ned said. "I am impressed. Learned that from the Injuns, did you?"

Westlake grinned but said nothing. At the thud of his knife, a black crow had lifted off from the barn roof and was now fluttering back to take up its former position. "Walt, show 'em what a musket can do in the right hands."

Walt casually lifted his musket from his crossed arms, put it to his shoulder, pointed, and pulled the trigger. The explosion and the crow falling seemed to happen at the same time. All four men stood and stared at one another.

"Well, now that we know we're all expert killers, why don't we eat?" Danny said. "I can't believe you made that shot."

Ned slapped his leg in amusement. "Walt has never shot anything in his life. That was only a joke, and I was sure he would miss." Walt shrugged and shook his head.

As the four men jostled toward the house, out the front door came running Danny's youngest brother.

"Hey, *bonjour*, Marcel," Westlake shouted. "Comment ça va? "

"*Bien, et vous?* "

"*Bien*," Westlake replied. "I'm doing well."

"I heard a gunshot so I thought maybe Danny had shot himself by mistake." Everyone laughed, again.

"I shot a crow off the barn," Walt announced proudly.

Danny punched Marcel in the shoulder.

"Come on," he said. "You can ask me your big question at dinner." Danny walked to the front door and looked over his shoulder at Westlake. "Let's eat, and you," pointing to Marcel, "*ferme la bouche.*"

The Parrish brothers frowned at each other, puzzled, so Westlake played interpreter. "That means, shut your mouth."

9

......

IN THE EARLY SPRINGTIME, Washington, D.C., warms up quicker than most parts of Michigan. By the end of March, after an extended winter, the warmer winds bring a certain optimism into the air, albeit not one that the visiting Michigan Governor William Hull was sharing, no matter how wonderful the breeze felt or how bright the sun shone.

Hull insisted he didn't want to do it. They had tried everything, and even flattery had not worked. They reminded him of the nine battles he fought during the revolution, a bullet ripping through his hat and another tearing up his boot. The Congress even voted him special thanks, as the bravest of the brave, but he still said no to their request.

Hull arrived in Washington expecting to be appointed secretary of war, but President Madison was sticking with his idiot friend, William Eustis. Hull liked Eustis, but everyone knew he was useless except the president, and he was the only one that mattered. Henry Dearborn had already been offered the post of commander of the U.S. Army, so that role was out too. What therefore could Hull do?

For the job of brigadier general and commander of the U.S. Army of the Northwest, the president had no one else to turn to, but that was Madison's problem. And since Hull was in town, he decided to get a few things straight with his president. Personally, he liked Madison but hated this city, so the longer he was there the harder it was for him to maintain his liking for Madison.

Hull set out today for the official residence of the president of the United States on Pennsylvania Avenue. In a foul mood, he stepped on to the road and spit a mouthful of chewing tobacco, which became a necessity when he was under pressure, and right now he felt plenty. A few minutes' brisk walk and he reached the president's door, where a stern black servant showed him directly into the president's office. Madison smiled and circled the large desk to shake hands with his visitor.

"William, how are you? A touch warmer here than in Michigan, I expect."

"But it's not making me feel any better, Mr. President. You know I'm only fifty-eight, but I'm just flat-out too tired for the field."

"I need you, William. Eustis and Dearborn need you too."

"I'm too tired."

"The country needs you," the president said gravely. He motioned to a cushioned chair for Hull to sit down.

This was the one argument Hull could not refute. His stomach clenched at the words, and he remained standing as the president strolled back to his own chair.

"With all due respect, sir, if anyone is to succeed in the Old Northwest, there are a few things they need from you." He chewed on his tobacco a little faster.

"Don't be shy, presidents need to know the truth. Large events are unfolding and if there's something I can do to ensure success, then ask away." Even as the president uttered the words, to Hull he didn't sound convincing.

"Hope you don't mind my tobacco, but it calms me when I'm nervous. If I agree to fight this war for you, I'd want to stay on as governor." Hull continued to chew, waiting for a negative reaction from the president, but none came. "And the Army of the Northwest has to comprise an independent command—no strange ideas coming from Dearborn. In order to succeed, I'd need at least three thousand men, preferably four thousand. Of course, some would have to be militia, but in that cast they must come from outside Michigan."

"Why's that?"

"A large part of Detroit is French Canadian and the rest of the population all seems to be related to someone on the Canadian side of the water. Heck, my own brother lives over there on the Thames River. Families aren't likely to fight each other."

"So troops have to come from far away to ensure a willingness to fight? Am I right?" The president frowned. "And please do sit down because you're making me nervous." He gave a small grin, but Hull still paid no attention to the chair.

"And they'd better be used to battling Indians, 'cause they're the key to this whole business. The British are continually stirring them up and heaven help us if we can't control them." Hull finally sat down and started looking for something on the polished floor. "Finally, we need a navy on the Great Lakes starting with Lake Erie so we can move our men and arms quickly. We need to control the lakes—they're another key to the affair. Well, that's my list of requirements, and I've said all I need. Do you have a bucket by chance?"

The president pointed to a copper waste container sitting by the desk, and Hull let fly with a gob of tobacco. Madison turned his head away quickly and Hull suspected he didn't approve of his visitor's chewing tobacco, or his list of demands. Yet he knew Madison was in a difficult situation since Congress was pushing him hard for war. The "war hawks" wanted to seize Indian lands and gain total control of the northwest trade in furs. The British had meanwhile given them every excuse to shout about preserving American honor. Pressure for war was mounting steadily, and Madison now needed someone to command the Army of the Northwest.

"William, I guess you've got me over a barrel, since I've no one but you. That means I can only answer yes to all your … let's call them suggestions. I won't ask you to resign as governor and I'll tell Dearborn you are to be left alone."

"Thank you, sir."

"You've got four hundred army regulars to start with, and I'll see what else I can do about arranging more. Your militia can come from Ohio and, if you're feeling a little tired these days, I've just the man to help you out in the energy department. He's Duncan McArthur and a little flamboyant, but he's organizing your militiamen even as we speak." To William Hull, the president was sounding like a salesman. "You know those relatives of yours may prove a great help to you. You've heard Jefferson is saying that taking Canada will be 'a mere matter of marching'—those are his very words—so this whole war thing might not be as difficult as you think."

"And what would Jefferson know?" Hull shook his head in disbelief.

Madison ignored the comment and continued, "As for the Indians, I know some are against us, but many of them are waiting to see which way events might go. A good show of force will tell them that we mean business. Your job is to cut a new road from Urbana to Detroit and secure the Northwest—our left flank, so to speak. When the time comes, you can cross the Detroit River and take Sandwich and Amherstburg."

Easy for you to say, thought Hull.

"Go on up and see your brother on the Thames. Meanwhile, Dearborn will arrange an attack in Niagara, to take some pressure off you. What do think?"

Hull nodded, chewing slowly, and doubted silently if Dearborn could manage such an undertaking competently.

"Once you can secure the Northwest, then Dearborn can take the army on up through Sackets Harbour and attack Kingston and Montreal without fear of his left flank going up in flames. As for the navy on the Lakes, you'll have to consult Eustis because on this one I can't promise you results. Funds are tight, but I'll do my bit. So what do you think—will you help us out?"

"You're sure—positive—that Dearborn will attack across the Niagara River?" Hull asked.

"Those are his orders."

"I guess we have a deal, then." Hull clasped the president's hand and backed away, then spit into the bucket again.

"Thank you, Brigadier General Hull." The president smiled. "I wish your army the best of good fortune. If it comes to war, God will be with you and the United States."

Their meeting had not lasted as long as Hull had been dreading. He had got most of what he asked for and he was now a brigadier general with a free hand to run the Army of the Northwest. He still had to meet Eustis about the deployment of the navy, but he knew that would be a waste of his breath. The less he saw of Dearborn too, the less interference he'd have to put up with. However, it would take time to train the militia and, the way the president spoke, war seemed imminent, so more important to his way of thinking was to track down this fellow McArthur.

Brigadier General Hull approached on horseback, along with a party of three officers. Almost two months had passed before the Army of the Northwest was finally organized, and it was time for a general review. Colonel Duncan McArthur, of the 1st Ohio Regiment of militia volunteers, sat upright in his horse. It stepped sideways and gently brushed against the leg of Colonel James Findlay, recently elected colonel of the 2nd Ohio Regiment. Each man now had approximately four hundred militiamen under his command. The 3rd Ohio Regiment was under the command of Colonel Lewis Cass, a lawyer and U.S. Marshall for the state of Ohio.

Yards away, Hull watched the militia officers snicker and joke among themselves. Tired and cold from the ride to Dayton, he knew he looked much older than his fifty-eight years and he suspected they were probably laughing at him. Governor of Michigan for the last seven years, with his receding white hair, a charitable description of him might be "distinguished," but the three colonels were in no mood to be charitable. They wanted action, and had already complained to Hull that his deliberate preparations were taking up too much time. He hauled up his horse in front of them.

"Congratulations from me are in order, seeing as all three of you have been elected to your militia commands, though I've no idea how any army is supposed to function as a democracy. Meet William Beall, assistant quartermaster general in charge of our supplies, and this is Robert Lucas ... and this, gentlemen, is Lieutenant Colonel James Miller, U.S. 4th Infantry, Army of the Northwest."

McArthur, dressed in buckskin pants and a brown homespun shirt, was first to respond.

"There's no problem over elected officers seeing it's the American way." He gave a thin smile, since the popular inclination was to keep away from anything that smacked of too much British tradition.

"I need no lessons from you about the American way. I was fighting for our independence while you were still in your diapers. Get it out of your head that everything British is always wrong and everything American is right. We need the best ideas, and I don't care where they come from, as long they're right, and voting on military decisions is a wrong idea." He could feel his face reddening. "One more thing, you'll address me as 'sir' from now on or you can return home immediately."

There was silence for a long moment. Then McArthur replied quietly, "Yes, sir, General Hull." Now it was the turn of the stocky Cass.

"General, we just want to get moving and attack the British, so what's wrong with marching now?"

"Did you check the powder in the magazines?" Hull asked him.

Cass shook his head no.

"McArthur, did you check the coverings of the cartridge boxes?" McArthur did not move.

"While you three were busy electioneering, maybe one of you should've noticed that we have no armorer to repair our weapons. Who of you wants to face the British with insufficient ammunition and no weapons? Ah, just as I thought, you think we should prepare and take our time. Maybe wait until the first of June, when we'll be sure of having everything we require."

No one said anything, but Hull knew dissension when he saw it, and these men were going to be difficult.

"I'm waiting for an answer, gentlemen."

"Yes, sir, we should wait for the ammo," McArthur replied.

"Yes, sir, we should wait," Findlay joined in. Cass just nodded in agreement.

"Good, well, that's something we all agree on. Now, after we leave Dayton, in a few days, we'll hit Urbana. From there on we have to hack our own road through the bush. I know some back trails that'll help, but there's going to be tough times ahead. Prepare your men for it and sharpen your axes. If the Indians don't get us, the mosquitoes will. Great to have you with us, gentlemen. Good day." A beginning at least, but not the one Hull had hoped for.

With constant prodding, Jonathan Westlake urged his horse slowly ahead while Ned and Walt Parrish followed. The melting snow left the well-worn forest paths soft with scattered puddles, the deeper levels actually under water. On this sodden ground, the men were fortunate to manage half the distance they had traveled on snow and ice. Most of the time, they walked beside their horses, listening to the sucking noise made by their hooves in the soggy mud.

Westlake's important question for Danny Lapointe was asking him to join them on their mission, but Lapointe had other plans. He was hiking back to Lower Canada, where his uncle had promised him a working farm on the St. Lawrence River, just west of Montreal. With no son of his own, his uncle wanted to leave his legacy in good hands, and Danny was his favorite nephew, the oldest boy in his sister's household. There seemed no one better for that inheritance to the old man.

Westlake was hoping Lapointe might change his mind, as he revealed the strategic significance of their quest. The young men had become close friends at school in Cornwall, a bond that had grown stronger during Westlake's previous trip to the Old Northwest. He could sense Lapointe's reluctance to say no. More than anything Westlake wished to share one last adventure together before Lapointe settled down to farm life, but nevertheless the men parted. Westlake continued on his way with the Parrish brothers while Lapointe would wait for the spring runoff before leaving his old Detroit home for good.

Westlake surveyed the forest, his eyes taking in each tree at a time. They had not met a white man or even an Indian since they left Detroit. They journeyed west, and to avoid the problems they had encountered at Fort Detroit, they stayed well south of Fort Dearborn, at the bottom tip of Lake Michigan. Westlake maintained in his head a map of the great inland water system with Lake Superior in the north and Lake Michigan and Lake Huron hanging to the south. He imagined the water flowing past Detroit into Lake Erie, then roaring over Niagara Falls into Lake Ontario, and finally finding its way out through the mighty St. Lawrence River to the Atlantic Ocean. All this vast extent of water carrying furs to buyers far away, men never to be seen. The entire water system covered a distance longer than from London to Moscow, which reminded Westlake that he had a lot of ground to cover, and speed was critical.

On one side of the path appeared a small clearing, twenty paces across, while on the other side of it the forest remained dense. Westlake turned to face his horse and pulled on the reins as the animal's hooves again became stuck in the mud.

"Make no sudden movements, gentlemen," a commanding voice boomed from the forest nearby. "That's right, just stay calm."

Westlake turned slowly to detect where the voice originated.

"You will drop your weapons gently to the ground, then one hand held in the air and the other holding your reins will do nicely." The voice carried a threatening tone.

Four men on foot sprung up suddenly from the forest undergrowth, aiming muskets at the travelers. Three of the men, close to the path, had filthy beards that reached their chests, and one of them, covered in mud from head to toe, grew out of the ground so close to Ned that he was only an arm's length away. Westlake had walked right by him. A fourth man stood at the edge of the clearing, close to a pair of horses carrying a single rider, who had emerged on horseback from behind some cedars. This fifth man on horseback gave the instructions.

Westlake noticed beneath the man's open greatcoat a well-worn British officer's uniform and an English cutlass. A naval man for sure and there was no mistaking his tone of authority.

"You three fellows have been hard to find. You headed out so fast from York to Detroit that we lost track, but then like fools, you get yourselves captured by miserable Sergeant Harris. That gave us our chance to catch up." As he spoke, his high cheekbones remained curiously still while the hooded eyes over a nose and chin that were too small for his face gave him the appearance of a great owl.

The tall man standing first in front of him slipped sideways on the uneven ground and bumped the muzzle of the rider's horse. From what Westlake could see, they could easily have been brothers. The officer tightened the reins, so the horse remained steady. Westlake calculated their odds, three against five; they had only a slim chance with those muskets pointed at their chests. He nodded to the Parrish brothers, and they followed his example as he slowly lowered his weapon to the ground.

"Now, here is what each of you will do," the man on horseback continued. "With one hand raised and the other holding the reins, each of you will now take three steps forward in front of his horse."

"Wait!" Westlake exclaimed, so the brothers stood still. "Who are you, and why do you stop us?"

"That's none of your business," the man on horseback replied sharply. "Just do as I order, and no one will get hurt—at least for now."

His men grinned and grunted in amusement, but Westlake and the Parrish brothers didn't budge. Westlake tried again, "We're ordinary fur traders, and residents of Upper Canada, so why would a British officer be threatening the civilians that he's sworn to protect?"

"Appearances can be deceiving, young man, and I'm sworn to protect no one but myself. You can feed all that crap about who you are to Captain Jackson, but I'll kill you if you say it again. Just do as I say. Now, step forward."

Westlake motioned for the Parrish brothers to comply, but on his third step Ned skidded in the mud and fell to the ground, in a splash. The mud-covered fellow closest to him was so startled at the sudden movement that when he jerked the musket it slipped in his grip and blasted its ball straight into Ned Parrish's chest.

"You bloody fool," shouted the man on horseback.

"Sorry, sir … an accident … It just went off."

At that instant, a tomahawk came whistling through the trees, cracking into the forehead of the assailant closest to Westlake. The man stood wavering, his hands briefly reaching for the axe, before toppling over backward with the handle jutting up out of his skull.

Westlake tensed, realizing that this was his chance. In a twisting motion, he reached for the knife at his boot and flung it hard at the attacker standing closest to Walt. The man fell sideways, clutching at his throat, where already the blood streamed through his matted beard. In a matter of seconds his eyes opened wider, and then wider still until they froze.

The commander in the saddle had quickly turned the horses to ride off to safety, the other man standing with him now running at the rear. Westlake grabbed for his tomahawk that was sheathed on his own horse.

As the man on foot turned back, he fired too quickly, the bullet smacking into the neck of Westlake's mount. The man stared when the animal staggered on its front legs, then he groaned as a hunting knife took him full in the chest, entering with such force that it buried itself to the black handle. He dropped to his knees and tumbled face forward.

Westlake gazed around in amazement as Walt took three giant strides, landing right on top of Ned's shooter, who was frantically trying to reload his musket. Both of Walt's hands gripped the man by his mud-smeared neck. He flailed against them, trying to break their grip, but oblivious to the pain Walt wouldn't let go. Even two hard punches to Walt's face produced no effect. Quickly the man's head turned red and purple, then he lost all strength and the struggle was over.

The only attacker remaining was the man on horseback, who had crashed off through the trees while his accomplices had died. Westlake ran the short distance to peer through the brush where the rider had departed the clearing and headed back into the forest. He turned his head to search for Ned's horse that had wandered off into the tangled forest. Westlake ran after it, grabbed its reins, and leaped into the saddle. He rode back a short way to snatch up his musket, then spurred the horse into a gallop. After stumbling in the mud, it regained its balance and found stony ground before Westlake guided it through the same opening in the trees that his quarry had chosen. But once inside the forest again, he could see no one, so he slowed the horse to a cautious walk and then stopped completely to listen.

There was no sound to be heard and no sight of their enemy, but he noticed that the trail ahead was covered with hoof marks and footprints, both coming and going. Clearly, the five men had traveled this ground before, perhaps while rehearsing their ambush. He considered whether it was possible to hunt the man down but could see no obvious way forward. Accepting defeat, he tugged on the reins to turn his horse back to Ned.

As he trotted into the clearing that had been the scene of the skirmish, he found the four dead attackers lying on the ground. His bleeding horse laid nearby and Walt knelt beside his injured brother. Westlake dismounted and crouched along side the pair of them.

"I strangled him with my bare hands," Walt murmured. "I swore I'd break his neck, Ned, and I did."

A slight smile came to the corner of Ned's mouth as he closed his eyes. "Thank you, Walter," Ned whispered to his twin brother from a face the color of chalk.

Westlake swung round at the sound of footsteps and found at his side the familiar face of Danny Lapointe.

"Your tomahawk killed the first man and I guess you threw the knife that killed the last one," Westlake said.

"I was too late for Ned. I watched it all from back there, but I had no idea that this stupid fellow was going to fire." Lapointe glanced down at Ned. "I've just circled the area and there are no more of them nearby."

Westlake nodded. "Let's take a look at Ned's wound," he suggested.

Walt glanced up at them but did not move away. He gently undid the buttons of Ned's coat and did the same with the shirt beneath, and then he drew up the undershirt so that the hole in Ned's chest was visible.

"There's little bleeding on the outside, but that ball has gone in deep." Westlake put his ear to the wound and held his breathe, listening carefully. "By the sound of the gurgling, it's lodged in his lung so it's very bad. Let's move him out of the mud and put some blankets underneath him to keep the dampness out." Westlake stood up and said to Walt, "For what it's worth, I believe that man fired by accident. Those bloody muskets can be touchy."

Lapointe shook his head. "Makes no difference to Ned. Accident or no accident, he's in serious trouble."

Westlake felt his hands start to shake and his head go light. He stepped over to a low branch, grabbed it, and he steadied himself while he retched. Lapointe followed him and watched as Westlake spit what was left in his mouth. "I've never killed a man before. It all happened so fast." He spit out bile again and took a deep breath. "I thought you were going to Montreal?" He felt Lapointe's hand resting on his back. "I'm okay now, Danny ... just shaky."

"I decided to go to Montreal, by way of Fort St. Joseph and

Michilimackinac." Lapointe grimaced. "It means an extra thousand miles to my trip, but the ice has broken in that Detroit River and now it's flowing too fast to cross. Besides, I knew you English could not make it without a good French Canadian along to guide you." He grinned, tapping Westlake's back twice, and moved to stand facing him. "I traveled hard to catch up even though I left only two days after you did. You three have been flying despite the mud."

"I sacrificed safety for speed, Ned's accident is my fault."

"That's crazy talk. You didn't shoot him."

"It'll never happen to us again, I swear. How's Ned doing, Walt?" Westlake asked.

"He feels hot, and look how flushed he's becoming." Walt took his hand away from Ned's forehead. "Is that where we're going, this Fort St. Joseph you mentioned?"

Westlake looked at Lapointe and shrugged. "General Brock ordered me not to inform you, in case we were captured. Our task is to find Robert Dickson, the red-haired chief of a Menominee band of warriors. Apparently, he's somewhere in Wisconsin Territory. After we find him, we head on to Fort St. Joseph."

A sudden wind gusted through the trees, and Westlake looked around instinctively to see if anyone appeared.

"We need to be ready in case any more of them come back."

"Why will this red-haired chief help you?" Walt asked.

"Brock's message, that I hid in the bottom of my boot is vague, but Dickson will know what it means."

"What if we can't find him?" Lapointe asked.

"We go to Fort St. Joseph and be ready to assist a Captain Roberts, should he receive orders from Brock to seize Fort Mackinac. Then we race like hell to tell Brock what has happened. To win a war against the Americans, General Brock needs the Indians on side, and to get the Indians, he'll need an early victory once war's declared."

"Christ, this is really serious business," Lapointe declared.

Westlake's hand gripped Walt's shoulder. "So that's our secret mission."

"Why would the Indians fight for Brock?" Lapointe asked.

"Tecumseh wants an Indian state, land between the United States and Upper Canada, but the Americans told him to forget that and then burnt down his home." Westlake scanned the trees as the wind again whistled through the forest.

"Brock will support Tecumseh's struggle with the Americans. The more the Americans settle on Indian land, the more angry the Indians become. Throw in the fur traders too, and at some point there has to be an explosion."

"I'm not leaving my brother here," Walt said grimly. "That bastard might come back."

"We'll make camp here for the night. Let's get a fire going right beside him."

On one side of the path, the ground rose higher and it was relatively dry. Lapointe gently took Ned's feet and Westlake lifted his head while Walt, who had laid out a bearskin, supported the wounded man's torso. As Ned groaned and gurgled loudly, the three men jumped in unison when Westlake's horse let out a piercing whinny.

"Tonight we guard in shifts, in case our friend on horseback returns. I need to put my horse out of her misery," Westlake said bitterly. "Walt, gather up the extra muskets and clean them thoroughly before they're reloaded. Once they're ready, we'll all be safer. We don't need to be shooting with fouled weapons."

"Hey, Johnny, what did they want with you?" Lapointe asked. "We can talk about it later, but do you think they were just robbers?" He waved Westlake away with his hand. "We need a roof over our heads or we'll be covered in dew before morning. I'll build us a lean-to over where Ned is lying and, along with a good fire, it should help keep us all warm."

"Before it's dark, I'll secure the horses and see if our dead friends here have any clues on them as to who they are," Westlake decided. "That owl-faced guy somehow knew we came from York."

10

· · · · · ·

From his office window, General Brock stared out at his small defenses, watching the snow melt. Behind the twelve-foot-deep ditch and the ten-foot-high stone wall created to impede invaders, Government House looked directly south toward the circular battery that protected it from attack across Lake Ontario. Built for Governor John Grave Simcoe in the late 1790s, its walls of stone slate had been hacked out of the Niagara Escarpment and floated here fifty miles by barge.

If the Americans were coming, Brock would know soon enough. An extra three hundred soldiers had arrived but with just fifteen hundred regulars to protect an area larger than France, defense was impossible. He hated that word and had told his officers many times that *impossible* did not exist for a British soldier.

"What is to be done?" Brock asked himself out loud.

If war came, he wanted to seize the initiative, but from Governor General Sir George Prevost, his superior in Montreal, he had clear orders to do nothing to provoke the enemy. And Brock knew Prevost was acting on direct instructions from England. He leaned over the top of his desk to study a map of British North America that showed him the obvious opening moves of a potential war. An American attack at Kingston and Montreal would cut off Upper Canada, and this had led Prevost to suggest the abandonment of the province so that he himself could concentrate his meager forces in Lower Canada, around Quebec City.

Brock had recently won an argument with him to use the defense of Upper Canada to delay an enemy attack on Montreal. Yet how could he be successful without provocative action and still stop the Americans from running unconstrained through the streets of York? Surely the British authorities would let him act in Canada's own interest. Then again, perhaps not, for their interests and those of Upper

Canada's were not identical. They were a long ways distant and didn't understand the situation he faced. If it came to a choice between following orders and achieving victory in war, Brock knew he would err on the side of winning, but God help the officer who disobeyed his orders and didn't produce victory. British military justice always was harshest on the defeated. He shouted out to the sleepy Private Burns, standing guard outside his door, "Find me Major Glegg! Quick, man, at the double!"

The York Volunteer Militia required expansion and hard training, but these citizen soldiers had to accept his demands on their time and labor. Untrained, they could lose their homes and even their lives to an invader. He wished he knew which of the citizens to arm, for there were so many recently arrived Americans that he ran the risk of arming an internal enemy. His military adviser, Major J.B. Glegg, would have to decide on an individual basis.

And Brock had no firm commitments among the Indians, yet without them he suspected the Canadas were doomed. They were the warriors he was desperate to have on side, but to bring the Indians over he needed a victory, and to have a victory required a battle, which was precisely what he had been instructed against. But he could plan for a battle now, and later hope for a change of heart in Prevost.

"You called, sir," Glegg puffed. Captain Nelles entered behind him.

"A bit of a run shouldn't have you panting, Major," he chided. "Transfer two hundred men immediately to Fort Amherstburg. If the Americans attacked us today, it would be either at Niagara or Sandwich, and right now we're weakest in the south. The sight of some fresh regulars will stiffen their resolve at the fort. Also, I have some work for you with the York Volunteers that we need to discuss. Have you heard anything yet from Captain Roberts at Fort St. Joseph?"

"No, sir, but it is early days," Glegg replied. "Our note will do the trick. He knows what to do."

"How about Westlake, anything there? It's been two months now." Brock looked to Nelles.

"I am afraid not a word, sir, but in this case, may I suggest that no news may in fact be positive."

"Wherever he is, we can only hope he is keeping his mind on his own business and not on everything else." Brock nodded. "Let's get on with our militia problems. How many more volunteers could we raise, Major Glegg? Do you think they would accept some extra training—some hard drilling?"

Glegg pondered the question before answering. "While they are volunteers, sir, they're also enthusiastic. It's plowing and planting time soon so this is our only chance to turn them into a proper fighting force."

"Get on with it then, and keep a sharp eye for these dammed American sympathizers. We don't need the American army knowing every bloody move we make." Brock tapped the table twice with his finger, as if to make his point. "I'll be leaving York shortly for Niagara before I must meet again with those scared chickens in the legislature. If this mess with the Americans gets any worse, I've decided to suspend all legislative sittings. The cowardly way those politicians talk, you'd think they supported the other side."

Walt Parrish sat beside his wounded brother, watching him closely by the firelight. Had they really come all the way from England to end up like this, with one of them dying in the middle of a forest? It just wasn't fair. Their father had run off before they knew him and their mother had done her best to raise them into their teens, but then she'd died after a long coughing illness. She'd never ceased cleaning other people's houses, washing clothes, darning socks, and knitting sweaters: anything to make enough honest money for their clothes, food, and shelter.

After she died, his brother and him had cried for a week. Her last request asked them to always stay together. "You've a better chance staying shoulder to shoulder," she coughed out.

To begin with, they slung barrels of rum imported from the Caribbean on the brand new quay of London's West India Dock, but the work there was infrequent, so they had drifted from the great inner city to its outskirts, stealing food wherever they went. Walt remembered his one and only victorious prizefight earning him a shilling that fed them both that night but his eyes had remained black for weeks. They got a few odd jobs painting rich men's houses but in the end barely escaped arrest after they were caught stealing from an owner's wine cellar.

They drifted into a life of highway robbery, and it was there they acquired a five-pound purse from a sleeping officer who belonged to a rifle regiment. How the man could sleep in a coach traveling those bumpy roads, Walt never figured out. "We're rich," Ned exclaimed as he counted the money in delight.

Walt shook his head and stared down at his sleeping brother; that rifle officer had chased them all the way from the southern edges of London to Portsmouth, where they escaped only by joining the army—"taking the King's shilling" —on the promise that they would ship out within the hour. A small boat took them out to a large ship and an hour later they set sail for Canada with the 41st Foot, still safely together and ready to begin a new life.

Walt Parrish realized the seriousness of their mistake within a couple of days because not only was he violently seasick but he was also unprepared for military discipline. After an entire month back on shore devoted to marching and drilling, he began talk to Ned about making a run for it. That's when they encountered Captain Nelles, who seemed to know exactly what they were thinking without ever their saying a word, and he firmly warned them they would be hanged as deserters. "Stay with it," he urged and promised to find a job for them. So while remaining rascals, they didn't run.

Captain Nelles kept good to his word, and here they were, stranded in the middle of a great wilderness. Just as they had decided to apply for some of that free land Westlake's uncle told them about, planning to be farmers, Ned gets himself shot. After all the pair of them had been through, it just wasn't fair. Walt put his hands to face and a tear fell to his cheek. He sighed, his chest heaving in despair. Happy the others were asleep and couldn't see him cry, he threw another log on the campfire and peered into a black forest. For the first time in his life, he felt really alone.

The sun started lighting the day a full two hours before the forest floor saw any shadows. Except for their little clearing, the trees were thick about them and while there was no wind, April makes for cool mornings in Michigan. Westlake shivered under their lean-to and opened his eyes to see Walt alternately staring into the forest and watching his brother. Ned had passed a peaceful night, but he looked flushed and almost motionless. They had to reach Robert Dickson and his Indian followers soon, but they couldn't simply abandon Ned. The bullet was lodged too far in his chest and just moving him off the path caused him pain, so transporting him any farther was not an option.

Westlake decided that, since they had to remain, they wouldn't waste time. Mentally he checked off the list of priorities for the day: breakfast first, some sleep for Walt, enough firewood to keep Ned and themselves warm. Then check all their weapons again, scout the area in a quarter-mile circle for their attackers, strip his dead horse, search the corpses one last time for any clue to their identity, and finally bury them before their rotting corpses started attracting predators. He yawned and stretched, watching his frosted breath hang before him in the air.

Lapointe had grilled him about the ambushers, but he had no idea who they were. Lying back, he pulled the blanket up until the coarse wool scratched his neck. Westlake closed his eyes and surprisingly Mary Collins's bared shoulder came into his mind.

Like a spark in a firing pan, it came to him. She had told him how a man in uniform had gripped her by the neck; that he dressed as a soldier but didn't act like one. The other men addressed him as "sir" and she had felt a sword pressing through his greatcoat as he seized her. Perhaps he was the same one who had led the attackers: the one dressed like an officer. But what was he trying to accomplish by pursuing and attacking Westlake? Revenge for Wagg's beating seemed unlikely, yet he seemed to already know where Westlake was traveling.

With breakfast over and Walt finally asleep, Lapointe chopped a two-foot-high wall of firewood to dry by the fire while Westlake watched the surrounding forest. When it was his turn to chop,

Westlake hacked at the wood with all his strength, angry with himself for the previous day's events. By the time they had finished, the wall of firewood stood four feet high, a reasonable barrier to any would-be intruders. Lapointe scooped up his musket to patrol the perimeter of their little camp.

Walt had now cleaned and loaded the four muskets taken from the dead men, so Westlake positioned them at intervals around their small camp, save for the one that shot Ned, which had to be laid gingerly on the top of the firewood. If attacked now, they had four extra shots to deliver before letting go with their own three muskets and another with Ned's. It would take a strong force to overcome them, but Westlake still felt he had failed. If Lapointe had not come along at that precise moment they might have all been killed.

Although he hated the task, Westlake had to bury his horse. Since it was too large to move, with his shovel's edge he cleared away some brush and then dug right beside the dead animal, thus allowing himself and Lapointe to simply roll the carcass into its shallow grave.

"You were lucky," Danny remarked, "that could have been you instead of the horse."

Westlake paused a while before he replied. "I made a mistake marching too quickly, without ensuring a proper lookout. It'll never happen again. I'm off to circle our camp twice, once at a quarter-mile radius and again at a half-mile. That'll tell us where we are and if anyone is watching us." Westlake picked up his musket. "When Walt wakes up, tell him to check the corpses again in case I missed something. Then you and he will have some fun digging the graves to bury them."

"Hey, Johnny, I'm not one of your soldier boys so don't order me about."

"Fine, don't bury them then, but they're going to stink soon and you'll have black bears on your ass."

"*Mon ami*, so you made a mistake and now you are angry," Lapointe snapped back. "Just don't take it out on me. We'll bury these dead guys in shallow graves, just deep enough to keep the animals away. I don't like bears anymore than you do, but remember, I don't take orders from anyone."

Westlake walked away in silence, and Lapointe called after him, "Hey, while you're out there, don't forget what Paxinos taught us."

"What's that?" Westlake turned back.

"Keep quiet and keep it sneaky." Lapointe grinned and raised his eyebrows.

Westlake waved to him and disappeared into the cedars.

By the time Westlake returned, the daylight was fading. In two great circles around their camp, he had padded quietly but found no trace of anyone. Just some fresh bear droppings and a few deer trails besides the tracks of their single horseman heading straight north. But why heading north, and where he was going, Westlake had no idea.

"Don't shoot, it's me, Jonathan," he shouted as he approached.

Lapointe appeared from behind their woodpile barrier and whispered, "Ned stopped breathing a few minutes ago."

"Oh God, where's Walt?"

"He's sitting beside his brother, holding his hand and talking to him as if he's still alive. Walt needs some time to feel bad."

Westlake walked a short way off and sat down on a log, putting his head in his hands. He'd thought Ned might die, but he hadn't imagined how terrible he'd feel when it happened.

Lapointe strolled over until his knee brushed against Westlake's arm. "Come on, Johnny, Ned was not going to get better. You already knew that. Did you see anything out there—any signs of the bad guys?"

Westlake shook his head to indicate no. "I can't believe this has happened to us. My Uncle George was right, we would be lucky to all came back alive." He rose and walked over to Ned's body lying motionless beside the fire. Walt still sat beside it, rocking back and forth, squeezing Ned's hand in the same gentle rhythm, as if he could bring back life to a stilled heart. Westlake touched his shoulder and felt him sob.

"I'm very, very sorry Walt. I didn't see it coming and I should have. Ned was a good man and he didn't deserve to die."

"Ned wouldn't want you to blame yourself. He slipped in the mud and that bastard jerked the musket, that's all that happened. But we'll never get that farm together, we'll never do nothing together again. Nothing … I feel like I've died." Walt's chin touched his heaving chest as he lowered his gaze to hide the tears in his eyes.

"I only knew him a short time and I feel so bad for the both of you." Westlake patted him again on the shoulder and stepped back to the woodpile. He picked up the shovel, headed a short distance into the woods, and began to dig. Careful to keep out of earshot of Walt, he chose somewhere not so far as to make it difficult to carry the body. Within a few moments, without a word said between them, Lapointe joined him in digging.

The fire sparked and hissed while Walt sat up through most of the night, peering into the darkness. Lapointe relieved him well before dawn, but Walt still did not lie down, he simply dozed off, sitting upright beside the body. Westlake slept soundly, exhausted from the tension. As the woods started to lighten, he woke knowing it was time to bury Ned's body.

"Where did you dig his grave?" Walt asked flatly.

"Just over there," Westlake pointed, stretching his arms to rid himself of the cold and stiffness.

"Let's get on with it, then. I want to leave this place." Walt spit. "If I ever find that owl-faced bastard, I'll rip his limbs off one at a time."

He carried his brother's body the short distance over to the grave. Then he jumped down inside and Westlake and Lapointe lowered the corpse into his arms. Gently, Walt laid the body out on the floor of the grave and climbed up, pulling on Westlake's hand for support. Walt touched Lapointe's shovel to pause him before he started shoveling again and then turned to Westlake. "Just a few words Jonathan—you know, like a real funeral, churchlike."

The three men stood, hats and mitts in hand, under a canopy of trees that arched overhead. Walt and Danny stood on either side of the grave, and Westlake at the head. After days of dull sky, the sun suddenly broke through the clouds, beaming columns of light through to the forest floor.

"I think we should bow our heads. I haven't done this before, so I'll just say what comes to mind. Ned was a good man that sinned only to get by in the world. He was quiet and often I thought he didn't understand, but I was wrong: he thought a lot about life. He had many questions, but I think he understood more than most. We feel like we ourselves have died, because our world with Ned in it is gone, but we have a responsibility now to remember his life and keep his spirit alive. We are better and wiser for knowing him. He loved his brother, and I am sure God has forgiven him his sins. I know all of us have. Amen."

Westlake raised his head to see Danny and Walt staring at him.

"That was beautiful." Lapointe touched Westlake's arm.

"Ned would've been happy with that, Jonathan, thank you," Walt said. "Those were very kind words for my brother. I even feels better. Let's cover him up."

Walt placed a blanket over Ned's head and body and then started the job of filling in the grave.

During breakfast, Westlake explained to them their travel directions. They would ride with muskets loaded across their horses, spread twenty yards between each man. The last man would keep a lookout behind, and the man in the middle would watch from side to side. Westlake had traveled this area before, so he knew that by heading south he would find Indians. Lapointe agreed that those Indians would tell them what they needed to know.

Just before leaving Walt handed Westlake a present. It was his brother's small knife, in a brown leather sheath, and with an appreciative nod he said, "Ned would want you to have it, Jonathan. Let's go. Right now, I just want to leave this place."

They saddled the horses, and Westlake tucked the knife through his waist belt and then led them away from the lean-to, the woodpile, and Ned's grave. He sighed with a mixed feeling of sadness but also relief. The wind increased as he glanced up at the heavy clouds rolling overhead.

Walt called out, "Goodbye, Ned." Westlake and Lapointe did the same, each giving a final wave to the grave, as the woods lost the sun and its cathedral of light vanished. It soon started to drizzle and the blood of wounds washed into the forest floor.

They headed south-southwest through the mud and the rain. It was time to find Robert Dickson.

11

· · · · · ·

MICHILIMACKINAC ISLAND

THE TWO MEN were almost touching, toe to toe, and the American customs officer reckoned he was in trouble.

"I'll not pay you a cent, seeing these are my provisions for my own personal use. Don't touch them or I'll knock you down so I will, I swear it. What's your name, laddie?"

The chubby customs man, just referred to as "laddie," had a loaded musket resting on his shoulder and was prepared to use it. A recent federal law, the Non-Importation Act, had to be obeyed. His job was to enforce that law and by so doing shut down the Canadian fur trade with Indians living on American soil. He took one step back.

"To you, it's Officer Bennett. Now, what value do you have packed on all those horses? You know better than to bring any goods across the border to trade with Indians."

"No more than a thousand dollars, I tell ye. I've been doing this for years without interference, and I'll have none now. You're getting me very angry, Officer Bennett. I don't know if I can stand much more."

Officer Bennett was a head shorter than the six-footer in front of him, so he knew he was no physical match. Under his fringed buckskin coat, this man from the forest sported muscular arms, broad shoulders, and a thick neck. A deep tan and shoulder-length wavy red hair made him appear like some kind of forest god.

And there was something else strange about him, for the four-inch fringe on the arms of his deer coat kept rippling in waves while his red hair lifted constantly in the breeze. He was standing still yet his necklace of bear teeth seemed to swing against his chest of their own

119

momentum. Everything about the man appeared to be moving, making it hard to focus on him precisely.

Bennett squinted, as if trying to view him at a distance instead of the arm's length that they stood apart.

"You've got a dozen horses tied together, packed to the sky, and you want me to believe all those supplies are for your own personal use. There's at least ten times the value you claim on those horses."

"Och, man, are you calling me a liar? I made a good bargain and bought these goods at a large discount."

"What you've told me is ridiculous, and you'll obey the law like everyone else passing Michilimackinac. What's your name, to begin with?"

Officer Bennett began to lower his musket, but before he could take aim his would-be smuggler snatched hold of the musket's barrel end and pointed it to the ground. He was laughing as he did so, but it was a nasty laugh.

"You think you can scare me with your toy? To survive in the north, you'll have to be a lot quicker than that." A second later, Bennett felt a pain to his jaw as his teeth snapped together and his head rocked backward. Then everything went dark.

"Oh that was a vicious punch, laddie, forgive me. When you wake up you're going to have a horrible headache, that's all. Serves you right, though, I tried to warn ye but you pushed me too far. By the way, since you asked, my name is Robert Dickson."

But that had been almost a year ago. Dickson leaned back on his elbows from the blazing fire, looking pleased with himself after recounting his tale.

Westlake suppressed a grin and watched him in admiration. It was the night of June 18, 1812, and Westlake, Lapointe, and Parrish had journeyed for more than fifteen hundred miles to catch this one man, the one the Sioux called Mascotapah, "the Red-Haired Chief." They had traveled west, then south to avoid Fort Dearborn, and then north after receiving word from a lone Indian the whereabouts of Dickson and his men. They finally caught up with him at a sharp bend in the Wisconsin River in Illinois Territory, at the Wisconsin–Fox Portage.

"You are a long ways from home, Mr. Dickson," Westlake said.

"Home? Here's my home." Dickson nodded toward the forest.

"I was thinking of Scotland."

"Aye, Dumfriesshire is a long way off, to be sure, but this is my home now, among these forests and these people." Dickson tilted his head toward the Indians camped beside them. "I fell in love with it here. They'll have to bury me in these forests, and that will suit me just fine."

"The Shawnee told me how you gave away your thousand dollars' worth of supplies to native families last August because they were starving," Westlake said.

Dickson chuckled. "I've heard things about you and the Westlake Trading Company, mainly about your father, but I won't hold that against ye. Rather ruthless methods your father has, I'm told. Anyway, it was ten thousand dollars' worth I gave away." Again, Dickson gestured behind him toward the Indians' fire. "What would you yourself do if your friends were starving? Remember, my wife, To-to-win, is sister to Chief Red Thunder. They're people just like you and me, and they were hungry."

"So the customs agent was right when he guessed the value of your goods?" blurted out Parrish. He put another branch on the fire, and the dead leaves flared bright, revealing a grimace on Dickson's face.

"Of course he was, the bastard. The Americans are only slightly worse than the British." Dickson laughed again.

"I'll agree with that one," Lapointe added.

"And don't get me started on France, laddie. We're still having a go at you lot on the continent."

"Hey, Red-Haired Chief, I'm not from France, and for someone who claims they know so much about the Northwest, you should know better. I'm Canadien and that's a big difference. I don't give a damn what is going on back in France or England, but if Johnny's right and the Americans are planning to attack Montreal, then I'll have to help stop them. It's no joke, eh."

"Westlake, your friend has no sense of humor," Dickson remarked.

"Just don't make fun of him being French. Without him, Walt and I wouldn't still be alive."

Westlake went on to tell the whole story about their detention at Fort Detroit and the death of Ned after the ambush. He described the four men they killed, the British Army officer with a face like an owl, and ended by asking Dickson who they might have been and why they had attacked. But Dickson had no idea other than he was sure the leader had acted like no British officer.

"I don't know how he knew about us or who would reward him, but he took off heading north." With a long stick, Westlake poked hard at the fire, causing it to spark, and he turned his head toward Dickson to listen.

"I can tell you this, laddie, you're not the first of Brock's secret agents to face trouble while trying to reach me. I hope you've noticed that we're already heading north."

On this news, Westlake sat up straight and attentive.

Dickson continued, "You didn't expect Isaac Brock to leave the war's opening salvo entirely in your hands. Yes, that's right, we're on our way to Fort St. Joseph. Another agent reached us earlier. Now read me the letter you have from our friend."

Westlake reached under his buckskin coat and slowly, gently, revealed Brock's letter. All the traveling and the strife made this moment possible. The others around the fire leaned forward, their eyes concentrated on the small envelope, while Westlake thought back to the cold cell at Fort Detroit, then of Ned and his grave.

He eased the note from the envelope and smoothed out the folds on his knee. With some difficulty he began to read out Brock's handwriting, holding it up to the firelight.

"Sir,
As it is probable that war may result from the present state of affairs,
it is very desirable to ascertain the degree of cooperation that you
and your friends might be able to furnish, in case of such an

Emergency taking place. You will be pleased to report with all practicable expedition upon the following matter.

    1. The number of your friends that might be depended upon.

    2. Their disposition towards us.

    3. Would they assemble and march under your orders."

"That's enough," Dickson interrupted. "It's basically the same note."

"There is one other important point he raises." Westlake paused. "Will you approach the Detroit frontier next spring?"

"Well, now you might begin to see the endgame, laddie."

Westlake had guessed from the beginning: it was all about Fort Detroit. He waved his arm toward the Indians and the forest beyond. "If we take Fort Mackinac quickly, especially with the help of Indians, it'll be the first victory of the war. The other tribes will come to join the winning side—the British side. General Brock knows he can't win without the Indians because he doesn't have enough troops. With them he has a chance and so, if he has the opportunity, he'll attack Fort Detroit and secure the entire Northwest."

"Brilliant, laddie, positively brilliant, Fort Mackinac first and then on to Detroit, you've figured out his whole book. But everything hangs on a victory up north, and that's why we're moving."

"If this chief already knew to head north before we even got here, my brother died for nothing," Parrish pointed out.

Before Westlake could reply, Dickson interjected, "Don't ever think that, Mr. Parrish, because maybe your owl-faced friend would have killed the first agent, if not for your diversion. Without that first agent, you might have been the only ones to get through. No, your brother was sadly one of the first casualties in a battle that will get very dirty. Besides, we're going to need all the men we can find to capture Michilimackinac, and I'm grateful that you three are with us."

"I'm going to kill that owl-faced bastard when I find him." Parrish muttered.

"Mascotapah!" one of the Indians called over from their camp.

Dickson stood up, and so did Westlake.

"We leave before first light tomorrow." Dickson's smile vanished. "I have one hundred and thirty Sioux, Winnebago, and Menominee warriors here. I'll send couriers to Brock, so he knows what we're up to. Remember, he wrote that note you delivered to me a good four months ago, so a great deal may have happened since then."

Dickson waved back to the Indian campfire to say he would be there soon.

"We travel up the west side of Green Bay, stay well clear of Michilimackinac, and head for Fort St. Joseph. We'll be there by month's end, and it's important no one knows what we're up to so anyone we encounter either comes with us willingly or they die." He slapped a mosquito at the side of his neck. "Get a good rest tonight, as we've a couple of weeks hard traveling ahead. Goodnight." And with that, Dickson marched away, his image fading slowly from the firelight.

Westlake nodded to his companions. "I think we had better get some sleep." He yawned; it had been a long day, and he thought about the journey ahead. The next part of his orders was to meet the officer in charge at Fort St. Joseph, and there help him to carry out Brock's wishes.

"Johnny, that talk of attacking Detroit is getting too close to my house, so should I be heading back home? And what about my uncle and the rest of my family outside Montreal?"

"I doubt there'll be any action from the British side until something has happened up north with us. Besides, Detroit may not be the focus of attack, it might be Niagara instead, although I would dearly like to meet up with Sergeant Harris again, only this time on my own terms."

"Then Fort St. Joseph here we come, but after that I have to head home," Lapointe decided. "My uncle in Montreal will have to wait."

"What about this Michil… place?" Parrish asked. It's in the north too?"

"I assume Brock's orders will be an attack on Fort Mackinac, on the island of Michilimackinac," Westlake observed, "otherwise he wouldn't be going to all this trouble. Assuming of course that war will actually be declared. Goodnight, gentlemen."

On the same day that his party reached Dickson, unknown to

Westlake, but true to Brock's thinking, war was duly declared on Great Britain by the United States of America. Upper Canada would be a convenient battleground, and an easy prize for the Americans, or so the thinking went.

"War was declared two weeks ago! You can't be serious, Mr. Shaler. Why would it take from June 18 to July 2—and at two in the morning I might add—to deliver this all-important message?" General Hull demanded.

"Wasn't my fault, sir. The War Office gave the bulletin to the post office. The letter was lost, and on finding it again, they gave it to me."

Hull hung his head and glanced sideways at Colonels McArthur and Cass.

"Do you see what I'm dealing with in Washington? They *mailed* me the declaration of war! First no ammunition, and now this, dating from June 18. It's unbelievable." Hull tossed the letter in the air and it floated to the floor.

"I missed you at that junction of the Maumee River with Lake Erie, so I had to keep on riding." Shaler trembled. "I've ridden eighty hours straight, or you wouldn't have the dispatch in your hand yet." Shaler held out his arms and moved his face into the candlelight. "My horse just now died. I'm covered in mosquito bites. That bloody Black Swamp is a bog from hell."

McArthur jumped out his chair. "You need not tell us, we built that road, and without it you would've taken eight hundred hours to get here. Take a look at this: ankles, wrists, neck, face, all eaten by mosquitoes." McArthur displayed the red welts where the bugs had feasted on his blood.

Hull eyed McArthur with contempt. War had been declared and yet the man's first thoughts were about his mosquito bites. Then Hull's own mind went back to the day before when he had loaded a schooner named the *Cuyahoga*, at the mouth of the Maumee River and Lake Erie. The ship carried all his correspondence from Washington, the excess military baggage, and thirty-five officers, men, and women now too sick to march. He'd put Assistant Quartermaster William Beall in charge. Colonel Cass had warned him that the *Cuyahoga* needed to sail right under the guns at Fort Amherstburg, but Hull had brushed his objections aside because at the time he had not known they were at war.

"McArthur, find Colonel Miller, and tell him that the entire camp must be woken before dawn. We march at first light, and I want to be in Detroit within three days."

The longboat pushed its way south out of the Detroit River and into the ripples of Lake Erie. Aided by the current and a light wind from the north, it needed only an easy pull from the eight seamen commanded by Lieutenant Frederic Rolette of His Majesty's Provincial Marine. In the distance, a schooner under full sail obligingly tacked toward them over the sun-drenched water.

Even after his grand experiences at the Nile and Trafalgar, Rolette felt a rush of energy on the eve of a confrontation, no matter how small the prospective engagement. He took a deep breath of the moist air and then exhaled slowly with a whistle, deliberately trying to calm himself. "Steady, now." The handle of the tiller rubbed smoothly against his skin as he lifted a hand to block out the sun in order to better see his prey.

The schooner continued across the waves until within minutes the longboat was only yards from its bow. Lieutenant Rolette cupped his hands around his mouth and shouted, "Down the mainsail and stand by to be boarded." Then he raised his pistol and simultaneously four of his seamen raised their muskets. The remaining four seamen struggled to keep the boat steady.

At least twenty spectators, men and women, had gathered at the schooner's rail, but no one replied. Rolette repeated his demand and added, "Now!"

Captain Chapin of the American schooner *Cuyahoga* took a step forward to reply, but Assistant Quartermaster William Beall, the officer in charge of Hull's supplies, moved in front of him to intercede.

"What's the meaning of this?" Beall demanded.

Rolette took a shot at him as the ship rolled, and the longboat bumped against its side. A woman screamed and Chapin yelled, "Get down." The pistol ball missed Beall's head by just inches, chipping the main mast. Chapin needed no more encouragement and the sails came fluttering down. As the longboat hooked on to the schooner, four seamen and Rolette himself clambered over the side, with cutlasses drawn. A pair of American officers had meanwhile drawn their swords to confront them.

"Drop your weapons, and get down below." Rolette pointed his sword at the men, who complied with his order. "You're now prisoners of war, so move!" Rolette's seamen nudged the officers and women below decks.

"We're not at war," a woman protested, frowning at the American officer beside her as they descended the steps.

"No one told me," he replied.

Another two seamen from the longboat jumped down from the side of the schooner and trained their muskets on Beall and Captain Chapin. Meanwhile, Rolette surveyed the deck, and he could feel the cutlass slide in his sweating hand. Something seemed odd here, since rather than a ship at war, the schooner appeared to be proceeding as if on a leisurely cruise.

"What's your cargo—any official correspondence?" Rolette's mouth went dry as he raised his sword to Beall's jowled neck, trying nervously not to slit the man's throat.

"Why are you doing this?" Beall asked again.

Rolette suddenly took hold of Beall's neck instead and rammed his head into the schooner's side rail. Beall's knees buckled and he slumped to the deck.

"I will not ask you again, and I'm going to find out regardless, but I would prefer that you to tell me now," Rolette demanded.

"For God's sake, tell him what he wants to know," Captain Chapin implored.

"We're the schooner *Cuyahoga* sailing for Fort Detroit, with thirty ill officers on board, under orders from Brigadier General Hull. We have all his papers and correspondence aboard, but they're private property," Beall protested.

Rolette took a step back, grinning, pleased that he could put Hull's paperwork into Brock's lap. He could not stop smiling as sheathed his cutlass and lifted Beall back on his feet.

"Thank you for your answers, sir. Now, to answer your question, I am Provincial Marine Lieutenant Frederic Rolette. We have seized your ship because a couple of weeks ago your country declared hostilities on my country. That is why you now have that nasty bump on your head. Simply put, sir, you and I are at war."

On June 30, 1812, surrounded only by a thirteen-foot-high cedar picket palisade in several states of disrepair, Fort St. Joseph did not present much of a military bastion. Along the east side of the fort, outside the palisade, Westlake observed at least a dozen civilian buildings where the ground sloped down toward St. Mary's River. He and the others plodded along a potholed road that eventually lead them past a huge wharf jutting into the water. A large two-storied blockhouse sat in the center of the fort, topped with a flagpole displaying an oversized Union flag that flew above the palisade. Only the flag itself, blowing straight out in the wind, appeared to him both new and well kept.

The gatekeeper slurred a challenge. "Who goes there?" Westlake identified himself and his party. But even as the gates were unlatched, a sudden gust of wind blew over a twelve-foot section of palisade next to the gates. Everyone burst into howls of laughter, the Indians hooting and stamping their feet. By now Westlake doubted the troops inside were in better condition than their fort.

Once inside, he counted ten buildings constructed of timber and stone, including the blockhouse itself, which he guessed to be about a hundred feet long. The troops, all forty-four of them, were the 10th Royal Veterans Battalion, specially selected for duty at Fort St. Joseph because they were nearing the end of their military terms and were thus considered by Brock to be less likely to desert. The sound of someone retching caught Westlake's attention, but when he looked, the man responsible had disappeared.

Twenty paces from the gate, a disheveled Sergeant James Baker introduced himself to Westlake and his party, his overfleshed face distinctly purple from too much indulgence. In a dismissive tone, he scoffed, "Who are you people?"

Westlake glanced over his shoulder at the Indians who had come to help. Tired after the long march, and near sick from being devoured by mosquitoes, he gripped his musket tighter.

"My name is Jonathan Westlake of the Westlake Trading Company. We've come here to meet Captain Roberts."

"From the look of the lot of you, you've no business in here. Get those Indians back outside immediately," Baker ordered.

The butt end of Westlake's musket found its target in the middle of Baker's chest. The sergeant stumbled backward to sit on the ground, with both hands nursing his chest.

Westlake strolled toward him. "I asked you a question and don't even need you to speak. Just point out the building that houses Captain Roberts."

Baker groaned and pointed, directing Westlake and his party farther into the fort.

"He gets dangerous when he's tired, eh." Danny grinned and elbowed Parrish in the ribs.

Captain Charles Roberts, a twenty-year veteran of the British Army and the fort's commander for less than a year, approached Westlake through the door of the blockhouse. He appeared genuinely pleased to meet his visitors.

"The infamous Robert Dickson, no doubt, and you must be Mr. Westlake." Roberts extended his hand. "You've both traveled a great distance. How are you?"

"Tired and hungry," Dickson replied.

"No trouble at the gate?"

"No trouble that I can think of. How did you know we were coming?" Westlake added.

"I believe, Ensign Westlake, that it is customary in our army to address a superior officer as 'sir,' even if your family has the ear of the major general."

Perhaps it was a hesitation or the paleness in Roberts's skin, Westlake was not sure, but he guessed that Roberts was ill. "Captain Roberts, sir," he replied. "However, as General Brock himself has ordered, it's also best that Parrish and I should not be recognized as serving in the army." With his thumb, he gestured over his shoulder toward Parrish. "We're fur traders, you see."

"Fine with me. I was informed of your coming by courier sometime ago so it's well that everyone's arrived safe and sound. You other two gentlemen must be the Parrish brothers?" Roberts again held out his hand.

"Everything did not go too well, I fear, sir," Westlake said. "This is Walt Parrish and this is Daniel Lapointe. Ned Parrish was killed when we got ambushed. Perhaps I can tell you about that after we've eaten something?"

"I'm sorry about your loss." Roberts gave Parrish a sincere nod. He then continued with some of his instructions: "Dickson, I want you and our Indian guests kept out of sight. You can set up camp on the land side of the fort, away from the river, and try to keep the number of your fires at night to a minimum. Don't light up the nighttime sky so Mackinac spies can guess what we're up to."

"We'll do our bit," Dickson said.

"We have limited rations of salt pork and biscuit and as you'll soon see, we make our own bread, which we consider a luxury. We'll set up a proper system for rationing, but today you are on your own except for bread and I'll have my men distribute some extra loaves."

"I can smell the bakery from here." Dickson grinned at Parrish.

Captain Roberts continued, "I suggest that the Indians should hunt and fish as much as possible, since we don't want to run out of food." There was strain evident in his voice and it showed on his face, which made Westlake wonder if the man was up to the task of dealing with an American invasion or perhaps all it signified was that he had been too long out of action.

"Dickson, I suggest that you start constructing some canoes, since we have nowhere near enough. You'll find that we have a wonderful canoe factory just outside the fort provided by the Northwest

Company. I'm expecting a great many Indians and other reinforcements to join us, so everyone will have to make an effort to get along.
We could be here for days or even months until war is declared. If it
ever is to be declared at all."

"We certainly don't mind lending a helping hand," Dickson agreed.
"Nice of a big fur company to lend us their factory."

"Mr. Westlake and his two friends will move into the blockhouse,
along with me. Quarters will be a bit cramped, gentlemen, but that's
the way it is. You'll soon notice that we have two blacksmiths working
at the shop yonder, so every man has a responsibility to have his sword,
knife, and axe repaired and sharpened." Roberts's face gave a twitch
under one eye, again showing his stress.

"Those possessing muskets must also have them checked for repairs.
One other important point to remember: stay away from the stores
building and particularly from the powder magazine or you'll be likely
shot." Roberts pointed out buildings where guards patrolled. Clearly,
the captain was determined he would not run out of food from theft,
nor would he risk being blown up.

"Mr. Westlake, after you've eaten and slept, perhaps we could have
a private chat. Otherwise, that's my welcoming speech, gentlemen,
and you're all dismissed." He looked relieved it was over.

Dickson walked among the Indians, and translated to them
Roberts's message. Some sat down where they were and ate while others drifted over to the bakery or went to inspect the blacksmith's
workshop. Demands for a ration of salted pork were quietly met in
spite of Roberts's earlier words. After a few parting words to Westlake,
and a promise that he would see him later, Dickson led most of his
followers out of the shaky confines of the palisade to pitch their tents
away from the sight of the river. St. Joseph Island turned out to be
much bigger than Westlake had first thought, so that once Dickson's
tents were pitched behind the fort, they remained well hidden.

Westlake sat up and perched on the side of the bed, his feet touching
the chilly floor. Like a horse that is agitated after a long run, he couldn't
relax. He closed his eyes, reliving his search for Dickson. He eventually

dozed off while sitting up, finally putting his head down on the pillow, but he couldn't stop thinking. Traveling through miles of forest, they had met almost no one—only the odd Indian who pointed them in the general direction to find the Red-Haired Chief. Westlake had listened in as Parrish told Lapointe how no one back home in England would believe him if he said that he had traveled twice the breadth of England and encountered not one other human being. The distances were unimaginable and so were those black flies that could remove a chunk of skin with a single attack. That scourge was followed in late May by hordes of mosquitoes that left Westlake itching from every bite.

Finally, they had caught up with the legendary Dickson and then the daily pace got faster until at last they had reached their objective at the top of Lake Huron, just as everyone—including the horses— was completely exhausted. Westlake rolled over to fall into a deep sleep.

The following morning he went straight from his warm bed for a plunge into the river. The water was so cold that Westlake couldn't endure it for more than a few minutes. Lathering himself with soap and diving under, the sheer cold helped him realize just how tired he was. Though he felt refreshed and somewhat rested, he was still weary. Too many months and too many miles of traveling had finally caught up with him.

He didn't know, and he wouldn't have cared, that Daniel Lapointe and Walt Parrish were currently resting in a drunken stupor, along with Robert Dickson and a few of the French voyageurs. In twenty-four-foot canoes, the voyageurs had paddled all the way from Montreal to pick up furs and then return the same way they came. Westlake spoke to no one as he ate, then went back to bed, happy to continue this pattern for a few days more until he was summoned for another meeting with Captain Roberts.

"I hope you've had a good rest, Mr. Westlake, because someone in your family's employ has arrived with very important news for you. David Hicks, meet Jonathan Westlake."

A head shorter than Westlake, Hicks had round brown eyes and puffy cheeks. The way he marched his wiry build across the floor and jerked out his hand reminded Westlake of a man that was play-acting the part of a soldier. He displayed a type of tenseness in his manner too.

"Mr. Westlake, I came straight from New York after I heard the news, just like your father directed. Of course, we'll get your furs out before trouble starts, now that war's been declared. The bundles here should be no problem, but the one's at Fort Mackinac—well, that's a different story, I'll need your help there." Speaking fast with a nasal sound, Hicks had an annoying habit of making too many assumptions.

"Did you just say that war has been declared, Mr. Hicks?" Westlake glanced at Roberts and raised his eyebrows, now feeling the tension himself.

"Yes, but we'll get the furs out, don't worry." Hicks pointed a thumb to his chest. "That's why I'm here."

"I swear to you, Captain Roberts, I had no idea Westlake Trading had furs here or at Fort Mackinac. I would have assumed that all the cargo would've departed by this time." Westlake was genuinely surprised. "How did you get here, Mr. Hicks?"

Hicks stared out the window toward the river, brushing back curly hair disheveled by the wind. "The *Caledonia* is approaching … with her brass cannons. I came by express canoe, of course. We have to send word to Fort Mackinac, to get all the furs out."

"You'll do nothing of the kind, Mr. Hicks," Captain Roberts interrupted. "In fact, as of right now you don't set foot outside of the palisade or you'll be shot. No one else could have traveled faster than you and Fort Mackinac must not learn that we are at war. I want such information confined within these four walls."

"But—" Hicks began to protest, then desisted under a glare.

Roberts shook his head and continued, "I can tell you that another of your company agents passed through on his way to Fort Mackinac a few weeks ago." Roberts smiled privately. "After a promise from myself to save the Westlake furs currently at Mackinac, he has conceded to act as my secret agent at the fort."

"Well, that's great news. If I were you, I'd—" Hicks jumped in.

"Mr. Hicks, shut up!" Roberts ordered him sharply. "This same agent is delivering a message to a man on Michilimackinac, but if he and his companions are caught, they'll be shot." He turned to Westlake. "Your father must be a wise man to have seen the war coming, and then take the appropriate actions—as did General Brock."

"My father is nothing like General Brock. He acts only in his company's interest, and he'll stop at nothing where money is concerned. I feel ashamed that Westlake Trading is involved in this whole affair." That his father's reach extended as far as Fort St. Joseph and beyond astonished him.

"Don't be naive, Mr. Westlake," Captain Roberts replied. "The Northwest Company is providing canoes, weapons, and men. The Southwest Company will be volunteering the *Caledonia*, her cannons, and her crew. And many voyageurs are willing to join us." Roberts pointed out the window.

"Your company will provide arms, intelligence, and also a few men. All of these are resources we desperately need if we're going to win. If Westlake Trading happens to profit in the bargain, then so be it."

"Yes, I agree with that," Hicks chipped in.

Roberts ignored him. "Even the Indians and Métis are here for something. Everyone acts in his own legitimate self-interest, Westlake. That's the way the world works. This coming war will be as much about furs as anything else. To many out there, the conflict is about the fur trade and nothing else."

Roberts edged Hicks to one side so he could get a good look at the *Caledonia* already in full view. "Now, Mr. Hicks, you'll kindly retire to the rear of the blockhouse, and not a word to anyone, understand? I don't want to have to shoot you, though the thought doesn't lack appeal."

"Understood, sir," Hicks replied. "I believe I know your … or should I say our agent. Mum's the word." Hicks put a finger to grinning lips. "You'll have no trouble from me, but please remember I've come all this way with just one purpose in mind: to ensure the safe passage of the furs. I'd therefore be much obliged if you'd keep that in consideration."

"Our duty now is to capture Fort Mackinac, so I could care less about the furs. However, by telling us that war has started, you've performed a considerable service to His Majesty's government. Once the fort is safely in our hands, you may take your furs and be gone. That's all, Mr. Hicks. I suggest you retire now."

Hicks gave a mock military salute, turned abruptly, and marched off.

"Well, Mr. Westlake, we must plan our attack. I've been thinking about how best to attack Fort Mackinac for a long time now. There's not much else to do out here."

Westlake had some questions, but before he could speak Captain Roberts held up his hand. "Please don't ask me about the other agent. He remains secret for now, but you'll meet him soon enough." He spread a map out on the table, placing his teacup at one end to stop it curling up.

"In this wilderness, it's safer to have a backup man, in case the first one fails. Your company sent two agents, taking no chances with the furs, and I don't blame them. Now, let's get down to business. This is how we capture Fort Mackinac."

12

......

Through the hot days of early July, Captain Roberts patiently planned his attack on Fort Mackinac and awaited a signal from Brock that would send his forces against the American enemy. Finally, on July 15, a courier arrived bearing the fateful instruction.

Adopt the most prudent measures of either offense or defense which circumstances might point out.

The very next morning, with flags waving, forty of His Majesty's 10th Royal Veterans Battalion paraded to the fife and drum out of Fort St. Joseph and down to the wharf. To an unpracticed eye, the marching red tunics, white cross-belts, and Brown Bess muskets at the shoulder gave an impression of invincibility, but with their incessant drunkenness, Westlake wondered if these men could fight as well as they could march. The short path down to the wharf ended at the *Caledonia*, which showed her two brass six-pound cannons secured tight.

Behind the regiment marched one hundred and eighty voyageurs and Métis, turned out in their red-and-black checked vests, with silk kerchiefs tied around their necks. Westlake watched them step lightly off the wharf into their Mackinac boats, looking more at home on the water than on land. For the fifty-mile journey, they added their ten boats to what was becoming Captain Roberts's armada.

Their boats were still inches from the shore when three hundred hooting Indians came charging round the fort and headed for their seventy canoes. Westlake noticed a fearsome warrior strutting along beside the Red-Haired Chief, his angry eyes accentuated by lines of charcoal-black war paint. A leather headband secured a single feather at the back of his shaven head, and on his chest was drawn a hawk's outline in gray pipeclay. He carried his musket lightly, a knife strapped to his hip and a tomahawk thrust through his belt.

Ensign Westlake, Daniel Lapointe, and Private Walt Parrish stood to one side observing the commotion as the flotilla prepared for departure. Westlake remarked how the fort may never see the likes of such a scene again, then he motioned to where Dickson's new canoe sat surrounded by a dozen others filled with natives holding their paddles at the ready. Captain Roberts approached them, resplendent in his dress uniform.

"I haven't had much cause to wear this, out here in our Canadian Siberia. And now that I have it on, I feel rather out of place, gentlemen."

Before Westlake or Lapointe could make a joke of it, Parrish spoke up. "Your appearance will tell the men that it's an important day, sir, if you don't mind me speaking out of turn." Roberts bobbed his head to express his thanks.

"Well said, Mr. Parrish, well said, indeed," Westlake remarked.

"I hope we can win this island without having to count on the way Captain Roberts looks," Lapointe added. "I mean no offense, sir." Roberts merely smiled, and Lapointe continued, "The Indians and the regulars look like proper warriors, but I have never seen voyageurs more deadly serious."

"Back home we have to club a man into joining the navy, yet these voyageurs are volunteering to lose their lives without a thought," Parrish said.

"Don't think they haven't thought about it. They know that Michilimackinac holds the key to the last frontier of the fur trade," Westlake explained, "so they fight to protect their livelihoods from the Americans. For some, the fur trade is all they've ever known."

"Enough chatter now, gentlemen," Roberts interrupted. "On to the *Caledonia* and then to Michilimackinac. We must be in position there before dawn tomorrow, or all may be lost."

The four men marched down to the wharf, up the gangway, and on to the boat, leaving behind a mostly defenseless Fort St. Joseph. Westlake wondered if anyone at Fort Mackinac yet knew that war had been declared. Perhaps Captain Roberts was right, and surprise was on their side … or perhaps he was wrong and the Americans were already waiting for them.

And what of the furs? Capturing them would make Westlake's father proud. He would be flabbergasted to learn that his son had been part of an invasion force to capture the island and also the furs. Westlake laughed to himself as the *Caledonia* lifted anchor, and he splayed his feet, holding the rail to keep his balance. A victory for Father and a victory for Brock too, through the capture of one island, how difficult could it be?

As Roberts had illustrated earlier, gigantic bluffs impossible to scale rimmed the island of Michilimackinac. The one exception, apart from the village shoreline, was a break at the far north end, where a beach met the water. With Fort Mackinac at the south end, it was a three-mile uphill march from the beach to reach the fort undetected. To Westlake, Roberts had explained how he planned to drag the *Caledonia*'s cannon up the hill to a crest of rock that rose some three hundred feet above the fort. A cannon on the heights could fire down into the fort itself, smashing and killing everything in its path while blowing holes in their walls from the inside out—through which the Indians and voyageurs could then attack. Roberts planned to be in position before dawn the next morning and issue a demand for surrender to the American commander, Lieutenant Porter Hanks.

Westlake's task was to ensure no resistance from the townspeople living outside the fort. They were to be escorted to an old distillery at the far end of the village, so Sergeant James Baker and thirty soldiers of the 10th Royal Veterans would aid him. Baker and his men therefore had to be told that Westlake was an ensign in the York Volunteer Militia.

Westlake knew he would be given no respect by Sergeant Baker. Like many soldiers of the Royal Veterans, the army was all Baker knew, and as his service time drew to an end, he was dammed sure that no infant militia officer was going to get him killed. When Baker received his orders from Captain Roberts that Westlake would be the officer in charge, it was obvious he was unhappy. Besides, from the time

Westlake had struck Baker on their first encounter, inside the fort gates, he had acquired an enemy.

Westlake had already attempted to approach Baker at the blacksmith's to discuss their task. Never making eye contact, Baker had turned his back as if to examine his newly sharpened sword. Westlake moved to one side, whereupon Baker had sheathed his sword with a snap, turned, and walked away. Frustrated, Westlake had kept the incident with Baker to himself.

Now that he was on a boat approaching Fort Mackinac, the thought of Baker's insubordination made him feel miserable. He should have dealt with Baker more harshly at the time, but it was too late.

Captain Roberts strolled along the deck and drew near to Westlake.

"How many people does my father have working up here, sir?" Westlake asked.

"Not near as many as the Northwest Company," Roberts replied. "Westlake Trading employs those who trade with the Indians further inland. However, these other men - these agents - are a different sort. You yourself don't look like a soldier, but you are. They don't look like fur traders, but they are. I mean men like Hicks."

"And who is this other man who works for my father, the one who came through before me?"

"You'll meet him after we land, Ensign Westlake." Roberts laughed and continued his stroll.

With the end of the day, the sky darkened and so too did the water, until everything was turning black. Westlake imagined what the long paddle meant for those in the boats and canoes; their muscles must be burning by now. In the fading light, he could just make out the northern tip of Michilimackinac Island, but his eyes must have been playing tricks. He could barely see the end of the *Caledonia* let alone those miles across water to the island. His hands gripped the rail, anxious to start the attack.

To keep hidden from the island, the armada tacked as close to the northern shore of Lake Huron as safety would allow. The canoes of the natives stayed within a few yards of land, followed not too closely by the Mackinac boats. On a clear sunny day it was no problem to see across the water to the island, but Captain Roberts had timed their arrival perfectly: all was now dark and nothing could be seen.

Roberts brought the *Caledonia* almost to a stop, after he'd been peering southwards for some time. Westlake noticed a warm breeze brush against his face, and just as quickly it was gone as they waited. Water lapped gently at the side of the boat in the darkness, till Westlake felt as if they were suspended in space. He stared up at an explosion of stars in the summer sky. A dense layer of cloud drifted by and, with the stars blotted out, the world plunged into sudden blackness. Slowly the stars re-emerged, and all the heavens shone once again. The stars seemed to extend forever, the quiet and stillness making him feel so small. He continued squinting into the emptiness that lay over the black water.

Out of the darkness a single candle flame appeared, and then it was gone so fast that Westlake was unsure if his eyes had played a trick on him. He searched the blackness until it showed itself again, and then vanished just the same. In a whisper he called out behind him, "Captain Roberts."

"I know," Roberts whispered back.

Some moments later the light reappeared, this time much closer. Without a sound, someone on the water had joined them. The candle moved from left to right and then up and down: to Westlake it looked like the sign of the cross rising miraculously out of the lake. Roberts lit his own candle and gestured in return: left to right and then up and down.

A small dory with oars extended edged closer, its lighted lantern, unshuttered, magically suspended over the water. The dory and lantern circled, floating in the darkness towards the unseen island.

Roberts said quietly, "Pass the word to follow that lantern - our beach is south-south-west. Light the lantern at the back of our own boat. "

The *Caledonia* swung into the wind as Westlake concentrated on the lantern floating over the water. It disappeared for a few seconds, finally reappearing again. Eventually, the light went out, but their course was set and the shape of the island - like a phantom rising out of the infinite darkness - soon came into view.

Parrish was at his side and Lapointe came up behind. "How can we trust this guy with the lantern?"

"Captain Roberts says we can but I don't know who he is. What I do know is that this attack is more like a raid by fur traders than a strike by the British army."

"Well, I'm not with either of those guys so I wonder what the hell I'm doing here," Lapointe muttered.

"Are you afraid of the dark or something? You're here because you're my friend, and to keep me safe." Westlake laughed.

"I thought that was *my* job," Parrish said.

"You're right, Johnny, I hate fighting in the dark, so you have to keep me safe."

"I wish we could land soon and get on with it." Westlake felt the boat slowing. The *Caledonia* came to a full stop, well out from the dory, and he assumed a good distance from the beach. An anchor made a great splash and Westlake thought if anyone was listening, their surprise attack had vanished.

The Mackinac boats that had shot passed the *Caledonia* to join the dory, were now coming back, after unloading most of their paddlers. A familiar face peered up from the water, then said in a gruff whisper, "Unless ye want to swim for it, I suggest you three explorers get into the damn boat."

Westlake was instantly over the side and into the boat, followed by Parrish and Lapointe.

"Mr. Dickson, sir, even in the darkness I can see that flaming Scottish hair," Westlake chuckled.

"Excess chatter will get us all killed, so just be quiet and paddle."

Westlake grimaced and nodded to the others to oblige. He felt foolish being admonished by Dickson, but the joke had allowed him to cope with his fear. Since he knew better than to put their enterprise at risk, he clenched his teeth and swore not to make another sound.

By the time their boat hit the beach, it looked like a whole army was disembarking. They found no American resistance, not even a stirring from the tree line. Westlake squinted over the water, where only the barest silhouette of the *Caledonia* could be seen; perhaps no one had noticed their coming. The natives hauled their canoes ashore while the voyageurs brought up their boats. Roberts stepped out of the darkness and, as if by some conjuring trick, behind him was a team of oxen. It was going to be a night full of surprises, Westlake concluded.

And he was right, for leading the oxen was a face he could never forget.

Captain Roberts made the introduction. "Mr. Westlake, I would like to introduce you to Mr. Bill Wagg, agent of the Westlake Trading Company. Mr. Wagg meet Mr. Westlake."

The two men were only inches apart yet neither moved nor spoke. Westlake could think of nothing to say, stunned by the sudden appearance of that same jowled face that had tried to kill him all those miles ago. His fists clenched, his jaw tightened and he almost exclaimed, "You're alive". Perhaps Mary herself was on the island, but he checked himself from asking, deciding that such interest in her was better kept to himself. One thing was certain; he would no longer be hanged for murder.

A hand on his sword, it was Wagg who spoke first. "Is this the same Jonathan Westlake that is the son of Richard Westlake, of Westlake Trading, my employer?" He whispered in a rasp.

Walt Parrish had moved up beside Westlake, with his knife already drawn.

Captain Roberts intervened, "Obviously his father is your employer. Is there something I need to know here, gentlemen? Can you both do your jobs without killing each other first? Answer me that."

The sight of Mary Collins limping across that dirt floor jumped back into Westlake's mind. "I'm pleased to see Mr. Wagg is alive and I've no problem with him currently, sir." Westlake successfully controlled his emotions, and his voice, but it was an act.

"Nor I with him, my main interest is to get that shipment of furs. I sent Mr Dousman to bring you here to the beach, and I've brought a team of oxen as you asked, though God knows why you need them. Until I've got my money for those furs belonging to Westlake Trading, Mr. Westlake's life is quite safe with me."

"Understand, both of you, that any insubordination that jeopardizes our mission will be met with the severest punishment." Roberts voice was strung tight.

Both men nodded to him in agreement but the Captain's eyes were fixed directly on Westlake.

"Yes, sir." Westlake confirmed, his thoughts in turmoil. Wagg working for his father seemed impossible, although he recalled that his father had hired some unsavory characters in the past.

"Let's get on with winning a war, shall we? This is Mr. Michael Dousman, who met us out on the water with the lantern. He's a resident on the island and an employee of the Southwest Company - who'll lead you and your men down the coast road, Mr. Westlake."

While Westlake and Dousman shook hands, Roberts continued, "Mr. Wagg will lead my group through the centre of the island. Meanwhile, Dickson, take a dozen men back to the *Caledonia*. The crew already knows that the sight of you means they're to swing out the cannon. Get that cannon back here as fast as you can."

Dickson started immediately for the boats as Roberts explained, "With the help of these oxen, the rest of us but for Westlake's troop, will drag the six-pounder through the forest to the crest overlooking the fort. The coast road is a little longer than our three miles but it's treacherous in places because it follows the cliffs. In the dark, you'd best tread carefully. I want no weapons going off accidentally, so you'll march with muskets unloaded."

"Yes, sir," Westlake replied.

"Take your thirty men and with Sergeant Baker, once you get there, round up the townsfolk into the distillery at the far west end of the village, just like we planned. All must be completed before sun-up, or our surprise is lost and so could be our battle. Let's be about our work quickly, eh?"

"Agreed, sir," Westlake replied firmly.

. . . .

"And Mr Westlake, accept no argument from these villagers. Use force if you have to, but I want them all under guard before sun-up. If you meet the enemy, you will engage them."

"Sir."

With thirty of His Majesty's 10th Royal Veterans, Westlake's troop marched two abreast off the beach heading towards the village. The road narrowed into a well-trodden grass path as it climbed up the hill, alongside the cliff face. Westlake then passed the word that they were to spread out and form a single file.

After the appearance of Wagg, it was difficult to keep his mind on his task, however, and he sent Dousman, Lapointe, and Parrish ahead to scout their route. They disappeared within seconds into the night. If the stars had not helped light their way, the march would have been hopeless, which set Westlake to thinking of the part the weather must have played in all the great battles of history. A few more clouds drifting in and they would have to halt, or else risk plummeting off the 150-foot cliff to their right. And where were the Americans, he wondered, since just a handful of enemy soldiers, hidden in the trees, could stop their progress by shooting the lead marcher. A hidden assailant in the dark would be impossible to locate, and the gunfire would alert the whole island. He decided that if the enemy were not on the road, then it was unlikely they were in the forest. While Captain Roberts would have a hard pull with the cannon, at least he'd be safe. Roberts was right; everything depended now on surprise.

Westlake slid on the uneven ground and stumbled to his left. A tree stopped him from falling over but he paid the price with a painful collision against his left shoulder. Trees to the left, a cliff on the right, he and his men had to stay precisely on the rutted path that climbed with every step. By resisting the urge to peer around, and by looking only at his feet and the path ahead, Westlake found he had little trouble navigating the climb, apart from the strain on his legs. He passed the word back for each man to do the same.

In front of him, Baker grumbled that he did not need anyone

telling him how to walk. Westlake nudged him forward and thinking of his recent lesson from Dickson, "Excess chatter will get us killed, so be quiet and just march."

But that comment from Baker made Westlake consider the men, and wonder what they thought of their young Ensign. He was decades their junior, but they followed him as if he was their wise old grandfather. If they wanted rid of him, all they had to do was give him a little push to the right. *It was an accident; he slipped and was gone before anyone could move; we didn't see him go; he just vanished* – these were all the things the men could say. It had been done before to officers seriously disliked by the ranks. Westlake hunched his shoulders up to his neck. It was like being back in school and hoping that everyone liked you, except now your very life depended on what they thought.

They had been climbing for some time when Parrish appeared out of the night. "The path at the top of this hill leads right to the cliff edge. Another twenty paces or so and everyone could tumble in for a swim, sir—that's if they survived rocks below."

Westlake passed the word back for an immediate halt before someone got pushed off the edge.

"Is it passable, Parrish?"

"Yes, sir."

"Well, would you tell the rest of us how you did that," Westlake demanded in a whisper.

"Me and Danny got scared, so we crawled for a bit on our hands and knees. If you're real careful, you won't fall over. Besides I can't swim, sir."

Even in the dark, Westlake knew Parrish was grinning.

Westlake ordered Baker, "Pass the word that we take fifteen paces more and then crawl on hands and knees until we're clear of the edge. Do not bunch up. Give each man room to crawl. Parrish, you know the way, so off you go. I'll go first from our group, and, Sergeant Baker, you'll follow."

Westlake counted off fifteen paces and then crouched to his knees.

He barely saw the back of Parrish's boots but knew he was down on his knees also.

"We's coming up to the tricky part, sir," Parrish whispered over his shoulder.

The path changed from dirt to stone to broken rock as it slid toward the edge of the cliff and to the water and rocks far below. Westlake reached forward, but a stone jerked clear of his hand and tumbled over the edge, taking a few smaller ones with it. His limbs stiffened and, after a few seconds, he heard them smack onto the rocks. His hand was cut and he felt a terror never known before. He willed himself forward, uselessly gripping on loose stones and wondering how anyone got past even in the daylight. The angle of the cliff face tilted toward the water just as a jagged rock surprised him by slicing through his buckskin pants and cutting into his shin. Westlake winced and stopped once again to wipe a drop of sweat that had made its way on to his eyebrow. Keep crawling, don't stop, he urged himself, and finally he was through to where the ground filled out between the cliff's edge and the path.

He did not get up immediately but felt safer crawling farther on to the soil before standing. His back ached and his hands had a hundred small cuts while his muscles felt strained and tired. The men behind him were more than twice his age so they would be feeling the hardship of it even more.

Clouds shifted and the reappearing stars gave a little more light to the path where Westlake stood with Parrish. He saw a small clearing only yards ahead, where travelers before them must have stopped after their ordeal with the cliff.

"Parrish, move to that clearing just ahead. I'm going to direct everyone else there for a rest. We need a break."

"What about Captain Roberts's orders, sir? Get to the village quick and all that."

"There's no point in getting to the village if we're all bloody exhausted when we get there. They need a rest and so do I. Head on to the clearing."

By this time Baker had come through, also cut and exhausted. He wiped his forehead with the back of his sleeve and in a whisper Westlake directed him to follow Parrish.

Ensign Westlake stood pointing each of the thirty men in turn toward the clearing.

"Why the break in our march?" Baker questioned Parrish.

"You are such a horse's ass, you wouldn't know a half-decent officer if you met one. Maybe he just thinks you are bloody useless and too old to fight, like I think." Parrish spit.

Almost half an hour passed before the last of the thirty redcoats came through. After a pat on the back to the last man, Westlake joined the men and sat himself down. Parrish sat beside him.

"Who was that fellow Wagg, sir?"

"I thought I'd killed him. It's incredible he's here." *Mary might be with him?* "We'll have to meet him again, after we've taken the fort. I can't believe he's working for my father."

They rested for ten minutes before he gave the order to march out in single file. The men began shuffling to stand. "That was a good show back there, gentlemen, but I'm afraid the hard part comes next," he said. "We have to take the village in silence, and without getting ourselves killed."

"Beg yer pardon, sir," Baker interjected, "but so long as the village ain't on no bloody cliff, it'll be a piece of cake for us lot." The men laughed, Baker grinned, and Westlake nodded. For the single kindness, that of a rest, Baker was with him.

The trail began to ease itself downhill until they approached the town. Westlake considered how the cannon was getting along, down the center of the island. If marching was difficult along the shore, it would be pitch-black in the forest, and being uphill the entire way, it would mean a long and strenuous haul through the woods. Still, Roberts had a few hundred men to take turns on the ropes while the others cleared the ground ahead and kept on guard for the enemy.

Their path leveled out, and with the sky beginning to lighten, Westlake distinguished Lapointe and Michael Dousman at the forest's edge. With Dousman added to their party, it would undoubtedly make things easier. "Let's get on with it, gentlemen. Load muskets and fix bayonets. We need to do this without a sound."

The thirty Redcoats crept, in pairs, down the road through the center of the town. Impossible as it seemed, no Bluecoat soldiers were seen from one end to the other. The Redcoats gathered at the opposite end of the town.

"Sergeant Baker, form two ranks on the roadway outside the first household and ready arms. Lapointe, Parrish, back to the other end of town. See that large building under the cliff?" Westlake pointed to the abandoned distillery. "Stand at the doors of it and watch the road … I don't want any surprises. We'll be sending you some company shortly. Well, be off then, at the double."

Westlake turned to the waiting men. "Mr. Dousman, kindly knock on the first door. Explain to them we're at war, and that the inhabitants of all homes here are requested to gather at the distillery, under the protection of His Majesty's government."

Dousman dashed up the stairs and knocked hard. After a few moments the door opened slightly ajar. He said something through the gap and within minutes a man and woman, barely awake, came scurrying out of the house. Without uttering a word, the pair headed straight for the distillery, whereupon the troop marched smartly toward the next dwelling, which was barely more than a small hut.

Westlake squinted up the road and saw Lapointe and Parrish usher the man and woman into the distillery, then shut the door behind them.

"Dousman, what did you say to get them moving so quickly?" Westlake asked.

"I told them the war started and there were hundreds of Indians on the island, just waiting for a chance to scalp them." He grinned. "I explained their only hope was to run for the distillery under your protection. Seems to have worked."

So it went, all through the small village, herding the inhabitants into the distillery. No one resisted. Westlake waved back to one family who had even shouted, "Good morning to you all." Out of the last house came a heavy woman with a blemished face, wearing a loose gown and pulling on the arm of her young daughter. After picking up the child, she marched straight for Sergeant Baker.

"My man's gone trappin' for over a year and I doubt he's ever comin' back." Her daughter tugged at the neck of the woman's gown, revealing her large breasts. "We can't defend ourselves. Are we gonna be scalped? If we are, I wanna know now." She put the child down and pulled her gown back into place.

At first Baker was surprised at the fearlessness of the woman, then flustered at the sight of her breasts. He clearly didn't know what to say.

Westlake intervened. "No, ma'am, you will not be scalped, but you must move quickly to the distillery with all the others."

The woman didn't budge, and scarcely paid any attention to him, as she stared at Baker, waiting for his reply. "I wanna hear from the man in uniform, the man in charge. Cat got yer tongue? What do you say?" Baker glanced at Westlake with a wide grin.

In his torn buckskins, worn through from miles of traveling, Westlake appeared anything but authoritative, so he gave Baker a nod.

"Yes, ma'am, my men will protect you—on that you have my word. Them Indians will have to kill all of us first before we would let them harm a hair on your pretty head. Sergeant Jim Baker at your service, ma'am. Now if you'd be so kind as to move into the distillery, for your own safekeeping, I'll come personally to see you home when this is all over."

The woman giggled. "Well, thank you, Sergeant Baker—special treatment, my word. Little Martha and me will be waiting for you." She gave Baker a sly look before trundling off with the girl, now under one arm.

Baker was pleased with himself, standing eyes front, and stiffly to attention, as Westlake had never seen him behave before. "Putting on a bit of a show for the lady, Baker? I hope the Indians are agreeable, and leave the inhabitants here with all their hair. Otherwise you're in for the fight of your life."

"Yes, sir."

"While you were flirting, some smoke rose from the crest above the fort. That's our signal that the six-pounder is in position to fire, so give me your sword, Sergeant." Both men looked up the hill, where more smoke had appeared. Westlake took a white towel from inside his coat.

"Don't let this towel fall off or the Americans might shoot you. Under this flag of truce, you'll escort Mr. Dousman into the fort and ask for Lieutenant Porter Hanks's unconditional surrender." Westlake knotted the towel around the end of the sword, then took hold of Baker's musket.

"Point out to Lieutenant Hanks that there's a six-pound cannon now aiming into his fort, which could batter him and his men to death. Tell him that he also faces a force of more than six hundred, of which half are Indians."

"That'll scare the hell out him, sir," Baker replied.

"Let Dousman confirm what you say. A fellow islander will be far more credible to the good lieutenant. If Hanks agrees to surrender, he must run up a white flag for all to see, and then you'll assemble him and his officers for Captain Roberts."

Both Baker and Dousman nodded their heads in understanding, then trotted up the hill to deliver the bad news to Lieutenant Hanks.

Westlake arranged six men to guard the distillery. The remaining two dozen he posted at the other end of the village, in case enemy troops should arrive. The sky brightened fast, giving Westlake a clear view of the deserted town.

"Why aren't we taking the surrender, sir?" Parrish asked. "We brought Dickson and the Indians here, and it was us who took the town."

"Our job was to merely deliver a message to Robert Dickson, and to help with the attack on Fort Mackinac. We've done that now. Remember General Brock's words, 'You don't exist,' so let's keep a low profile. Mr. Lapointe, what do you think is in those warehouses by the wharf? Let's go have a look."

The three men approached the first warehouse, and Parrish snatched up a long-handled axe leaning against a woodpile. Above the large door someone had nailed a block of wood carved with the words *U.S. Army. Keep Clear.* The door was bolted shut, but with two swings of the axe,

Parrish snapped the peg like a twig and the door swung open. Lapointe aimed his musket at the opening, and Westlake peered inside. No sound or movement came from within. Westlake pulled the door wide open so that the early-morning sun could light up the interior.

Parrish walked inside. "Would you look at those furs, they must be worth thousands. Who do they belong to? Ours for the taking?" He laughed. There were stacks of beaver pelts from the floor to the ceiling, with bundles of black bearskins near the door.

"I'm afraid not." The nasal tones of Mr. Hicks were with them again. "My God, look at that poor fellow." An acute stench encouraged Hicks to hold his nose. The single bear carcass, rotting by the door, was covered in flies, a great hoard of which lifted off when Hicks waved his arm at them. He was accompanied by a soldier whose shredded red coat looked as if held together only by its white cross-belt.

"It seems I'm expendable, so I've been sent by Captain Roberts to confirm the village is secured and that Sergeant Baker has gone to request surrender."

"We saw smoke and assumed the cannon's already in place, so Baker left some minutes ago," Westlake replied.

Hicks said to his partner, "You know what to do, run back to Captain Roberts and tell him the news." The man ran off, the back of his coat looking comparatively new. "Pulling a cannon up that bloody hill in the dark was a nightmare I don't wish to live through ever again. Look at me, I'm cut to pieces and worn out. You should see the others: those red-checked shirts are torn apart."

Hicks's face and hands were covered in small red cuts and his blue coat had multiple tears. "As for the furs, there's about fifty thousand dollars' worth and they belong to the Westlake Trading Company." Hicks stuck his head farther in through the door still holding his nose. "You see, Bill Wagg, like myself, was sent by your father to secure several large shipments of furs. The first shipment was at Fort St. Joseph, as you saw for yourself. The second shipment you are now looking at. Are you pleased?"

Any mention of Wagg brought with it confused emotions. Of course Westlake was relieved to see Wagg alive, but Mary Collins would remain at the man's mercy, and perhaps that of his associates. If Wagg and Hicks were being employed in case of war, to what lengths would they go to secure the furs?

"Parrish, get back to the distillery and fetch two men to guard this door. No one is to get in or out. When you come back, stay with them." Westlake turned to Lapointe. "Do you mind watching the furs while Mr. Hicks and I have a chat?"

"No problem, but I am not sure I can be trusted with all this loot." Danny laughed.

"Hicks, let's go for a stroll."

A short walk from the wharf, down to the water's stony edge where the air had a fresh taste to it, and the two men were completely alone with only the lapping waves. The early sunlight glittered off Lake Huron. "Mr. Hicks, when did all this planning start between my father, Wagg, and yourself?"

"Your father employed Wagg last year in London when talk of war heated up again. Mr. Westlake sent Wagg to Upper Canada with instructions to secure the furs as fast as possible." Hicks reached down, drew his arm back, and then skipped a stone across the water. "He says he was attacked in York, but the bastard probably deserved a punch-up. He claims it delayed his arrival here, yet all's well that ends well, as they say."

Westlake looked back toward Fort Mackinac and saw a small white flag of surrender now fluttering in the breeze. Sergeant Baker had done his job, and Lieutenant Porter Hanks had made the right decision. A massacre would have ensued had there not been surrender. Captain Roberts would be pleased with himself and his bloodless victory. Perhaps war was easier than he thought.

"And what of yourself, when were you told to work with Wagg?" Westlake asked.

"You do not have that quite right. I was not working with Wagg until I met him here. I got my marching orders by courier from your father in late February this year. If either side declared war, I was to race for the furs at Fort St. Joseph and then proceed on to Fort

Mackinac to seize the furs here. I'm a simple backup plan in case Wagg himself didn't make it through this mosquito-infested wilderness."

"So Wagg is working alone?"

"Wrong again. Within reason, we're both allowed to pay people as we see fit. I hired transport to get me here or I never would have found the godforsaken place."

"And Wagg, who did he hire?"

"There are bullies in this world, and then there are some that are real evil. Wagg hired the latter, I'm afraid: a bastard named Carson Stone. He's ex-British Navy who now works for himself and sometimes the Americans. How he stole the officer's uniform he wears only God knows; and who knows why he deserted—maybe gambling debts or a duel over a girl? He despises me and my humor, rotten shit that he is."

"What does he look like?" Westlake could barely breathe.

"I wouldn't say this in front of him, but behind his back everyone jokes about how he has a face like an owl. It's quite funny, really."

Westlake turned to the lake, and pressed his eyes shut. He'd guessed as much before he asked the question, but it was still a shock to hear that his father had indirectly employed the man responsible for Ned Parrish's death. Such a disaster.

"What did Wagg hire Carson Stone to do?"

"You seem fairly intense about all this, Mr. Westlake. I had the impression that you could care less about the furs."

"Answer my question. Why did Wagg hire Stone?"

"I don't know all the details, but Wagg needed someone to tell him of British or American movements toward the Old Northwest—apparently that's where we are now. You see, Wagg had to be first to get to the furs if there was war or risk losing them. I hear the Americans are snatching anyone who travels past their forts."

Westlake groaned, thinking back to the vindictive Sergeant Harris and his troop.

Hicks continued, "Imagine if Fort St. Joseph had surrendered to the Americans, the furs would've been lost. Or what if Captain Roberts had seized Mackinac without our help, the furs could've been lost again. Stone was supposed to stop anyone who looked like a courier, find out their purpose and who their message was intended for. He would even delay them, if necessary, while Wagg made his way north. The money paid to Stone yielded nothing, if you ask me."

Westlake remained puzzled as to how Stone knew that he and the Parrish brothers would be traveling past Fort Detroit. "Was he to use force?"

"Wagg gave him free rein, but personally I think old Bill is afraid of Stone. I guess Stone, being an evil prick, would use force, for sure. He tried to intimidate me last night, but I told him to push off. Tell your father from me that he can keep the both of them."

"You mean Stone is here? On this island?"

"Of course he is, although he stayed well clear of Captain Roberts. Lucky for him the night was darker than a blackie's ass. Wagg sent him off only an hour after we landed, lazy bastard."

Westlake turned Hicks by the shoulders back toward the village with a hand under his arm.

"You stay with the furs, Mr. Hicks, as you're employed to do, while I go and meet Mr. Stone. One more thing, did Wagg ever mention that he was traveling with a girl?"

"Not to me, but he said he had someone staying with his boat near our landing place in case the attack failed. Probably was Stone's idea to cut and run if things went poorly. You know how most bullies are cowards deep down."

Westlake left Hicks with the furs and collected Lapointe and Parrish. On the way up to the village he explained all that he heard from Hicks. If they saw Stone, they needed to capture him, but how to do that he wasn't sure.

"Stone will hang for any number of reasons, so we have to capture him—not kill him. Do I have your word on that, Parrish?" Westlake demanded.

Parrish walked on in silence.

"Mr. Parrish, I asked you a question."

"Yes, sir, I won't kill Stone."

Not bloody likely, Parrish thought.

154

Westlake spotted Sergeant Baker traipsing back alone from the fort, where Dousman had remained to assist with surrender arrangements. If Captain Roberts felt Lieutenant Hanks was good to his word, he had the power to parole the captured enemy soldiers. With the village under control, Westlake put Baker formally in charge and told him about the cache of furs in the warehouse.

The three men continued their climb up the hill to the fort, where they met Captain Roberts coming out through the gate. Westlake congratulated him on his victory and asked the whereabouts of Bill Wagg. Roberts informed him that, as soon as the white flag of surrender went up, Wagg had headed back toward the landing. He was traveling alone, as far as Roberts could see, and no, Westlake could not go after him.

"This isn't personal, sir," Westlake lied. "There's a civilian that was left behind with Wagg's boat who could now be in grave danger. I give you my word that I won't harm Bill Wagg, but please let me go, sir."

"There's more to this than I care to guess about. On your honor, Westlake—Wagg is not to be touched. You must return immediately after you secure this civilian you mention."

"Yes, sir. Thank you, sir."

Westlake and his two friends turned and sprinted back along the shore road. Even in daylight the path came too close to the cliff side for Westlake's liking. It was a miracle that not one of the Royal Veterans had gone over the edge. At the slanting shale, Westlake kept running, using his momentum to keep him upright. When his right foot slipped out from under him at the last yard, his knee smacked down hard on loose rock but he rolled safely over to the grass. While there was no need to crawl in the daylight, Lapointe and Parrish secured each footstep as they proceeded. Though a piece of shale broke loose and rolled off the cliff to smash on the rocks below, the two men managed to cross without incident.

Westlake was up and running again. Wagg had at least an hour's start on them, but if he had dithered, they might just catch up with him and Stone at the shoreline. Westlake felt the strain in his leg muscles. The lack of sleep and a night of marching began taking their toll, so his pace slowed as he descended to the beach. Suddenly Parrish shot past him, and Westlake yelled out to remind him of his promise to capture Stone alive.

Lapointe caught up with Westlake and they paused inside the forest's edge, trying to catch their breath. Indians and voyageurs now covered the beach, climbing into their canoes and pushing out the boats. Westlake peered around the throng of bodies, but he could not see Mary Collins so he stood up on his toes and peered over all their heads but saw no sign of either Wagg or Stone. Parrish came striding back with a shake of his head. Westlake scanned the water beyond the shoreline, but Lake Huron lay flat all the way to the horizon.

A shout from the water's edge caught his attention. "Do you three loafers want a ride back to the village?" Dickson asked.

"Have you or your men seen Bill Wagg in the last hour?" Westlake yelled back.

Dickson turned to ask the men in his transport canoe the same question. One native gave him an answer. "He says he saw two men and a girl at the shore some time ago."

"Ask him which way they went."

After consulting the man again, Dickson replied, "He didn't watch them further and has no idea where they went. Now, do you want a ride or not?"

There was one man who might know which way Wagg was traveling.

"We'll take your ride," Westlake said. He had urgent business with Mr. Hicks.

He stepped into the bow of the canoe, followed by Parrish and Lapointe. On their way back, he glanced up at the gap in the path that deteriorated into broken shale, and from the water, the angle looked almost vertical. The waves of Lake Huron smacked against the base of the cliff, and Westlake noticed the eyes of both Lapointe and Parrish open wide as they too saw the cliff-top path suddenly crumble away.

"*Mon Dieu.*" Lapointe shook his head.

The village wharf was packed with natives and voyageurs, but Hicks still sat on a wooden barrel outside the storehouse of furs. He jumped up and called out to Westlake: "One of Baker's men just told me you've captured two hundred and fifty-three gallons of whiskey, to say nothing of guns, ammunition, blankets, and provisions. Captain Roberts says he could hold off a whole army with what he's captured. I'm getting drunk with Baker tonight."

"We need to talk again, Mr. Hicks," Westlake said.

"More furs in there, if that's what you're wondering." Hicks pointed to the small building next door.

"No, unless that's the other cache of furs you and Wagg were sent to safeguard. You said earlier that you were sent for 'several caches of furs.' Where are the rest of them?"

Hicks laughed. "At least now you're starting to get the point. This is all about money, the value of the furs."

"Where are they?" Westlake grabbed the startled man by the lapels of his coat.

"We got everything at Fort St. Joseph and all the furs here, so the only ones remaining should be in Fort Detroit."

"That's where Wagg went?"

"He didn't confide in me, but I can guess as much," Hicks replied. "It's where he should be going at least."

"Where's Captain Roberts?"

"Persuading the villagers to take the oath of allegiance to King George. Most of them started off as British, so I don't think it'll matter much. Dousman is the only islander to be exempted from the oath. These fur traders think they own the place."

By midday the village was alight with cooking fires, so that the smell of burning maple and pine wafted through the air. Parrish was scooping a handful of water out of the lake to drink when his stomach growled and he realized that he'd missed breakfast.

Captain Roberts had come striding through the distillery doorway. "No, Mr. Westlake, I cannot let you go tearing after Bill Wagg. By now he'd be far down Lake Huron, well on his way to Detroit. You, on the other hand, are going directly to General Brock, and you're leaving forthwith." Roberts slapped the gloves he held in one hand across the palm of the other.

He pointed to the wharf where Dickson was building a fire. "Robert

Dickson and a small squad will escort the three of you to York. You'll be carrying from me the news of our victory here. The general must know straight away, so there'll be no time for any sideshows, understand? I'll give you a letter before you leave."

Westlake wanted to speak but realized he had no hope of being heard, as Roberts kept right on with his instructions.

"You can get something to eat here and then collect your things back at Fort St. Joseph, but I want you on the water, and soon. Dickson and his crew know the way, so you three just help out where you can. There're some tough portages ahead of you, but for God's sake keep pushing."

Parrish grinned at Westlake as if he was looking forward to it.

Roberts continued, "The tribes will be more likely on our side now, and the sooner General Brock knows of this victory, the better it'll be for all. I'll allocate a share of the prize money for each of you. My guess is ten thousand pounds sterling in value here, so each of you should get at least ten pounds. Goodbye." Roberts extended his hand to each man in turn. "Say hello to the general for me."

"There's a start on that farm you've been talking about, Parrish," Lapointe said.

"He's right," Westlake added. But as Parrish stared at this boots, downcast, Westlake suspected he was thinking about Ned and all that his brother would miss.

Some whooping and hollering close by caught their attention.

Although the Indians behaved well throughout the capture of the island, they were becoming restless, and Captain Roberts had let loose some cattle for slaughter. By the time Westlake got back to the wharf, Dickson was roasting several thick chunks of beef.

They had not eaten or slept for more than twenty-four hours so Westlake and Lapointe were hungry, but they waited until most of the blood had been cooked out of the beef. Parrish was never fussy about how his food was prepared, so when Dickson handed him blood-soaked hot beef skewered on a stick, Parrish bit into it instantly, staining his chin red.

"Here's your note from Captain Roberts, Ensign Westlake," came a voice beside him. "I've been asked to inform you and Mr. Dickson that you may leave at any time, so long as it's soon."

"Sergeant Baker, what a nice surprise. Some meat to appease your hunger?" Parrish suggested. He held out the remainder of his beef, dripping with blood.

"No thank you, Parrish. I haven't gone Injun yet. Besides, I have to escort a certain lady back to her home and it wouldn't do for me to see her with my face covered in blood. The good captain has seen fit to let all the civilians out of the distillery, now that they have sworn allegiance to His Majesty."

Westlake held out his hand. "It was my pleasure to march with you, Sergeant Baker." He winced at the strength of Baker's grip.

"I've met all kinds of officers from India to this wilderness here and you'll make a fine one if you stick with it. That is, if you don't get your head blown off first, sir."

"Then I'm lucky that I'm not in the regular army." Westlake laughed. "But it's strange, Baker, I could have sworn you didn't like me at first."

"I didn't … sir. Goodbye." Baker gave a casual salute, offered a wave to Parrish and Lapointe, and marched off to meet his new female friend who was waiting at the distillery for her personal escort home.

"Goodbye," Westlake hollered. As for getting himself killed, he didn't think so, but finding his own female friend required a new strategy.

13

· · · · · ·

Sergeant Frank Harris stepped out of the longboat and on to the shores of Upper Canada. "We're here, finally. Now let's kill the bastards," he said.

"Sergeant Harris, less foul talk if you please. It's Sunday morning and God has granted us this beautiful sunshine for our crossing. Do not try His patience, or mine." Captain Daniel Jackson leapt out of the longboat to scan the tree line thirty yards away for any sign of Redcoats. He was sweating both with nerves and from the heat. Beyond the beach, where the sand ended and the brush gave way to trees, something moved. Jackson shot up his hand for the others to stop, and everyone crouched, clearly expecting a blast of musket fire. He squinted in the sunlight to see a bush rocking in the river breeze, nothing more—nothing to do with a musket. He had expected this landing to be more difficult.

"Clear the beach. General Hull is right behind us. Harris, hurry your men up and secure that building ahead." Jackson pointed to a new, two-storey brick house with a wooden veranda. "Take down that British rag and put up the Stars and Stripes. People should know we're here, since they've been waiting long enough for us to arrive."

So on July 12 the Americans had come to Canada. And Captain Jackson was correct: the Upper Canadians had been waiting for them, especially those with sympathies toward the republic. But, with problems mounting, Jackson had wondered if the U.S. 4th Infantry was ever going to invade. For more than a week, General Hull had been trying in vain to cross the Detroit River. Colonel Cass complained that the campaign was stagnating, but when it came time to cross, there were not enough boats. Colonel McArthur promised he would keep them supplied with rations, but how realistic was that when the supplies lines stretched back more than two hundred miles to

Dayton, Ohio. Colonel Findlay's militia threatened to desert if they didn't get started soon, but on the first invasion date three hundred of them would not budge an inch past the river. Jackson had already warned Hull that their terms of duty did not require them to fight on foreign soil.

"What am I to do with you louts?" Hull demanded. He called the militiamen every despicable name he could think of, from coward to traitor, but they would not move. Then he tried praising them for their patriotic march through the Black Swamp. He could imagine no finer fighting force, he said, yet nothing worked. At last he threatened to hang those who wouldn't follow orders, and this was enough to finally make some jump. Even so, on the day the U.S. Army of the Northwest invaded Upper Canada, at a small town called Sandwich, more than a hundred militiamen stayed behind.

Of course, the moment the 4th Infantry was on Canadian soil, Hull was flooded with advice from his three militia colonels. Charge Fort Amherstburg immediately and catch them by surprise. Keep moving and don't stop until we attack York. Torch everything and string up British sympathizers. Jackson turned his head as a single cannon fired from somewhere miles to the south of them.

"So much for your advantage of surprise, gentlemen," Hull said. "They obviously have their cannon ready while ours remain in Detroit. As for supplies, what do you three suppose we should eat—just these unripened peaches?" He waved his arm at the rows of peach trees that surrounded them. "Have you thought of the Indians? My personal plan is not to get scalped. It would be much wiser to set up a breast-work to ward off attacks."

"Let me go and forage east of here for supplies," McArthur volunteered. "I could be back in a few days, when you're ready to move."

"Now you're thinking," Hull replied. "See that brick house yonder? It's the house of a British militiaman, Colonel Baby, and it'll now be my headquarters. Report back to me there in three days."

McArthur saluted from his horse and galloped off before Hull could change his mind. Hull looked happy to see him go, and Captain Jackson suspected McArthur was just as happy to be gone.

Colonel Cass and Lieutenant Colonel Miller were ordered to reconnoiter five miles south, as far as the Canard River, and find a way across it, preferably a bridge. They were to meet force with force, if challenged. Colonel Findlay was to secure the landing from counterattack by building breastworks around the camp.

Hull had given all the complainers something to do and now he grinned. "Lieutenant Colonel Miller has departed and left your orders with me, Captain. I assume you don't know how to build gun carriages." Hull handed Jackson his orders.

"Sorry, sir," Jackson replied.

Jackson had watched Hull fret over the lack of heavy guns, and in the end, Hull decided to float them across the river before attacking the fort. Two weeks to build new gun carriages for the twenty-four pounders and mortars was too long to wait, but to lay siege to a fort and then storm its walls, cannons were required to make breaches. Otherwise, storming the walls meant an escalade, and considerable slaughter on both sides. Jackson hoped Hull would wait for the cannon.

Captain Jackson's orders were plain enough, or so they seemed. Attached to Colonel Miller's regular army, he and his men were to secure the right flank of their reconnaissance force by eliminating any resistance from the farmhouses along the Detroit River. Since they were short of rations, everyone was expected to contribute. He and his men were also to act as a foraging party as they proceeded downstream.

The first building they came upon was an abandoned log cabin with a veranda. Except for a few tools, its owners had carried off the entire contents. The next few farms were similar: nothing had been left for the invaders. Made of brick and stone, the last farmhouse along the river was a more substantial enterprise, with outbuildings. One large barn contained bales of hay, tools, a wagon—and four horses.

"Sergeant Harris, see if these people are still around. The place looks occupied." Captain Jackson pointed to it from his horse.

A moment later Harris reappeared. "There's a women named Iris in the back bedroom."

Harris took only two steps away from the front door when a voice behind Jackson said, "Put your hands in the air and stay away from my house. It's private property."

Jackson remained still and gazed down at Harris. "Do as he says, Sergeant Harris."

Jackson turned his horse and half-heartedly put his left hand in the air while holding the reins with his right. He studied the fellow with interest, a man he guessed to be in his late forties. It took someone special to take on more than a dozen men single-handedly with one musket. He must have hidden in the barn during their cursory search knowing it would come to this confrontation.

"You give orders sharply for a farmer," Jackson remarked.

"What right do you have coming on my land?"

"You're an ex-military man," Jackson guessed. "We're at war now and the U.S. Army has taken over this territory. We need supplies, for which you'll be paid."

"I doubt that very much."

"Put your musket down. You cannot possibly shoot us all before we kill you and everyone else in the house."

The man paused to study them. Jackson knew he wouldn't run because his wife was still inside, but he also could not kill them all. One, maybe two, and then they would have the farm and Iris at their mercy.

Jackson turned in his saddle to assess the impression given by his troop. Harris appeared rough and he strode with an assertiveness that suggested a type of recklessness. He was what a dangerous man looked like, even if he was also heavy and disheveled. And his hungry troops stared at the farmer with the insolence of soldiers let loose for a weekend of mayhem. The man would never make a deal with this lot so Jackson made a decision.

"I give you my word, sir, that you and your wife will not be harmed." He was saying it to Harris and his own men as much as to the man with the musket.

No one moved, then slowly the musket was lowered.

"Captain George Moore, retired." The man offered his hand.

Jackson agreed to leave him tools enough to work the orchard and vegetable garden, and a month's food. Three of the four horses were taken while the wagon was loaded with provisions and all the weapons found in the household. Moore appeared satisfied enough.

Private Rufus Boggs was detailed to take the wagon back to their Sandwich camp, except that Boggs disappeared by the time the troop was preparing to leave. "Sergeant Harris, where's your man in charge of the wagon?" Jackson demanded. "We have to move on." Harris opened his mouth to speak just as a musket shot cracked out from somewhere at the back of the house.

Moore's eyes widened in alarm before he bolted through the front door. He raced through to the bedroom to find Boggs leaning against a wall, clutching his left shoulder.

Iris had produced her own musket from under the blankets. She now sat up in the canopy bed and reached for Moore's hand as he came in to the room.

"What's going on?" Harris had followed Moore.

"I just poked my head in the door, and the witch shot me," Boggs cried in pain.

"If it was just your head in the room, then how could I shoot you in the shoulder?" Her blue eyes set in defiance, Iris gripped the quilt just under her chin with knotted hands.

"You've shot me, you bitch," Boggs yelled in outrage, and he lunged at the bed with his army knife held high. The woman screamed and pulled the blankets over her white hair as Moore shouldered Boggs aside and reached for the knife. Boggs tumbled off the bed with Moore on top of him and the knife beneath him. Moore continued to struggle, but he soon felt the body under him go limp. He stood up quickly and rolled Boggs on to his back. The knife was imbedded in his chest, up to the handle: Rufus Boggs was dead.

The entire episode happened in seconds. Moore heard Iris sobbing, still hiding under the covers. Then the world for Captain George Moore went black.

"Rufus was just checking to make sure the lady was alright when she shot him, then Moore pulls a knife and finishes Rufus off. There was

nothing I could do, so I butt-ended old Moore in the head, sir."
Sergeant Harris tapped the stock end of his musket with the bloodied
knife he had pulled from Boggs's chest. He was panting after dragging
Moore by the collar out through the front door.

"Let me see that knife," Jackson said. Harris handed it to him,
blood still running over the blade.

"This is one of our knives. How did Moore get one of our knives?
It probably belongs to Boggs. Don't you lie to me, Harris, does Boggs
have his knife?"

"I couldn't find it, sir."

"I ordered everyone to leave Iris Moore alone. I checked her room
myself, and there was no one else in there. Boggs had no right being
in her bedroom." Jackson spit out the words with disgust.

"They were to turn over all their weapons, sir, no exceptions. So
what was she doing with a loaded musket in her bed? And Moore
doesn't get to kill one of our wounded men just for being in the wrong
room, sir." Harris was shaking with resentment.

"You're forever finding ways to try me, Harris. Settle down now.
I've heard gunshots toward the Canard River." Jackson called over to
one of the men, "Haggard, tie up Captain Moore and throw him on
the wagon. Put Boggs's body there as well, and take the lot back to
camp. I'll sort this out after I return. Don't touch Mrs. Moore—or I'll
shoot you myself. Understood?"

"Yes, sir." Haggard nodded in agreement.

"The rest of you, let's move at the double."

The balance of the troop jogged inland while Jackson galloped
ahead of them. Ten minutes later, he slowed his horse to a walk as he
approached the backs of U.S. Army regulars. "Lieutenant Colonel
Miller?" he inquired. A man pointed ahead to his left.

Miller was sitting on his horse inside a stand of birch trees as
Jackson trotted up behind him.

"I heard musket fire, sir?" he began, then tugged the reins so the
horse stepped back lightly.

Miller poked his head cautiously around the large birch. "You
couldn't have heard our muskets from here all the way to the Detroit

River. What you heard was Cass's men firing inadvertently as they moved toward you and then circled around back of the Canard River bridge." He pointed across the small wooden bridge to the far side. "I told them to run with muskets unloaded, but our militia friend Colonel Cass believes he knows more than us regular army types. Now, of course, the enemy knows we're here."

"What are we facing—a detachment of regulars?" Jackson scanned the bridge. He was expecting to see Redcoats but saw no one.

"Cass was to take the bridge from the Amherstburg end so we didn't have to run across in the open. But maybe he can't move, I don't know for sure. We'll try to help him from this end."

"My men will be down this road any minute, so can we be of assistance, sir?" Jackson prayed for a chance to tackle the real enemy instead of confronting just local farmers. He glanced at the bridge again, but the Redcoats remained hidden.

"Certainly you can help. Take the Canard bridge." Miller grinned, gesturing with a grand wave of the hand.

"Gladly, sir." Jackson touched the front of his hat in gratitude.

In his red coat with white cross-belt, young Private John Dean of His Majesty's 41st Regiment crouched behind the bridge post. His friend and fellow sentry of the same regiment, Private James Hancock, hid beside the post that stood on the other side of the road. The British detachment guarding the approach to Fort Amherstburg had retreated even as Cass's noisy militiamen had tried to encircle them by crossing the river upstream. This left him and Hancock trapped, alone between American forces approaching at either end of the bridge. The bridge itself at their back was thirty yards of planked logs. They had now turned to challenge the militiamen who had got around to intervene between them and Fort Amherstburg.

"Remember what Captain Moore said," Hancock whispered from across the road. "Keep your head down!"

John Dean did not feel that jovial. In the sun's heat, he fingered a warm pewter button on his coat and wondered how they were to get back to the fort, or even if their orders would allow them to leave their position at the bridge. A musket banged out and the ball whizzed over-head. The enemy then strode into view as a group of Ohio militiamen, dressed in gray and brown homespun, came marching down the sun-baked road.

"I'll fire first and then you fire while I reload, so don't shoot right away," Dean hissed.

"After you've fired, slide halfway down the hill, but make sure you can still see the road," Hancock urged. On either side of the bridge posts, a few trees growing separate from the dense line of cedars offered shade from the sun but also some cover for the two sentries.

Dean aimed at a militiaman not thirty yards away and the man col-lapsed, bawling and holding his shin. All the other militiamen scattered instantly off the roadway, and Hancock fired too late, just as the last one dove behind the trees. Dean had slid down the grass, sure that Hancock would have done the same.

Within seconds, a volley of shots rang over his head, but they were too high so Dean guessed the militiamen had no idea that he and his partner were now hiding farther down the slopes leading toward the river, on either side of the bridge. He waited briefly until another volley hammered the right plank of the bridge and then he smiled: they were firing blind. The first man he had shot suddenly stopped wailing and the forest went quiet.

Three militiamen stepped onto the roadway in a crouch, and he took aim at the closest. He fired, but the man stumbled at a crucial moment so the ball sped past harmlessly. The second man, wearing a raccoon hat, spotted the smoke drifting from Dean's location and stood up, knowing it would take the shooter time to reload. He took one extra peek to be sure and then pointed his musket.

This time it was Hancock's turn to fire. His ball cracked the man's cheek, smashing through his jawbone and tearing out half his face. The raccoon hat flew in the air as he jerked his head, gripping at his face. He tumbled off the road into the undergrowth and Dean heard him moaning until someone shouted at him to shut up.

Both sides of the road filled with angry militiamen firing in an uncoordinated volley. No bullets came close to the sentries lying in the cedars, but the bridge above them thudded repeatedly, the balls splintering its upright wooden posts. Dean crawled back up the embankment, to the base of his bridge post. "Hold your fire, James," he whispered loudly. "Don't let them see our smoke unless you have a clear shot." Sweat trickled down his brow into one eye and he let it sit there, stinging, rather than take a hand from his musket.

Militiamen peered from the cover of the trees trying to see how many men were guarding the bridge and exactly where they were located. Dean watched as, on the left side of the road, they tried to draw him out by appearing for a moment, firing, and then disappearing back into the safety of the forest. He stayed hidden, head down, but with all the action in front of him, he'd not thought to look back down the bridge behind him.

A volley from the militiamen whizzed passed his head and along to the far end of the bridge, where someone hollered, "Down." Dean peered toward the shout and glimpsed a troop of Bluecoats hustling behind the bridge posts at the other end. The militia's volley had caught the U.S. Army in the open. They were coming from both sides and Dean's stomach tightened until he felt he was going to throw up.

"Any wounded?" Jackson asked.

"Not bloody likely. Those backwoods bumpkins couldn't hit anything, right, boys?" Harris laughed and the men laughed with him as they crouched for cover.

"There are twelve of us here, so let's show our militia friends how army regulars take a bridge," Jackson chided in a raised voice.

Enthusiasm for battle was starting to take hold. "We'll split up, six on either side of the bridge, but in pairs of three. My three will fire first, followed by Harris's group. As we reload, the three behind us will advance and fire, to ensure continuous fire. But we keep advancing, understood?" The men nodded in agreement.

"Good. Now stay down for a moment." Jackson eased his head up and surveyed the distant end of the bridge.

"This is Captain Daniel Jackson of the U.S. Army speaking. You're surrounded. Surrender and you will not be hurt. Refuse to surrender and you face certain death." Jackson ducked down again.

"They're not going to give up that easy, sir." Harris licked his lips. He crouched lower, then toppled over to one side.

"Shut up, Harris. I don't expect them to." Jackson raised his head, secretly hoping for a white flag on the end of a bayonet, but he saw nothing. "I was speaking for the benefit of our own side. Now, when we charge the bridge, our own militiamen will know that we're U.S. Army and won't shoot at us."

"That's why he's a captain—smarts like." Tapping the side of his head, Harris laughed, and the men tried to join with him, fighting their nervousness.

"God help me, Harris, in any other army you would be shot for your mouth. Get ready to run on my command. Thirty yards, and don't stop."

Dean considered the offer to let them surrender. "How many of them do you figure there are on that side, James?" He gestured toward Jackson's troop.

"I don't know, not that many that I could see. We can't just give up this bridge without a fight."

"Then let's show 'em what we're ma ... made of." Dean tried to speak, but his mouth was too dry for the words to come without stuttering.

"I'm with you, John," Hancock said.

Dean replaced the ramrod under his Brown Bess, noticing his hand shaking. Thudding footsteps across the wooden planks told him that the U.S. Army was now coming. At twenty yards, he stood up and took aim at the bulky soldier coming straight down his side of the bridge. Dean fired, the ball creasing the left arm of his attacker and lodging itself in the rib of the man behind him. The second man fell, howling in pain.

Harris winced from the sting in his arm and slowed to a cautious walk.

Jackson held up his hand for all to halt and pointed toward a lone Redcoat. "Fire." But Dean was already down and loading before any of the racing balls could reach him. Another Redcoat stood up, thinking that the attackers would be reloading, and fired directly along his side of the bridge at an officer. In his nervousness, he aimed high and the ball whistled harmlessly past Captain Jackson.

No longer able to aim his own musket, Harris drew his sword and pointed it at the standing figure of Hancock. "Fire," he yelled as the rear group of three men stepped up beside him.

The balls tore into both of Hancock's thighs and dropped him to the ground. "Oh God, my legs … John, my legs," Hancock yelled in panic.

Dean rose to fire, but Jackson was waiting for him on the other side of bridge. Dean had risen only partly out of his crouch before Jackson gave the order to fire. One ball struck home, smashing Dean's right forearm. He dropped his musket and rolled to the ground clutching his wounded arm.

Hancock shouted to him, "Fix your bayonet." Unable now to stand, Hancock rested on his knees with his own bayonet pointing upward. Harris and his men crossed to the other side of the bridge and charged at him.

"You must yield!" Jackson shouted

His shout came too late as Harris parried Hancock's bayonet aside and stabbed him through the shoulder. "You bastard, you shot my arm," Harris screamed, his face contorted and flushed red from his sprint across the bridge. He ripped his sword from the boy's body deliberately, twisting it to inflict agony.

"That's enough, Sergeant," Jackson ordered.

The blade had ground against bone and tore its way out, leaving Hancock with a hole in his shoulder. He tumbled backward down the embankment under the bridge and splashed into the river, his blood streaming out into the current.

Dean would not yield and tried to fight by gripping his bayonet in one hand while his right arm dangled uselessly by his side. Jackson pushed the bayonet away and knocked the fellow down with the back of his gloved hand. From the grass, Dean managed one glance up at Jackson's concerned expression before fainting.

"Well done, Captain. The militia is still lost in the woods, it seems." Miller chuckled as he rode up to the bridge. "Any casualties?"

"Harris, are you hit?" Jackson asked.

"Someone else took that ball meant for me … right in his ribs, sir. I'm fine," Harris lied, for his bicep stung like a scald. He gestured to a man lying on the roadway surrounded by others.

"You men, get that soldier out of the water and try to stop his bleeding. What happened to this one?" Miller looked down at the unconscious Dean while a couple of them scrambled down to retrieve Hancock.

"He fainted 'cause he was scared." Harris laughed, but no one laughed with him.

"This man continued to fight with just one arm, Harris, and my guess is that he fainted from pain." Jackson pointed to the other arm bent in a strange position. "That lad in the water fought from his knees after he couldn't stand. Can you imagine, even with your small brain, how hard this war will be if every British soldier fights us with the courage of these two? The pair of them managed to hold off a militia regiment and our entire company!" Jackson's exhaustion in the July heat was becoming evident. He felt dirty, and with the back of his hand, he wiped the sweat dripping from his forehead.

"Captain Jackson, we'll make camp here," Miller ordered. "I'll inform Colonel Cass. Meanwhile, take care of your wounded."

"I have to ride back to Sandwich, sir. We sent a wagon back there with supplies, also a prisoner and a dead soldier … one of ours, I'm afraid."

"I'm sorry," Miller replied. "While you're there, you can tell General Hull that the bridge is secure, and the way is now clear to Fort Amherstburg."

Bill Wagg sat upright in the stern of their sixteen-foot canoe and paddled with an uneven stroke. He felt the heat of the sun beating down on his neck and hunched shoulders. His stepdaughter, Mary, sat in front of him, and he saw her struggle to keep stroke with Carson Stone in the bow. *It's a wonder she hasn't left me*, he mused, but then again where could she go. She'd get much worse treatment if left to her own resources.

Carson Stone was another matter though, too quiet and always brooding, best kept where he could be watched. It was evident that he terrified Mary. Wagg had caught Stone staring at her more than once, and each time it made him anxious. Something terrible would happen by remaining close to Stone for too long, but Wagg had to keep pushing on to Fort Detroit, and for that he needed the other man's help.

They were paddling down the western shores of Lake Huron, under a blue sky and over glistening water. The canoe was too large for their purposes, but it was all Wagg could buy on a moment's notice. His problem was that no one in the vessel knew how to properly handle a canoe. This led to a zigzag pattern across the water, which was adding miles to their journey. But the current was with them so that even if they floated all the way, they would reach their destination eventually.

Now that war was declared, Wagg had to rescue the last remaining cache of furs destined for the Westlake Trading Company, and that meant traveling to Detroit. Nothing was going to come between him and those furs.

Carson Stone had demanded that they escape Michilimackinac Island immediately. The idea of being trapped on an island side by side with the British Army was too much, even for him. If Wagg wanted to keep the man's protection, then he had to keep Stone concealed and away from the Redcoats; and capturing those furs meant protecting Stone.

Of course, for Wagg the overwhelming shock of the night had been confronting Jonathan Westlake. Out of the blackness had appeared those angular features, working alongside the British Army to capture Fort Mackinac. What a surprise it had been and Wagg wanted to kill him right there. He took his hand off the paddle and rubbed his forehead, which was paining him still after five months of healing. The canoe slid sideways.

"Keep your damn paddle in the water back there," Stone yelled from the bow. "We're too far out in the middle so stay closer to the shore. I'm not drowning myself needlessly just for some goddamn furs."

Wagg splashed his paddle back in the water and strained on his stoke to bring the vessel back on course just as a gust of wind sent ripples over the water.

From London to York without incident, and the first trouble I encounter is with the boss's son. Where did he come from? Wagg wondered. He shook his head and glared at the shoreline half expecting to see Westlake waving to him with both arms from a rock. *It's lucky I didn't kill him. The boss would never forgive me for murdering his son. I'll have to get my pay first—and then kill him.* Wagg laughed to himself quietly, not wishing to attract Stone's wrath further.

Then he recalled Stone's tale about the ambush: four men dead in the blink of an eye. One man with a tomahawk in the skull; the knifing of another through the throat from thirty feet; Stone's brother shooting Westlake's horse and then taking a knife in the chest buried to the handle; the fourth man must have been beaten to death. Stone said Westlake was so quick he barely saw him move, and it was all Stone could do to escape with his own skin intact. Wagg had never seen Stone express fear, but at that moment, during his story, Stone could barely breathe. If Stone had all three captives surrounded, with their hands in the air, Wagg wondered how Westlake did it all so fast. Perhaps he would never know, but without a doubt Westlake was a killer.

Wagg frowned. *Maybe I was the lucky one. Knocked out cold in that cabin, if Westlake had wanted to, he could have finished me off in York.* But something had stopped him. Beyond the water, Wagg studied the shore again to see nothing but miles of rocks and trees. He remembered striking the back of Westlake's head with the birch log, and the red poker burning through the sleeve of a buckskin coat, but he could not recall receiving the blow to his own forehead. To Wagg's thinking, Westlake should have killed him, but for some reason the young man hesitated, and that meant he had a weakness.

Wagg had so far kept Westlake's presence on the island to himself; it had been dark and there was no purpose in upsetting Stone. Just get the furs was all that mattered. After seeing Stone off the beach, Wagg had given him the job of packing the canoe with their hidden supplies of food, clothing, and weapons. All Wagg had to do was run from the cannon above the fort, back down the same path the cannon had hacked out through the forest. The three of them would be off before anyone but Captain Roberts knew. Wagg had left Hicks in charge of the furs, and the moment the surrender flag went up, Wagg had gone, stumbling off to the beach. The plan had worked perfectly.

Wagg peered up at the sky as the canoe turned to shore for their second night out of Fort Mackinac. The wind picked up so that the ripples on the lake became small waves while some puffy clouds, drifting out of the southwest, had turned dark. From the stern of the canoe, Wagg called out to Stone, seated forward, "I meant to tell you that I met a friend of ours on that island back there, but in all the mayhem, I forgot about it. When I was handing the oxen over to Roberts, who should appear out of the darkness but that damn fellow, young Westlake." Wagg concentrated to keep up his stroke. He had expected some reaction out of Stone, but instead it was Mary who twisted around.

"What, he was there! He was there the whole time, and you said nothing?" She slumped forward and stopped paddling.

Wagg stared at her, thinking back to the cabin and what might have taken place with him lying unconscious on the floor—Westlake standing over him—ready to crush his skull with the birch log.

Stone did not miss so much as a stroke. "Then we should have killed him back there in the dark."

Wagg had other thoughts now, for he had just figured out what had stopped Westlake from killing him. *Another weakness in the fellow*, he thought.

In the smooth rhythm of the native's paddling, Westlake dozed, sitting upright in the center of the canoe, puzzling how to get Mary Collins out of Fort Detroit. Her surprised face on his return to her cabin in York made him grin. He jerked out of his reverie when Parrish asked Dickson if birchbark canoes were hard to make. Parrish had been absentmindedly stroking the smooth side of the birch until his finger had caught on a sticky seam, which set him to wondering about the craft's construction.

Westlake kept his eyes shut, remembering how Paxinos had constructed a birch canoe with little more than a knife. This was after they had destroyed a canoe by running some whitewater rapids that turned out to be too shallow. The rocks had sliced the bottom of the craft lengthwise, like a jagged knife through an apple. For its replacement, he recalled peeling the birchbark off a large fallen tree, then suspending the frame of the new canoe on four thick posts.

"The gunwales and ribs - closely laid mind you - from bow to stern are all made of cedar strips," Dickson explained. "Once they're in place, more longitudinal cedar ribs are sheathed over the top. I make 'em specially thin so they're flexible and easy to work with."

That day with Paxinos, Westlake had built a fire to boil the fibrous roots of a cedar tree used in sewing the strips of birch to the gunwales. The same hot water was then used to soften pitch from a pine tree. After using the pitch to seal the birch seams, Paxinos took no chances of a leak, so he sewed extra strips of birch over the same seams and sealed them again with more pitch. Westlake could see it all again in his mind, as if it was only yesterday.

"But what do you use to sew the cedar roots to the birch bark," Parrish asked.

"Ah, you've been listening closely Mr Parrish. We use what's called a square-bladed awl - a wonderful little tool, and I wouldn't want to be without it," Dickson replied.

Westlake added, with his eyes still closed, "And when they're finished they sometimes paint a design on the bow, maybe a hawk or a bear - usually something powerful."

"You're awake, so get paddling. I don't have time for painting pictures myself, but some do go in for that type a thing ... Land ho." Dickson pointed out Fort St. Joseph's wharf, now within sight.

At the fort, there was almost no one to greet them. An enemy force could have taken it for the asking. Just a cook, a baker, and several guards remained.

"There looks to be no threat of rain, so load up your belongings if you have any. I want the canoes ready to go at first light," Dickson said. "And don't get so drunk that you can't get up or I'll leave you behind."

No one paid any attention to Dickson's instructions about drinking. From the two hundred and fifty-three gallons of whiskey captured at Fort Mackinac, each man had stolen at least a canteen's worth of the rarified spirit, but first the canoes were packed with provisions and readied for traveling, as Dickson had asked. Outside the bunkhouse, fires blazed to cook more raw beef, then finally the serious drinking began. Westlake guessed the singing would last all through the night, but since most of the men had been awake for just shy of two days, the whiskey knocked everyone out.

Halfway through his own canteen, Westlake found he had to excuse himself. He staggered away from the campfire and back to the bunkhouse, his head lowered and feeling sick to his stomach. Never a big drinker, he still hated to miss the fun of a party.

With his legs wide apart, and his arms outstretched against the wall, his stomach began to heave uncontrollably. Shaking and sweating, he couldn't stop himself from throwing up. Between heaves he swore out loud that he would never drink that much again.

"But do you make that promise to God, sir?"

He heard a voice and answered. "Yes, I promise. Just let it stop." Westlake was on his knees, hurling up the last of his beef supper mixed with the whiskey. He looked up at the night stars, but even that slight movement made his head dizzy so he returned his gaze to the grizzled contents of his stomach.

"But I thought you didn't believe in God, sir." Someone laughed.

"I never said that. I'm just not sure." Then he realized the voice belonged to Parrish. "I'll believe in him if he can stop this retching, I promise. Now, go away."

The heaving had already stopped, and even his breathing returned to normal. His head hung lower, and it looked to Parrish that Westlake was about to pass out or fall asleep. He reached down and slid his arms under Westlake's from behind, pulling him up and throwing him over his shoulder, for the short trip to their bunks.

"It's lights out, sir. We have a long pull before us in the morning." Parrish chuckled because Ensign Westlake had passed out.

The following morning, Westlake was conscious of a hard grip on his shoulder as he was rocked back and forth.

"Wake up, laddie. I can leave anyone else behind, but Brock would have my hide if I forgot you."

Westlake struggled to open his eyes. "God, my head hurts." His own voice sounded foreign. He sat up and put both hands over his ears.

"Don't you look a sorry sight. No respectable young lass is going to have anything to do with a fellow looking as terrible as you. Here, I brought you a mug of coffee, being the kind gentleman that I am. We have to be off so ten toes on the floor."

The sun had barely touched the eastern sky, but the Red-Haired Chief seemed already in fighting form. Westlake took a sip of coffee and moaned again. "My stomach is too shaky to drink this." He pushed the coffee back into Dickson's hands.

"Can't wait all day so it'll have to be the voyageur's hangover cure for you. Into the river, now."

"That's the last place I want go—the water's freezing in that bloody river."

"We can do this the hard way, with me dragging you, or the easy way on your own. So which will it be?"

Westlake tried to stand but sank back on to the bunk. Dickson reached down with a hand and drew him to his feet. Westlake took three steps and a knee buckled so he had to grab the wall before passing through the door. His head throbbed with every step to the water's edge. Indians started to hoot and jeer as they saw him test the water's temperature with his foot. *It's barely light, so how can they see me?* His stomach gave a slight heave just from the sip of coffee. Too late, he felt Dickson's hand on his back, pushing him hard so that he plunged straight into the river.

Like a cold knife splitting his head, the water made him wince and close his eyes tight, the pain worse even than the red-hot poker searing his arm. He was aware of tightening his stomach to the point where his body was almost rolled into a ball. *Start swimming or sink farther.* He stretched his limbs out and kicked, and as his head broke the surface of the water he gasped for air.

"You're feeling better already, aren't you? I can tell," Dickson goaded.

"Go to hell, Dickson. If you're still there when I come out, I'm taking you back in here with me." But shouting made his head hurt, so Westlake went quiet and closed his eyes.

"That's the spirit, laddie. Drink some fresh water. It will help settle your stomach. See, you're fine now."

Parrish ran up behind Dickson, still tucking in his shirt. "What's all the commotion about?"

"Mr. Westlake here decided to go for an early-morning swim. The water was a might chilly, I expect. Get him out. We push off in half an hour." Dickson strode back to the fort.

"Sir, you have to stop playing about now, the chief says we push off soon," Parrish shouted.

"And you can go to hell too," Westlake hollered back, his head still pounding.

Westlake had packed his gear and was leaving the wharf when Lapointe called to him from along the shore.

"Hey, Johnny! I'll see you sometime, eh!" He gave him a big wave.

Westlake jumped down and jogged toward him. "I knew you'd be heading home."

"You saw where my family lives—right in between Detroit and Sandwich. The Americans think we're *Canadien* and the British think we're American. It will be very dangerous for us in this war, so I must go home."

"Stay close to the shore. Go down the Michigan side of Huron, it'll be faster. "

"I'll be there in a few days, no problem. I paddle with the current and it's all water, no portages."

"Thanks for saving our necks in the ambush. We'd have died without you."

"I'm sorry about Ned. Are you going after that owl-faced guy?"

"I have to get to Brock now, but one day I'll meet the bastard again. We had a great victory at Fort Mackinac. Tell your brother what you did: how you took the whole village by yourself." Westlake laughed and reached out for Lapointe's hand.

"Best of luck."

"You too, Johnny. Stay at our house if you ever come back to Detroit."

Lapointe stepped into his small canoe and Westlake pushed him away from the shore. With a few stokes of his paddle, Lapointe was heading south to Detroit. Westlake remembered that Mary Collins was there, and wished he were going with him.

They were flying through the North Channel of Lake Huron. The big canoe sat a mere eighteen inches above the waterline and this seemed to Parrish to be a bit too close for comfort. He imagined all eighteen men floundering in the water at the first giant wave.

Parrish never liked the water, especially swimming, which he didn't do very well. As the wind picked up behind them, a small wave splashed a few drops over the side, and that was all he needed.

"Chief Dickson, do you think we should have packed some more supplies in this canoe, since we can still float." Parrish laughed but not convincingly.

"Ah, do I hear sarcasm. You look nervous, Mr. Parrish. Just keep up your stroke."

"I'm not a swimmer."

"We're carrying exactly half what this canoe can hold. If I piled in the other half, it would still be six inches above the waterline. Under those two oilcloths, we have stored three hundredweight of biscuit, one hundredweight of pork, a bushel and a half of peas, and a very small amount of whiskey. Maybe a little less of everything now because we've eaten once."

On mentioning whiskey, Dickson winked toward Westlake, who paid no attention.

"Throw in about thirty other packages, an ax, a towline, all our personal belongings, a sponge for bailing, a kettle for coffee, and a good quantity of gum, birchbark, and cedar roots in case you wreck the canoe, and you've half what the men would normally carry on a trip to Montreal. As we're only going to York, we've stocked more than enough."

They paddled well over seventy-five miles that day, and no more water entered the canoe, so Parrish was happy. To their left, the not-too-high mountains of La Cloche rose in their beauty. Except for a midday meal, they paddled all day and put in to a sandy beach well after the sun was lost, leaving them minimal light to make camp.

To calm his jittery stomach, Westlake had eaten only his rations of fresh bread taken from the fort's bakery. He drank water out of his hand, scooping it up from the side of the canoe. It was all his stomach could digest without starting the heaves. He had just managed to force down some weak tea before he saw Dickson posting Indian guards around their camp for the night. He was asleep before saying goodnight.

For the second morning in a row, Westlake felt a hand pushing at his shoulder.

"Not you again."

"Come on, laddie. Do you have need of a river swim again?"

"It's still dark." Westlake rubbed the corners of his eyes and looked up to see Dickson.

"We need to be off as soon as the sun starts to brighten the eastern horizon … if it does today." Dickson studied the sky while some low-lying dark clouds scudded past. "The wind is up and when the waves fight the canoe's hull, it makes for a tough paddle."

"The coals are still hot." Westlake held his hand over the fire pit. "I'll get it going so we can have some coffee. Do you want some of my bread warmed up?"

"I want to be on the water." Dickson stared into the fire as some dried twigs brought it back to life. "We have to leave the shoreline for a while, so I only hope the weather holds—although I don't like the look of it."

At the end of a long stick, Westlake began toasting a chunk of bread over the growing flames. Others were beginning to stir in the camp, and within minutes some were packing to leave. He felt the breeze on his face as he scratched his head and yawned.

"Parrish, wake up." Westlake pushed his companion's hip with the tip of his boot. "I have coffee and toast for you. You should be grateful, you great oaf, so just get up."

"Yes, sir, I am grateful, but I'm also still half asleep."

Within thirty minutes the canoe was on the water. As they passed out of the North Channel into the open water of Georgian Bay, the wind seemed to increase with each passing minute, and with it came rising waves. Westlake noticed how the odd one with a whitecap reached over the side and trickled into the boat. His heart began beating faster and it was not just from the exertion of paddling.

He searched for the shore and guessed it would be a long pull if they had to make an emergency landing. The sky continued to darken until the morning light looked more like early evening. They were now inching forward against a strong wind.

A loud crack in the heavens, followed by a jarring bang that vibrated through each man, was enough for Dickson to get the men stroking for shore with all their strength. Lightning lit up the entire lake, for a moment turning its surface to silver. The water, solid and threatening, appeared to stop moving.

In the flash of light, Westlake saw not another soul on the water, as if they themselves were the only humans left in the world. He knew that Dickson had gambled with the weather, but now it was too late for blame. Rolling thunder farther away followed more lightning, and a series of booms shook the canoe again and again. At first, the sound and fury was followed by quiet, when the sudden disappearance of the wind made the world feel still, and not a drop of rain fell. The canoe picked up speed, and Westlake nodded to where few random drops hit the water. Then the wind returned in force to snatch at his hair and the spitting drops turned to sheets of what felt like pellets striking his face, sweeping across his sight to fade away in front of the canoe's dash for the shore.

"Stroke. Stroke. Stroke," Dickson hollered out the rhythm.

Westlake paddled for his life, his hands aching from squeezing the paddle. He strained his muscles, watching with each passing minute the waves get larger until they began to wash over the side. Land was within reach, but as they approached, the shore presented a wall of minor cliffs and boulders that the waves smashed against only to explode and come crashing away again. The canoe was taking on too much water to stay afloat.

"There," said Boucher, a Métis seated in the bow, pointing to a small inlet.

"It's too risky between those rocks," Dickson yelled above the rain, his soaking red hair plastered to his face.

"What choice do we have?" Westlake shouted. "Boucher is right, we should make for the crease or we sink regardless." With a shrug, Dickson steered them toward the inlet. Another crack of thunder overhead, and Parrish ducked his head as if it was aimed at him directly. With the canoe taking in water and the waves crashing around them, Dickson now struggled to steer.

Giant boulders, motionless in the water, rushed toward them. Dickson cleared the first rock, and the wind forced them to brush against the second, but there was no damage to the vessel as yet. They were within twenty yards of the shore when a single rolling wave lifted up the canoe so that it had no steerage whatsoever. The wave collapsed beneath them and Westlake jerked as the stern of the canoe hit bottom first, whipping the hull forward across a stationary rock the same width as their boat. A jarring snap and the canoe had split in half, throwing everyone out.

Westlake hit the water face first and he tried to swim, but another wave surged over his head and drove his upper body under. Seconds later, he was astonished to find his hands groping the lake's stony bottom. He struggled to get his feet under him and stand up straight while he wiped his eyes even as the rain and the waves kept coming at him.

"Good God, we're in only five feet of water. Parrish, where are you?" He saw a hand go up and he waded over. In panic, Parrish thrashed with all his might against the water, his feet kicking hard at the surface. Westlake grabbed him by the collar and pulled him upright.

"Stand up, stand up, for goodness' sake." The water streamed off Parrish's face as he took a deep breath and fell sideways, only to bob back on to his feet.

"Where's Dickson?"

Parrish looked around him and pointed, "There, sir." Then he stared down, through the water, at his feet. "I'm standing!" he yelled and held up his arms to the sky to show his thanks for salvation as thunder boomed overhead like so many cannons.

Dickson snatched at floating packages and waded to shore. The Indians did the same, each rescuing a few packages. Some were already returning for their second load.

Westlake smiled. "We need to help them, Walter, now that we know you're not going to drown."

"Nothing funny about it, sir. I was sure we was done for. I never drank so much water in my life."

On shore, Dickson looked downcast and apologetic. He had returned to the water many times, to gather parcels, and now he sank to his knees on the stones. There was nothing remaining in sight to bring in from the waves. Whatever they hadn't found was lost to Georgian Bay.

"Sorry, young Westlake. First thing this morning, I knew that with the wind up, it would be rough going. That damn storm just came up so fast."

"You got us safely through the first few boulders—that's what saved us. I'll bet there's no bottom on the other side of those rocks." Westlake pointed to the row of pink and gray boulders cutting off the tiny inlet where they squeezed through.

"Our half-and-half friend picked the right inlet then," Dickson said. "We were lucky to hit a shallow bottom as we did."

"What do mean, half and half?" Parrish asked.

"Boucher's half French and half Indian," Dickson replied. "Known to you as *Métis*."

"It only got shallow so fast because Parrish tried to drink the lake dry," Westlake joked, wiping away rain from his forehead.

"I'm very happy to amuse you, sir," Walt protested, "but the docks of London aren't the best place for learning how to swim."

"You did fine—and standing up was your key to victory. Let's get off this exposed shoreline and into the trees. We need a fire, food, and then a new canoe." Westlake glanced at the sky. "Although this rain has to stop before we can do much of anything." He turned to question Dickson, who waved him off.

"I'm already way ahead of you, Westlake, my lad. I have the awl here in my belt, and we'll teach Mr. Parrish to sew a canoe together before this trip is out."

14

· · · · · ·

DINNER WAS GOING to be perfect, Elizabeth Westlake thought, feeling proud of herself. The smells of roast duck, rabbit pie, and rising bread combined to spread a heady aroma throughout the house. When she saw him arrive, she'd light the candlesticks on her dining-room table, now covered by her best white linen. She would show what a real home should look and feel like. Maple Hill was ready.

Elizabeth stared through the window and down the hill, knotting her hands anxiously. It had started again: her absent son's return was almost all she could think about. The worry that had left her in February, with his homecoming, had returned to afflict her in March. At first she took walks in the woods, but this only gave her more time to brood. She didn't know where he was or if he was safe; she didn't even know if he was alive. Going for rides on Warman helped, but nothing could postpone the worry for long.

In the early spring, with its cool nights and warm days, the maple trees annually oozed their sap. Elizabeth herself supervised its collection and boiling so that she had more than enough maple syrup for the household, with cases left over to sell to the garrison officers. It was only a diversion, something different to think about, but now with the most important officer in the land coming for dinner, perhaps she could concentrate on other matters tonight.

At the end of a road lined with maple trees on both sides, she saw his horse arrive at the foot of the hill. In full dress uniform, he was approaching at a controlled trot. Elizabeth wondered if he had any more news for her as she patted her neatly curled hair. Surely Brock had not dressed so splendidly just for dinner at Maple Hill? As he came into clearer view, his expression seemed distant, the way it always looked when he was worried. She headed for the door, but the manservant, Joseph, was ahead of her.

Brock brought his horse to a halt and dismounted. Joseph took the reins and Brock gave him a nod.

Elizabeth stood in the open doorway of the great oak door. "Welcome to Maple Hill, Major General. Do I not warrant at least a smile?"

Slowly a smile crossed his face. "Mrs. Westlake, if the day ever dawns when there's nothing left on this earth to make me smile, one look at you will change that in a heartbeat."

She offered her hand and he raised it to his lips, holding on a moment longer, exploring her blue eyes.

"I'm afraid I've not dressed to do justice to your uniform. Could we perhaps be expecting the Prince Regent for dinner?" Elizabeth teased as she proceeded inside.

Brock closed the door behind them, then undid his dress jacket and laid it on a nearby chair.

"Apologies for my overly formal appearance, but I've been trying to impress on our illustrious legislature that we're at war. These lawyers don't seem to give a damn that Hull's army has reached Detroit. Can you believe they're even debating a new school bill?"

"They think the Americans will win, so they're careful not to offend them," Elizabeth replied.

"I've sent Lieutenant Colonel Proctor and two hundred regulars to Fort Amherstburg. Henry's a good man, and he'll stiffen their resolve. Almost half the militia melted away once they heard Hull was in Detroit: four hundred men back to their farms in a flash and there is next to nothing I can do about it."

"Isaac." Elizabeth tried interrupting him, but Brock was lost again in his thoughts.

"In the event Hull invades across the river, I've moved more troops from Niagara to Fort Erie so they can make a dash for Amherstburg." Brock turned to the window, gazing southwest in the direction of his troops.

"But they are not so far away from Niagara that I can't call them back if the Americans attack Fort George. I've also sent men down the Thames River to calm the residents. Half the population are cheering for the Americans, and the other half are indifferent."

"Isaac," Elizabeth tried a second time.

"The Loyalists are almost the only ones I can count on. They are flocking to the York Volunteers. That's the militia Jonathan's in. I'm—"

"Isaac, where *is* Jonathan?" Elizabeth cried.

"Elizabeth, you've never before raised your voice to me." Brock jerked his head away from the window to face her.

"I'm sorry, but you're giving all these details except the one that's vital to me."

"Of course, I should've told about your son first. I apologize. These damn legislators have put me in a foul mood. I should dismiss them all and declare martial law."

"Jonathan?"

"I've no specific news of him, other than what I told you last week. I'm sorry."

"I was hoping for just something," she said. Robert Dickson's courier had reached Fort George and reported the tale of Jonathan meeting the Red-Haired Chief and how they were heading to Fort St. Joseph as planned. The courier described the forest ambush and its consequences. In turn, Brock had assured Elizabeth that Westlake was uninjured but that one of the Parrish brothers had lost his life in the ensuing struggle.

"We'll know more shortly, I suspect," he ended. The smell of hot rabbit pie on the table attracted his attention. Brock lifted its white cloth cover and broke off a piece of crust to taste. Elizabeth, however, wanted to know all he could tell, and at this point she saw no harm in pushing further.

"There must be *some* news," she insisted. She could see the hesitation in Brock's face, deciding what he could say safely.

"After our last dinner I sent a note to Captain Roberts at the fort, ordering him to use his discretion to either attack Michilimackinac or defend his own fort, as the circumstances warranted. If he's the officer I think he is, he would have attacked immediately, assuming the conditions allowed."

"When will we know?"

"Any day now. By God, we could use news of a victory. Defeat would make mobilizing the militia impossible, and the same could be said about the Indians. We need both to have a chance."

"And Jonathan would have gone along to fight with Roberts, if he was needed?"

"Elizabeth, Jonathan was sent up there to give us an early victory in case of war. Yes, he would have gone with Parrish, Dickson, Roberts—and hundreds of others. He'll be safe, I assure you. Parrish will guard him carefully as ordered."

She tried to keep her face relaxed, but her mouth tightened as she looked up at the ceiling, feeling the tears well up in her eyes. Brock stepped around the table, his arms holding her, reaching around to caress her head against his chest.

"Perhaps I've said too much. Jonathan is much stronger you think. He may be a little impulsive, but he's a smart lad. I'm more concerned about you, my dearest."

Elizabeth let Brock hold her. A big man, she needed his embrace, his strength, both comforting and tender. Her husband had been away for more than a year and she really did not miss him; there were times that she could hardly remember his face. Compared to the man who now held her, Richard Westlake was barely a shadow, but he'd come home soon and she knew that Isaac Brock had to be warned. She'd agonized over her decision to reveal the news and worried about the difficult conversation that she knew would follow. Where would it lead? Probably back to loneliness.

"Last week, I received Richard's letter sent from England. Would you like to see it?" She sighed as she turned away from Brock's embrace, wiping a small tear from the corner of her eye, and then straightened her back.

"I do not think it is appropriate that I read another man's letters to his own wife," Brock declared.

"Do other things with his wife but not read his letters?"

"That was unfair, Elizabeth. If you don't love him and he does not love you, then tell him so."

"Read it out loud." She drew out the letter, hiding under a white napkin. "It's important to me that you see for yourself." Elizabeth placed the single folded page in his hand.

Brock unfolded it and began to read:

"Dear E.
Sailing home in the fall. Furs over there taken care of. Company well positioned. It does not matter who wins the war, London and Paris will still need furs.
Making my plans accordingly. Main thing is to stay safe.
Yours, R."

Brock laid the letter on the table in front of her and took his seat opposite her. There was no "How are you, hope you are well" and no "I love you." Her husband did not even use her name, or even sign his own. It was more like a letter to a business acquaintance than to a loving wife not seen for more than a year.

And clearly Richard Westlake could care less who won the war. Elizabeth noticed how Brock clenched one fist, and she knew his thoughts, for her husband's indifference bordered on treason. Men were going to die, but as long as the furs and his own profits were safe, Richard Westlake was ambivalent about the well-being of the Canadas. Brock's thoughts, his actions, and his very life were in direct contrast.

"Do you want me to hate him, Elizabeth? I cannot do that."

"That's not why I showed you the letter."

"There are men like him everywhere. In peacetime, we need them to conduct commerce. They don't understand how dramatically the rules of business would change against them if the Americans are victorious." He shook his head. "When business profits conflict with the interests of the state, then the nation's interests must win out. And they will, if I have anything to say about it."

"But what am *I* supposed to do?" Elizabeth held out her hands on either side of her, an empty feeling in her stomach.

"Let's get Jonathan home first. You'll feel better then. As for Richard, you yourself must decide, and you have time. The fall is a long way off and a great deal can happen between July and October. Perhaps it would be best if I made my departure now, so excuse me." Brock stood and started reaching for his jacket.

Elizabeth jumped up, ran to his side, and grabbed his arm in fear of losing him.

"You'll do no such thing. I need you here with me now." She embraced him tightly but did not begin to cry. "I'm sorry I hurt your pride," she said with her head still pressed against his chest, "but I have a son and you to lose. Sometimes the thought of it is too much to bear alone."

Brock said nothing but merely took her in his arms. "And I feel I have the same to lose—plus this small concern of mine called the war."

They held each other close.

"Please stay, Isaac. I'm asking you." She could feel his chest heave.

"Let's eat that duck, then." His face broke into a grin, and he kissed her on the cheek.

Elizabeth Westlake sighed in relief. She had won a small battle.

The rain's patter on the hull of the canoe was intermittent. The wind gusted and died just as quickly, leaving Mary Collins guessing at the next unfamiliar sound she would experience. She sat upright on a blanket, beneath the overturned canoe, her knees under her chin and her arms wrapped around her shins, thinking of her situation. For the fifth day in a row, it had either drizzled or rained hard. Further travel on the lake was impossible at present not because of the rain but the unending wind that whipped the water into white-capped waves so that any attempt at paddling would result in swamping their craft.

Each morning, Carson Stone entered their tent to play cards or just talk with them, but on this day he was staring at Mary in a different way. More interested in his whiskey, Wagg had not noticed, or at least did not let on he had. Stone's look had made Mary feel frightened and alone, she was not sure why, so she announced that she was going outside for a while and snatched up a blanket as she lifted the tent flap. Stone joined Wagg with a swig from the bottle.

After her own father had run off with another woman, Mary's

mother had taken up with Wagg in the very same week. At night, from her own room, Mary would listen to their sounds of intimacy. Within a year her mother had died of fever, entrusting her daughter to Wagg's care, and the following month Mary was on a ship bound for a different life in the New World.

With the canoe turned over and each end of it resting on a hump of rock, the rain bounced off, preserving the ground dry underneath. Mary had listened for hours to the sound of the rain, thinking back to her trip through the ice and snow, every step north a step farther from Jonathan Westlake. When they passed through Fort St. Joseph's wobbly gates, she had met Captain Roberts and Sergeant Baker. The sergeant had taken a shine to her, but with his purple face, he was clearly too old to begin married life again. As for Roberts, he had been ill from the time they arrived until the day they waved goodbye to him from their canoe.

Wagg was inexperienced in canoe travel, and even on calm water, every shift in his weight and the whole craft would tip immediately. After five days to travel less than a hundred miles, under sunny skies, Mary's palms blistered and her shoulders ached. She had never cried or asked for pause, but now shook her head in wonder, just happy to be sitting here immobile on a rock.

Inside Fort Mackinac, Lieutenant Porter Hanks had gone out of his way to make her feel at home. The temperature had dropped, and with the rain falling, he would not allow Wagg to make her wait outside while they talked. Hanks led her into his private kitchen while the men conversed in his office so she listened quietly, straining her ears at the door. Wagg could be heard laughing when, twice during their meeting, Hanks ran to relieve himself from some strange stomach ailment.

During these conversations between Wagg and Hanks, Mary learned that her stepfather worked for Richard Westlake. The entire trip from England to Fort Mackinac had all been about furs, Westlake Trading furs. Wagg informed Hanks that the company was based out of New York City, and he needed a favor—a favor that would be paid for with information. It cost Hanks nothing, so he agreed to store the furs for a short time under the protection of the U.S. Army. Wagg's information was that the British were making plans to seize Fort Mackinac the moment war was declared. Hanks laughed and said that he had guessed as much, but the British had less than sixty drunken old men for their "invasion." He appreciated Wagg's gesture, and the furs were safe, but for the present there was no war so there was nothing to worry about.

At first, Mary did not understand what she was hearing. They were friends with Captain Roberts, or so she thought. She had no idea that Wagg would betray Hanks also, when it became convenient. At that moment the furs were safe, and that was all that mattered to her stepfather.

At Fort Mackinac, Stone had appeared out of the darkness. She wondered how he had found them amid such wilderness, until she learned it had all been prearranged. Around the campfire, his story about coming upon Westlake and his companions seemed too contrived. The Jonathan Westlake she knew would not kill all those men for no reason, but, for sure, the incident had left Stone terrified of him.

Overhead, the dying wind gave a last gust that rocked her canoe. She never even heard Stone come up beside her, so when he began to speak she gave a little jump.

"You know, I'm not an entirely bad fellow. Your father thinks I'm worthy of employ so that must tell you something." He paused.

Mary heard the wind go quiet and the waves subside.

"You've traveled an enormous distance with Bill and should be proud of yourself. Any lesser woman would've collapsed long ago. I too have a great deal of experience and know the ways of the world. I'm not that much older than you, and men my age have taken younger brides." He waited, expecting a reply. When none came he tried again. "Mary, give me a chance," he pleaded.

A pair of scuffed black boots, the toes pointing toward the lake, revealed that Stone was standing directly beside her. "What are you doing here, Mister Stone? What are you searching for?" The rain had now finally stopped.

"You know what I'm looking for. When we get our hands on that last cache of furs, I'll be wealthy enough to start over, so nothing will come between those furs and me. Then I'll have enough money to buy land."

"I thought you might be searching for love, and that's why you're talking to me."

"Don't be naive, girl. We could maybe learn to love each other, but you can't have love on an empty stomach." His words were somewhat slurred.

She heard the effects of cheap whiskey consumed during hours of playing cards.

"I think you need some idea of what love means before you can find it. Otherwise, how will you know what to look for?"

"All this talk about love … Mary, I can protect you." Stone walked slowly around to the other side of the canoe.

"From men like yourself?"

"Why must you be so cruel? I see the way you look at me—the disgust."

"You almost strangled me once and threatened to kill me, so how else should I see you? I'm not a fool."

"I'm sorry, I'd been drinking then, but that's all in the past," Stone bellowed, his agitation rising.

"So I'm to live in fear of you each time you drink—like today, like now."

"I could just take you, if I so chose." His voice hardened. He kicked the canoe and it rolled over to one side.

Mary crouched lower, staring straight out over the vastness of Lake Huron, careful not to make eye contact with him. "My stepfather would never let you." She shifted on the rock. "You would have to fight the both of us." Mary hugged her knees tighter, her heart beating faster.

"Don't be so sure of that. Old Bill may not want to risk everything on your behalf, and, besides, he's passed out after all that cheap whiskey." Any shred of gentleness was gone from the man's voice, and he spit the words out angrily. His hooded eyes blinked, glaring down while his fist opened to reveal long dirty fingers. Mary suspected those owl-like facial features had left Stone spurned and humiliated by women too often in his life.

"If you even touch me, you'll never be able to sleep securely again. I'd kill you the moment I got the chance," Mary said, putting up a brave front even though she felt stricken with panic.

Stone flew on top of her before she could move, his body pressing heavily upon hers. She felt the same terrifying grip tightening around her neck, until she could hardly breathe. He stank of stale whiskey and sweat.

"Have it your way then, I gave you your opportunity. Now I know where I stand. Make a sound and I will kill you and your stepfather too." His knees forced her legs apart while his free hand fumbled and tugged at her clothing. "You're going to do me a little favor."

Mary tried to call out but could make no sound with his hand grasping her throat. Besides, what if Wagg heard her and Stone did kill him? From the corners of her eyes, tears trickled across the side of her face. The hump of rock that had been her seat now jabbed into her back in rhythm to Stone's movements, the pain inside her increasing with each thrust. Across the water, the storm and the winds rolled farther away and Mary desperately held on to the boom of distant thunder.

In Georgian Bay, on the eastern side of Lake Huron, the front of the storm blew with all its might. Westlake stared out across the inlet where their canoe had broken its back on the rocks, realizing it a miracle that no one had drowned or been dashed to pieces. There was nothing to stop the wind sweeping across the lake and into the bay until it collided with the shoreline. Trees bent to its will and the waves soaked the huge rocks outlining shores composed of pink granite and green forest. The race to recover their belongings from the water and then build shelter from the elements had drained his remaining strength.

Day after day, the storm raged, the waves lashing the shores unceasingly. Westlake knew they would have to build another canoe, and to this end the Indians worked through the thunder and rain without stopping. Four stout posts, cut and pounded into place, would hold the frame of cedar strips. They collected bark from the birch trees and then cut long fibrous cedar roots to sew it to the canoe's framework.

In their tents, meanwhile, pine gum was boiled to form the pitch that sealed the seams. Thwarts or crossbars were cut in preparation for the first letup in the driving rain.

The worst of the weather diminished on the western shore of Lake Huron in the morning, and the eastern shore felt the same relief in the late afternoon. Immediately, Dickson had every man working on his assigned task for the canoe's final construction, and with everything prepared, the construction of a sleek new vessel came together like magic.

The following afternoon, Dickson gave Parrish the job of applying pitch to the seams of the bow, but every few minutes a different Indian would come to inspect his work. Their stern faces would nod and go back to their own work, only to be followed by another inspection by a different Indian. Parrish applied the pitch carefully with his swab, knowing that he was under close eye. He had followed Westlake's advice and added strips of birchbark over the seams and resealed them for safe measure.

At the end of one such inspection, he hollered, "What's with all the curiosity in my work?"

"They've never seen a British soldier make a canoe before, and naturally they don't want to drown," Westlake explained as he checked the strength of the crossbars beginning from the stern.

"Blimey, they don't trust me, then?"

"Aye," Dickson said. "I have a rule that I live by. So remember this and apply it throughout the course of your life. Are you listening, then?"

Parrish nodded.

"It's not what you *expect* that happens," Dickson continued, "it's what you *inspect* that happens. Do you understand that?"

"We make things happen by inspecting—to make sure instead of just expecting things to work out, right?"

"Now you know why the Indians keep inspecting your work," Dickson replied.

"Why don't you give them something else to do? I've had enough inspections."

"Parrish reckons we have too many chiefs and not enough Indians." Westlake laughed.

"No, we just have too many Indians inspecting my work." Parrish didn't laugh and Dickson was no longer paying attention.

"It was a joke, Walter. In this case, you are the Indian and they … just forget it. If Lapointe were here, he'd understand it, but you guys have no sense of humor." Westlake stepped back and admired what they had constructed. This canoe was sleek and built for speed, all twenty-four feet of her. He knew Dickson would have them paddling it early the next day.

Since the wind had disappeared during the night, they paddled out of the inlet just as the dawn's sun touched the water. Mist still hung thick over the surface and Westlake stretched out his arm to feel the side of a boulder covered in dried moss while the canoe slid past the pink rocks.

Dickson had them flying through the mist within a couple minutes, the canoe lifting out of the water and making its own waves. Westlake felt a fresh breeze, and the speed of the canoe and the wind lifted his blond hair as they shot along the eastern shore. Every stroke of the paddle broke the glasslike surface of the lake. As the sun struck the water harder, the mist ascended and then vanished before them. To his left he saw the trees and rocky shoreline flitting past, but one look at the sky told him their luck would not last. The sun was barely above the treetops before a heavy bank of black clouds began packing the western heavens. He pulled until his muscles burned.

"How much would I pay to buy a canoe like this one, sir?" Parrish asked.

Before Westlake himself could reply, Dickson said, "I thought you didn't care for the water. Last year, I sold a big one like this to an American for fifty dollars."

"Whew! Flying along this way makes me feel free, like I've never felt before." Parrish smiled with his eyes. "But where would I find a big enough crew to paddle it? Maybe I need to become a voyageur. Would you happen to have a place for me in Westlake Trading, sir?"

"Up there is the mouth of the French River," Dickson pointed. "If you want to join the fur trade, you take the French to Lake Nipissing, catch the Ottawa River on the other side—and it will take you all the way to Montreal. That's the main fur-trade route, Parrish, and I didn't want you to miss it."

"I can just see myself in a canoe, with fifteen others, paddling for freedom. No more parade-ground drills in the bloody sun for Walt Parrish." He stared out at the river.

"There's always a place for paddlers—*comers and goers*, Parrish. During this war it's going to get a little crazy, but my father normally pays eighteen pounds sterling a year for paddlers. And if you can do Mr. Dickson's job, I mean, steer the canoe, and hopefully not on to the rocks, the pay is fifty pounds." Westlake grinned at Dickson. "That's at least three times or even more than a good farmhand would make in any year."

"If it were me, I'd also aim to be a guide, so the pay is then eighty-five pounds a year," Dickson continued. "That's for the run from Montreal to Lake Superior. Starting in the wee hours of the morning, eighteen-hour days, and covering maybe a hundred miles a day if the weather holds. I'll tell ye it's a tough go, so it is, and not every man has the fortitude for it. You'll lose weight, and that's a promise, seeing they all do."

At the mention of weather, Westlake glanced skyward again. The sun had disappeared behind black clouds, the wind increased, and the waves sprouted into whitecaps. Dickson did not want a repeat of their last adventure and so steered for shore. They managed to find shelter behind an island, where the waves were half as high as they were on open water, then the canoe slid on to a sandy shore for the midday meal.

Not for the first time, the natives caught and cleaned some fresh-water bass. Cooked over the open flames, the bass made a tasty dish. They waited several hours, sipping on their hot tea, but the rain never came and the black clouds slowly turned to gray. Then the wind started to quiet and Dickson had them back in the canoe, paddling at a fever-ish pitch. They had a good two hours on the water before the sun went down, and Dickson had no choice but to steer again for shore.

"We probably got in sixty to seventy miles today. I'd like to do at least that tomorrow, if you soldiers can handle the pace," Dickson announced.

"The sooner General Brock knows about Michilimackinac, the better, and we can handle any pace you can move at." Westlake wouldn't be outdone by Dickson, and he had started thinking about a trip to Detroit. "Let's leave before first light."

Day after day, they labored down the eastern shores of Georgian Bay, getting ever closer to Fort York. In the wide spaces under a canopy of blue sky, Westlake had time to contemplate home. No longer a possible murderer, he wondered how Brock would greet him after these many months. At least he was bringing him news of victory.

His thoughts were interrupted when Parrish inquired if the voyageurs brought their own food. Parrish was now dreaming of freedom, and a life of canoes across open water; forget farming, he wanted speed and adventure. He'd never been to the rivers Dickson had named, but he maintained that if other men could do it, so could he. Westlake explained that all food for voyageurs was packed and provided by the company. The comers and goers were given everything for their journey except their own paddle, an item that was considered as personal as man's shirt.

"If I only have to bring my own paddle, then I'm in," Parrish declared. He gave a pull so hard that it lifted water and splashed his friend directly behind him. Westlake laughed and, with his own paddle, poked Parrish in the ribs.

Westlake reminded himself that he was in a familiar situation. Only five months earlier, he was fighting the winter weather and yearning for home. Now here he was again exerting all his efforts to accomplish the same goal: to get home. This time he was determined not to stay long for he needed a favor from Brock—one that would help him see to some unfinished business in Detroit.

15

· · · · · ·

ON THE WEST SIDE of Fort Detroit, Captain Daniel Jackson contented himself with the knowledge that the guides sent to find the supply train were the best that could be found. The river shoreline, the route they would normally ride, strayed directly under the guns of Fort Amherstburg. Travel by water was out because the British controlled the lakes so the only safe route was farther inland, the same route watched over by the Indians. Although the Wyandot were still friendly, no one wanted to bet his life that they would stay that way.

No, as Jackson therefore ordered his guides, the safest way to journey south was to sneak past the Indians and stay concealed for the entire trip. He didn't tell them that the 4th Infantry had rations for only thirty days; instead he demanded they did not return without acquiring those supplies. In the morning light, Jackson watched the backs of his men disappear beyond the forest edge before he turned his horse back toward Fort Detroit. Hungry, he decided to breakfast first and then cross the river to learn more of Hull's progress.

On the Canadian side of the river, Colonel McArthur had been away for five days and was now back preparing for another foraging excursion. Tales already spread of his plundering and devastation along the Thames River. He was hot, sweating, and wanted to be again free of General Hull's authority, so he kept his report to a minimum.

"Wagonloads of flour, vegetable sacks, herds of cattle, and a flock of Merino sheep, sir. The details are in the lists." He placed the papers in front of Hull and took a step back. "My men carried off farming implements and building tools. Any settlers showing resistance had their farms put to the torch, sir."

"What about new settlers from the United States?" Hull asked.

"They're either with us or against us, sir."

"Even if they're with us, you're too damned harsh. You've got the whole Thames Valley against us, as if we're an occupying army of oppressors."

"I thought we were, sir."

"Just take it easy, and that's an order. Dismissed."

"Sir." McArthur saluted, gritting his teeth.

His meeting with General Hull over, he rode around behind the brick house that served as Hull's headquarters. Some thirty yards to his right, he spotted a small wooden barn, a horse and wagon outside, and a group of blue-coated soldiers lounging in the morning sun. He spurred his horse in their direction, his foul mood evident even as he spoke.

"Who is in charge here?"

Every soldier snapped to attention except Sergeant Harris, who had been lying flat in the wagon and now jerked himself upright. "Sergeant Harris at your service, sir." He slid off the back of the wagon, came to attention, and squinted in the sunlight. McArthur suspected that Harris had been dozing.

"What do you think you're doing, lying about like this? We're at war, for Christ's sake." McArthur reined in his horse, as it twisted its head in defiance and rose up on its back legs. His hat, with a long white feather, shifted to an odd angle, and he adjusted it to sit better on his head.

"Just like ordered, sir, we's guarding a murdering prisoner what killed one of my men while resisting our foraging." The other Bluecoats relaxed from their formal attention, inching closer to hear the conversation.

"If he resisted by killing an American soldier, he should be dead himself. Did you burn his place to the ground?" McArthur scanned Harris up and down and noticed his suspenders were undone. The only thing holding up his pants were his two arms tight to his side.

"We did nothing but took the prisoner to this barn and tied him up, sir." Harris pointed. "Maybe he got roughed up a bit, though."

"How far is the man's house? Did you leave anything worthwhile behind?"

Harris's face brightened, his tone becoming more confident.

"About three miles south along the shore. Everyone in between here and there had already cleared out, sir. There's a good wagonload of supplies there—all kinds of stuff we left behind on orders from Captain Jackson."

McArthur knew this man was covering himself. If there was to be any trouble for leaving behind supplies, then Harris was taking no part of the blame. "Do you know who I am, Sergeant? I'm ordering you now to return to that farm, take what's left of value, and then burn everything else to the ground."

"There's an old lady inside the house, sir, what started all the trouble; name's Iris." Harris was going to suggest that they burn the house with her in it, but McArthur interrupted.

"An example has to be made, Sergeant, are we clear? Tell her to get out, though I appreciate your concern for her well-being."

"That's the kind of fellows we are, sir." Harris grinned, showing his remaining two front teeth, then he lowered his gaze.

"About this prisoner—is it certain he killed one of your men?"

"Seen it with my own eyes, sir. They was standing not five feet away when he stabbed our man Rufus Boggs. And Rufus was a good man, sir. This news'll probably kill his poor mother."

"Ya, Rufus was a good lad," the men around Harris joined in.

McArthur clenched his fists as his horse twisted round again in frustration. Within seconds, McArthur's entire face had turned red. "You cannot just shoot this prisoner, see," he continued in a whisper as he leaned from the saddle toward Harris's ear. "However, when you come back from his farm, if you untie his hands and feet, and leave the barn door open, he may even try to escape." McArthur reached up and grabbed his hat before it fell off completely. "You'd be obliged to stop him then."

"Yes, sir. My pleasure to be of service, sir." Sergeant Harris gave McArthur a salute as the latter spurred his horse away and into a gallop.

Iris Moore was a tough woman. In her teens, she had followed her young husband's regiment from England to Boston and then to New

York. After the Revolution, Captain George Moore decided that America had no place for him, and so Iris had followed her man to Upper Canada, to establish a farm on the banks of the Detroit River.

Iris had never spent a day sick in her life, but this last winter had struck her down with the ague while caring for the Baby family. She had gone to bed with a blistering fever, and there she had suffered through the spring and into the summer. She still needed an afternoon nap to make it through the rest of the day.

Iris guessed the Americans would cause trouble, but Captain Jackson had assured her that she would be left alone. When that soldier had come charging into her room, she uncovered her musket and shot him. The action seemed reasonable enough to her.

After they had taken away her Captain, staying by herself in the farmhouse seemed impossible. She figured that if Harris backtracked, she'd be finished, so the next morning, after a full breakfast of cheese on toast and steaming tea, she bundled the rest of the cheese into a cotton bag, collected her brooches and necklace, and set out on their one remaining horse to Fort Amherstburg. When the Captain returned, she'd be gone, but he'd soon guess her whereabouts. The Moores had several friends in and around the fort, but she would go looking for the Captain's special friend, Lieutenant Rolette. He would know what to do.

"Lads, you all heard the colonel: direct orders right from on high to a lowly sergeant like meself. We're back in business, and we have some pleasant work to do." Harris dropped his musket to the ground and began reattaching his suspenders so there was no chance his pants would fall down. "Porter and Morrison, stay here and guard the prisoner. The rest of you fine fellows into the wagon and back with me to that farm. We've a score to settle with that old bitch what shot our young lad."

Anxious to get started, Harris jumped into the wagon taken from Moore's farm and snapped the reins. The horse jerked the wagon around to face the road leading south along the river. Several soldiers piled into the back as the wagon clattered down the stone road with a couple of men following on foot.

Between Moore's house and the barn, Sergeant Harris brought the wagon to a halt. Not used to such pace, the old horse heaved and frothed at the mouth. The soldiers clambered out of the wagon and a few of them followed Harris into the house. He came out first, moments later, shaking his head. "Trimble, go check inside the barn."

Trimble ran over, stuck his head inside, and yelled back to Harris, "Nothing here, Sergeant."

Harris gestured to the barn again. "You two, remove any tools and stow them in the wagon. Then, Trimble, fire that barn." He strolled back to the house. "Let's see what old Iris has left us to eat and drink, Haggard. Looks like the witch has fled."

"At least I won't get shot," Haggard chimed in.

"Shut up, you coward, or I'll shoot you myself."

Fifty yards away, Iris Moore herself and Lieutenant Frederic Rolette of the Royal Provincial Marine were peering through the cedars. Try as he might, Rolette had not been able to dissuade her from returning to her home. His warnings on the dangers of American patrols having no effect, he decided he could not let her go alone.

"We're too late," Iris whispered.

"No, we're right on time," Rolette replied. "Any earlier and we'd be inside the house, either captured or dead. We should be going now, Iris—we're of no use here."

"But I just wanted my clothes and our family Bible ... my best dress from England. There must be something we can do. I could shoot one of them from here."

"There are almost a dozen of them, Iris. They'd be on us in no time, and we'd both get killed. Unless you want to watch your house burn, we should push off while we can. Perhaps I'll journey upriver later and take a look."

Sergeant Harris tore open a cupboard door. He knew Moore must have wine somewhere, but all he found was some leftover bread and cheese. He filled his pockets and then thought of the cellar, realizing the wine would be cooler if kept there. He searched for a door in the floor near the back of the house but found nothing.

There surely must be an entrance to the cellar from the outside. He kicked open the back door of the house and picked up an axe leaning against the woodpile. Built completely of stone, the cellar was not directly connected to the house but had been dug into the ground only a few yards away. The door slanted at a forty-five-degree angle to the ground itself, and with just one blow its lock shattered. Harris yanked the door skyward and flung it to the side before he descended some steps and with a second swing of the axe tore off the lock on another door. A musty humid smell wrinkled his nostrils, and he stepped backward from the cellar's damp. Then Harris thought again about the wine, took a deep breath, and stepped forward, reaching out to touch a slimy stone wall.

His eyes slowly adjusted to the dark, and he could see even better by jamming the door open with the axe. The cellar was about seven feet high, three paces long and two paces wide. Along the wet walls were rows of wooden shelves containing apples layered with straw to keep them fresh. In the center of the cellar, at the very back, was a small table on which stood nine bottles of claret. He grabbed one bottle, chiseled out the cork with his knife, and guzzled some of the contents.

"Oh, that's what I needed." Harris sighed out loud to no one. He then snatched a second bottle and climbed up into the sunlight. The smell of smoke from the burning barn made him smile.

Harris re-entered the house through the back door and announced, "My lads, the claret is in the cellar. I've already got mine. Never say that Sergeant Frank Harris doesn't share his good fortune with his men, so help yourself." To show off his loot, Harris raised his arms above his head, holding a bottle in each hand.

Trimble was first out through the back door, breaking the hinges as he pounded it open. The other's crashed through in pursuit, eager to get at the wine. Harris meanwhile climbed into Moore's soft bed, where he swallowed cheese and guzzled wine until he fell asleep.

A short time later, he felt a hand nudging his shoulder.

"Sergeant Harris, wake up," Haggard urged. "It's time to fire the house."

"I'm not asleep, lad, just resting a wee bit."

"Let's fire this house and then go kill old man Moore."

Harris perked up at the idea of killing. "Set the curtains and this bed alight first, that'll get things flaming just fine." Harris yawned. "Seems a shame in a way. I'm kind of partial to this room. You know this is the first real bed I've slept in since I can't remember."

Harris staggered out the front door and eyed the smoldering barn, then he hollered to his men to get aboard the wagon just as the farmhouse started to fill with smoke. He took a last swig of the claret and threw the empty bottle to smash against the front door of the burning house. The other bottle he concealed inside his jacket, and at a snap of the reins the old horse jerked the wagon forward. A little ways down the road, he turned back with a grin from the wagon seat to see flames burst through the bedroom ceiling and a great plume of black smoke escaped skyward.

Inside the cavernous barn, Captain George Moore had slept on the straw-covered floor. His head had ached so bad from the blow delivered with a musket butt that he had been sick to his stomach for the first two days. Since Harris had tied his hands and feet together, there was no chance of him escaping and, thus secured, he had taken considerably more punches to the ribs from Harris so that now he was content to have some time to himself. He worried about Iris, how she was coping without him, and who might help her during his absence.

One evening, well after sunset, four officers had begun arguing at the back of the barn, where Moore could see and hear them through the cracks in the wall. Three militia colonels wanted to attack Fort Amherstburg immediately and were threatening to leave with all their men, or even arrest General Hull, if they didn't get their way. Another officer, a Lieutenant Colonel Miller, reminded them that he was a proper soldier who followed orders. And, besides, Miller agreed with Hull that they needed artillery to smash down the fort's walls if they were to succeed. It might take two weeks to build their carriages, but they wouldn't win that battle without artillery. Miller was convinced that, angry or not, they had to wait.

The next morning, Moore sat up, his back resting against an upright beam, and glanced again at the same wall: a possible mutiny? A split in the upper command, two weeks to build the gun carriages— he had vital intelligence for the commander of Fort Amherstburg. Porter and Morrison came and untied his hands and feet so he could eat and relieve himself but just as quickly bound them again. To get this information out, he had to escape somehow.

Now, for the first day in some time, his head didn't ache. From the brightness of the sunlight seeping through the rear of the barn, Moore guessed it was midday when Porter and Morrison returned to slice away the ropes that bound him; and he couldn't believe his good fortune. Porter explained he was still a prisoner, but he no longer needed to be tied, and they'd bring him some food in an hour. Something was strange, though, because the two soldiers left the barn door unfastened. Moore stood up slowly and stretched his legs, clutching the square beam beside him for support. The barn walls were full of cracks and as Moore peeked through at the front, he reckoned there must be a dozen soldiers hiding behind his wagon with their muskets at the ready. His old horse was heaving anxiously, like it was going to collapse any minute.

Moore limped quickly to the back, where he had noticed the brightest sunlight. Barn repairs were only partially finished here, and he soon found a small gap between a couple of boards possible to squeeze through. He poked his head out, looking both ways, and saw no one. The enemy was so sure he would go out through the front door they had left open that they had posted no guards to the rear. In just a few seconds, his heart thumping, he edged through the boards and set off into the wooded area directly behind the barn. He was going home.

Sergeant Harris enjoyed the agreeable haziness brought on by Captain Moore's wine, and so didn't mind basking there in the sun, waiting for his prey to fall into the trap. He was in no hurry therefore, but after half an hour, when there was still no sign of Moore coming through the barn door, he suggested that Porter and Morrison take a look inside. After Porter peered in and shouted the alarm that Moore was gone, Harris jumped down from the wagon and ran for the barn, drawing his sword. He began stabbing at the straw bales like a madman, furious that Moore was cheating him.

"Here's how he got out," Morrison yelled from the far end of the barn.

Harris saw the hole with dismay. "Get out and around to the other side." He pushed Morrison in front of him as they both raced out of the front door.

"Haggard, take this lot and follow his trail. He must have gone in there." Harris pointed to the forest ten yards away. "My guess is he'll head straight back to his farmhouse. If you can catch up with him, just shoot him. You don't have to wait for me. Morrison and Porter, you're with me in the wagon, and we'll try to cut him off on the road. He has to cross it at some point."

Harris ran back around the barn and leapt in to the wagon, taking up the reins. Morrison and Porter jumped in behind the driver's bench, but when Harris snapped the reins the wagon didn't move. The old horse had finished its work for the day and had no energy left. Harris drew the whip and laced the animal's back three times, but it didn't move an inch.

"Let's go, lads, at the double. I'll kill this brute later. Christ, I wish I hadn't drunk all that damn wine." Harris belched and spit. "But if I can run after drinking, you lot can keep up with me. Fall behind and you'll see the same fate as that stupid horse." Harris cursed and jogged off down the lane, with Morrison and Porter running behind him.

George Moore was frantic; the forest was dense, but he could not take the chance of being seen on the road. If he were caught now they'd shoot him for sure, so he was running for his life. He kept his hands and arms high in front of his face, to block the branches that constantly slashed at him as he plunged deeper into the undergrowth. His left thigh started to burn where his old battle scar glowed red. It wouldn't be long before they discovered his escape, he imagined. Out of breath, he came to a small stream and flopped down beside it, putting his entire head underwater. He swallowed three or four great gulps and rolled over, gasping for air, while he counted off another thirty seconds. With a last small sip of cooling water, he raised himself to go.

For another half-hour, with his remaining strength, Moore limped directly south. When he figured he'd covered the three miles needed, he slanted his path off to the right, to meet the main coast road. His face and hands lacerated with minor cuts, he was happy at last to find a narrow trail that led out of the forest and up a hill. He struggled to the top and couldn't believe his eyes: his farmhouse and barn were both smoldering in the midday sun. The barn had burnt to the ground except for the eastern wall, which stood alone among the whiffs of smoke drifting upward from the charred ruins. The odd orange flame flared in what used to be his house, but he knew on first glance that there was no hope to save anything. At the top of the hill he collapsed to the ground and put his face into his hands. A life's work gone, and then he realized there was no sign of Iris.

As Moore stumbled down the hill toward the house, he fell, rolled over, and got up again. His safety was no longer a concern, for now he thought only of Iris. He crossed the road and hobbled down the lane toward the smoking ruins. A few room partitions remained half standing and the stone fireplace, although perfectly upright, was blackened on every stone. For some reason the front door and its frame remained untouched, ready to welcome visitors even now. He limped to the back of the house, to their bedroom, surveying the smoking floor inch by inch, but there was no sign of any human remains. Relieved, he took a deep breath and then began to sob. It was too much to bear.

A musket shot banged from somewhere, and Moore heard the ball thud into the ground beside him. A second musket fired, and the ball plucked at his left shirtsleeve: another few inches and it would have penetrated his heart. He threw himself flat to the ground and crawled toward the stone cellar where he saw the door lay open. Moore stared back along the lane for sign of his attackers but could see nothing. Only the river might offer him a chance of escape.

The Americans had taken everything, but being army and not navy, he hoped they hadn't thought to look for his little canoe. On sunny days, it had been a great joy to take Iris for a leisurely paddle on the river. Now this canoe would have to save his life.

Such thoughts of better days ended as a group of his pursuers crested the hill. He didn't stop to count them but crawled another few yards on past the cellar, then rose to his feet to run for the shore. Again, two muskets shots echoed, only this time they were closer, and a ball creased the outside of his left thigh. Moore fell to the ground, his leg searing in pain. But he was determined to reach his canoe, and he stood up to limp on again, his heart pounding in his ears.

"Got him," he heard Morrison crow. "Old bastard."

"That was my ball, reload. We have to close in. He's wounded, but I can see him moving. And here come the rest of our lads. Porter, move your arse forward." Harris began waving his arm for his men to spread out, then ran toward his victim, chuckling.

Moore reached the shoreline, churned his way down the embankment, and there was his canoe, waiting. "Thank God." He rolled it over and snatched up one of the paddles he'd concealed underneath. Three muskets shots exploded over his shoulder, two balls zipping the water and one whistling overhead. His left leg felt like fire, but his fierce effort of will powered the canoe into the water even as his feet slid, giving way in the sand.

Someone fired just as Moore fell into the floating canoe. They would be on him in seconds. Out of breath, he sat up and took two strokes with the paddle and heard shouting behind him.

"I've got him now." Morrison raised his musket to fire at the canoe only fifteen paces away.

Moore looked back, his paddle raised for another stroke, understanding that the soldier about to kill him was the same man that brought him food while he was captive. Moore gazed at the muzzle end of the musket, waiting to die. The bang, when it came, was much louder than it should have been and seemed to echo all the way up the river. He squinted back toward the shore and then stared in astonishment. Where Morrison stood a split second before, there was now only half a man—then the hips and legs toppled over.

"Captain, keep your head down," came a new voice. Moore glanced out at the river and there, only forty yards away, was Lieutenant Rolette in a gunboat alongside a smoking cannon. Eighteen men were pulling the craft toward him. Rolette had aimed the gun himself and was frantically reloading.

Moore paddled with the last of his strength.

"My God, would you look at that," Porter gasped. "Morrison was there only a second ago." Harris grabbed him by the shoulder and tugged him to the ground.

"And you're going to end up just like him if you don't stay down. That was chainshot," Harris barked. "Lay flat and aim low. Try to get off a shot without getting yourself killed."

Porter fired and watched as his ball struck the canoe. Harris fired too, his bullet also striking the canoe, and he heard Moore yell in pain.

"My ball must have gone clean through the side and got him again. This bastard won't die. Christ, get down, Porter," Harris ordered.

Nine of the twelve seamen on the gunboat downed their oars at once and wrenched up their muskets to fire.

The volley sailed passed Harris and thudded into the tree trunks beside him. One of his soldiers behind screamed as a ball tore through his shoulder.

The canoe and the gunboat had gently bumped together and some of the crew were pulling Moore up and over the side. The boat had steered between the canoe and the shore, so Moore was now protected from further fire. The empty canoe drifted downstream, and the gunboat circled round to reach the center of the river as the seamen pulled hard on their oars until the current was pushing them out of range.

"Keep firing," Harris ordered. "Aim low, and we may get lucky."

This time, nine seamen on the gunboat's starboard side suddenly raised their muskets to fire.

Harris yelled again, "Everybody down." The volley crashed out, and the balls flew overhead.

"That was close enough, thank you, Sergeant," Porter said.

"We're up against professionals, lads. Let's get off a volley of our ... stay down!" Harris yelled. The cannon that had been used only the once, to cut Morrison in half, swiveled back to face the shore. Reloaded, Harris knew that, with his men bunched around him, it could kill all of them in one blast. But the cannon had swung round only to make a show, and thus force Harris to pause long enough to give the gunboat more time to pull away with the current, heading farther downstream.

Harris and his men fired from their prone positions, but it was of no use. The seamen merely cheered and held up their middle fingers as the balls hurtled past harmlessly. The gunboat was out of effective musket range, and Harris cursed, "Shit!"

Moore lay in the bottom of the boat and reached up to shake Rolette's hand.

"Welcome aboard, Captain Moore. Think you're going to make to it?" Rolette smiled.

"That was some piece of work, sir, and I thank you for saving my life. Have you seen my wife?"

"Just like the Nile, did I tell you I fought with Nelson? We crushed the buggers ,you know. Iris is fine—angry but fine. She forced me to come back here this afternoon to salvage your belongings from the house. If she hadn't, you'd be dead."

"That's my girl, tough as nails. She'll argue you to death, but I wouldn't have any other. My leg's burning like hell." Moore gently rubbed on his leg where the bullet had pierced his pants. "And I've some news for the fort's commander. God, that was a close one."

"Lucky you kept your head down." Rolette laughed as the tension of the battle gave way to relief.

"Good advice at any time," Moore replied.

A large canoe approached the shore at Sandwich, and Captain Jackson watched with suppressed laughter as it struck the dock bows on. Paddles thrashed as the man in the bow used his own paddle to push off from the dock, attempting to lay the boat in parallel. The vessel swung with a breeze so that on its next attempt the canoe again struck the dock bows on. Since the second effort had been for nothing,

Jackson reached out a hand and took hold of the man in the bow, dragging the canoe in alongside the dock.

"Christ, Stone, I hope you're better on a horse than you are in a canoe. Why didn't you just beach her?"

"Thanks for the hand or we might never have got in. We've important news for you, so we steered for the dock—though not too successfully." Stone turned to stare at Wagg and then back to Jackson. "So, you conquered Canada with little resistance, I suppose."

"Just enough to cause some difficulty."

"This is Bill Wagg and his daughter, Mary Collins. Any news yet of our furs at Fort Detroit?"

"Pleased to meet you." Jackson headed along the dock to where Wagg was still sitting in the canoe and shook his hand. He then extended a hand to Mary.

"Captain Daniel Jackson at your service, Miss Collins. May I help you out of the canoe?"

Mary reached up as Jackson gave her his right hand and guided her ashore with his left. She was much lighter than he guessed so that when he pulled, she almost flew out of the canoe and into his arms. For a brief second it looked as if they were embracing. Stone scowled when Mary laughed in Jackson's arms and said, "Thank you."

"I thank you too, ma'am." Jackson looked just as surprised. "I haven't enjoyed a hug in long time."

"And I haven't really hugged you yet, Captain Jackson," Mary nudged him away and stepped farther on to the dock.

"Then I can't wait." He grinned. He studied her plain round face and yet noticed there was something striking about her.

Stone coughed. "The furs, Captain Jackson. The fort is sealed and when we asked after you, they said you were here. Any news of our furs?"

Jackson glanced away from Mary toward Stone, who had remained in the canoe.

"In case you haven't heard, war has been declared and I've not had the time or inclination to look for your damn furs ... excuse my language, Miss Collins. They're just not on my list of priorities. Now I have to report in to Lieutenant Colonel Miller, and you said you had important news."

Wagg had climbed out of the canoe and approached Jackson, holding a document in his fist. "This gives me authority to move those furs on behalf of Westlake Trading. It's signed by Richard Westlake himself."

Jackson paid him little attention, choosing instead to focus on Mary. Her eyes had caught his attention—dark, with just a hint of something concealed within.

Wagg continued, "We're hoping to be shown some consideration for our efforts. We've come a long ways to inform you that Fort Mackinac has fallen to the British."

"My God, when did this happen?" Jackson's expression turned grave.

"We've been up against the elements ever since," Wagg added. "Bloody near died, we did. The fort fell on July 17, so that would make it ten days ago. Although it seems like we've been traveling on Lake Huron for a lifetime."

Jackson asked about the number of British soldiers involved in the attack and the number of casualties. He asked how the fort was taken, if Indians had assisted, and if fur traders joined in the assault. He asked every question he could think of and after he assured himself that Wagg was telling the truth, he said, "Would you mind coming with me to my commanding officer." It was not a request.

At the headquarters building, Jackson asked for Lieutenant Colonel Miller. "This better be important," Miller said.

"Fort Mackinac has fallen. These three have a story to tell you," Jackson answered, gesturing to his companions.

"And you believe them?" Miller asked.

"Yes, sir." Jackson nodded.

"Then they might as well tell General Hull himself."

They were ushered into what used to be a parlor and now served as an office for General Hull. After Jackson had made the introductions, the three travelers were asked to sit. Wagg told their story convincingly, and Hull's face remained impassive. But Jackson watched him turn pale as he slumped in his chair on hearing the worst news imaginable.

Hull had one vital question for Wagg and his companions. "How many Indians were with this Captain Roberts?"

"The beach was littered with their canoes for as far as I could see," Wagg replied. "Hundreds, more likely thousands ... very hard to tell. The whole episode was terrifying, with those savages running everywhere."

"You seem to have fared for the best," Miller remarked sarcastically. "You would do well to tell us all the details truthfully." A secretary handed him a note.

"We paid one Indian three times what that canoe was worth just to escape with our lives."

There was a knock on the door and Jackson opened it to usher in a couple of Indians. They approached Miller directly and looked small standing beside him. One of them could barely keep his eyes open as he whispered in the colonel's ear.

"These men are in my employ, and it seems Mister Wagg is telling us the truth," Miller declared. "Fort Mackinac has fallen to the British, they confirm it." Miller wrote something on a blank sheet of paper, signed it, and handed it to one of the Indians.

"See the man outside and he will show you where to go. I'll talk to you later." Miller put his hand on the man's back and guided him to the door.

"General Hull, unless you have further questions, sir, I'd like these three to go along with Captain Jackson now and record everything they can remember."

Miller looked to the general, who shook his head. "No more questions."

Jackson saluted and marched off into the next room with his companions following. Two hours later, he emerged with his written report. His instructions from Miller were to keep their three visitors close by. Their testimony would be reviewed and considered line by line when they'd be interviewed once again.

On horseback, Jackson escorted their carriage to the first empty farmhouse lying south of the headquarters building. A log building with two bedrooms and a planked floor would more than suffice for his three guests. The travelers descended from the carriage and climbed the steps to the farmhouse porch. As Mary went inside to inspect her new home, Jackson nudged his horse up alongside the veranda.

"You said you work for the Westlake Trading Company, Mr. Wagg, and that those furs rightfully belong to them. You wouldn't by any chance know of a Jonathan Westlake?"

"Of course—that's the son of the owner, Mr. Richard Westlake," Wagg replied with a laugh. "Do you know him?"

"Stone, care to add any more?"

"As he says, Westlake is the owner's son." Stone had hesitated and spoke with a grim face.

Captain Jackson studied his expression and guessed there was something left unsaid. "Well, I suppose that clears up one mystery for me. The young man is obviously who he claims."

Just then Mary stepped out on to the porch, and Jackson spoke directly to her.

"You'll be safe here with your own room, and perhaps I'll drop in for a chat later, if you wouldn't mind. If you need me for anything, Miss Collins, go back to headquarters and just ask for me." Jackson swung his horse round to Wagg and Stone.

"Though your escape seems a little too easy for me to believe in, you've nevertheless done us a great service by delivering the news, bad as it is. If you want my help with those furs, just sit tight for a while." Not waiting for a reply, he spurred his horse and trotted away.

16

......

THE CANOE SLID south out of the main channel of Georgian Bay, behind
a long point of land that cut the wind down to a whisper and thus made
paddling easier. Westlake was soaked in sweat, and his arms, shoulders,
and back ached from a long day's pull. The sun was blistering, but the
passing air cooled him as he stroked. He glanced to his left and marveled
at the length of beach alongside them, its sand sparkling in the sunlight
as they flew by. If only he could stop for a swim.

From the time the poor weather had released them, Chief Dickson
had set a rapid pace. In the morning darkness, Westlake could barely
see the outline of the canoe as they pushed off from a rocky shore. The
mist had wavered in mid-air as it rose in vertical columns up from the
lake. As on every morning, a unique music had greeted them as the
sun rose to light the water and set off the haunting song of the loon.

Westlake had developed a new respect for the comers and goers of
the fur trade, or *coureurs de bois*, as the French called them. Every muscle in his body was toned and strengthened with each hour of struggle
on the water. He had endured the rain and the sun, so that his face
and hands now had a smooth tan. Even his blond hair had whitened
in the constant sunshine. From the stern, Dickson had chided him
that there was nothing like a good paddle to build a boy's body into a
man's. "You should find a lass now while you finally look presentable."
He laughed.

Parrish meanwhile passed the entire day by singing strange English
ballads. The wilderness flitted by them and Westlake felt as if he were
the only human ever to have seen it. He guessed this must the reason
for Dickson's intense love of the north. At a stop for their midday meal,
Parrish stepped outside the camp to relieve himself and spotted a solitary deer. He immediately ran back to pick up his musket and a few
of the Indians followed him to watch the farce.

Westlake saw that the deer was two hundred and fifty yards off, too far for even the best of shots. Nevertheless, Parrish pulled a paper cartridge from his pouch, bit off one end, and spilled a thumbnail amount of powder into the pan, then closed the frizzen. The remaining powder he poured down the barrel, followed by the cartridge and ball, which he stuffed in hard with his ramrod. He rehooked the ramrod back in place. The Indians shook their heads and gestured with their arms, as if to say the shot was too far to succeed. Westlake watched as Parrish crept behind a tree and cocked the musket hammer into place.

The deer must have sensed that the forest northward of it had suddenly gone too quiet because it raised its head and froze. Boucher, the Métis, had crept around and behind the deer, and at the first snap of a twig the deer was fleeing right toward Parrish. At twenty yards, Parrish stepped out and fired, aiming just behind the deer's shoulder for its heart, and a second later the creature staggered to the ground. The Indians jumped with laughter and began slapping Parrish on the back. One of them even picked him up in a bear squeeze until the man looked like he might pass out.

Chief Dickson was not amused by the incident. They had made good time traveling and he wanted to maintain the pace, but the Indians would not take a further step without first skinning the deer and preparing its meat for travel. Already they claimed Parrish owned a magic musket that could never miss. Westlake himself suspected it was simply a lucky shot.

Once they were on the water again, Dickson commented, "You two have come a long ways. Mr. Westlake has proven to be stronger than I thought, and Parrish now has my friends thinking he's magic."

"Over two thousand miles and we're not finished," Westlake replied. "I'll be happy to sleep in my own bed again. Where to now— the bay seems to end up here?"

"We are taking the Nottawasaga route to York, and this is the mouth of the river itself." Westlake started to speak, but Dickson held up his hand. "I know, you're going to tell me there are other routes, but this is the one I know. So we don't get ourselves lost and I get you back to York quick as I can, this is the route we'll be taking." Dickson steered them into the mouth of the river, and Westlake turned to glimpse the glistening waters of Georgian Bay for the last time.

For a while the Nottawasaga River ran straight, but it soon started to twist around until they were heading back north. It turned on itself yet again, went east through a small lake, and then straightened up before it began a series of rapid sharp turns. Although it was a broad river, the forest hugged its banks and in places angled over the top of them so that Westlake felt strangely confined after being out on the open lake. After a short time the river straightened again, whereupon Dickson announced that they had reached Willow Landing.

"Well, Mr. Parrish, you're soon going to find out what a portage is like because we have to hike nine miles on foot across to Kempenfelt Bay. From there we'll paddle through Lake Simcoe down to the Holland River, where it ends thirty miles north of York at the Holland Landing. Then it's back to hiking, but we'll leave the canoe behind, to be carried down after us."

Dickson sent off six natives to scout the route ahead and four to watch their backs; he was taking no chances of an ambush this close to York. The canoe weighed more than four hundred pounds, and although many times Dickson had carried a similar canoe with just three men, he said that, with all the extra men available, they'd travel faster if four men now did the carrying. Anyway, their provisions had been mostly consumed so that the load per man was light. Parrish begged to be allowed to help carry the canoe, and eventually Dickson relented.

"Your orders, as I remember, were to guard Mr. Westlake and you can't do that from under a birchbark canoe. Take the stern for a short while and give me that musket. Only for a short time, mind you, or Brock will have my hide if anything happens this close to home."

Parrish joined Boucher and two Indians as they rolled the canoe over and hoisted it above their heads. The nine-mile portage followed a route traversed over many years first by natives, then by the military and fur traders alike. The forest on either side was dense, but the path itself was well worn and therefore easy to navigate. Parrish hummed to himself quietly, his head hidden under the stern.

"Keep a sharp eye, Mr. Westlake," Dickson said. "We're at war and I wouldn't like to run into your forest friends again."

"That's strange, I'm dying for a chance to kill owl-face."

"Yes, and die you might in the trying. You may want revenge for Ned Parrish's death, but it won't bring him back."

"What else would you want if you were me?" Westlake asked stubbornly.

"There's an old Scottish saying I particularly like: When one starts out on the road to revenge, dig two graves. One is for your enemy, of course, but the other is for yourself."

"That hasn't seemed to hold back the Highlands clans from fighting, but I asked what you would do," Westlake persisted.

"Stone would be a dead man, for sure—but I would remember that old saying and remain extra careful." Dickson turned away. "Parrish, your time at playing voyageur is up, Mr. Westlake here is making me nervous, so take your musket and move over to our right flank. And don't shoot one of my lads by mistake."

Parrish let the other three men under the canoe take the weight as he ducked out and accepted his musket from Dickson. "Not too bad that," he reported. "Kind of light weight, if you ask me." He headed off toward the flank.

The canoe reached Kempenfelt Bay without incident well after the sun went down and they all settled down for a meal of Parrish's venison. Even though he was exhausted, Westlake plunged in to the water. Cool and refreshing, he dove under, feeling it rush over him and wash away the day's efforts. In anticipation of tomorrow, he had difficulty falling asleep at first, but he was so tired that thoughts of his report to Brock and anticipation of Maple Hill soon came to end. The next thing he felt was Dickson pushing on his shoulder, again.

"Sunshine on the portage, young fella," Dickson was shouting. "This will be the last time I have to wake ye. Ten toes on the forest floor, if you please."

Dickson already had the fire roaring, and it cast the only light in the camp for there was no sign of the sun. Westlake was the last to rise and had just enough time for some weak tea and a biscuit before the canoe was back in the water. Kempenfelt Bay turned out to be long and windy, but they were through and around Big Bay Point in less than an hour. Lake Simcoe proved to be a bigger challenge, where the wind picked up as they rounded the point and the waves buffeted the side of the canoe. Westlake eyed the western sky but saw no evidence of dark clouds. This close to York, Dickson would not be stopping. Westlake paddled full out for as long as he could and then rested his paddle along with the others as the canoe drifted into the mouth of the Holland River.

"How much farther, Chief?" Westlake asked.

"The Holland River is not that long." Dickson raised his eyebrows. "We'll hit Holland Landing in no time, so keep paddling."

"I prefer the open water to this," remarked Parrish, pointing to the swaying reeds on either side of the river. Instead of the loon's call, the constant song of red-winged blackbirds rang out. They flitted from one waving bulrush to another, pecking at insects.

At Holland Landing the canoe was pulled on to shore, where they strapped on their packs and then started the thirty-mile march to York. Westlake looked back for Parrish and saw him shaking hands with Boucher and the three Indians who would now carry the canoe to York. Parrish rubbed his fingertips one last time along the canoe's rough stern as he said goodbye. Westlake gave the men a wave.

Dickson shouted something in Sioux. The Indians laughed and waved too.

Again Dickson sent scouts to the front of their route and assigned two men to their rear. The terrain sloped toward Lake Ontario, but the way to York was by no means all downhill. Westlake crossed numerous streams and skirted bogs, and much like the nine-mile portage, the path from Holland Landing to York was well traveled and relatively smooth.

Dickson then set a torrid pace, but Westlake had been hiking for the past year so at one point in their march, he ran on ahead of Dickson, turning backward to grin as he went by.

"Don't you be cheeky, laddie, or I will have to teach ye a lesson."

"I prefer paddling to marching," Parrish announced. "And I'm starving."

"You can go a while longer, and then we stop," Dickson replied.

Within the hour they came to a small stream, where Dickson laid down his pack and scooped up water in his cupped hands for a drink, Westlake and Parrish following his example. When the rear scouts caught up, Dickson motioned for them to fetch the others up ahead. They were soon all sitting around the fire, eating the last of the venison with their mugs of tea.

"Last stop before York," Dickson declared. "Just a few minutes more rest."

"What's in this war for you, Chief Dickson?" Westlake asked.

Dickson stretched out both his hands, then folded them behind his head of long red hair.

"The Americans have come flooding into the Old Northwest—soon my people will have no land of their own. What choice do we have but to fight?"

"Do you think you'll get better treatment at the hands of the British?"

"It's in their interest right now to help us. Without the tribes, the Canadas will fall, and Brock knows this better than anyone. So we get blankets, weapons, and food in exchange for our loyalty and eventually our blood." Dickson sat up straight and scratched his head. "But to answer your question plainly, the British won't be much better than the Americans once they no longer need us. Yes, that's the way it is: even in victory, the future looks grim for us."

"I'm sorry."

"So am I, but we can't be naive about it. Time we were going again."

They reached York just as the sun was touching the treetops under the western sky. And by luck, the path from Holland Landing had led them close to Maple Hill.

"Mr. Dickson, my home is just a short distance over that path so I'll say goodbye here and see you at headquarters tomorrow." Westlake shook the man's hand in thanks and turned. "Parrish, you're with me."

"Straight home now, mind ye," Dickson yelled to them from behind.

The old barn stood three hundred yards to the east and Westlake sprinted the entire distance, leaving Parrish far behind. He unlatched the wooden bar securing the door, and as it swung, he was greeted by the familiar smell of animals and hay that told him he was home. Warman shuffled sideways in his stall, and Westlake slowly held out a hand to let the horse remember him by sight and smell.

"There, big fella, it's just me." He rubbed the horse's nose and patted his smooth neck.

"Put your hands in the air, if you please," a voice demanded.

"Point that musket elsewhere, Joseph. It's me."

"Master Westlake, this is a surprise. Your mother heard an intruder and Neville is coming around the other end. I should stop him immediately. Good to see you again, sir."

"Go get Neville and come back here, I need both Warman and Berton saddled and ready to ride."

"It'll be done in a jiffy, sir. Just like the last time you returned: lots of charging around, excitement, and secrets. We're at war with the United States, you know, and I've joined the York Volunteer Militia, sir." Joseph gave a mock salute and ran off.

Westlake's mother appeared in the doorway, musket in hand. She stood motionless and stared.

"I had a terrible feeling you weren't coming back, Jonathan."

Westlake turned his head and saw her with the musket resting across her arms.

"Mum, you know I'll always come back to you, and Maple Hill." He smiled and laughed. "By the way, Wagg's alive and I'm not a murderer."

"I know." She returned his smile. "My goodness, look at you. You've filled out and grown another inch. Come and give me a hug."

She embraced him, and he was reminded of the love he had felt for her from the time he was a boy.

Just then, Walt Parrish marched into the barn with Joseph and Neville at the business end of his musket. "These gentlemen want to question me, so I thought we could all talk together—you know, friendly like." Parrish poked Neville with his own musket and the man took another step forward with his head bowed in shame.

Westlake laughed. "Put down the musket, Parrish. These are good men. And meet Mrs. Elizabeth Westlake." Westlake turned to his mother. "This is Walt Parrish, my guardian angel."

"You have done your job well, Walter, and I thank you for bringing my son home to me in one piece."

Even in the fading light, Parrish visibly reacted to the beauty that was Elizabeth Westlake. She was everything the soldiers in the fort had talked about, for report of her appearance at the officers' dance had spread to the lower ranks like a speeding bullet.

Parrish swallowed hard. "My great pleasure to meet you, ma'am. Just doing my job, although, if I may say so, they were the most pleasant orders I've had to follow."

"Since you've already met Joseph and Neville," Westlake said, "let's saddle up the horses. We have to be off." Before his mother could protest he continued. "We have news for General Brock. We've had a great victory at Michilimackinac without a shot fired. He must know this directly." Westlake put up a hand to silence her, indicating that no amount of argument would dissuade him. "I'll be back soon, I promise you that. And I've an interesting story to tell you about Bill Wagg."

As soon as the horses were saddled, Westlake and Parrish were off at a trot. They took a familiar back lane on the west side of Yonge Street, where Westlake felt the warm wind in his hair. They passed the house where he had met Mary, and he wondered if she was truly in Detroit or if Hicks could have been mistaken and then his stomach tightened as he thought of her traveling with a man like Stone. Surely Wagg would prevent Stone from harming Mary. He didn't know that for sure, but he did know he had to find her and the sooner the better. He pressed Warman to a gallop, as if his next trip to Detroit depended on this race to headquarters.

The gates to Government House were sealed shut, but when Westlake was challenged he announced that he had an important message from Maple Hill for Captain Edward Nelles. He and Parrish dismounted and waited only a few minutes before the gates opened. A soldier took charge of their sweating horses.

In the office of the headquarters building, Captain Nelles was checking through some lists from Quartermaster Puffer. His oak desk was large, similar to Brock's, but he sat on a wooden chair instead of the comfort of Brock's black leather one. When he saw Westlake's face he jumped up from behind his desk, the chair knocking backward.

"Don't say a word yet." He put both his hands on Westlake's shoulders and turned him around. "Come with me."

Westlake glanced back to see the same expression on Parrish's face as when they had approached the Michilimackinac cliffs. Parrish had once told him that he hated being in the company of officers; that he never had any luck around them. Now he felt trapped and Westlake knew the feeling. They marched down a short hallway, and Nelles knocked on another door. Westlake had been in this room before and he grinned at Parrish with eyes wider than normal. A voice from within called, "Enter." By now Parrish looked like he was going to faint.

"I have two people who wish to see you, sir," Nelles said.

"At this time of night, Edward. Are they mad?"

Nelles glanced back at Westlake and Parrish and motioned for them to step close up behind him.

"Perhaps I should have said that I have two people whom you wish to see, sir." Nelles swung the door open to reveal fully his two companions.

Brock was sitting behind his desk, with a white quill pen in his hand, and with the Union Jack draped from a pole behind him. He dropped the quill, but before he could say a word, Westlake spoke out.

"Victory at Michilimackinac."

Brock pounded his desk with the flat of his hand.

"Or perhaps I should say, victory, sir. Forgive me, but I've been in the bush too long, sir." Westlake laughed, stepped forward, and then gestured to Parrish.

"By God, well done, both of you." Brock hurried around his desk. He was not wearing a jacket, and his white shirt was unbuttoned halfway down his chest. He shook Westlake's hand and then immediately stepped past him and grabbed the right hand of Parrish.

"And a pardon for him, as agreed," Westlake mentioned.

"And a pardon for you too, Parrish. Victory at Michilimackinac, yes." He was shaking the man's hand with such vigor that Parrish was barely able to keep his head steady.

"Let's have some port to celebrate. I need all the details now. Your mother will be pleased to have you back safe." Brock hesitated just for a moment and turned back to Parrish. "And we should have a special toast to the one who gave his life so that our mission might succeed. I heard the news via courier from Mascotapah. I am sorry, Parrish."

Westlake gave Parrish a puzzled frown.

"Robert Dickson, Mascotapah. It means the Red-Haired Chief," Brock explained.

"We've heard the word used but didn't know until now what it meant," Westlake said. "Foolish of us never to have asked. He's acted as our escort all the way from Fort Mackinac and is currently not far behind us."

Nelles poured wine from an opened bottle sitting on the table. He gave each man a glass and they raised them, repeating after Brock, "To victory at Michilimackinac." Brock took a sip. "To Ned Parrish, who gave his life to protect Upper Canada." They raised their glasses again and toasted Ned. It was the twenty-ninth day of July.

Westlake looked at Parrish, whose eyes had filled with tears on hearing the toast to Ned. If only Ned could have seen his brother shaking hands and raising a glass with General Brock. Westlake sensed how he felt and swallowed hard with a lump in his throat.

"To Ned," Parrish said again, raising his glass with a quivering hand. The others repeated his words and drank with him.

Westlake told his story backward, beginning with the capture of Fort Mackinac. Brock would let no details be left out, and at the table Lieutenant Nelles took notes as fast as he could write.

"That's a great number of voyageurs volunteering to fight. Sounds like the army helped them instead of the other way around," Nelles interjected at one point.

"Because they know their livelihoods are at stake, sir," Westlake said. "Chief Dickson and his Indians were just as enthusiastic."

He recounted their trip across the water in the dark, from Fort St. Joseph. He described Captain Roberts's plan to haul the cannon up the center of the island and above the fort, so that by dawn Lieutenant Hanks would wake to the threat of cannon balls ripping his stronghold apart from the inside out.

"Brilliant," Brock agreed.

Westlake told them also of Parrish, Lapointe, and Dousman finding their way forward along the cliff, in total darkness, of Dousman assisting in the roundup of the villagers, and of the Indians being on their best behavior after the surrender. Brock quizzed him about numbers of men, who did what, and when they did it. Westlake took his time, and just as he had rehearsed it many times in his mind, he described the capture of soldiers, weapons, ammunition, and food.

When he came to Hicks, Stone, and Wagg, he took a sip of port first and put his glass down on the table.

"I know that Wagg is alive, which means I'm not a murderer. I saw him there on the island. He and another man named Hicks apparently work for my father. They were sent to Upper Canada to secure three large caches of furs at Fort St. Joseph, Fort Mackinac, and Fort Detroit." Westlake shook his head and tasted the port. "Naturally, I couldn't stop thinking that this was a dead man who had been murdered by me and yet here he was—a miracle."

He waited for any questions, then continued, "While they may have helped us, we should remember that they did so only to secure those furs, and not because any profound allegiance to King George. I'm telling you this because Hicks believes Wagg has now gone to Detroit to secure a final cache of furs. Once there, you can bet that he'll start working for the Americans, sir."

"The girl Mary would not be with him, would she?" Nelles asked.

Westlake ignored the comment and kept going with his own line of reasoning. "He's traveling with a man named Carson Stone, who's a suspected deserter from the British Navy. This same man, dressed in a British officer's uniform, ambushed us with his gang of four others. They killed Ned Parrish and we can identify him." Westlake paused to allow Nelles time to catch up with his writing.

"You did well to escape with your own lives. It seems, Parrish, that you and your brother kept Westlake here safe, and for that I congratulate you. How did Stone know where to find you?" Brock asked.

"Truth is, sir, that Mr. Westlake and his friend Lapointe kept me alive. Once those men shot Ned, it was two against five. If Lapointe had not come along at the right time, we'd not be here to tell the tale, sir," Parrish said.

"Very commendable of you to be so honest. You've had a change in character, I see. Surely, Parrish, you must have had some small part in the fight," Brock replied.

"I only strangled one of them, sir. And then, with a twist, I broke his neck for good measure—like I told him I would." Parrish grinned. "Mr. Westlake knifed one through the throat and Mr. Lapointe axed one, splitting his forehead, and then knifed another one in the heart, sir."

"Quite graphic." Brock winced.

"There must be an informer inside these walls, sir. That's how they knew where to look for us," Westlake declared.

"Why would the informer be here and not at Fort Amherstburg?" Brock asked.

"We never even went to Fort Amherstburg. We took my Uncle George's horses, and I gave him the note for replacements?"

"That was wise," Brock added.

"I'm learning as I go, sir. Stone probably informed Fort Detroit of our coming. But who told Stone—now that's the real question." Westlake paused again and took a sip from his glass. Brock walked over to the window and returned to his seat without saying a word. He began to drum his fingers on the table.

"At Detroit, they held us for weeks. A Captain Daniel Jackson of the U.S. 4th Infantry sends his regards, sir."

"A traitor between the walls of this fort? I don't know who that could be, but I have my suspicions," Brock said. "Some of these Loyalists are not so loyal, I fear. Just a few, thank God, and the rest form our backbone,"

"Well, that's it—our whole story, sir." Westlake sat back and finished the rest of the port in his glass, already feeling its effects on his head.

"Very good, but I may need to ask you some questions later, probably about Fort Detroit." Brock slapped the table and again shouted, "Victory!" He continued in the same excited fashion. "You know what this means?" Nelles put his quill down, grinned, and prepared to listen, though Westlake suspected Nelles had heard the speech many times before.

"With Forts St. Joseph and Mackinac in our hands, we control the far northwest. And our people are now armed and supplied up there. Most importantly, with this victory the Indians will fight with us and against the Americans." Brock punched the air with his fist. "I cannot imagine a single tribe staying with the Americans—even the Wyandot may come over. By King George, now we have a chance."

Westlake watched Brock's elation, realizing that if he was ever going to get a positive reply to his unusual request, now was the time to ask.

"If you think it would be appropriate, sir, I'd like stay at Maple Hill for a day or two and then leave for Detroit." Westlake waited to see the reaction on Brock's face, but there was none evident. "With Walt Parrish, sir."

"You presume a great deal, Ensign Westlake, but I suppose after two thousand miles, you both deserve a rest." Brock thought again of the victory at Fort Mackinac. "Yes, of course, go and enjoy some home cooking." He remembered Elizabeth's wonderful dinner of roasted duck. "And I might as well join you, on your trip back to Detroit. I'll bring some men with me—say about two hundred."

Westlake could not believe what he had just heard, and he pushed back from the table. All this, and only to catch Stone?

"You see, while rescuing Mary Collins from the clutches of Stone is important to you, unfortunately we'll have another job to do."

Brock's expression turned serious, the cheer of their victory already vanished. Nelles leaned forward with interest, knowing that a decisive turn in Brock's thinking had taken place.

Westlake remained perfectly still and he held his breath, waiting.

"I have some news for you too, Ensign. General Hull and the U.S. Army of the Northwest have invaded Upper Canada at Sandwich, and his force now threatens Fort Amherstburg."

Westlake thought of his Uncle George and Aunt Iris.

"My intention is to oppose Hull there, and push him back across the river into his own damn country. If the opportunity presents itself, and I can't imagine why it won't, we will seize Fort Detroit," Brock concluded.

"We've a great deal to prepare," Nelles warned.

Brock stood up and was followed by each man. He stared directly at Westlake.

"Go home, get some rest, and take Parrish with you. Well done, again, to the both of you. You have three days off before we leave for Fort Amherstburg, from where, if God is willing, we will invade the United States."

Westlake rode back to Maple Hill in silence, his mind spinning with thoughts of imminent revenge.

The eggs and toast were perfectly cooked, exactly as he liked them. There was always something special about breakfast at Maple Hill— the slowness, the smells, or just being with his mother again, Westlake knew it was perfect. He sipped at the hot tea and ran his forefinger along the surface of the maplewood table. Each time that he went away, he would dream of these moments of buttered toast dipped in egg yoke. After months of eating stale bread and salted beef, he could only think of one word for such a breakfast: *perfect*.

Parrish remained asleep, giving an opportunity for Westlake to have a private conversation with his mother. He laid his fork down on the plate, aware he was eating too fast.

"You need a haircut with scissors," Elizabeth smiled and tussled his sun-bleached hair.

"I use my knife in the bush. Away." Westlake waved her back.

"Your father is coming home," his mother announced. "When exactly I'm not sure, but sometime in October he should be back here in York." Elizabeth eyed him, as if watching for a reaction.

What did she expect from him? he wondered. Although his father had been gone for more than a year, he had not forgotten the man's single-mindedness. His father was all business, focused to the point of obsession, with no time for idle talk. He was like Brock in that, yet he knew the two men were somehow different. "What's the difference between General Brock and Father?" he blurted out.

"Why would you ask that?" Elizabeth replied sharply.

Westlake wished he had not asked the question, but he continued, "I know they are similar in many ways, yet there's a difference between the two of them. Have you thought about it?"

His mother stared at the table and Westlake suspected she was avoiding his eyes.

"Your father is concerned about business, and only business. This leaves little room in his life for anyone he's with, and unfortunately this includes our family."

Westlake listened to his mother choosing her words carefully but sensed a tension about her that he had not noticed before.

"Of course, he's been a good provider." She held out one hand and gestured to the room, as if to say, Look around you. "In his own way, I know he loves us."

Westlake took another sip of his tea. Elizabeth did the same, but with a quiver to her hand she replaced her cup in the saucer and continued.

"On the other hand, the general always seems to have concern for the people around him. Whomever he is with, he cares about their well-being and this engenders a certain loyalty to him." Elizabeth recalled the fun with Ensign Simpson, and the care Brock had taken not to undermine the young man during dinner. She continued, thinking out loud, "And his job is not about one company but rather for the general state of Upper Canada, where sometimes the interests of a single business collide with those of the country."

Westlake had been watching his mother develop her thoughts. They had often spoken like this when he was younger. She'd say, "Let's talk about the world," so they would pick a big topic and argue it out, whether it involved politics—which was her favorite—or even religion. He came to see that his mother was far more than just a housekeeper; she had a keen mind and was in great part his teacher. But now it was different: while there were larger issues, for sure, this time it was personal.

"I used to think Father was perfect, and the fur trade the only thing that mattered," he said. "Now I know he is only about saving himself, and greed, and Mr. Brock is about saving the country and honor."

Elizabeth rose from the table, picking up a towel, and went to the brick oven beside the kitchen fireplace. "No one is perfect and I think you're being a little harsh." She removed two hot loaves of bread and then a steaming rabbit pie after wrapping the cloth around each.

He breathed in the aroma before she put the pie back in the oven. "Do you realize that it was men employed by Westlake Trading who killed Ned Parrish and nearly killed Walt and me? Father hired this miserable creature, Wagg. Wagg hired Stone and his cronies. Indirectly, father hired the men that killed Ned!"

"Your friend Walter said that Ned's death was an accident."

"Westlake Trading was responsible for Ned's death. Primarily the men that actually killed Ned are responsible but, indirectly, also Father."

"Then you should add that the rest of us that form the company may also have some responsibility."

This was something Westlake had not considered. Unsure of where the line on responsibility got drawn, now he had another reason to feel guilty about the entire affair, for he too worked for Westlake Trading. He was not finished, though. "Wagg and Stone have more than likely gone to Detroit, where, just as they worked for the British up north, they'll help the American side in Detroit in order to get hold of those furs. This means that Westlake Trading will actually be aiding the enemy."

Elizabeth shook her head and went back to the oven with her cloth in hand to inspect the rabbit pie and hold it directly under his chin. He could taste it from the waves of heat on his nose, but he pushed it away.

"Come on, be serious, Mother. Father should be charged with treason."

"Well, what can I do, I'm baking a pie. Can't we order Wagg to stop? Look at that." She eyed the brown crust, pleased with her work.

"Wagg wouldn't listen to us, but I'm going there to stop him. What

Father doesn't understand is that by helping the Americans, we could recover the furs but lose the war—and that includes Maple Hill."

"I don't think anyone in York thinks American soldiers would cause us harm." Elizabeth frowned. "So many of our friends still live in America."

"You should wake up from your dream. What's good for Westlake Trading is not necessarily good for the country." Westlake felt his voice rising, but he kept himself under control.

"You sound like that journal you wrote, but I guess you're right. I just need time to think about this. Must you really leave now?"

A voice interrupted.

"Good morning, everyone. The new Walter Parrish at your service. Sleeping in that big bed is heaven itself. Blimey, that pie smells wonderful." In the doorway to the kitchen, Parrish put his nose in the air and inhaled deeply, then stretched both his arms. "Does it always smell so great in this kitchen or are you doing this just for me?"

17

······

FORT DETROIT

YOUNG ENSIGN ROBERT SIMPSON had wanted to join the army from the day his father brought home those tin soldiers painted like the men of the 48th Highlanders. By seven years of age he could name and describe half a dozen regiments and tell you the names of their battles, the dates, and the officers involved. He wanted to become one of those soldiers, and nothing would dissuade him. The day he put on his red coat, with the officer's sash and sword, was the happiest day of his life.

Rumor was that his family had influence at Horse Guards in London and that it was somehow obscurely related to the King, but no one knew for sure, and the other officers were afraid to ask for fear of causing offense. His father had blocked a posting with Sir Arthur Wellesley in the Peninsula War; there was too much slaughter there. The West Indies was out too, as everyone posted there died of fever. The 41st Foot in Upper Canada would therefore do just fine, a little cold in the winter perhaps but that would serve young Robert right for worrying his mother with his soldiering ambitions. At least they could count on one thing: there would be no real fighting.

Yet war had found Ensign Simpson, and he could not be happier with a chance to show his father that he was a man, and a real soldier. The fact he would be fighting Americans and not the French was a little strange but not too much of a bother. If General Brock said these former Englishmen were the enemy, then that was good enough for him. Perhaps if he did something particularly heroic, even King George might notice. General Sir Robert Simpson sounded much better than merely Ensign Simpson. He wondered if he had said it out loud and looked over his shoulder in embarrassment at his two new companions.

233

If Westlake and Parrish had heard anything, they were not showing it; they were both paddling as hard as their muscles would allow.

Westlake was pleased to be back on the water because sitting around Maple Hill arguing with his mother had bothered him. He felt free again on the open lake: traveling somewhere at least gave him the illusion of progress. But for Parrish it was a different story, and he told Westlake that never in his life had he enjoyed such luxury as in recent days. He wished Ned could have seen him, for Maple Hill was the life they dreamed about: a kitchen where meals were served and eaten at a table, like a real family; and sleeping in the same soft bed every night, instead of never knowing on what piece of earth your head would rest. When he was finished with the army, he was going to lead the life of a gentlemen farmer, and that was all he wanted to think about right now.

On only their second day home, a visit to Maple Hill by Captain Nelles, with direct orders from Brock, had lasted no more than thirty minutes. He apologized to Elizabeth for the absence of the general himself. Brock had another task for Westlake, again out of uniform, and it was a mission of three parts. Westlake was not to come back to Government House but rather proceed directly to the wharf just east of the garrison. Ensign Robert Simpson and an express canoe of six Indian paddlers would meet him for a trip to Burlington, from where they would collect five horses and ride to Port Dover, acting as an escort. Sergeant Archibald Stamp and Private Fred Burns would be accompanying Simpson. At Port Dover, Simpson was to procure enough boats to carry two hundred men. General Brock himself was going to Fort Amherstburg.

Nelles paused in detailing the orders. Westlake could see he was struggling with what he wanted to say next. "May I help you with something, Captain?"

"This is somewhat difficult to say, after your recent success. However, Ensign Simpson is energetic but not wise about traveling through the bush. I'm sure he is brave enough, but General Brock asks that you avoid all scuffles—just get to Port Dover and complete the first part of your task. In other words, and these are his own words, 'Try not to kill anyone on the way.' I simply need a 'Yes, sir' here, Mr. Westlake."

"It's not my fault that Wagg almost died, and I have no guilt about the death of those four bushwhackers." Westlake had not been in a fight since then, although he knew he would have certainly killed Carson Stone if given the chance at Fort Mackinac.

"Mr. Westlake, I need an answer."

"Yes, sir, I won't kill anyone … unless it's absolutely necessary."

"Thank you. And that goes for you too, Parrish."

"Yes, sir," Parrish confirmed.

"You must proceed from Port Dover to Fort Amherstburg, and there report to Lieutenant Colonel Proctor that the major general is on his way. Then you're to find Tecumseh and deliver him a message. The trouble is that the last known whereabouts of Tecumseh is in American territory. That's all for now. I have some further instructions that I'll explain on the way."

"When are we to meet Ensign Simpson?" Westlake asked.

"I'm to deliver you myself. In two hours from now, he'll be waiting with a canoe at the wharf. He won't leave without you, but I would ask that you both pack in a hurry."

There was no point in reminding Nelles that he was promised three days' rest, and this was only the morning of the third day. After Westlake packed and said goodbye, he heard his mother quietly curse General Brock.

Now they were flying across a choppy Lake Ontario, in company with Ensign Simpson, Sergeant Stamp, and Private Burns. Westlake was wondering why Simpson had turned around in the canoe. He heard him say something, but with the noise of the paddles and the wind, he couldn't make out a word. They kept on paddling, and with the extra paddlers, they reached Burlington just after midday.

At the Burlington dock they were met by a man holding the reins to five horses. Simpson handed the man an envelope, and he was gone.

They set out, Westlake taking the lead and Parrish the rear, with Simpson, Stamp, and Burns in the middle. The road out of Burlington was wide and clear, and Westlake set off at a slow trot that he gradually accelerated to a gallop, covering as much ground as possible while their way was safe. The horses were strong and they continued at full speed until the road narrowed to a path and the forest closed in, every corner offering a suitable place for an ambush. Westlake put up his hand to slow the pace to a walk.

"Ensign Simpson, I suggest we stop here for a break. The horses are winded and we need to eat, sir."

Simpson turned his horse. "Dismount."

"Parrish, make a circle on foot, a hundred paces out. I don't want any surprises," Westlake ordered. "Burns, you guard our rear, and Sergeant Stamp watch up front. You can have a break once Parrish returns. Come on, Burns, don't drag your feet." The two Redcoats marched off to either end of the camp.

The day was hot, typical for the end of July. A single white puff of cloud drifted above in an otherwise blue sky. Westlake pulled his canteen from the saddle and swallowed a mouthful of water. He undid his pack, placed a newly baked loaf of bread on his lap, and broke off a chunk of cheese.

Ensign Simpson sat himself down beside a tree with a piece of salted beef. He brushed at it, trying to get the mould off, and then glanced at Westlake's lunch. While the food provided for officers was generally good at the garrison, Simpson was feeling hungry and Westlake's food looked much superior.

"Where did you find that beef? It looks rancid." Westlake ripped off a chunk of bread and then some cheese and threw them to Simpson one a time. "You can thank my mother for this."

"That's very kind, Mr. Westlake. Much obliged to you and your mother. This damn beef from old Sergeant Puffer is likely to kill a man. I refused to talk to him, so I guess he gave me the worst bit of the lot."

Simpson bit into the lump of cheese as if he had not eaten in a week and washed it down with water. "Excellent, this. You really must invite me over to Maple Hill for a home-cooked meal some day." He bit off a mouthful of bread, rolling his eyes to indicate approval.

Westlake was a little surprised by such forwardness for they had barely spoken and yet the man was already inviting himself to his home. And how could Simpson know where he was from? Before he could to ask, he received the answer.

"You're obviously the son of Mrs. Elizabeth Westlake, since you look so alike. General Brock told us all that she was from Maple Hill and there can't be that many Westlake families in York." Simpson almost said something more but then must have thought better of it.

Westlake waited in silence. Simpson was the type of individual who would eventually betray himself with his own words, but he too had gone quiet.

A breeze came out of the west, moving the humid air enough to remind Westlake of the heat. In the western sky a few clouds appeared but nothing that threatened rain. A wheezing Parrish appeared out of the bush beside them to report that he'd seen nothing.

"Sergeant Stamp—and you, Burns," Westlake called them in. "I will stand guard forward while you eat. Mr. Simpson, would you mind looking out back—the way we came, sir? Burns needs to eat."

"Are you not being somewhat cautious? Parrish has just told us he's seen no one." Simpson rose as Parrish and Stamp seated themselves on the ground to eat.

"No, sir, I'm not. Your musket's loaded, I trust." Westlake did not explain himself but turned and walked twenty paces farther down the path.

Over the course of the evening and the following day, Westlake learned everything he wanted to know, and more, about Robert Simpson. He really was a distant relation to the royal family, being German on his mother's side. With power and money, the Simpsons were used to getting their own way.

"The war is my chance for advancement, since there are always offi-cer casualties. At least it's better than supervising repairs to the palisade around York garrison." According to Simpson, the incessant drilling demanded by Brock only accentuated the frustration of accomplishing nothing during a time of war. By the time they reached Port Dover, late the following day, Westlake was ready to say goodbye to him and anxious to reach Amherstburg.

The narrow path widened so that they could have ridden four

abreast, but Westlake kept them moving single-file and twenty paces apart. There was no one in sight as they approached the shore of Lake Erie, and the landscape around them was flat, with broken stone and brush forming the shoreline. Compared to the docks at York, the wharf at Port Dover was a modest affair, being only a few paces wide and twice as long. Tied up alongside were two fishing boats that would each hold eight men. Westlake stopped and dismounted while the others drifted in behind him.

Simpson gestured to the fishing boats; he had his first transports.

Westlake squinted over the water toward a double-masted schooner anchoring offshore. She looked about eighty feet long and at least twenty feet wide. Her mainsails were already down and her twin square topsails were dropping. Westlake heard the splash of an anchor and saw the launch slap the water. Since the Provincial Marine controlled the lake, there would be no threat from the schooner or the launch and the ship had no cannons mounted. Three native canoes paddled out from behind the bow and pushed toward the shore.

"That's your prize transport, sir. She should carry a good eighty men in cramped conditions, and with her is my ride." Westlake pointed to the canoes. "We may be in luck, Parrish. Sergeant Stamp, Burns—stay here and keep a sharp eye inland." Westlake ran along the wharf and waved to the canoes. One of them came dockside while the other two stood off. Westlake indicated where they had to go and then returned.

"We leave when the commander of the schooner says so, since it seems he employs them in some way, but it cost me the rest of that cheese and all of my bread. Parrish, I hope you loaded up with food before we left Maple Hill."

Parrish grinned and stared at the ground in embarrassment.

"I thought as much. Well, at least we won't starve before we get to where we're going. This'll cut days off our journey."

Westlake turned to Simpson. "Here comes the launch party so please do not address Parrish or me by rank. These men don't know we're military and we need to keep it that way, sir." Simpson opened his mouth as if to speak, but Westlake cut in, "Thank you, sir."

When they reached the wharf and tied on, three of the seven men in the launch stayed in their seats, muskets resting across their arms. The other four disembarked, also armed with muskets except for their apparent leader. He marched forward with a confident bounce to his step, his men hustling along behind as they tried to keep up with his pace. The man had a rather serious face with the rugged features of one used to being in command, although he appeared not much older than Westlake. He stepped off the wharf and glanced back toward his ship, then bobbed his head and smiled—the serious expression gone.

"Look at her, gentlemen. Isn't she a beauty? Feast your eyes on the *Nancy*."

They all watched the schooner swing and tug gently on her anchor. At her bow was an elegant figurehead of a slender woman wearing a feathered hat, with her arms folded across her breasts, while her fashionable white dress appeared to flutter in the wind. Her carver had taken great care to endow her with the grace of the ship itself.

"Yes, and now in the name of His Majesty the King, I impress her and all your crew into service for the defense of Upper Canada. She now belongs to me." Simpson said it with a flourish as Sergeant Stamp took two firm paces forward to stand beside him, a hand resting on his sword.

"Can you sail, fella? Do you know these waters, then?" the man asked with a hint of a Scottish accent.

"Er, well … " Simpson said.

"Just as I thought. Then I think she remains mine since, between the two of us, I'm the only one that knows how to sail her. And, for your information, she's already in the King's service." The man held out his hand to Westlake. "Alexander Mackintosh. This is my crew, and better seamen do not exist."

Westlake shook their hands in turn. "My name is Jonathan Westlake. This is my friend Walt Parrish." He pointed to the others: "Sergeant Stamp, Private Burns over by the trees—and this is Ensign Simpson of the 41st Foot." Mackintosh shook all their hands but held on to Simpson's just a little longer and stared him in the eyes.

Before there could be trouble, Westlake continued, "I've heard of you, Mr. Mackintosh. I believe you're the son of Angus Mackintosh, who helped build the Northwest Company. I'm the son of Richard Westlake, of Westlake Trading, but not so famous."

"I know your uncle, Captain Moore. The Provincial Marine runs out of the docks at Fort Amherstburg only a few miles from where he lives. He speaks very highly of you."

Westlake nodded to the wharf. "Perhaps you can help me with your Indian friends." While they walked that way, Westlake explained their need of a ride. And he also asked for some leniency for Simpson.

Mackintosh laughed, explaining that he had encountered worse officers than Simpson. "Wait till you meet Proctor," he added.

Westlake asked after his uncle, but Mackintosh had been busy on the lake and had heard nothing specific. He explained that many of the families near Sandwich had simply abandoned their farms when the Americans invaded; perhaps the Captain was among them. Westlake didn't think either the Captain or his Aunt Iris would go quite that easily.

A canoe wouldn't be a problem, Mackintosh confirmed after talking with the Indians at the wharf. The two men headed back to the shore. With Mackintosh beside him, Westlake approached Simpson to tell him of his plan.

"Captain Mackintosh has generously agreed to release a canoe," Westlake explained. "He and the *Nancy* will wait here meanwhile for General Brock's arrival."

"You've told him of our mission?" Simpson exclaimed. "General Brock's arrival was to remain secret. I hope we can trust this man."

"Ensign Simpson, my family used to live in Michigan Territory," Mackintosh intervened. "When the British handed Fort Detroit over to the Americans, we left everything behind and built a new house on the British side of the river. We own two ships, the Nancy and the *Caledonia*, both of which we voluntarily put at the disposal of the Provincial Marine. I certainly can be trusted, but what has your own family done for the war effort?" Mackintosh asked.

"I'm sure the lieutenant will learn that all Canadian fur traders have the same interests as the Crown," Westlake said. "Let's be off, shall we?" Mackintosh marched toward the wharf while Westlake went back to his horse alongside a red-faced Simpson.

"I leave you safe and sound," he said quietly. "Thank you for keeping our secret. Our job is done here and I hope you find the rest of your boats. General Brock is counting on you, sir." He lowered his pack and musket from his horse.

"I know my duties, Mr. Westlake, and you may carry on with yours." Simpson leaned forward as he lowered his voice. "But what exactly are they now?"

"If I told, I'd have to kill you, and you would miss your big promotion, sir."

"I say, steady on." Simpson's eyes widened. "That's a little extreme, don't you think?"

Westlake laughed, reaching over to shake Simpson's hand. "Best of luck." He then took Sergeant Stamp's hand and said goodbye to him. Burns had stayed apart and simply nodded. Parrish waved from the wharf.

They threw their packs and muskets to the natives in the canoe and climbed down after them. With the blades of their paddles thrust against the dockside, they pushed off. A few minutes later the canoe was well out into the lake, and Westlake waved to the launch with his own paddle. In less than an hour, they were crossing a large sandbar that seemed to stretch forever toward the middle of the lake. The heavily laden canoe slid over it with only a few feet to spare.

"Do you want to know what I think about Ensign Simpson, sir?" Parrish asked.

"Not a word." Westlake held up his hand. "I know what you think, Parrish, but for now, just enjoy the lake." They paddled into the sun as it descended in the western sky, the lake shimmering in front of them.

"You people in this country have a lot of lakes, and I seemed to be required to paddle across most of them," Parrish said. "I even used to think there was a lot of water in the old River Thames back home."

"I thought you wanted to be a voyageur ... paddling all day on open water, singing at nights by the campfire."

"Changed my mind, didn't I, sir. A fellow has a right to change his mind. Ned was right: settle down, work a farm, and sleep in one of those soft beds like you have at Maple Hill. That's my dream, and now I've the ten pounds coming to me for the capture of Fort Mackinac—that's a start on getting myself a bed like that."

The Indians had begun eyeing the shore for a suitable campsite. Unlike the deep waters of Georgian Bay, with its shores of giant boulders and sheer cliffs of pink granite, Lake Erie was comparatively shallow, with level shores of pebble stones and sandy beaches. Inland, the terrain looked good for farming, and farmer Parrish was now on the prowl for agricultural land.

"Do you think this is a good place to set up a farm, sir?" he asked.

From the moment they had departed York, they had been traveling southwest. Westlake knew that farther south meant shorter winters and longer growing seasons, which gave the farmer a better chance at success.

"Wait till we get farther. Captain Moore will show you where's best to start."

Westlake thought about his own agenda. He'd meet Proctor and track down Tecumseh, but he'd also find his uncle and Mary Collins. If he had to kill Wagg and Stone, then so be it. Westlake wondered if Mary still cared for him or perhaps found someone else. As for love, what was that? When he thought she might reject him, his stomach clenched and he assumed that meant being in love. He had to get to Detroit.

The Indians guided the canoe to a chosen spot on the shore. Westlake guessed the site was familiar to them because a campfire was still warm from its last visitors. Elizabeth had crammed Walt Parrish's pack full of food, and they stuffed themselves.

Parrish volunteered to take the first watch, announcing that he had some thinking to do about farming and had better get started.

"Captain Jackson's guides have disappeared—probably dead by now." General Hull pointed to the map. "Your orders, Major, are to take two hundred Ohio volunteers south and bring back my supplies from the Raison River."

"The militia will make amends for not crossing into Canada, sir. They're a little unruly, but this is their chance to become heroes." Major Thomas Van Horne imagined himself leading a triumphal procession of three hundred cattle and seventy pack mules into Fort Detroit.

"Watch out for those damn Indians," Hull warned.

Van Horne inspected his militia as they trooped through the fort's gates, pushing and elbowing one another for position in the column and laughing together. They carried with them their own knives, tomahawks, and muskets. In their buckskins and faded homespun, they blended in with their natural surroundings. Van Horne just hoped that what was lacking in discipline would be offset by backwoods cunning. He had already sent his two best men, Ranger Captain McCullough and scout Robert Lucas, ahead to warn of danger.

In the early morning of August 5, 1812, McCullough and Lucas crouched motionless in the mist. The moisture that dampened McCullough's face merged with the sweat that he now wiped away from his brow with the back of his hand. He peered through the trees, searching for any movement.

"Get the men and horses. We mount up and ride for Maguaga. Will you look at that mist rise off the river."

"The village will be empty, sir. They've just gone over to the British on the news of Mackinac's fall," Lucas said.

"If there's one Wyandot left, I'll get me another one of these." McCullough held up an Indian scalp hanging from his belt.

Since the war had been declared, McCullough was the only man so far to take a scalp, on either side, considering it a trophy. He laughed as Lucas jerked his head away in disgust.

McCullough approached Maguaga, riding slowly, his musket resting across arms, his aide walking beside him. With the warming sun, a slight wind lifted the mist halfway up the walls of the village wigwams. His eyes darted from house to house, but no one came charging out, nor was there any sound. He shuddered and spurred his horse from a walk into a slow trot.

On the other side of the village the road forked, one side staying with the river and the other curving away inland.

"Lucas, take a man and go right. I'll stay on the river side."

Farther down the river road, McCullough slowed his horse so his aide could catch up on foot. To his right were tall stalks of green corn waving in the morning breeze. *Peaceful*, McCullough thought. *A good place for an ambush.* He didn't like his position, but he edged his horse forward, with his musket at the ready, as a crow flapped away beside them, lifting itself off a stalk of corn. Startled, McCullough jumped in his saddle, but he managed not to fire. He shook his head. "Next I'll be jumping at bloody ghosts."

Paxinos slapped at a mosquito landing by his ear and then stared at his shaking hand. Kawika frowned and turned away. They had seen the large body of soldiers leaving the fort, and Paxinos knew the scouts of the Long Knives were nearby, but he couldn't see them. They were walking right into his trap, the same as before. Days previous, he had killed a guide not far from here, on the other fork in the road—away from the river. He was thankful his man had died quickly with no sound; just one bullet was all it took. The other guide had screamed as the musket's shot had torn away his face. He was then tomahawked and stabbed repeatedly by Kawika. Paxinos hid his face from his friend, feeling sick to his stomach at killing his first man.

Now, two more white men gradually came into view, turning their heads with each step, their focused gaze seeing everything. They seemed to know that Paxinos was hiding there, and he was sure they would spot him. Perhaps he would die this day while the white men would live. When a bird fluttered up from a corn stalk, the two men jumped but held their fire. They walked directly past him, not noticing his four friends lying flat amid the corn a few yards off the path.

Paxinos rose slowly along with Kawika, both their faces painted with charcoal stripes. As he looked at his friends, he realized why white men were frightened of them: their appearance, inhuman and beast-like, scared him too. He stared back down the road to ensure no one followed the white men. With a sharp nod, he and his friends jumped out onto the path. Too late, the rustling stalks made the white men turn. Paxinos fired with the others. The tall man on horseback was hit three times, the bullets tearing into his chest. He toppled off his horse to the ground, already dead. The man on foot had crouched, so only one bullet had found its mark, penetrating through his left shoulder. Under the pain, he fired his musket high and then fell to his knees, lifting his right arm in a futile attempt to ward off his attackers. A tomahawk sliced down, breaking his raised arm; a second one slashed across his neck. He took Kawika's crushing axe to his forehead and fell backward, dead.

The Indian scalp hanging from the rider's belt only enraged Kawika even further. While grabbing the rider's hair in one hand, he reached for his knife with the other and sliced just under the scalp, to leave the top of Captain McCullough's skull a bloody mess. Kawika then cut the rawhide string suspending the dried scalp from McCullough's belt. The Indians pulled the two corpses into the cornfield, and Paxinos waved his arm as a signal for his group to run. The entire ambush had taken less than three minutes.

They ran hard until they were out of breath, then walked for a while, trying to catch their wind before running again. Rounding a sharp bend in the road, Paxinos collided with a white man running toward him. Impacting shoulder to shoulder, they bounced off each other and ended up lying on the ground. Two Indians leapt on the man, ready to dispatch him with their tomahawks, but Paxinos shouted, "Stop, find out who he is first."

"We should kill him," Kawika argued.

They lifted the little man to his feet, his eyes grown wide in alarm, his whole body shaking as he rubbed at his bruised shoulder. Whether from his physical exertion or fright, the man's cropped brown hair was standing straight on end.

"What is your name? Where are you coming from? Where do you live?" Paxinos demanded in English. The man's fate would be decided in the next few moments, but the fear on his face kept his mouth shut.

Kawika raised his tomahawk, and the man spoke quickly. "I come from visiting my father in the south. You know the mill? I live near there, on the river at Fort Detroit. My name is Tremblay."

"Kill him quickly and let's go." Kawika pushed for a decision, but Paxinos paid him no attention. His friends would do as he told them, if he could stay calm.

"Who are neighbors to your farm? I will know if you are lying. Hurry with your answer."

Tremblay heard the question, but his white face had now turned ashen. Paxinos suspected that the man couldn't think due to his fear.

"Speak," Kawika shouted at him.

Tremblay panicked, watching the other Indians raise their tomahawks. "The Robichauds are to the north and the Lapointes to the south," he blurted out. He gagged and looked like he was about to throw up.

"So you know the Lapointe family?" Paxinos asked.

"Many times we work to help each other. They're my friends, like family," Tremblay pleaded.

"Then know that this day your friendship with Danny Lapointe's family has saved your life. Run away. Go, now!"

Instantly, Tremblay was off, scurrying down the road toward Fort Detroit.

"Why let that white man escape?" Kawika said. "We should have killed him."

Paxinos waved an arm, indicating for all of them to start moving again, but an angry Kawika raised his own arm to hurl his tomahawk into the departing back of Tremblay. Paxinos grabbed his hand from behind and kicked his feet out from under him. Kawika hit the ground hard, Paxinos landing on top of him before he could move. Paxinos still grasped the shaft of the tomahawk, pressing it across Kawika's throat, as he gave an angry grin.

"That man is the friend and neighbor of our own friend. At Prophet's Town, when the Long Knives came to destroy our village, a white man helped us carry the little ones away! That same man is the good friend of Lapointe." Paxinos was pressing down on the shaft so that Kawika could hardly breath.

"Enough now, can we go?" Paxinos waited for a sign that the fight was over. He eased off the pressure, and Kawika nodded to indicate it was finished.

"Who is this friend of Lapointe?" Kawika rubbed his throat.

Paxinos laughed, running with the others as he remembered that day the white boy asked if he could stay with the Indian village to learn their ways. They hunted together and fought each other, as brothers do. He thought back to that incident when the soldiers were entering at one end while he and his friend were scrambling out the other. His new friend could run fast even while he was carrying the child. Paxinos was proud of his friend and knew that if he had a brother, this is how it would feel.

"You could not harm him, for you would have to kill me first. Even then to overcome him you would need five warriors or maybe ten, and most of them would die before you got to harm him. I think the Great Spirit watches over him."

"But what is his name?"

Paxinos let the warrior wait for an answer, but after a few paces, he turned his head so that they were face to face. "He is like my brother and his name is Jonathan Westlake."

Jacques Tremblay kept running until his heart felt like it was going to explode. He pelted along the road until his legs finally gave out, then crawled on hands and knees over to a tree. There he threw up his breakfast. Twice more he spit trying to get the sour taste out of his mouth. Behind him, a squirrel skipped across the road, but there were no painted warriors to be seen. His fingers wiped some of the sweat from his brow. He was safe now. "Damn Indians," he muttered to himself. "Where the hell did they come from?"

From behind him came a deep voice that said, "They live here."

"Aahh!" Tremblay yelled and he almost jumped into the air.

"Apologies. Did I scare you? My name's Robert Lucas."

"You scared the shit out of me!" Tremblay yelled. "I almost died of fright, *mon Dieu*." Tremblay clutched a hand over his pounding heart.

Lucas started to laugh, but Tremblay cut him off. "First those damn Indians nearly kill me and now you creep up behind me. My heart might give out right here." Tremblay clasped his chest now with both hands and tilted his head back to take a breath.

He then told Lucas his story, beginning with the journey from his father's farm. Some Indians had attacked farmers west of the River Raison, so that his father was forced to flee for his own protection. On the road home to Detroit, Tremblay had spotted the tail end of a large body of Indian warriors, so he had headed inland, across Brownstown Creek, far upstream from the warriors. Where these Indians were now, he didn't know, nor did he know where the Indians were that had just surprised him. Tremblay didn't care; he just wanted to run off in the opposite direction, back to his home.

Lucas watched the road, expecting to see Captain McCullough come into view, as he listened carefully to Tremblay's story.

"Frenchmen have lied to me before, but any man who throws up his breakfast must be telling the truth. How many Indians did you see?" Lucas asked.

"Are you crazy? I didn't stop to count them, but there were lots— all over the place."

"I'd better get you to Major Van Horne."

"Which direction is he in, *monsieur*?" Tremblay asked, not yet prepared to move an inch.

"Not far down this road." Lucas pointed in the direction from where he had come, toward Detroit and away from the Indians.

"Jacques Tremblay, at your service." He held out his hand. "That is the right direction for me, so let's get going." Tremblay glanced one last time over his shoulder, checking that the road was clear. "And no more sneaking up on me, if you please, *monsieur*, I've had enough of that already."

Lucas laughed as his eyes continued to search the road because he had yet to see Captain McCulloch.

Paxinos was running hard again. They had lost time over Tremblay, but at least he didn't have to kill the man. Now worried that soldiers would be chasing close after him, he stopped only to quench his parched mouth at the Brownstown Creek. He then splashed through the river in the one place he knew was fordable, driving his knees forward under the water with the musket held above his head. His companions climbed up the embankment and pressed on through the bushes that ran alongside the river. Suddenly a large arm reached out, clutching Paxinos under the chin. For a second his feet could not reach the ground, and his head snapped back so that he was looking up at the clouds.

"You may stop running now. You are safe."

Paxinos opened his mouth to speak, but no words would come. He bent over, putting both hands on his knees, trying to catch his breath again. On each side of him, he saw that his friends were safe.

"Tecumseh!" he exclaimed. "We counted many more soldiers, then we ran away. More than two hundred are marching this way." He gasped for air between his words. "We have just killed two scouts."

"Good. We wait for them, then. With your friends, we are now twenty-five while they are two less." Tecumseh grinned.

"But how can we hold them when there are so few of us?"

"How loud can you and your friends shout?"

"We can yell like ten men." Paxinos laughed out loud, but Tecumseh patted the air as if to calm them down.

"Quiet. We shoot and then scream, shoot again and then charge them with bayonets and tomahawks, but we keep screaming. They will run like rabbits." Tecumseh nodded knowingly, seeing the battle unfold in front of him. He pointed to the river. "We will wait until they are in the water, and then we kill them."

18

......

WITH EACH STEP along the worn path the angle of the trees changed, and Major Van Horne studied them constantly for movement. Captain McCullough had disappeared and, after the news from Tremblay, Van Horne ordered his men to march in double columns, their primed muskets resting across arms but pointed toward the forest.

Between the columns, a precious cargo of leather mailbags rode on horseback. They contained General Hull's official correspondence addressed to Washington, in which he outlined his plans for the future conduct of the war. More important, Hull had sketched the problem of dissension within his officer corps.

Van Horne had detailed a detachment to protect his rear plus another to guard his cautious advance. Although past experience led him to distrust intelligence from Frenchmen, he decided that, with or without the news from Tremblay, his orders were to break through to the supplies at the Raison River, and he would do so in spite of any opposition.

Van Horne galloped ahead to where Scout Robert Lucas had halted the advance party at Brownstown Creek. The road ran down an embankment into the water and up the other side between thick hedges, this being the only place to ford the river. Van Horne saw it as a perfect site for an ambush. "Keep an eye open and ready your weapons for crossing." He held up a warning hand and spoke in a whisper.

Although his advance detachment stopped, the main body did not halt similarly behind them but continued to march until they too were lining the edge of the riverbank.

"I don't see any danger, but we have yet to reconnoiter the other side, sir," Lucas said. The main body then began to bunch up so that the entire force jostled together down the embankment in an unstoppable mass of men and equipment.

"Ambush," Lucas hollered but not soon enough.

Van Horne stared in horror as the entire far side of the river exploded in fire and screaming. One blast shot the horse out from under Lucas, causing it to slide down the bank. The rider leapt clear but fumbled his musket as it went down with his dead horse. Other men dropped dead beside him as he thrashed on the ground searching for a weapon.

Tecumseh now recognized his opportunity. He had formed his warriors in two ranks, thirteen in the front and twelve positioned a step behind, spaced out at least two yards between each man. This gave the enemy an exaggerated sense of the number of warriors they faced and their front would extend fifty yards across, firing deep into the ranks emerging from the river. His men would not fight independently, as they usually did, but would attack in a coordinated unit—as white men fight.

Once Van Horne's men descended to the water, Tecumseh had raised his musket and his front rank sprang up from the bank opposite. They screamed as they fired, the sheet of flame from their muskets spitting bullets. Only ten yards away, the Bluecoats died as every ball found its mark. The Indian chief scanned the embankment for his next target before directing the fire from his second rank into the midst of a mounted column. Men and horses toppled down the embankment, whereupon he shouted for his warriors to fix bayonets.

Van Horne tried to direct the fire of his militia, but most of the men were still clawing their way up the embankment. His right column was fleeing, but the mounted left column stood firm and tried to return fire through the smoke. The smoke burned his eyes so that he could only squint. Opposite him, the riverbank erupted in a sheet of flame for a second time while only ragged individual volleys responded from his own men. The deafening screams of the Indians convinced him that he faced an enemy in the hundreds. Indian bayonets flashed through the smoke as every warrior now charged. Van Horne's stomach squeezed in terror, and he shouted for a general retreat so as to form a new line some way back from the river. But the panic in his men's eyes, as they clambered up the bank, told him it was now hopeless.

Beside him, Lucas held up a hand, trying to get the men to reform, but the terrified soldiers shoved him aside, throwing down their muskets in order to run faster. Even the mounted men galloped straight past Van Horne toward safety, which meant his only hope for personal survival was to turn and run with them.

The Indians chased Van Horne and his men for three miles before giving up. When finally Van Horne stopped retreating, he watched Lucas fall to his knees and throw up.

When Paxinos and the warriors returned, Tecumseh brandished his musket above his head, raised in a frenzied cheer. Paxinos joined in song until his voice was hoarse.

"Only twenty-five of us against two hundred and fifty Long Knives, yet they ran. Remember always this day here at Brownstown!" Tecumseh bellowed.

Paxinos felt the man's strong grip on his shoulder and he saw Tecumseh smile. He handed the chief several leather bags of mail and watched for his reaction to their contents. Tecumseh studied each bundle, putting them aside, until he opened a black valise marked *Confidential*. One by one, he read the letters and reports signed by General William Hull.

"You must take these to the British and give them only to a man named Proctor in Fort Amherstburg." Tecumseh held out the valise to Paxinos. "You will share the news of our victory with the Redcoats, then you must return here. The Long Knives are coming back, you need to be wary," Tecumseh warned. "They will kill you instantly if you are caught."

"I will cross the river at the fort," Paxinos replied. "I can do it."

Slumped at the massive front gates of Fort Amherstburg, Lieutenant Colonel Henry Proctor stared across the Detroit River and spit out, "Damn, damn" to the wind. Sent by Brock to take command from the fort's shaken commander, he had arrived a little more than a week previously. Morale had dropped to new lows, and even his sixty reinforcements from the 41st regiment failed to stem the tide of militia desertions, which had to stop soon or he would have little hope of defending the fort. The problem seemed more burdensome the more he thought about it. He gave a sigh, noticing how the air from the river was smelling thick, like it was about to rain.

Previously, Proctor had commanded at Fort George, near Niagara Falls. There he had drilled the 41st Regiment into a fighting unit to be proud of, and he was determined to do the same at Fort Amherstburg. The son of an army surgeon, he had joined the army in 1781 and never left, rising steadily through the ranks. One year short of his fiftieth birthday, all his experience told him that what he needed most was a victory.

Proctor had considered a night action but decided against it because he knew a failure would cause the entire militia to desert. The wind rose and the river's waves pounded the shore, sending up a spray that moistened his face. In the middle of the river, the trees on Grosse Island bent under every new gust. He surveyed a western sky darkening with scudding black clouds. *If it was going to rain, let it rain bloody hard on Hull and his tents of invaders. The worse the weather for them, the more fortunate for us.*

A small canoe approached, with a single paddler. It didn't settle beside the docks but came in on a wave just a few paces north. The handful of soldiers on watch ran to the canoe and grabbed hold of its occupant, after which one soldier sprinted toward the fort and came to attention in front of Proctor.

"A young Indian has a black valise that he says is for you personally, sir. Says it's from a chief named Tecumseh. Do you want him here, or would—"

"Do you not know of Tecumseh? Of course I want the fellow here. Fetch him."

The Indian approached warily with an escort gripping him by each arm. His large brown eyes darted all around him before finally resting on Proctor.

"We just killed seventeen Long Knives at Brownstown Creek—twenty-five of us with Tecumseh against two hundred and fifty enemy soldiers."

"What did you do exactly?" Proctor asked with a frown, wanting to shake the young man into standing up straight.

"They all ran away, but seventeen of them are dead." Proctor watched the Indian hold up his fingers to count. "We won," he said.

"Very good." Proctor nodded but still wondering what the young fellow was about. "What's your name?"

"These are from Tecumseh." The young man held up the valise. "They are letters from the chief of the Long Knives, the one they call Hull. Tecumseh says important for you. My name is Paxinos, but are you, for sure, Proctor?"

At the mention of Hull's name, Proctor began to realize the potential of this delivery, and any traces of his reserve were gone. "By God, if you have dispatches from the enemy, they are indeed vital." He rummaged in the valise until he found the letters written by Hull himself. "We won a battle, you say?"

Paxinos nodded.

"Then well done indeed. My name is Proctor, Lieutenant Colonel Henry Proctor. Did you hear that, lads? A victory at Brownstown Creek." He turned and waved a fistful of Hull's letters in the air.

He grabbed Paxinos's hand and shook it, the impact of the young brave's words finally understood. "And we have captured Hull's despatches. Go tell everyone. Go now, quickly," Proctor urged the men who stood immediately around him.

They lifted their muskets in the air and shouted, "Huzzah," then they split up and dashed off in different directions.

"You must come into the fort and dine with me. I want to know everything about this battle you fought."

Proctor laid his hand on Paxinos's arm and led him through the gates of Fort Amherstburg. "Major Muir, over here, if you please," he beckoned. "Hull has been denied his supplies again. Join us for our midday meal, Major. Paxinos is going to describe the Battle of

Brownstown Creek, so we'll hear of the victory first-hand. This'll put some backbone into the militia, eh? No more damn desertions, I trust."

"Thank you, I will, sir, congratulations." Muir smiled and held out his hand to the young Indian warrior.

Congratulations indeed, thought Proctor. *My luck is improving and the war has just turned a corner.* With a renewed gust of wind, the river air smelled even fresher. He led the way to dinner with his head up, shoulders back, and chest thrust out. The weight of the world had just vanished with one word: victory.

At first light, the sky had been packed with clouds, but the air was windless. Lake Erie remained flat and calm, and the Indians wanted to make time while such weather allowed. Now that the canoe came round into sight of the Fort Amherstburg docks, the wind was blowing hard again under a darkened sky, and from the whitecaps on the river, Westlake knew this was going to be no easy landing. However, the native paddlers timed the waves so that the canoe hit the shore with the least possible impact. Just north of the docks alongside a smaller vessel the Indians leaped over the side to hold the canoe's bottom away from the worst of the pounding.

Westlake jumped out into shallow water, feeling his boots slide between the stones. Parrish carried their packs to the shore while holding his musket above his head with one arm. Though Westlake had motioned for the Indians to join them, they had already leaped back into the canoe and were paddling south, toward the river mouth.

The three sentries posted at the north end of the fort charged over to intercept these newest visitors. Muskets at the ready, one of them demanded to know their business. Westlake and Parrish picked up their packs and struggled up the embankment toward them.

"Point those bloody muskets away," Westlake ordered. "We're here to see Colonel Proctor, so take us to him straight away."

"Another canoe for Colonel Proctor," remarked one sentry to another. The three soldiers shouldered their muskets. "Follow us."

The great gates of Fort Amherstburg opened up, and Westlake and

Parish headed inside along with their escort. A young, thin-faced ensign approached, who was told of their business. He reappeared a few minutes later to say that Colonel Proctor was having dinner and did not wish to be disturbed.

"You'll have to return to him, Ensign. Tell him that I carry a message directly from General Brock," Westlake explained.

At hearing Brock's name the man stood very still.

"Go now," Westlake ordered.

The fellow tore off again. This time when he returned his face was red and he was panting. "The colonel will see you now. Follow me." He staggered and Parrish caught him by the arm.

"Are you all right, sir?" Parrish asked.

"This has been the worst summer for heat and rain … I have the ague."

Lieutenant Colonel Henry Proctor never liked to be disturbed while eating dinner, especially when he was also entertaining. He had gathered a group to celebrate a victory, and listen to a tale of battle, but a message from General Brock could not be ignored. He was pacing back and forth at the door to his headquarters when Westlake arrived.

"Well, man, speak up." There would be no niceties of introduction.

After traveling thousands of miles, while risking his life and those of others, Westlake took instant offense at the lack of a proper greeting from this colonel.

"I bring news from General Brock, sir," Westlake reported as evenly as he could.

"Spit it out then, man. My dinner is getting cold."

"General Brock is on his way to Fort Amherstburg with reinforcements, sir. You are to organize for an assault on the enemy and immediately prepare gun carriages, if you have not done so already."

Proctor unfolded his arms from in front of his chest and stepped away from Westlake, staring at the ground. He looked like a man who had just been poleaxed in the back of his head.

"You men will join our militia, and I'll speak with you again later. What are your names, by the way?" Proctor asked.

"That's not possible, sir. General Brock's immediate orders are that you're to assist us in finding Tecumseh." Westlake had been instructed by Nelles to ask for Proctor's assistance, but the colonel's shoddy welcome had made him angry so he turned that request into an order. Proctor simply stared at him, not used to being ordered about by a man dressed in buckskins.

"Tecumseh will then accompany me here for a meeting with the general. You're to prepare for this meeting by gathering information for a possible attack on Fort Detroit—after the enemy has been cleared from these shores, sir."

"Good God, is he mad?" Proctor blurted out.

"This is Walt Parrish and my name is Jonathan Westlake, sir," he said sharply as Proctor reeled in front of him. He wanted to ask, *How is your dinner now?* but kept silent before making his request. "We're hungry, sir, having forgone breakfast to bring you these orders. Before we set out looking for Tecumseh, we'd like to eat."

Proctor ran his hands through his hair in private turmoil. "Yes— yes of course. You should join us for dinner now," he replied. "There's someone here who may be able to assist you in finding Tecumseh." Proctor led the way back indoors with Westlake and Parrish behind him.

They entered a room furnished with a long dining table covered in white linen and crowded with guests. Paxinos instantly called out, "Jonathan!" leaping up from the table to embrace Westlake in a bear hug. His relief at seeing a friendly face here was obvious. On the far side of the table sat another familiar figure, Captain George Moore.

"Uncle George, how are you?" Westlake exclaimed. He hurried around the table and the two of them shook hands.

"You're looking well, young man, and you've grown even more," Moore said. "The bastards shot up my bum leg again, so I can't dance as well as I used to. Do you happen to remember Lieutenant Rolette here, of the Provincial Marine?"

"Of course," Westlake said. "And you remember Walt Parrish."

Parrish shook hands with the pair of them, then Moore asked, "Did you not have a twin brother with you at the farm?"

"Unfortunately, Uncle, he was killed on our way to Fort Mackinac," Westlake interjected.

"My God, I'm sorry," Moore said.

"Am I the only one in the room who doesn't already know you, Mr. Westlake?" Proctor said with a frown. "If you were present at Michilimackinac for the victory, then we have two battle tales to hear about before the dinner is finished." He then introduced Westlake to Major Muir and his friend, a man named Thomas Verchères de Boucherville, who was a storekeeper and fur trader.

Great plates of roasted chicken and steaming whole potatoes were served with goblets of wine. Walt told his story of near death by drowning in five feet of water when their canoe crashed on the rocks; the comic relief in the middle of dinner. When Paxinos gave his account of the Battle of Brownstown Creek, there was no humor in anything he said. Though his fellow natives had been outnumbered almost ten to one, seventeen American soldiers had been killed to the loss of one Indian, a chief coincidentally named Blue Jacket.

"Tecumseh says the Long Knives will try again to retrieve their supplies at the River Raison so I must go back," Paxinos concluded his tale.

"We'll go with you," Westlake decided. He wiped his face with a napkin and looked for Proctor's approval.

"Major Muir, you will accompany these men to Tecumseh," Proctor ordered. "Take a detachment of the 41st and provide all possible aid. Lieutenant Rolette, can you get them across the river with whitecaps showing?"

Rolette stood up to signal the dinner was over. "In long boats, sir, it will be a tough pull, but we'll manage. I should be off now to arrange them, if you want us to depart immediately."

Major Muir gave his compliments on the fare and announced that his men had been praying for this order. He would co-ordinate his embarkation with Rolette. De Boucherville, who had not said a word all evening, departed with him.

Westlake went to his uncle's side, motioning for Parrish to join him.

With support under each arm, the Captain was lifted from his seat and Westlake handed him his crutch.

"I'm staying in a bloody tent, with your Aunt Iris, until we can get our bearings," Moore explained. Seeing the puzzled look on Westlake's face, he continued, "The bastards burnt down the farm. Of course, that was after Iris shot one of them. Goddamn Sergeant Harris was no help."

"Harris? I know him." Westlake glanced at Parrish.

"Of course, you do, Mr. Westlake, who don't you know?" Proctor interrupted from the door. "But should you not get moving with your friend Paxinos? You'll have to inform me at another time of your exact duties for General Brock."

As they made their exit, Westlake turned back and offered his hand to Proctor. "Thank you for dinner, sir, it's much appreciated." He pointed to Parrish and then back to himself. "General Brock says it is best if we do not exist."

"Goodbye, Uncle."

"It's dangerous over there, so be careful," Moore called out.

The young men left the room, leaving only Moore and Proctor behind.

"Care for another coffee, Captain?" Proctor offered as he reached for the pot.

"Thank you, but Iris will be giving me the blazes if I am out too long on this bum leg."

"No wonder your nephew has the ear of Brock, having been at Mackinac. I thought you might tell me a little more about him—like what the hell he does in this army, exactly."

Moore was making his way slowly, limping to the doorway. He raised his cane and jabbed it at the door, which had swung half closed, then turned back to face Proctor. "I would think, for a man like you, that would be self-evident," he said before hobbling on his way. Then, over his shoulder, he added, "Ask General Brock."

19

• • • • • •

HULL NEEDED to know just what they were prepared to do. Six officers, all but one with their arms folded over their chests, gathered around the dining-room table in the unfinished Baby residence that served as headquarters for the U.S. Army of the Northwest. Their determined eyes kept a focus to their immediate front, and the lack of conversation only served to add even more tension in the room. The wind was up, and the smell of the Detroit River was strong throughout the house—and indeed the entire village of Sandwich. An early August breeze made the stifling humidity just bearable. With a white napkin, Hull mopped a few drops of perspiration from his forehead.

Colonels McArthur, Findlay, and Cass were conspiring against him; the rumors had been rampant for days. Of the four officers in his upper level of command, only Lieutenant Colonel Miller of the U.S. 4th Infantry would stand with him. Hull wondered if they were as prepared to fight the enemy as they were ready to do battle with him. The room darkened as the remaining light from the sun was clouded out, and Miller asked Captain Jackson to light the four tapered candles on the table.

Hull had ordered barges built to float his cannons. Anchoring in midstream, they were to blast a hole in the fourteen-foot-high palisade that surrounded Fort Amherstburg. Although the artillerymen thought the idea daft, they were willing to give it a try.

Reports from Captain Jackson told of a ravelin—a thick dirt mound—in front of the main gates. Five deadly cannons stood guard behind those gates so it was no use attacking there. The palisade ran completely around the fort, forming a perimeter of more than three thousand feet, but Hull knew he needed to make a breach only twenty feet wide for his soldiers to pour through and overwhelm the defenders.

Of course, the barges would have to survive a British onslaught from the one-hundred-and-eighty-ton brig *Queen Charlotte*, armed with ten twenty-four-pounders and six long-barreled twelve-pounders. Two other armed British ships would also join the attack on the barges, namely the *General Hunter* and the *Lady Prevost*. These ships of the Provincial Marine would have one job: to sink his barges before they could do any damage.

Hull figured most of barge crew members would die because in the unlikely event that they survived the onslaught of the Provincial Marine, the odds of their dodging cannon shot from the fort were slim. Stationary shore batteries almost always won out over unstable ships, whose floating cannons rolled on the waves. With the weather worsening, the barge cannons would have little chance to make their breach. They may get off a few blasts, but the barges might be sunk and the artillerymen all dead before they found their mark. Hull began to doubt the wisdom of his own plan, and his stomach tensed.

He now had a different question for his conspiring colonels and their men. If this attempt to breach the walls failed, would they stand the unceasing musket fire while escalading the walls of Fort Amherstburg? He told them of the casualties his men had taken during the Revolutionary War while attempting a similar venture. This escalade would be even more dangerous. He nodded to Captain Jackson for him to detail the fort's defenses.

Jackson unrolled a drawing and put two candlesticks at one end to keep it flat while Miller placed two at the other end. The chart showed how Fort Amherstburg had at each corner a diamond-shaped earthen bastion that contained four cannons. Therefore, each bastion allowed a pair of cannons to fire in two different directions at any time.

Jackson tapped a stick on one bastion to show that, because of its diamond shape, the men in the first angle of the diamond could fire back at the fort itself if need be. This meant that anyone attempting an escalade would, on their approach, have to face fire from one hundred and fifty loopholes in the palisade as well as the crossfire from the cannons. The fire would be rapid, as the men at the loopholes could have as many as three loaded muskets each at the ready.

After tugging the bottom of his jacket into place, Jackson sat down but continued speaking. "If we're lucky enough to survive the fire coming from the fort, we run down into a three-foot ditch that's a killing ravine six feet wide. Climbing the ladders, we have to face more musket fire, only this time it'll hit our backs, which are unprotected from the enemy in the first angle of the diamond." Jackson threw his pointer on to the chart and looked to Hull to show he was finished.

Despite all their previous bravado, none of the militia colonels had anything to say, so Miller concluded with a summary of the problem at hand. He insisted that his U.S. Army regulars could face the firestorm, get up the ladders, and battle over the top of the palisade and into the fort. From British militia deserters, Captain Jackson had received information that the fort's militia had dwindled to half its original strength and therefore now stood at barely four hundred.

However, in addition to these four hundred militiamen, once over the wall, the attackers would face at least three hundred and eighty-five British regulars and four hundred Indians. Even if all four hundred and fifty regulars of the U.S. 4th Infantry made it over the palisade, a very unlikely event, they would be overwhelmed by almost twelve hundred defenders.

Hull wanted to know if the sixteen hundred and fifty Ohio and Michigan militiamen would be ready to follow the regulars through the firestorm and over the wall. Otherwise, he'd lose the bulk of his regular force to slaughter, and all for nothing. As he turned to the three militia colonels for an answer, McArthur pushed himself back from the table and walked over to the nearest window to see a blackened sky. Findlay glanced up at McArthur's back while Cass just stared at the floor, saying nothing: they were waiting for McArthur to break the silence.

"Yesterday, we were committed to attack, and that was by your order. The barges are ready and my men are anxious to get at it. Now it's August 7 and you're having seconds thoughts, but why?" McArthur walked backed to his place at the table but did not sit down. He rested the heels of his hands on the back of his chair and peered down at Hull.

Hull chewed on his tobacco a while longer, considering his three options. He could make the attempt on Fort Amherstburg, knowing that even if he captured the fort he could not hold it without supplies. He could retreat to Fort Detroit and defend the town, with the river between him and the British. However, even here he needed supplies to hold the town for more than thirty days. His last option was to fall back to the Maumee River, where more supplies were already accumulating. With hordes of Indians descending from Fort Mackinac, militarily this was his best option, but it meant abandoning Detroit. This would go against his orders, and to Hull, it just didn't feel like the right thing to do. After all, he was also the governor of Michigan, with a responsibility to protect its residents.

"As much as the three of you are in favor of attacking the fort, there are stories that the militia will not escalade the fort's walls under fire. The regular army will be wiped out, if the militia won't follow them." Hull paused to let this comment sink in and to dab away the sweat on his upper lip. "I want your guarantee that you'll lead the militia personally and that they'll follow you over those walls."

For a few moments the colonels were silent. A mosquito landed on Findlay's cheek and he slapped it away before it could bite. "My men are keen to attack, but they don't really understand what an escalade means. I'm afraid that once they witness the reality of a firestorm, they'll wilt. I can't guarantee anything unless we put a troop of regulars behind them, and then shoot every man that fails to advance."

"That's about the truth of it, I agree, sir," Cass said.

"Unless given a direct order from General Hull, I'm not in the least willing to start shooting our own militiamen," Miller replied.

Again, the room went silent. Hull sat motionless, wondering how he had got saddled with such a poor group of commanders. A frantic pounding on the door made all six men jump in their chairs. Jackson opened the door and put a hand to his forehead when he saw that it was his own man, Sergeant Harris.

"We've captured a man who says there are boatloads of bloody Redcoats on their way to Fort Amherstburg, sir." Harris came to attention and saluted. He saw McArthur and nodded to him but the colonel took no notice.

"How many boatloads and where are they?" Jackson asked.

"My prisoner's out here, sir. Says ten boatloads and a schooner, all packed to the gills."

"Captain Jackson, see this man for yourself and confirm what the sergeant says," Hull ordered.

Jackson closed the door behind him and the discussion continued. Hull demanded to know how the regulars could be expected to attack without knowing for sure if the militia would follow them. The militia colonels had no answer. Jackson re-entered the room and confirmed the prisoner's words. At the same time he handed the general a hand-written note brought by a recently arrived courier from Fort Detroit. With confirmation that British troops were approaching, Hull made his decision.

"Gentlemen, we have Indians pouring down from the north and Redcoats coming up from the south, and we've yet to break through to the Raison for fresh supplies. Attacking this fort is madness, so we should retire to the Maumee River, or at least fall back on Fort Detroit."

Before he could continue, McArthur was on his feet. "It's an outrage that we don't attack the fort, but I can guarantee that my militia will head home if we retreat to the Maumee, sir."

Cass and Findlay nodded in agreement: their men would also desert if Hull retreated to the Maumee.

"So you can guarantee their desertion but not their willingness to fight," Hull yelled. "So be it, we'll fall back to Fort Detroit. Prepare for this action tonight, and collect all the government stores—burn whatever we can't carry."

The three militia colonels stood up, gave him quick salutes, and departed sharply. Hull approached Miller, who was gathering his hat and speaking to Jackson.

Hull interrupted them. "It's kind of sad, but one gun carriage is now finally ready if we wanted to attack the fort." Hull waved the note Jackson had handed him moments before.

"That was very nicely put, sir, desertion versus fighting, but you've made the right decision. What would we have done with the fort had we captured it?" Miller asked and then answered his own question.

"Merely burned it and departed, perhaps. We certainly couldn't have held it."

"We won't hold Fort Detroit either, without supplies," Hull said bitterly. "Immediately on our return, organize one-third of our forces for a breakthrough march to the Raison River. You must bring back those supplies. Use the new gun carriage and take the nine-pounder, then blast the hell out of anyone who gets in your way."

"Our midday meal will be served soon, perhaps we should discuss those plans further before we eat," Miller suggested.

"May I be excused, sir?" Jackson asked. "I'll return in time for lunch with my friend, as discussed. "

Hull nodded his approval and waved his hand to say go. Jackson saluted and marched out of the office into the darkened day's light. Hull watched through the window as he untethered another horse before mounting his own.

Jackson rode straight south to the nearest farmhouse, the extra reins held tight in his right hand. The sky convinced him that at any moment he'd be drenched in a sudden downpour. Reaching his destination, he dismounted and tied the reins of both horses to the veranda railing. In two steps he bounded up and knocked hard on the door. It creaked open and Bill Wagg appeared but did not invite Jackson inside. Instead, he stepped out onto the veranda, with Carson Stone trailing after him.

"The army is heading back to Fort Detroit, gentlemen," Jackson said, then explained that they were to gather their belongings on the wagon and take it to their canoe. Although he'd always known the whereabouts of their furs, Jackson had wanted Wagg and Stone delayed. Now he told them that he'd located the furs in Detroit and they were welcome to them after the exodus from Canada.

Something bothered him about Wagg. He already knew how Stone had deserted from a British ship, and that the man would kill anyone if it suited his purpose. Betrayal was how Stone lived, but Wagg concerned him even more because he couldn't figure out what game the man was playing. Was it really just about furs? Stone must have been terrified to find the British Army landing on Michilimackinac Island; yet their escape had seemed too easy. Perhaps they worked with the British. By the same token, they had risked their lives in canoeing to Detroit with the news of Fort Mackinac's fall, and although it had yielded nothing, Stone had warned him about couriers traveling to the Old Northwest even before war was declared. Jackson was confused by it all and so he looked for answers elsewhere.

"Where's Miss Collins?"

"She grew tired of playing cards and went for a swim. Although, with this sky, I'm sure she's better staying out of the water," Wagg replied.

"You have two hours, gentlemen, and don't be a minute late. Miss Collins will join you there, but until then she's safe with me." Jackson had remounted and was again holding the reins of the extra horse.

"What do you want with her?" Stone demanded, his face betraying an anxiousness that Jackson had not noticed before.

Jackson wheeled the horses about. "Two hours, Stone. Be at your canoe or I will leave you here for the British … to hang." He spurred his own mount into a slow trot and tugged on the reins of the second horse.

Stone stared after him and spit out, "Bastard, I'll show him yet." He spied along the side of the house toward the river, but Jackson was well gone. Mary had to keep her mouth shut. He needed just another day before the furs were in hand and before Wagg had to pay up.

"She doesn't really know anything, so you needn't worry yourself," Wagg assured Stone, moving to the end of the veranda to stand beside him. "You should be happy that you minded your manners with her. We need Jackson on our side until we have those furs. Then you can kill him if you wish, but first let's get what we came for."

Stone smirked. He knew, or at least hoped, the girl was smart.

A distant rumbling across the Detroit River told Mary to swim back to shore. The clouds began flickering with flashes of light, and as she swam for the beach, she heard Jackson calling out.

"May I ask you to lunch with me, Miss Collins?"

266

"I won't come out of the water until you turn those horses around."

"I agree, let's not have the horses getting too excited." Jackson tugged on their reins and he turned his own head away. A few minutes later, he turned back, just as Mary tucked a white blouse into a long blue skirt billowing in the wind.

"I have no proper dress for lunch, but I should at least dry my hair." She began rubbing it vigorously with a towel.

"The wind can dry it as you ride." Jackson handed her the reins to the second horse.

"Do I have a choice?" She sighed.

"No."

Indeed, by the time they arrived at the Baby residence, her hair was almost dry. Escorted to a den, where she found a small mirror, Mary brushed it carefully while she was left alone. When Jackson returned to present her to General Hull and Lieutenant Colonel Miller, every black strand was neatly in place. She glanced at Jackson with a frown, even before he made the introductions.

"No need to be worried, my dear. My daughter will join us in a jiffy," Hull said, to reassure her. "In the meantime, let's begin our luncheon. I'm half starved from all the tension."

On a long table covered in a white linen cloth, roast chicken was served in great platters surrounded by halves of peaches. Steaming potatoes accompanied a type of green vegetable that Mary had never seen before. A glass of red wine was waiting beside each plate, and a fresh set of candles burned at the center of the table.

"Captain Jackson tells us you were at Fort Mackinac. Surely, it must have been frightening with the British and Indians everywhere?" Miller asked.

Mary studied his face, seeing there the sternness of Carson Stone yet without the meanness of spirit. She took a bite of chicken just to give herself time to think of an appropriate answer.

"We left there early in the morning by canoe, so I didn't really see any British. The only Indians I saw were the same ones who sold us the canoe. They were very nice."

Hull's face brightened at this news and he nodded to Jackson, as if to say continue. Jackson put down his knife and fork and with a napkin wiped the corners of his mouth before he spoke.

"Are you sure you saw no Indians? We've been told they were everywhere."

Mary sipped her wine. She realized she was eating the roast chicken too quickly, tearing at the skin when she should be savoring it.

"Their canoes were spread thick all around the beach, but I didn't see many actual Indians. Once my stepfather had paid our money for the canoe, we got out of there fast. I think Mr. Stone was particularly worried that the British might catch him." Mary laughed and the men at the table laughed along with her, then shot one another a glance.

Too quickly Miller jumped in. "How many canoes would you say were on the beach, taking a guess?" It sounded like an order so he continued quickly, "Would you like some more chicken?" He picked up the platter and set it down beside her plate.

Mary picked out a wing and took a bite, staring at each of their faces in turn. Jackson meanwhile leaned forward as if eager to hear her response. These powerful men were hanging on her every word, but she couldn't figure out why. Feeling the sudden pressure, she continued chewing slowly, watching them assess her face and her every word.

"You could hardly see the beach because of the canoes everywhere," she finally replied. "As far as my eyes could see, there were hundreds, probably thousands." Mary had exaggerated, hoping that thus she might curtail the interrogation.

Hull slumped back in his chair, and no one said much after that until Miller excused himself and headed off, sneezing and coughing into another room.

Coffee was served in china cups, and Mary sensed that the meal was ending prematurely. So she added, "Actually, there were only two canoes full of actual Indians—one with five and a bigger one containing twelve, but I assumed they were both there to guard all the other boats."

Hull swallowed and stood up, his chair scraping on the floor, his white napkin still hanging from his shirt collar. The other men stood too, placing their napkins on the table. Although Hull's daughter had still not arrived, Mary guessed her luncheon was over.

"Thank you for joining us, Miss Collins," Hull said.

She and Jackson walked from the residence down to the waterfront, where she asked him why they had wanted to question her.

"You are potentially our most honest observer of the Indians assembled at Fort Mackinac. If you saw five hundred canoes that could hold ten men each, or you saw one thousand boats that could hold five men each, either way five thousand Indians are on their way to kill us."

"Surely you will not just take my word for it," Mary said, now worrying over her exaggeration.

"Miss Collins, where do you go from Detroit?" Jackson changed the subject. "Any plans? What will you do?"

"My stepfather tells me little, but I think we are now off to New York. Westlake Trading has an office there—or at least I think they do." She jumped as lightning cracked directly overhead.

"Would you consider, after the war, Miss Collins ... " he began but stopped mid-sentence and then tried again. "I'll have some land, and my earnings after the war ... after all, I'm an officer. Do you understand?"

She watched Jackson struggle with the words like a man who had forgotten his carefully memorized speech. And she felt a kindness from him, warm and genuine.

"I'm sorry, but I don't. Are you asking me a question?"

"May I see you again when the war is over, Mary? There, that is what I'm trying to say. Is that clear enough?" He sounded just like a soldier.

"Why not?"

"Well, maybe you'll get married or what have you. I don't know really, but I thought it was the proper thing to ask."

"You're a good man, Captain Jackson." She touched the back of his hand. "I think we'll always be friends."

By the time they'd reached the wharf, Jackson had explained where Mary and her two male companions were to go when they reached Fort Detroit. Once they reported to the main gate, they'd be escorted to a small house outside the fort, north of a mill situated on the riverside, where most of the townspeople dwelled. From there, Jackson would arrive to show them the warehouse that stored the Westlake furs.

They stepped onto the ramp that descended to the dock, and Jackson offered her his arm. She slipped her hand under it and headed down to where Wagg and Stone sat waiting for her in the canoe. The waves had not diminished from the early afternoon, and the sky continued to threaten rain.

Almost as an afterthought, Jackson said to her, "I recently met someone else from Westlake Trading. Your stepfather and Stone say they know him, a young man named Jonathan Westlake."

Mary turned back toward him, and he knew in an instant that he had a competitor for her hand. The way her face lit up told him. She said nothing, though, but proceeded to step into the canoe.

Jackson held up his hand to Wagg and Stone before they could speak.

"Miss Collins knows where to go, so I'll see you tomorrow and show you the warehouse. Now get going before the wind gets any worse." The canoe pushed off into the breeze, Wagg and Stone paddling hard for the short ride across to the American side. Mary turned her head, and Jackson waved and with a smile on his face mouthed, "Goodbye."

The clumping of feet on the dock behind him belonged to his sergeant, and Jackson swung round. "Yes, Harris, how can I help you?"

"A message from Lieutenant Colonel Miller, sir." Harris saluted and handed him a sheet of paper.

In the wind, Jackson unfolded the note and gripped it carefully on each side to read Miller's scrawl: *Who did you leave the furs with at Fort Mackinac?* Of course, Jackson thought, that's what was bothering him. How could Wagg leave the island and yet feel assured that his furs were safe if he was not in league with the British? Or perhaps Wagg was simply on the side of whoever could guarantee him his furs at any moment.

In the gusting wind, he swung round to call out, but the canoe was well out of earshot. Wagg would be delayed a little longer, and there would be no furs for him tomorrow. Jackson was marching south with Miller to rescue the supplies, and that would give him time to think.

"Harris, prepare the men to retire to Fort Detroit. We're going home."

"Detroit? I thought we were going to Fort Amherstburg to kill some bloody Redcoats, like."

"Damn your eyes, Harris, you will call me sir. And the next time General Hull needs advice on strategic planning, I will be sure to give him your name. In the meantime, prepare your men to leave. Are we clear?"

"Yes, sir," Harris replied, sounding disappointed. "I only thought …"

Jackson pointed him to the shore. Harris had a way of making him feel miserable.

So on the night of August 7, 1812, the U.S. Army of the Northwest departed Canada in small boats heading for their home shores.

20

• • • • • •

WESTLAKE WAITED for the enemy. Nearby, Parrish leaned behind a tree. Most of the Redcoats could keep still, watching for the enemy across the ravine, but for these two men who had been traveling for months, men used to constant movement, the waiting was frustrating. Westlake couldn't stop fidgeting; he would stand watching, then crouch for a while, only to stand again, holding each position for just a few minutes before repeating the ritual. He would even have lain down, but the ground was still soggy from yesterday's rain.

To make matters worse, Major Adam Muir would allow them to have fires until only seven o'clock in the evening, and then just for cooking. Westlake was more damp than actually cold but knew their ambush had to be concealed. They comprised a hundred and fifty militia and regulars of the 41st Regiment, along with more than twice that number of Indians, amounting to more than four hundred men in total. This made for enough campfires to light up the night sky once darkness was upon them, but dousing them by seven gave them plenty of time to hide their light before the August sunset. To combat the dampness, Westlake used the heat from the glowing embers to warm a covering of small stones.

Parrish was acting like he'd been sent back to hell. Having relieved himself behind his tree, he then realized he had just messed up his hiding spot. So he found another tree, nearer to Westlake, that offered suitable cover and stood still, doing nothing, just waiting. *Next I'll be doing bloody drills again.* "I might as well be back in the regular army," he said to Westlake. In fact, he was already back in the regular army, except that the army didn't know it. As far as Major Muir was concerned, Westlake and Parrish were two good friends sent by Lieutenant Colonel Proctor just to help out.

Westlake watched the sky clouding over again. The temperature was already dropping; perhaps more rain was on the way. For August 9, it was not a promising start to the day. He rubbed his hands vigorously to dispel the morning chill.

When some had suggested they break camp and head back to Fort Amherstburg, deciding that the Americans were not coming, Tecumseh would not listen to them. He insisted that the enemy would have to travel this way to resupply Fort Detroit. His spies had also told him that a mountain of supplies waited at the River Raison for the white general.

"General Hull has tried to break through the river road before and he must try again or else give up Fort Detroit," Tecumseh explained. "Remember Brownstown. They have no choice." He even insisted that if the Redcoats wouldn't help him, he'd wait here with his warriors alone.

Such arguments were compelling and the man's commanding presence convinced Major Muir to hold firm, so the 41st dug in close to Brownstown Creek, occupying the center of the line while the Indians on either side covered their flanks—Tecumseh on the western flank, farthest from the Detroit River. Westlake and Parrish provided liaison between the 41st and the Indians forming the eastern flank, nearest to the river.

Two days previously, Paxinos had led Westlake, Muir, and the entire detachment of the 41st directly to Tecumseh. The Provincial Marine, under the command of Lieutenant Rolette, had landed them near the Brownstown Creek. The small flotilla had reminded Westlake of their attack on Michilimackinac, and he thought back to Captain Roberts and Sergeant Baker. That seemed like ages ago, but it had only been a few weeks.

Westlake had followed Paxinos across a stream to ascend a small grassy hill. At the top of it, sitting motionless near a small fire, all by himself, rested the great bronze warrior. From a distance, with his head tilted to one side, Tecumseh appeared pensive, his arms bent across his chest and his legs folded under him. But on the approach of Muir, he rose and waited to shake his hand, watching the Redcoats and militia march into his camp and spread around him. He nodded in approval. When Paxinos introduced his white friend, Tecumseh's face broke into a broad grin.

"Jonathan Westlake, the young prince, will always be welcome wherever Tecumseh lives. I know the story of your bravery at Prophet's Town, to save a little one before the Long Knives burned my home." Tecumseh continued smiling. "With my heart, I thank you." He touched his chest with his hand in a closed fist. "Paxinos has chosen his friend wisely."

He reached out and took hold of Westlake's shoulder while he shook his hand in a firm grip. Taller than Westlake, when he smiled his oval face seemed to say that he had known him his entire life. There was an immediate sense of community radiating from within this man, as if he had Westlake's best interests at heart. This then was the allure or charm that Westlake had heard so many speak about.

"General Brock sends word to you that he is coming. I'm to take you to meet him, sir," Westlake said.

"First we defeat the Long Knives again. When I meet General Brock, it will be with news of another victory." Tecumseh turned to Major Muir. "Thank you for coming."

"Colonel Proctor sends his respects. Now, how can we assist you?" Muir asked.

The first few drops of rain hit Westlake's face and he shook himself from the memory of that encounter a couple of days ago. He tucked the musket under his arm, to keep the firing pan dry, before huddling closer to his tree. There was still no sign of the enemy.

After introducing Tecumseh to Westlake, Paxinos had been sent far ahead to scout for signs of an advancing enemy, and no one had seen him since. The rain stopped again; perhaps they were going to be lucky and stay dry. Just then, a boy of no more than thirteen ran up from behind. Somehow, Mathew Tucker had managed to join the militia, and Westlake wondered if the boy's mother knew what he was up to.

"Are you Mr. Westlake, sir?"

Westlake grinned, knowing that the boy already knew his name but clearly took great pride in playing at being a soldier.

"Compliments from Major Muir. Be so kind as to find the scout Paxinos and report his sightings forthwith to the major."

"Please tell the major that I'm happy to assist. And, Tucker, you keep your head down, this isn't a game." The boy was off running before Westlake could say any more.

He gestured to Parrish to start forward. Sometimes even officers cannot stand the boredom of waiting for battle, and he supposed that Muir was feeling anxious himself.

They had traveled more than three miles by leapfrogging each other's position, only one man showing himself at a time, when Parrish pointed out something at the edge of a cornfield, almost by the side of the road. Parrish dropped to the ground and crawled forward, his musket raised. Westlake stared at it for a few moments longer but the image didn't move, not enough to even breathe. Through the cornstalks, he ran forward to the cover of the next tree for a better look, just as the stench made him retch. The torso of a man, covered in flies and half eaten away by animals, stood impaled on a stake.

Parrish covered his nose and entered between the rows of corn, but no sooner had he circled behind the corpse than he bolted out of the field again.

"There are two more beyond, just like that mess you can see," he called softly to Westlake. "I nearly ran full into one—and, God, they stink." The thought of dead men rotting on staves made Westlake feel physically ill.

"We put them there to scare the Long Knives," came a voice close by.

"Ahh, crikey, where did you come from?" Parrish sputtered. "You scared the shite out of me!"

"Sshh!" Paxinos held a finger to his lips as he rose up from the hedge beside Parrish. He had been lurking there the entire time while Westlake was peering at the half-eaten corpse.

"You must keep quiet," Paxinos said. "If the enemy is close, they will hear you."

"Well, don't creep up on me like that," Parrish grumbled.

"There's something about you, Parrish." Westlake was laughing. "When you're frightened, you look funny as hell."

"I'm happy I amuse you, sir. This place gives me the willies."

"Move forward now in a circle toward the fort. If they're coming, they must pass this way," Paxinos interrupted.

Followed by Westlake and Parrish, he crept off the road to where the cornfield gave way to forest. They traveled close to the shoreline of the river and then crossed the road again, all the while edging closer to Fort Detroit. Another few miles of cautious movement and suddenly Paxinos slashed his hand downward.

Westlake dropped to the ground instantly. A small advance guard of infantry was not twenty-five yards away from them. The voices sounded familiar, but he was too fearful to look up as the Bluecoats sauntered by, watching the trees. Westlake remained flat, almost gripping the dirt, knowing that they had little time to escape if a larger force was coming behind.

Then the earth began to rumble and the uneven beat of a drummer told Westlake that this was not just another foraging party. He raised his head ever so slightly to see hundreds of Bluecoats proceeding in two ragged columns. A single horse galloped into view from beyond the front of the right column. Westlake ducked his chin to the dirt so fast that the impact jarred his neck. As the first rider passed by, the ground vibrated to the clump of cavalry hooves. When Westlake spotted the artillery, he knew it was time to go.

They slunk away, bellies to the ground, and then ran south to avoid the advance guard, who had stopped to stare at the decomposing corpses. They pressed on farther, sprinting full out so that by the time they reached the 41st Regiment, Westlake was ready to throw up, his sides aching. Parrish fell to his knees beside him, sliding off his musket and pack, and rolled over on to his back, panting. To Westlake's surprise, men were crossing the road to the river by the dozens.

The young boy, Tucker, who had delivered the original message from Muir went scurrying by until Westlake reached out and grabbed him by the collar.

"Where is Major Muir?" Westlake panted. "Take me to him right now."

"We're going home to Fort Amherstburg."

Tucker then saluted and beckoned Westlake on to follow him. The boy spurted ahead and pointed out Muir not twenty paces away. Westlake reached him, still puffing, and even before he spoke Muir demanded to know what had taken him so long.

"Paxinos was heading north, to make a final circle across the river road. We joined him and—"

"That's no excuse for tardiness. You were to report directly back—"

"The enemy is coming, by the hundreds, sir," Westlake interjected. "Your troops are heading the wrong way."

"Boy," Muir called out, "tell your captain to turn everyone around and get them back to their original positions." Tucker darted off again, his head turning every which way in search of his captain.

"The leading enemy scouts are far upstream. The main body may not reach the Brownstown Creek before nightfall," Westlake explained.

"Then perhaps we should move forward somewhat, if we are going to engage the enemy today," Muir replied, thinking out loud.

Paxinos had gone off to find Tecumseh, and now led him back toward Muir. Tecumseh's thinking was obviously the same as he explained his plan to Muir.

"We must march forward three miles until we arrive between two small hills. Paxinos can lead you from there." Tecumseh pointed out the direction.

"Where is this place you mention?" Muir asked as his grumbling men filed past.

"We will fight near an Indian village, a good place for us to defeat the Bluecoats." Tecumseh smiled. "The village of Maguaga."

Lieutenant Colonel James Miller of the U.S. 4th Infantry sneezed and then sneezed again. In an involuntary reaction, he squeezed his knees and his horse took that as a sign to move, bolting ahead until the cursing Miller could rein the beast in. He favored this mount because it responded so quickly to his instructions, but that also meant it could be a little sensitive. Miller patted its neck until the horse calmed down, and somewhat embarrassed, he twisted his neck around to see if anyone had noticed. Captain Jackson, riding ten yards behind him, suppressed a grin and nodded.

"Bloody Jackson never misses anything," Miller mumbled to himself.

He tugged a handkerchief from his left breast pocket and blew his nose, being careful not to make any sudden movements with his legs that the horse might misinterpret. He replaced his handkerchief and, with a forearm, wiped his brow. Almost four o'clock in the afternoon and his fever worsened by the hour. It had started days earlier, on the Canadian side, and now the ague was striking him hard.

Yet despite his illness, he had accomplished much in a short time. Only two days before, General Hull had ordered him to rescue the vital supplies from the River Raison. The following day, after the entire army had slunk back across the river, Miller had put together a force of more than six hundred, composing a third of Hull's effective fighting force. In addition to two hundred and eighty regulars, he handpicked a company from each of the Ohio and Michigan militias, including their cavalry detachments. An artillery detachment accompanied the force, armed with a six-pound cannon and a howitzer. He gave the advance guard to the competent Captain Jackson.

Miller had led two smartly marching columns out of Fort Detroit in the late afternoon of August 8, heading south down the River Road. By the time they had reached the Rouge River, seven miles south of the fort, the sun was setting and he called a halt, ordering Jackson to secure the perimeter.

It was time to dig in and make camp for the night, and Jackson left nothing to chance. "Sergeant Harris, have those men put their backs into it. I want that abatis higher," Jackson ordered. "Do you want us all scalped in the night?"

The next morning's march started well, the columns forming up with the regulars on the road itself and the militia on either side to protect the flanks. The advance guard of U.S. 4th Infantry regulars was far in front of the main body as Miller judged it would hold fast better than untrained militia, although Sergeant Harris had taken the assignment as punishment for his slackness in constructing the breastworks the night before. Miller sneezed again, as they came to an open field, where he saw a chance to ride off the road to the rear of the advance guard.

"Captain Jackson, give my compliments to Lieutenant Markham and let me know how things are coming along at the front."

"My pleasure, sir."

Jackson spurred his horse to a trot and he caught up with Markham just as a putrid smell assailed his nostrils. The horse reared back on its hind legs, sensing the sudden alarm of its rider.

Young Lieutenant Markham wrinkled his nose and wheeled round his brown mare. With a giant white plume attached to his hat, and dressed in a clean blue and gold uniform, he looked every inch the picture-perfect officer. "I wish to report the rotting bodies of some of our dead soldiers around that next bend, sir," he announced in a formal manner. "Unfortunately, they have staves rammed up their … ahmm … into their bodies, so that they are decomposing while standing up, sir." His plume gave a wave as he put his hand to his hat in salute.

"Tell Sergeant Harris to keep going. I don't want the main column bunching up with the advance guard," Jackson ordered. "We'll cut those corpses down on our approach. Keep your eyes open, Mr. Markham." The lieutenant saluted again before galloping off. As Jackson studied each side of the road his stomach muscles tightened, but he assumed it was merely from the stench so he spurred his horse and galloped back to Miller.

Lieutenant Markham brought his horse to stop beside what looked more like a half-eaten scarecrow than a dead comrade. Harris leaned against a tree upwind from the cadavers so only when the wind subsided could he or his men smell the decomposing flesh. He grinned and waved casually to the lieutenant.

"Captain Jackson says that you are to push on, and make sure you keep well ahead of the main column." Markham started to retch but checked himself. "And no slacking, Sergeant, unless you want to end up like these poor fellows."

"Wouldn't think of it, sir … Watch out, you're almost stomping on our old friend, Ranger McCullough, sir."

Markham's horse had edged off the road and the lieutenant saw that under cover of bark, there lay a body bloated and half-eaten by wild animals. "Christ," Markham exclaimed, the corpse almost under foot. He spurred his horse but was too late as the horse's rear hoof crushed the remains of McCullough's chest before galloping off.

"We haven't been down that road yet, sir."

"Keep these men moving, Harris. Enough of your idle chatter."

"Yes, sir, suit yourself, sir."

Westlake estimated that he had advanced three miles to reach the edge of a forested ravine. Just then Paxinos held up a hand signaling they had arrived. Some Redcoats eased partway down the slopping side, where they lifted and sorted logs to cover themselves and waited, again. At the top of the ravine, the Indians were positioned on the far left and far right, hidden in fields of tall corn. Westlake himself was with the militia, on the right of the main body of 41st regulars, and next to the Indians covering their flank to the river. Behind some fallen trees, he met once again the same man who had remained so quiet during Proctor's dinner: Thomas Verchères de Boucherville.

"*Monsieur*, you must fix a twig with a leaf on it to your hat. None of us have uniforms, so otherwise we don't know friend from enemy. Without your twig I might shoot you." De Boucherville pointed to his own hat with its brown twig and he laughed. "So why are you here?"

Westlake was surprised at the question, then realized he was a stranger to these militiamen, who all knew one another's families and minded their own business. The twigs were easy to break but gave Westlake time to think of an answer while he offered one to Parrish and jammed another though a hole in his leather hat.

"The Americans are holding some furs in Detroit—Westlake Trading furs—and I want them back," Westlake lied.

"They'll be in that big warehouse down by the mill." De Boucherville leaned back on his elbows, his gray wool shirt gaping open to halfway down his chest.

"How would *you* know where they keep my furs?"

"Many years I have traded furs here so I know every building in Detroit, and furs are always traded down Trappers Alley. Believe me, I know what I'm talking about." The man beside him nodded as if to confirm this was right.

Westlake wiped a bead of sweat from one side of his forehead. After running back from the American advance, and the subsequent march from Brownstown, he was happy just to sit down behind the log pile and peer out across the ravine.

He hoped de Boucherville wouldn't mind if he asked him the same question. "Why are you here?"

"I have set up a new store in Amherstburg. When the Americans captured Sandwich, they stole everything from everybody, and I don't want them taking my store like the bastards who took his house and all his food." De Boucherville gestured with his thumb to the man lying beside him.

"Jean Baptiste Baby. Pleasure to meet you, *monsieur*." The man reached over de Boucherville and shook Westlake's hand. "Do you know, before this war I even had dinner with my friend William Hull. I know his family well, but after the war began he took my home for his headquarters and everything I had and just said, "Times have changed." I'll kill him now, if I ever get the chance."

Westlake nodded, detecting how hatred breathed inside this camp. He returned to marking time, but he didn't have long to wait. Across the ravine, an officer appeared wearing a startling blue and gold uniform and riding a well-groomed mare. He paused on his own side of the ravine, right at the edge. For a second, Westlake suspected that he recognized the trap, for his horse checked and whirled around as it sensed danger from its rider. The officer looked back across the ravine again, carefully scanning the far side.

The men had been given strict orders not to fire on the advance guard. Major Muir wanted to draw in the main force and get off the first volley before the enemy could fully deploy. But someone could not resist the easy target, and the crack of a musket broke the quiet as a puff of smoke rose over to Westlake's right. Militiaman or Indian, he couldn't tell who had fired, but the advance guard had now met opposition and within minutes the American army would be deployed—out of column and into files. The cannon would be readied and the militia, with cavalry support, would protect their flanks. All hope of ambush was gone.

The officer mounted on the beautiful mare rolled his head back. His hat with its white plume floated to the ground before his body rocked forward. He slumped to one side, tumbling out of the saddle, the reins still clutched in his right hand. The horse stood motionless, waiting for his instructions.

Lieutenant Markham realized he was looking at an ambush the moment he saw the ravine. His sturdy mare stepped to one side, but he twisted it back so that he could get another view. The logs placed conveniently across the edge of the ravine had little patches of red showing in between the cracks. *Stupid Redcoats, Captain Jackson has to see this.*

Markham heard the bang of the musket and briefly felt the pain of a bullet ripping through flesh and bone in his neck. He had only time left for a wince. His assailant had aimed for Markham's lower chest, but the accuracy of the Brown Bess was poor at best and the bullet drifted off target up to his neck. Even at the range of forty yards it was a lucky shot. The ball sped through Markham's neck to the top of his spine, where it ricocheted upward into his brain. He was dead in less than a second.

Sergeant Harris ran forward a few paces, temporarily forgetting his own safety. His feet carried him just far enough out of the woods to see the ravine and then Lieutenant Markham's body hit the ground. Harris dove for the grass, edging backward on his belly, crawling until he was sure he was out of sight. The ravine appeared still until he spotted a patch of red halfway down the hill opposite, between the breastworks. He studied the hill and discovered more red scattered along the top.

From the rear of the advance, Captain Jackson had galloped forward and demanded to know who had fired. Harris waved for him to keep back.

"They've shot dead Lieutenant Markham, sir. The enemy's not forty paces ahead," Harris replied. "Along a ravine edge."

"Have your men hold their ground and return fire immediately. I'll inform Colonel Miller." Jackson galloped off.

The main columns had gained on the advance guard and had heard the bang too. "Lieutenant Markham's been shot, and Sergeant Harris is holding a position on our side of the ravine ahead, sir," Jackson reported to Miller. Their horses stepped around each other.

"Thank you, Captain. Assist where you can, if you please. We'll join you at the double and give them a proper thrashing," Miller declared. Jackson saluted and spurred his horse away.

Behind some large trees that roughly lined the crest of the ravine, Sergeant Harris crept forward. He waved his arm downward as Jackson approached and pointed to Markham's body, where a pool of blood welled out from around the dead lieutenant's head. "The shot came from that direction, although I can't see much there, sir," Harris explained, himself well hidden behind the solid trunk of a maple tree.

"Colonel Miller is bringing up the main column, and there's a dozen men directly behind me. Form them into a perimeter on our right. No panic, though, just like on the parade square, form three ranks."

For a few minutes, Jackson merely observed, taking in the relative positions of the two forces. At the bottom of the ravine, something moved to his left.

"Sergeant Harris, prepare your men to fire on my command, but first rank only. Targets are Indians on the move to your left."

"Make ready," Harris ordered. "Present." Two dozen Bluecoats stood beside him.

Jackson looked back to his men. One soldier's teeth were chattering, so he reached out and gently pushed a finger up under the man's chin, simply to close his mouth. "You'll be fine, young man," he said, with a smile.

"There are your targets." He pointed after a moment. "Just the first rank. Fire!" The muskets banged out, and in the small ravine, the sound was amplified like a crack of lightning.

With their position known, the Indians screamed and returned fire.

"Now the second rank, while they think we're reloading, present. Fire! Third rank, present. Fire!" The muskets spit their lead and an Indian with his face painted red toppled to the ground.

Again the Indians lurched forward, firing individually. Captain Jackson turned back to Harris and his men, ignoring the threat approaching behind him.

"We will hold this ground, gentlemen. No running."

"My men don't run—do we, boys?" Harris grinned and held up a fist. "We're here for the killing, sir."

Another volley of musket fire cracked out from across the ravine. Harris plunged to the ground as bullets struck trees and broke off branches all around him. A soldier of the advance guard keeled over, apparently dead, but with no wound that Harris could see. This time the smoke was directly in front of them while the Indians came charging from their left.

"First rank, make ready," Jackson shouted. The Indians were only yards away but slanting even more to their left, taking cover behind trees and boulders.

"Steady now. Present, fire! Make ready." Jackson felt horse hooves pounding the earth behind him, meaning the cavalry had arrived in front of the columns of Bluecoats that had now swung into line. "Thank God for that. Now swing round the cannon," he mumbled to himself.

Lieutenant Colonel Miller trotted into full view of the enemy, as if out on a leisurely stroll. "Load the cannon with canister, and prepare to fire on my command," Miller ordered. "This will give them something to think about."

On either side of Jackson, the entire ridge filled up with soldiers of the U.S. 4th Infantry. Opposite them, a line of Redcoats, with militia on the flanks, suddenly stood up and fired. At least a hundred muskets split the air with deafening reports that made his heart pound. Men dropped to the ground all around him, crying in pain. Some were clutching their bellies, others their limbs. One man dropped his musket and held an ear cut loose in his hand. He said nothing but stared at Jackson, as if unbelieving of what had happened.

The ravine filled with drifting smoke until Jackson could no longer see clearly over to the British side. Smoky shadows of Indians edged closer to his immediate left. The ragged sound of their musket fire was unceasing and getting much louder.

"God damn!" A random bullet struck Miller in his left forearm. Jackson watched the colonel wince and grit his teeth in pain. "Cannons ready?" Miller yelled.

"Yes, sir," came the reply.

"Fire."

Jackson felt his body shudder at the cannon's boom and watched as Miller's horse reared back, throwing its rider to the ground. To their left, the shrieks of the attacking Indians ended as abruptly as the crash of the cannon, and an odd silence descended on the battlefield.

A single Indian, far in advance of his group, came running through the advance guard. He dove for Miller, his tomahawk raised. Jackson calmly raised his pistol and fired into the man's chest, the warrior tumbling dead to the feet of Miller's horse. Miller now remounted, gripped his bleeding arm, and sneezed. "Oh God, not now." He sneezed again. "Thank you, Captain Jackson. Make ready to charge these Indians to our left. Cavalry will assist you. Cannon ready?"

"Sir." Jackson saluted, his lungs choking on the smell of burnt gunpowder.

"Fire!" Miller shouted, and the cannon roared to life. "Give them a volley, Captain, then thrash them. We've already cleaned away most of them for you."

Jackson commanded, "Fire!" and watched Sergeant Harris squeeze off a round as the musket jerked back into his shoulder. "Make ready," Jackson yelled. The smoke was now thick on both sides of the ravine, trapped between the two small hills, and he quickly wiped his eye with the back of his hand.

"Fix bayonets," Jackson shouted.

His eyes burned from the smoke so he couldn't see more than twenty feet in front of him, just enough to watch Harris fix the bayonet to the end of his musket and then turn back to Porter, grinning like some kind of madman.

"Well, boys, this is what we's been dreaming of," Harris spit. "Let's do some right killing."

Jackson saw Porter laugh, his ragged hair standing on end. Some cavalry had by now moved in behind them. An Indian suddenly charged out of the smoke, and Porter stabbed him in the belly with his bayonet before he had time to react. Harris clubbed the Indian's head from the side for good measure, and the man crumpled to the ground.

"Advance." Jackson drew his sword. His heart was still racing, yet he felt surprisingly calm.

With blasts of canister, the musket volley, and now glimpses of cavalry, the Indians knew it was time to retreat, backing away slowly at first and then at a run. By the time Harris had advanced down the slope, they were in full retreat.

"Come back, you cowards," Harris yelled. "Don't you want to fight me? Frank Harris is here."

But all Jackson could see now was their backs, bouncing through the woods as they fled.

From behind his barricade, Westlake had watched the impeccably dressed officer fall from his horse and seconds later another Bluecoat appear and then disappear just as quickly. "I'm sure that was bloody Harris, the bastard. Parrish, did you see him?" Westlake grabbed Parrish by the shoulder.

Parrish shook his head and said, "Best hold our fire. We'll get our chance at Harris, never fear."

For a few minutes there was no sound. Rain clouds moved across the rays of the sun, and the ravine darkened. The boy messenger, Mathew Tucker, came running by to shout that Major Muir was asking everyone to hold their fire. His request made no difference to the Indians who were protecting their right flank. Once the first bang was heard, they continued their sporadic shooting.

Across the ravine, dozens of muskets exploded. Westlake tensed, waiting for the bullets to reach him. He could see branches falling over to his right and assumed that was where the volley was aimed. Another blast, seconds later, had Westlake gripping the ground. "Christ, did you imagine, Parrish?"

"Never, sir. That crash of muskets scared the hell out me. If I had a hole, I'd crawl in it, so I would."

Westlake dared to put his head up again but only for a second. He looked to his right and this time he saw an Indian fall. Tucker then shouted from behind him, "Major Muir says that the militia right flank may return fire at will."

"Take cover, you little fool," Westlake called out, but the boy darted away.

He heard someone to his right shout, "Make ready, present."

"Well, Parrish, that's you and me." Westlake stood up and looked around briefly for Sergeant Harris. On the order to fire, he pulled the trigger, pointing in the direction of the dead officer's horse. The entire right slope of the ravine filled with smoke, and both men plunged back to the ground. A moment later, the air was split with another deafening blast. Westlake felt the ground tremble.

"Hell's bells, that was cannon shot," Parrish said.

Westlake poked his head up to see a shower of canister ripping through the trees to his right. Some smaller ones broke or tilted sideways, and nearby he saw three Indians fall, holding their bellies.

To his left, in the center of the British line, a body lay across a fallen birch log, its red coat torn to shreds. Other than this one man, the canister seemed to have done little damage.

The ridge of the ravine opposite jumped to life with the enemy. From one end to the other, as far as Westlake could see, blue-coated soldiers of the U.S. Army surged forward. Immediately, every Redcoat in the line rose and fired from Westlake's side. He watched as Bluecoats dropped amid the deafening crash. One man held his eye, screaming, then tumbled dead to the bottom of the hill.

The American cannon blasted again, the sound of it rebounding off the low hills. The valley was entirely filled with smoke and Westlake could not see more then twenty feet ahead. He rubbed his eyes, but that made them burn even worse from the hanging fog. The acrid smell made it hard to breathe. When an order to advance was shouted, he couldn't tell if it was intended for his own side or the other. He turned his head quickly, cocking his ear in the direction of the order. Tucker came running directly up behind him, and Westlake yelled at him again to stay down. Musket fire echoed, and he watched in horror as the boy was knocked off his feet. Westlake scrambled over to him and lifted his head.

"I warned you to stay under cover, Mathew." The boy gripped his chest where the musket ball had entered, and Westlake watched as his little hand filled with blood. "Oh, my God," Westlake said in despair. "Oh, no."

"Am I a goner, then, Mr. Westlake?" the lad asked in his pitchy voice. He inhaled a short whisper of a breath, then stared straight up at Westlake, his body gone limp.

"No, no. My God, Parrish. Look what we've done. Young Tucker is dead."

"What we've done, sir? They shot him, not us," Parrish replied.

"We shoot at them, so they shoot back. We might as well have shot him ourselves, I should've spotted him coming sooner." Westlake laid Tucker's head down and closed his dead eyes with one hand.

"I'm sorry, sir, but that's an odd way of looking at things, if you don't my mind saying." Parrish shrugged.

"Everyone that shoots is responsible for every death that occurs, seems clear enough to me." Westlake crawled back to his hiding place as another blast chipped the fallen tree and the soil around him.

De Boucherville was now bleeding after being hit in the thigh. He ripped off a piece of his shirt and tied it around the wound. "Can you see anything?" he asked.

Westlake shook his head. "Parrish, are they our men?"

Parrish wriggled out from their hiding place. "I can't see any better than you two. Maybe its bloody Harris, and they're trying to outflank us."

The group of militiamen to his right was now firing at figures running past them, skirting the river road. Westlake peered into the smoke. He couldn't tell who they were, though they returned fire. Then the smoke cleared enough for him to see that the militiamen had fired at allied Indians who were now firing back. Westlake ducked for safety under the fallen tree, and to get out of the chaos.

In mid-August, the ravine should have been bright with sunlight, but with the vapor of battle and the black clouds that had moved overhead, it appeared more like the ominous darkness of an early twilight. The first few drops of rain struck the leaves above him and again Westlake tucked the firing pan under his arm.

A bugle then sounded the signal to advance. The firing to his right had ceased, so he glanced to the center and saw that some Redcoats were advancing while others were not. Men who had joined the attack late were retreating, so Westlake assumed they had missed the signal instructions. The Indians protecting the right flank were already in full retreat. Now the center faltered and then collapsed as the men realized that others were edging backward. More chaos followed. The British center fired a final volley, and the Americans replied instantly. Both banks of the ravine were covered in smoke, which worked well to cover the retreating Redcoats.

"What do you want to do?" Parrish asked.

Westlake glanced down at de Boucherville, who was tying another strip of cloth around his leg. "Well?"

"I cannot run on this leg, if that's what you want to know. You lot must go and leave me here."

"Baby, you go, and we will stay here with Thomas," Westlake decided. "Let Major Muir know that we're here."

Baby looked hesitant, not wanting to leave his friend behind.

"We'll be fine, but one of us must get to the major and tell him of our predicament. Only go quickly, while there's still a chance of escape." The rest of the militia on the right was pulling back, and Baby joined them. No one fired on either side, mainly because no one could see a target. Thick yellow and white smoke sat motionless in the ravine, choking each man and burning everyone's eyes until it drifted away.

"Parrish, while we have time, help me haul that branch over our fallen tree." The two men dragged a thick-leaved branch over their hiding place and then threw an extra log on to flatten it down. They crawled back into their cave, and within minutes of Baby leaving, the raindrops turned into a downpour. The smoke melted away and Westlake, through a crack, could see the Americans in discussion. He hoped they would keep debating a while longer, for it was growing darker by the minute.

"Do you wish us to pursue them, sir?" Captain Jackson asked. "There's not a man left standing on the other side. If it's true that Tecumseh himself was on their left, he's now in full flight." Jackson used a hand as cover for his eyes, the rain bouncing off the back of it. "You've won a victory here, sir. Congratulations."

Lieutenant Colonel Miller knew he had a victory, but his body was burning with fever. Where he took the bullet, his arm stung like a thousand bee stings, and he could not stop sneezing. The force he had defeated had been substantial, and he worried that they would return, but all he wanted now was to lie down.

The rain was unceasing and Miller was soaked to the skin. To his fevered mind, pursuing the enemy was out of the question. His orders, to a disappointed Captain Jackson, were to make camp right where they were, at the top of the ridge.

Since his men had thrown their packs down in their rush to the ravine, the Indians had snatched and gone off with them. Miller therefore ordered runners to circle back to Detroit and order up fresh supplies. Inside one of the few tents available he blew his nose and lay down.

Sergeant Harris cursed his orders to patrol the perimeter and then start constructing breastworks. In the rain, he stumbled down the ravine and clawed halfway up the other side. His gang halted when he scratched himself and sat down on a log resting over stack of branches. Though he did little of the work himself, he loathed building defenses just to abandon them the next morning. Except that he had learned their value at Prophet's Town, where the lack of breastworks and trenches had allowed the Indians to charge right through their camp, shooting and hacking away. That meant he had to dig and build; he knew it and he hated it.

In fact, if his thoughts were known, he despised the army and its regulations. Even as a sergeant, he had occasionally thought of running but had no idea what to run to. He had no skills, like a baker or a tinsmith, and was only good at bullying and thieving—and besides, who would join him on the outside? At least the army provided him with a gang ready to do what he ordered, and the war always gave him a chance at pillaging. Having filled his canteen with old Moore's last bottle of wine, he now swung his musket over his shoulder and took a swig before using his sleeve to wipe away a dribble from his chin. What he needed was more opportunity to use his exceptional talents in killing and plundering. Maybe something like that would happen soon, he hoped.

"We should be chasing bloody Redcoats instead of prancing around in the dark. I can't see a damn thing, so let's find some place out of this rain." Harris motioned with his hand for them to move on.

Westlake, Parrish, and de Boucherville had been expecting to be captured, but with Harris gone, they now crept slowly east toward the river, at first crawling through the mud and then, once they had crossed the road, supporting de Boucherville under each arm so that they could walk. By three in the morning they had reached the river, but finding no boats there, they made do with a makeshift log raft that was no more than two paces square.

"We're directly across from the northern tip of Grosse Ile. We have to float the raft straight out and then down the other side of the island toward Amherstburg, where the marine patrols will see us," de Boucherville explained. "The current will want to take us south immediately, so we'll have to fight against it. Once we reach the northern tip, it'll be easy to float down the east side with the current. The hard part is heading straight across."

"It's only a hundred yards across," Westlake said.

"What are you thinking?" Parrish asked.

"You two get on the raft. We have no paddles, so I'll get into the water and kick, holding the raft."

A few yards from the shore, the raft was clearly too heavy for

Westlake to push by himself, and in the current they were losing ground by the second. Parrish took off his coat and then started to take off his boots.

"But you said you can't swim," Westlake said from the water. "You'll drown."

"But I can hold on to the raft and kick as well as you can," Parrish replied as he slid into the water and took hold. The effect was immediate: the raft rose a few inches out of the water and, with two men pushing, it floated easily toward the island. Even in the dark, the outline of the island soon came into view. They had misjudged the end of Grosse Ile by several yards, but it was not long before Westlake found his footing and he and Parrish began walking the raft around the island's northern tip.

"Okay, everybody onto the raft and let the current do its work," de Boucherville urged. Pelting rain caused a thousand white splashes all around them as they turned out to the main channel where the current was running fast. The raft picked up speed, and Grosse Ile drifted by on their way south to the fort. Westlake lay back on the raft, his eyes closed, recalling that his mission was to bring Tecumseh to Brock. Where Tecumseh was now, he had no idea.

"There's a cutter over there—wave your arms and yell." De Boucherville interrupted his doze.

In the breaking dawn light and the pounding rain, Westlake realized they were fortunate that the cutter heard their calls for help. By noon, Thomas de Boucherville, wet to the skin, was back in his own bed at home, blood still seeping from his wound. Westlake meanwhile asked a neighbor to a fetch a doctor. He returned to find Parrish already stretched out on one of two bearskin floor rugs. The rugs were dry, however, and they were as good a place to sleep as any.

21

••••••

GENERAL BROCK FUMED. He had planned for a rapid trip to Fort Amherstburg, but events had conspired against him. There were simply not enough vessels. And then, after arriving at Port Dover, he had lost an entire day waiting to have his boats made lake-worthy. With the news of victory at Fort Mackinac racing through Upper Canada, he could transport but half the five hundred men who had scrambled to join the York Volunteer Militia.

Strange, he thought, that the populace was prepared to defend their homeland yet the legislature of Upper Canada, full of businessmen and barristers, seemed so timid and unable to defend their own interests. If the war was lost, they hoped there would be no harsh American reprisals if they had done nothing offensive ... or so their thinking went.

Still, Brock had made progress: the government had authorized an increase in the size of the militia and given him the money to make it so. That accomplished, he prorogued the legislature and sent the conspiring lot of them home. He would not have to work with them again—at least for the short term.

And advancement was made on another front too. On his trip to Port Dover, he stopped to visit the Six Nations Mohawk reserve. While his reception was cordial, it had not been the overwhelming success he had hoped for. Even with the victory at Fort Mackinac, these Indians chose to commit only sixty warriors for his battle with the Americans, not much but the Mohawks had clearly chosen a side and it was his. He considered this a victory in its own way.

Now he paced his tent on the northern shore of Lake Erie, considering what Hull could be up to. Perhaps he'd broken through Tecumseh's blockade and been resupplied; or perhaps Hull had built his gun carriages and his cannons had blasted holes in the walls of Fort

Amherstburg. At least it would be one hell of a fight, for Proctor might not be bold but he would go down fighting. On the other hand, if Tecumseh maintained his blockade, Hull could not hold out for much longer. Sooner or later he'd have to get more supplies or face retreat, perhaps even surrender. "But first I have to get there before I can accomplish anything," he reminded himself out loud.

"Captain Nelles, does Simpson have our boats ready yet?" Brock called out through his tent door.

"The *Nancy* is already loaded, sir," Nelles replied. "The rest of the boats but one have been repaired and caulked and their men are standing by to break camp. But I'm afraid some foul weather's rolling in."

"Signal Captain Mackintosh to get the *Nancy* underway. We depart forthwith," Brock ordered. "And tell Ensign Simpson to ready my boat, but don't forget that last one. Finish its repairs, and it can bring up the rear. We need as many men at Fort Amherstburg as we can possibly float."

Ensign Simpson angrily called out the names of men who would serve as oarsmen in the major general's boat. The truth was that he was miserable with himself. Along with Sergeant Stamp and Private Burns, he'd searched everywhere for suitable vessels to transport Brock and his men to Amherstburg, but they could find only nine old cutters that leaked. The boats should have been scrapped, but he had no option, so the men began their repairs. Gone were Simpson's days of joking and bravado: he had let Brock down and for that he would never forgive himself. Thank God, he still had the *Nancy*.

Brock arrived on the wharf dressed in his cloak and uniform, and the scowl on his commander's face made Simpson shudder. Nelles took the boat behind. The wind was up and the waves rising as the sky darkened; it was going to be a nasty pull against the current.

Brock's boat pushed off from the wharf while the *Nancy* made full sail for Long Point. She stopped abruptly only a short time later. Loaded with provisions and men, the schooner sat deep in the water and ground to a halt on a sandbar that extended far out from the shore.

It was Simpson himself who organized the ropes attached to every boat that eventually pulled the *Nancy* free. The men were exhausted after the effort, but no one complained.

"That was a job well done, Mr. Simpson. Good show." Brock had watched and nodded in admiration.

"Sir," was all Simpson replied, but the men had heard Brock's comment and that was enough. Simpson may have had difficulties securing enough boats, but that was now behind them. He felt relieved. He had helped free the *Nancy* and for that he was pardoned, redeemed by performance. Everyone pulled a little harder, at least until it started to rain. Great sheets of it swept across Lake Erie, driving the little flotilla shoreward. Not wishing to be caught on a lee shore, the *Nancy* had already dropped anchor well out in the lake.

"Put in at Port Talbot. We've no choice," Brock ordered as raindrops dimpled the lake around them.

The boat turned and headed to shore when a jarring halt threw everyone forward. Simpson apologized for falling against the man next to him. "What's the problem, Sergeant Stamp?"

Stamp leaned over the side of the boat, pellets of rain bouncing off his back. "We've hauled up on large flat rock, I'm afraid. What should we do, sir?"

Simpson shook his head. Every problem possible was finding him and all in front of General Brock. They sat in the rain without moving. One man kept bailing, and Simpson wondered if the water inside the boat came from the lake or from the sky. Before Simpson could respond to Stamp, Brock had his cloak off and was over the side, in the water in full uniform.

"Gentlemen, I'm going to need some assistance."

Simpson was stunned, along with everyone else.

"Now! If you would be so kind," Brock ordered. Their trance broken, the men heaved themselves over the sides and into the water.

Simpson leapt into the water and put his shoulder to the stern. "Heave!" he ordered. "Well, I did not mean you, sir."

Brock grinned and jammed his shoulder to the stern for the first push. The boat inched forward. "And again," Brock shouted. Everyone heaved and the empty boat scraped its way off the rock. They piled back in, clambering quickly over the sides.

"Seems the vessel is much lighter without me in it." Brock laughed at his own joke. "This calls for a drink, I say." He opened a small liquor case. "Do me the honor, Sergeant Stamp, and share this among the men. Cheers, gentlemen, we will win this war one way or the other."

Warmed by the rum and their general's appreciation of their efforts, they pulled for shore, and that night the story spread to the other boats. The supreme commander had jumped into the water in full uniform to help the men push a boat off a rock and then followed it up by giving every man a drink. Ensign Simpson repeated the story half a dozen times to the other officers, and overheard Sergeant Stamp do the same with the sergeants. "It was me he asked to pass out the rum," Stamp insisted. The episode was something to tell his grandchildren, for Brock rated next to God.

The following morning the waves of shallow Lake Erie pounded the coastline, and it looked to Simpson that they might lose another entire day, but soon the wind subsided enough for them to give the lake a try. Rain continued to pour, and in the open boat he was soon soaked through to the skin. They had gone only twelve miles before the strength of the storm forced them to again put into shore.

"I'm sorry, sir," Simpson shouted above the thunder. "It's not going as I had hoped."

"Not your fault, Mr. Simpson, not your fault at all. Get the tents up quickly, though, before we all drown," Brock ordered.

The next morning, the weather was no better: the rain torrential, the wind and waves hammering the shore. Summoned to Brock's tent, Simpson took along Sergeant Stamp. Soon after their arrival, Captain Nelles put his head through the tent door, water dripping from his face. "Sir, you called."

"Find me a damned horse. Rain or no rain, I'm riding the rest of the way," Brock stretched an arm to pull on a black Hessian boot. "Tell anyone else that can find a horse they're welcome to accompany me, but I don't plan to stop until I'm at the fort. The convoy can proceed in haste once the weather clears."

"There's a farm a quarter-mile back, sir, so we can check there." Nelles motioned with his head for Simpson to follow him.

An hour later the men returned with four horses saddled and ready to go. In seconds they were off, splashing through the mud and rain. Simpson was happy for the chance to sneak off with the farmer's wife for a few quick mouthfuls of eggs and ham while Nelles had examined the horses. Remembering the magical appearance of lunch provided by Jonathan Westlake, he had under his jacket a warm loaf of fresh bread too. He smiled, feeling its heat on his belly as they galloped toward Fort Amherstburg.

Captain Jackson loved being a soldier, but he detested filth. The rain left the ground soggy, and soon all the men, including officers, were mud-spattered. His boots and trousers were now sopping wet and covered in dirt. From his log perch, high at the top of the ravine, he brushed a mucky leaf from the sleeve of his jacket. His thoughts drifted back to the opening gunshot of the engagement.

Jackson had been prepared for battle, yet that first bang of the musket always shocked him. The unexpected crack in the air signaled that men would once again deliberately set out to kill each other. Why that would surprise him, he didn't know, especially since he trained soldiers to do this very thing. His men had responded with speed, dropping their packs, advancing on the double, and taking with them only weapons and ammunition. Each man acted in accordance with his training and Jackson was proud.

However, the Indians had stolen every abandoned pack, and now with no tents and no provisions, Miller's entire force of more than six hundred men was forced to spend the night in the open air, in the rain, without food. In the chill of a damp morning breeze, cold and hungry, men everywhere were sneezing and coughing, their morale deteriorating fast. Jackson overheard the injured, crying quietly to themselves, and it still jarred him when the odd man let out a scream.

He had counted the casualties from the previous day's battle, men he knew personally: eighteen dead and sixty-four wounded. One corpse looked unrecognizable, with half its face blown away. He rolled the man over and saw, from the other half, that this was a man whose wife he knew was expecting their first child. And so it went on, man after man, each with his own family story that was forever ended.

 Of the British, who had vacated the field, he counted only six dead, plus four wounded men that he had captured. He did not know any of their names, of course, and today he was not in a mood to care. The Indians had somehow managed to carry away many of their dead and wounded, so he had no accurate numbers to report for them. That meant casualties on the American side of eighty-two, and on the British side only ten—plus an unknown number of Indians. *Not exactly a stunning victory for the good guys,* he thought.

Miller's couriers returned by boat the following morning bringing with them a barrel of pork, two barrels of flour, and some whiskey. Jackson's men had found potatoes growing nearby, and when cooked in the grease of the pork, they made for a tasty treat. They gulped down their food as if they had not eaten in a week, so that all these new provisions were consumed in one sitting.

The open boats had departed with the wounded, but there was no word as yet on replacements. Now it was well after midday and Jackson sat waiting on a log in the rain. Sergeant Harris approached casually, as if he was just passing by, but Jackson suspected he must want something important because Harris addressed him only on rare occasions. Harris surveyed the ravine, careful not to make eye contact.

"Are we going on then, Captain?" he asked nonchalantly. Water dripped from his hat on to his shoulder and Jackson watched it fall to the ground. Harris stood in one of a thousand eddying rivulets running from the top of the hill to the gully at the bottom of the ravine. His uniform was soaked and his boots were waterlogged, one of them coming apart at the seams so that a couple of toes were showing. Sloppy and unkempt, like every other man in this victorious force, nevertheless he pressed to move forward and engage the enemy. Jackson didn't like Harris, but he guessed that even ruffians had their better points.

In fact, Harris's small troop had been badgering their sergeant all morning to get moving, anything rather than just sitting there in the rain. They were anxious to get dry and the only way they could do that was to get to the River Raison. So Sergeant Harris was their reluctant emissary, sent to ask a simple question of their captain. Harris kicked at a loose stone with his good boot, hoping for Jackson's reply.

"We're waiting for word from on high. We need supplies and reinforcements, a tent or two might be a help." Jackson tilted his head and looked skyward, searching for a break in the solid grey clouds.

"But we're the same distance from the Raison as we are from Detroit. Why not march forward, now that the Brits are beaten, sir?" Harris asked. "The scouts have seen no one ahead. We could reach our supplies in a day or two."

Jackson had asked the same question to Miller. Why not push on and take advantage of their victory? The answers were not convincing.

"What if the British have laid another ambush? If they get behind us, we'll be cut off without any supplies. I'd have to surrender the entire force," Miller replied.

Jackson was for smashing their way through, using cannon, muskets, and sheer force of numbers, but Miller just groaned and rolled over on his cot. Jackson persisted and asked for the chance to make a breakthrough on his own. He gave up when he realized that the feverish Miller had gone to sleep.

Late the same evening, a courier stumbled through the breastworks from Fort Detroit. First lost in the dark and now close to exhaustion, Miller allowed the man to sit down while giving his report. He wiped mud off his chin with fingers, leaving filthy streaks on his face. Jackson sneezed and wondered if this courier had crawled all the way from Detroit.

General Hull's orders were that if the force had not yet moved to within striking distance of the River Raison, they were to return to the fort. No more supplies or reinforcements would be coming. Miller therefore gave the order to break camp and return down the river road. Jackson heard the men grumble, but most were happy that at least they were moving.

"I don't like this idea of always retreating," Harris said to his men a little too loudly so that Captain Jackson could not help but overhear.

"We beat the British in Sandwich and now here at Maguaga, but we always retreat," Porter added.

Jackson felt much the same way but could not let such insubordination pass. "You have your orders, Sergeant Harris. Stop the complaining and let's go home. Perhaps you'd like to do one final patrol around the perimeter?"

The following day, in the afternoon, Jackson and his dejected force straggled into a rain-drenched Fort Detroit. A long march under dire conditions left many men too ill to look after themselves. Jackson himself was shivering and hoped he wasn't catching Miller's cold. Even as they passed through the main gates, the rain whipped up again as the weather turned on them for a final lashing.

He watched Harris drop from exhaustion in the first dry place he could find. The muck had soaked and rotted away the threads in his well-worn boots so that now his toes stuck out at the end of both boots each time he took a step.

Lieutenant Colonel Miller was carried directly to the surgeon for treatment of his wounds. Jackson helped him down from his horse and assigned two men to assist him. With Miller's fever raging, Jackson understood why a trek to the Raison River was unappealing.

Jackson himself had a different agenda. While he was thoroughly unhappy about the retreat, he now had one thing on his mind: a good hot bath. After an hour of soaking in a hot tub of water, he'd shave and then take a short nap. He would subsequently rise to eat some hot rabbit pie, then put on his dress uniform and pay an evening house call on young Mary Collins—and her stepfather, whose name he could not quite remember.

When Westlake awoke, he was surprised to see a crowd of men in the room, though Parrish was gone from his side. A little man with a half-moon scar on his cheek and a shining bald head was washing his bloody hands in a basin. His white apron was stained with blood and Westlake assumed he was a doctor. Someone had built a crackling fire so that the room seemed too warm. The patter of rain on the roof reminded Westlake of being soaked when he first entered the cabin. He gave a shiver in the heat, nonetheless.

"Will Thomas recover the full use of his leg?" Westlake rubbed his eyes and yawned. The little man turned to see who had asked the question.

"And you're Jonathan Westlake, I understand?"

Westlake nodded.

"Well, it's lucky you and your friend carried him back before that wound got infected." He tossed Westlake a musket ball. "That's what I picked out of the gash, but some fragments remain that were impossible for me to reach without carving up even more of his leg. I'm worried the puncture may still become infected."

"Shawnee medicine will heal him," said someone from the corner of the room.

Westlake stood up and was astonished to see a familiar figure.

"Tecumseh, I thought I'd have to go back to find you. General Brock may have already arrived at Fort Amherstburg."

"I have sent Paxinos to an Indian woman who will make a cake for the wound," Tecumseh said. "My friend Thomas will be fine and in a few days his leg will heal."

Parrish came through the door just then with a bundle of dry firewood, although where he got it Westlake had no idea. Without being asked, Parrish explained, "From the barn next door," meaning he stole it.

Westlake walked over to de Boucherville's bedside as the wounded man held up his hand. Westlake held it in his grip. "You'll get well again." There was a rolled-up blanket at the foot of the bed, and Westlake pulled it up to just under de Boucherville's chin.

"The general has not arrived," Tecumseh continued. "I will be back in two days. For now the Long Knives have halted their expedition at Maguaga."

"I assure you that General Brock will come. Where will I find you if you don't come back in time?" Westlake asked.

"We harass their army every step. Do not come to find me. Stay.

Take care of my friend Thomas." Tecumseh waved goodbye. "I will see you in two days."

Late that afternoon, Paxinos arrived back with the cake dressing for de Boucherville's leg. The rain had diminished to a drizzle and the fire was burning low, just enough to keep out the damp. Westlake watched Paxinos gently apply the poultice to de Boucherville's wound and then bind it with a clean white cloth. De Boucherville smiled his thanks but did not speak.

"I have seen this work many times. You will be running soon," Paxinos joked. De Boucherville finally closed his eyes.

"Let's eat," Westlake said. "Apparently we're in the company of a kindly storekeeper who has helped many of his neighbors through difficult times. Look at the food they keep bringing us." On the table were peaches and pears, carrots and corn, pies of pork and rabbit, along with basins of cooked potatoes.

"I love the smell of that roast pork," Parrish remarked. "Can I fetch you something, Thomas?" But de Boucherville was already asleep, so Parrish shrugged and pulled a chair up to the table.

The two days went by quickly and the rain finally stopped. The skies cleared to reveal they could still be blue. Westlake bathed in the river, washed his clothes, and ordered Parrish to do the same.

"But why, since it seems like forever that I've been in the rain?" Parrish asked.

"Because both you and your clothes stink. If you march with me, you're not going to stink."

When the second day came, it was almost midnight before Tecumseh returned. De Boucherville's door was barely open before he announced, "Your general has arrived. The Long Knives have returned to Fort Detroit. They did not break through to the Raison."

"Let's go then. I wouldn't like to keep our general waiting. You can tell him yourself about the American retreat," Westlake said. Paxinos rose with him.

Parrish stayed with de Boucherville, which suited him fine. The less time he spent in the company of officers, the better.

Westlake, Paxinos, and Tecumseh marched to the front gates of Fort Amherstburg, where the guard opened them after Westlake asked for Brock. Once inside, it was a subdued Ensign Simpson who came out to meet them. He said nothing but nodded to Tecumseh in recognition and then turned to head along the same path to the building where Westlake had first met Proctor.

A warm August breeze caressed Westlake's face and he stared skyward. The northern sky was brilliant. On August 13, 1812, the Milky Way gave off a strange luminosity, as if some spirit had turned up its brightness for the occasion. Those midnight stars lit the way to headquarters.

The party reached the main doors, and Simpson nodded to Westlake and Paxinos as if to say, "Wait out here." But Tecumseh said, "They come with me."

The group entered the hall, and Westlake turned to the waiting room where he and Parrish had waited for Proctor. Tecumseh started to protest, but Westlake held up his hand.

"It's fine," he said. "You should have your time alone with him."

The door across the hall opened and Tecumseh entered the room, trailed by Simpson. Westlake heard Brock speak first: "The Gracious King from across the water offers his greetings, as do I, to the famous warrior, Tecumseh." The door closed.

Westlake looked around the plain waiting room. Chairs were organized in a semicircle around an unlit fireplace while straight-back chairs with no cushions were placed at a few small tables arranged outside the semicircle. The floor was somewhat uneven, and he sat down in a chair that tilted.

Paxinos remained standing. "What will they talk about in there?"

Westlake was pondering the same question. He was half wishing that he'd stayed with Tecumseh so that he could listen to them talk. Whatever they spoke about, however, it wouldn't be idle chatter. They would not discuss the weather, unless to understand its impact on the war. Maybe they'd talk about Tecumseh's concept of limited siege. Soldiers could come and go from Fort Detroit, but no supplies would get through from the south. Surely Tecumseh would describe the victory

at Brownstown and the battle at Maguaga, or perhaps they would deliberate on what to do next.

"I don't know," Westlake replied. "Whatever it is, something
important will happen. The world will then change. That's what men
like them do." It reminded him of why he was so happy after he left
school, thinking back to the time before his first great trek on behalf
of his father. He wanted to make a difference, to do something signif-
icant, so that his life would have meaning. Mary's face jumped
unbidden into his mind.

"Tecumseh has told the tribes how you saved that boy at Prophet's
Town," Paxinos blurted.

"What made you think of that? Why would he say it when *you*
saved the boy?"

"We saved him together. I never told you, but that boy was his
nephew." Paxinos raised his eyebrows twice with a grin. "All the tribes
now know your name. You need only say it and you will be safe."

Westlake went to speak and decided enough had been said. He
needed time to think of his plan to find Mary.

An hour passed, the door opened, and Tecumseh appeared striding
across the hall and into the large waiting room. Westlake stood up and
stepped around from behind the small table.

"We can win with this general!" Tecumseh stretched out his arms
to slap Paxinos on each shoulder. "*This is a man.* " He clenched
Westlake's hand hard. "He calls his officers to meet now. Come, you
will be alongside me."

Proctor was seated beside Brock as they entered the room and he
gave Westlake a curt nod. Lieutenant Colonel John Macdonell and
Major Glegg, two of Brock's senior officers, were seated at the far end
of the dining-room table with a man whom Westlake had never met.
Brock stood up when Tecumseh, Westlake, and Paxinos appeared.

"Welcome back," Brock said. "I see that you have found my friend
Mr. Westlake for me."

"Wherever Tecumseh travels, Jonathan Westlake and Paxinos are
welcome."

"I understand that you know these young men too." Brock turned to Proctor.

"We had dinner together, and it seems there are very few men of consequence that are not acquainted with Mr. Westlake, sir," Proctor replied with a note of condescension in his voice.

"I don't know everyone here, sir." Westlake indicated a man at the end of the table.

"Ah, Colonel Robert Nichol is our new quartermaster general of the militia." Nichol came and clasped hands briefly, then went back to his chair. Captain Nelles hurried in late and shook hands with everyone, with a special greeting to Westlake. Proctor shook his head, bemused.

After calling the meeting to order, Brock explained how the Americans outnumbered them greatly. From the secret notes seized on the ship *Cayuga*, he assessed the enemy strength as approximately twenty-two hundred men while the force at his own disposal was barely thirteen hundred.

However, he reminded them that judging from the confidential papers captured at the Battle of Brownstown Creek, they were facing a demoralized army. Rumors of plots and petitions against General Hull had been substantiated in correspondence issuing from the general himself. Captain Moore had confirmed this from the arguments he had overheard between the four colonels.

The question Brock had for them now was what were they to do next: attack Detroit or not? He went around the table for the opinion of every officer in turn. They were outnumbered and pitted against a fortified position, so they each urged caution—except for Nichol, who pressed for an attack. Tecumseh was adamant as well; attacking Detroit immediately was their only option. Could the artillery be moved in time was his only question. Proctor, who was himself against crossing the Detroit River, nevertheless replied that his gun carriages were ready as ordered. Brock asked if they could think of anything to be gained by waiting further. There was no response.

Westlake studied each man for a sign as to what they were really thinking. They had each made their case either for or against attacking Fort Detroit and now, with nothing more to be said, they waited for Brock's decision. There was a long, silent pause in the room. To Westlake, the world seemed to hold its breath.

"Mr. Proctor, we need those gun carriages moving north tonight. I want a battery built directly across from Fort Detroit, near that Baby residence. Do the job as quietly as you can. I do not wish to tip our hand too early."

"Too early for what, sir?" Proctor shifted in his chair.

Brock ignored his question. "Mr. Glegg and Mr. Macdonell, I'm going to need a letter drafted to General Hull, and you must call up all available militia tonight."

Now it was not just Proctor shifting in his chair; even Tecumseh leaned forward over the table. Westlake sat as if frozen and found that he really had stopped breathing. When Brock stood up, everyone else stood with him, whereupon Westlake inhaled a single long breath.

"I've listened and taken into consideration your views, for which I thank you. Instead of any further advice, I entreat you to give me your hearty support. I have decided to invade the United States. We'll cross the river and seize Fort Detroit."

22

· · · · · ·

REVENGE NOW DROVE George Moore as he remembered the smell inside the smoldering ruin of his house. His artillery consisted of two mortars, two long twelve-pounders, and one long eighteen-pounder. A curtain of young oak trees concealed the battery's construction in front of the Baby farmhouse, halfway between the residence itself and the Detroit River. The original Baby home was a small wooden building that stood somewhat to the left and also helped hide the battery from peering eyes over in Fort Detroit. In blazing sunshine, Moore waved an encouraging hand to his small detachment as the creaking ropes of the gyn lowered the last cannon onto its mount.

"Clear the gyn away now and prepare to load," Moore instructed. "I want to be ready to open fire as soon as we cut down those oaks." Men trained to use artillery were in short supply, and this battery was simply intended to harass the enemy. Breaching the walls of the fort would fall to the more experienced artillerymen in the main attacking force under Lieutenant Colonel Proctor. "And that little building has to go," Moore pointed. "That's the one ... tear the damn thing down."

Two riders approached from the south, and Moore squinted to see that they were coming on hard. A long message from Proctor, Moore guessed. He limped toward the cannons, surprised to see that the riders were his nephew and Parrish.

"Seems they're short of artillerymen, Captain. Can you aim these beasts?" Westlake chided from his horse.

"Trial and error, young man, trial and error. Everyone has to pitch in, eh. I've done this type of thing before—long ago, mind you."

"Orders from Colonel Proctor, commence firing at four o'clock, but only if Officers Glegg and Macdonell are back from the other side." Westlake dismounted and handed his uncle Proctor's note. "I heard General Brock has asked the Americans to surrender."

"I hope they don't until we can get off a few shots at them. It'll feel good to get some payback after those bastards burned down my house." Moore slapped one of the cannons and felt the steel's warmth from the sun. "Put your horses in the barn behind the main house. That's where they kept me prisoner."

The men maneuvered the tripod of the gyn out of the way. To Moore, cutting down the young oaks did not appear too great a task, but the wooden building was sturdy enough to give them problems. He watched Westlake give his reins to Parrish and then stare across the river toward the farms located there. A look of panic came over his nephew's face.

Westlake glanced at the battery, then back to the farms, and back to the cannons. "Uncle, that's Danny Lapointe's farm. You have to fire directly over top of it." Westlake pointed over the water to the farm immediate opposite. "I need to warn Danny now before it's too late."

"You can't do that. What if we open fire and you're still there? We could kill you."

"That's exactly why I have to try. You won't get it perfect every time, so the first shot that goes astray could kill the Lapointes."

"What about your orders to assist us? Besides, American patrols are going to see you coming across the river."

"Your men will have to remove that building without us. I need a boat, Uncle. Danny would do it for me." Westlake's jaw was set and his body strained like a horse ready to bolt.

The passion in his words told Moore that there was no stopping his nephew. "All the boats around have been commandeered for the invasion, but you'll find an old rowboat in the barn—or at least it was when I was laid up in there."

"Thank you, Captain." With a mock salute Westlake was off, running to rejoin Parrish.

"Remember, four o'clock—and it's almost three now!" Moore shouted after him and considered how he would tell his sister, Elizabeth, that he bombed her son to death on the sunny afternoon of August 15. He watched Westlake speeding away, waving his hand behind his head to say goodbye. "Young fool," Moore said to no one. "A good lad but, my God, he is stubborn, just like Elizabeth."

They reached the midpoint of the river and there switched tasks, with Parrish bailing and Westlake rowing. Their old boat was sinking faster than they could bail. The more water that got in, the slower they traveled. The afternoon sun blistered, and by the time they reached the American side of the river, not only was the boat sinking but they were both exhausted. They rolled over the sides of the craft onto the sandy beach and lay there flat on their backs to catch their breath. The last voice that Westlake expected to hear that afternoon was the one that now broke the silence.

"Well, lookee what we's found. Trying to invade America all by yourselves? Stupid assholes." Sergeant Harris kicked Westlake hard in the ribs. "Get on your feet. What are you doing here? And where is the other one that looks like him?" He pointed his musket to Parrish. The three men with Harris turned back to scan the river for Ned.

Westlake got up slowly, holding his side, and Parrish followed. Harris had Porter, Trimble, and Haggard with him, all with loaded muskets jammed against their shoulders and aimed at their two captives. Four against two: difficult odds but not impossible. Westlake glanced at Parrish, and from that one look Parrish knew what he was thinking.

"Point your muskets away. Those things go off too easy. What are you doing here?" Westlake asked in return. With a nod from Harris, Porter hammered Westlake in the back of the knee with the butt of his musket. Westlake crumpled to the ground, where Porter kicked him again in the ribs. When Westlake groaned, Parrish made to move, but Trimble clubbed him in the back of the head. Parrish staggered but remained standing.

"You really don't get it, do you? There's a war on, and I can kill you if I want," Harris hissed between his front teeth as he hung over Westlake. He was perspiring from the day's heat, and drops of sweat fell off his nose onto Westlake's face. "Now answer my question, with no more lip, or I'll shoot you right here."

Westlake rolled over on the sand, felt the back of his knee and winced. It pained but nothing was broken. Porter smiled down on him, happy to see he was hurt. "We're here to visit friends." Wary of another blow, Westlake stayed on the ground.

"A bullshit story if I ever heard one." Harris raised his musket and looked behind them, back to the boat. "So where is your brother— what's his name, Walt or something?"

"He's dead. I'm Walt. It was Ned that died."

"Ned's dead? That rhymes, fellas, Ned's dead." Harris laughed and his patrol laughed with him, but he could see that Parrish was angry and so trained his musket on him. "You know, I remember this story now." Harris held up his finger as if to show it had just dawned on him. "Our friend Carson Stone told me about killing Ned by accident, and then you two murdering his four men, nasty bastards that you are. Did you know that one of them was his own brother?"

Neither Westlake nor Parrish moved or spoke. "I think there could be some money in their skins, boys. Stone would repay us kindly if he could kill these two. Says he's coming into a packet once he gets those furs. I says we take them to Stone."

So Carson Stone was in Detroit, and to Westlake that meant Wagg and Mary were probably here with him. It sounded like he didn't yet have the last cache of furs, which meant there was still time. But that time was running out because he knew that it was almost four o'clock.

"Let's take these scum to Stone and watch him punish them for killing his brother," Porter spit. "I need some extra money anyway. Get up, you." With the barrel of his musket, Porter jabbed Westlake in the back to make him move.

There was no hope for them unless Westlake got the patrol distracted. When they met Stone, Westlake was sure they would soon die, which left the Lapointe family still in danger. Time for action was disappearing fast.

"What time is it, Parrish?" Westlake got to his feet and took a first step but not fast enough for Harris. Westlake felt the butt end of a musket to his back, shoving him forward. At the same second, the battery opened fire across the river. The sand trembled, and with just flat water between the cannon blast and their ears, the reverberation shook them physically.

Everyone instinctively hunched away from the blast. Everyone except Westlake, who stumbled straight into Trimble, drew the knife from the sheath strapped to his leg, and stabbed it hard up under the man's ribs and into his heart. He was pulling his knife out again before the others realized what he'd done. Parrish lunged at Porter but lost his footing on a sandy rock and fell flat just as Harris raised his musket and pulled the trigger. Westlake saw Porter take the full blast in his stomach, where Parrish's head had been a split second before. Porter's eyes widened at Harris in disbelief, then gaped at his own blood as it oozed red between the fingers now clutching his stomach.

Westlake threw Trimble to one side and instead seized Haggard from behind, pressing the knife against the man's neck. "Don't move," he hollered.

For Parrish it was too late. Despite the shock of killing one of his own men, Harris had raised the butt end of his musket and cracked Parrish in the head while he still lay face down. Harris kicked Parrish savagely in the side, then raised his musket to stave in the back of his skull.

Westlake ripped the knife hard across Haggard's jugular, slitting his neck open wide, and then in one fluid motion he pulled his arm back and let fly the weapon. It tumbled once in the air before slicing into Harris's chest, embedding itself deep into his left lung. Westlake watched the shock appear in Harris's eyes.

Harris held the musket above his head for a second longer, then let it fall to the sand. He dropped to his knees, pulling at the knife in his chest with both hands, not willing to give in to death, but his strength was gone. "I always knew you's was bad news," he spit out. His eyes closed only to open again and take one last spiteful squint at Westlake. Then he fell back dead, his eyes open.

"Walter," Westlake called out, but Parrish lay face down in the sand and did not answer. "Walter, answer me, for God's sake." Westlake pulled Parrish by the shoulder until his body rolled over. A wave had covered him in wet sand and Westlake desperately felt for a heartbeat.

Parrish suddenly groaned, with his eyes still closed. "I must've hit my head." He felt the back of his skull and found a large egg-sized bump.

"You scared the hell out of me. I thought you were dead."

Parrish opened his eyes to see Westlake kneeling beside him. He started to laugh, but his head ached too much and he stopped. "Scared you, did I?" He slowly sat up and gazed around at the four corpses while rubbing the back of his head.

"Crikey, did you kill 'em all?"

Westlake helped him to his feet. "I'll tell you later. We're out of time and we still have to warn Danny. Can you walk?" Westlake looked down at his hands and frowned, "Christ, I'm shaking."

Parrish tried a few unsure steps, using Westlake for support. Westlake reached down and drew his knife out of Harris's dead body, wiping the blade in the sand. Parrish picked up their muskets from beside Haggard's corpse.

"I didn't think Haggard was such a bad fellow," he remarked.

"He wasn't, and neither was Trimble—just on the opposite side to us."

"I'm happy that other bastard got what he deserved," Parrish growled as they passed by Harris. His eyes were still open and a seagull had landed on his chest.

Up the embankment they stumbled, arm in arm, and after a few minutes, Parrish began to heave. "Sorry, that bash in the head has made me sick to my stomach."

"Harris always made me sick too." But this time Westlake didn't laugh at his own joke. "We can't stop here because there could be another patrol along at any moment." They pressed on, along a worn footpath leading to the Lapointe farm, briefly halting whenever Parrish needed to throw up. After a few minutes, they were close enough to call for help.

Danny and Marcel appeared together, rounding the back of the barn. "What the hell are you doing back in Detroit?" Danny grinned.

"You have to get your family away from here. Did you not hear the cannon?" Westlake demanded.

"That was just practice or something. Those foolish English wouldn't be shooting at our house," Marcel replied just as a second blast went high and far to their right.

"My Uncle George is positioned across the river with cannon and mortars, and your property is right in line with the fort. How many shots will it take before one falls short and hits the farmhouse? They're not expert artillerymen, remember." He was speaking fast. "Sooner or later they'll hit your home. Get your family away now."

Parrish began to retch again, and Westlake eased him to the ground. "What's wrong with him?" Marcel asked.

"I'll tell you later. We ran into a patrol and had to fight to get here."

"Marcel, he's right. Let's get everyone out. We'll move north up the river, to the empty place, near the mill." Danny turned to Westlake. "The Robichaud family has gone back to Trois-Rivières until this stupid war is over. If we borrow their place for a little while, they won't mind." Danny tugged his brother's arm and they hurried away. He shouted back as they ran, "Did you kill the whole patrol, Johnny?" Westlake made no attempt to answer him. "Oh shit, he did, that crazy English."

Westlake stayed with Parrish, and it was not long before the entire Lapointe family—mother, father, and two sons—were scurrying down the hill carrying some kitchen utensils and a clock. A third mortar blast occurred as they reached them. Straight over their heads it whizzed, smashing through the roof of their farmhouse. Westlake could hear the shell crash through the upper floor, exploding as it penetrated the ground floor, blowing out all the windows and most of the wall that faced him. They dove for the ground as one.

"*Mon Dieu!* Is everyone safe?" Monsieur Lapointe asked. He stood up again and helped his wife to her feet. "That was close." He then patted Westlake on the back. "*Merci*, Jonathan."

"Goddamn British, they have no sense. Don't thank him—it's his bloody uncle who can't aim that damn cannon." Danny was looking back at the house. "It will take a year to rebuild."

Madame Lapointe had not yet said word, trying to bear the situation as best she could. Now she sobbed and held on to her husband.

"We shouldn't stay here. I'm sorry," Westlake said, feeling responsible for his uncle's actions. "I'm truly sorry." He looked for signs of another enemy patrol. When he turned back, Danny's parents were already walking away, hand in hand.

Captain Jackson knew that his general badly needed a break from the tension, but instead the pressure only grew. Behind his desk, General William Hull pursed his lips and spit toward a bucket filling up with gobs of chewed tobacco. In yet another attempt to reach the supplies at the Raison River, he had sent Colonels Cass and McArthur south, with three hundred and fifty men. The conspiring militia colonels had so far made it difficult for him to concentrate on strictly military tactics, and Hull appeared relieved to have them out of the fort for a short time.

With Lieutenant Colonel Miller ill with fever, Colonel Findlay had reported to Hull his estimate of the number of Indians flooding down from the north, and it was not good news. One Indian every twenty seconds was seen passing through the gap in the forest; that made three per minute, or one hundred and eighty per hour. The Indians were first spotted well after dawn, but it was now four o'clock. A steady stream over eight hours meant almost fifteen hundred Indians, and they were still coming.

Jackson frowned on reading Findlay's report; there were too many warriors coming out of nowhere. Something was strange here.

"Bloody Indians, and now this." Hull chewed faster, throwing a note on his desk, then leaned back and spit again. The sound of cannon fire made them glance out the open door, but then they continued as if nothing had happened.

"May I, sir?" Jackson asked. Hull nodded and Jackson began to read the letter.

"The force at my disposal authorises me to require the immediate surrender of Fort Detroit. It is far from my intention to join in a war of extermination, but you must be aware, that the numerous body of Indians who have attached themselves to my troops, will be

beyond control the moment the contest commences. You will find me disposed to enter into such conditions as will satisfy the most scrupulous sense of honour.

Brock had signed the letter, asking for nothing less than the surrender of the fort to prevent a massacre. Jackson watched Hull chew even faster as the pressure on him grew.

"I told them more than an hour ago that we could meet any force. They can go to hell, but these Indians are unnerving," Hull said. "What is it you have for me, Captain?"

Jackson put Brock's surrender demand back on the desk and took out another note from his breast pocket. "This morning we caught a Sergeant Archibald Stamp trying to hand this over to an Indian on the north side of town." He placed the brief note in front of Hull. It was addressed to Captain Roberts, Fort Mackinac: *You need only send another five thousand natives to our cause.* A Lieutenant Colonel Proctor had signed it. "Stamp is currently under guard along with that wounded man, Dean."

"Is this likely, Captain? Five thousand?"

"I've asked Carson Stone and Lieutenant Hanks to join us." Jackson walked to the door and called out to the two men. The second blast of cannon fire seemed louder, but again no one paid it any attention.

Stone appeared in the doorway, as usual strangely dressed in his British officer's uniform, and took one cautious step inside. His owl-like face appeared wary, as if he was about to steal something or perhaps have something stolen from him. The sentries at the door seized the brace of pistols tucked into his belt. In contrast, Lieutenant Porter Hanks seemed happy to be of service. Although he had given his parole at Fort Mackinac not to engage in fighting unless exchanged, he was desperate to be of some usefulness.

Jackson asked each man in turn if it was possible for Captain Roberts to send five thousand Indians south from Fort Mackinac. Stone repeated that it had been dark when the Indians arrived there but that they seemed to be everywhere. He reminded Jackson that when he and his companions had escaped in the early morning, there were canoes as far as the eye could see. "Yes, I think it's possible he could send five thousand Indians."

Eager to satisfy, Lieutenant Hanks wanted to give a more complete report. The cannons across the river erupted again, and this time there was a crash somewhere to the north end of the fort. A woman screamed.

"See to that, will you, Findlay? Make sure that all the women and children are lodged in the root cellars. They'll be safe there, and we don't need them getting in the way."

Findlay marched out and Hanks continued. "Of course, I was on the inside of the fort and the Indians were on the outside, so I would not see them as well as Mr. Stone. However, I find it hard to believe that there would be that many, and Roberts would not want to send them all, for then he'd have none to help defend Mackinac, sir," Hanks reasoned. "Unless they were eating him out of house and home, so he wanted to get rid of them."

Except for the sound of Hull's rapid chewing there was silence. Jackson paced quietly, thinking there were just too many Indians unaccounted for, everywhere. To him, Findlay's report seemed exaggerated. Stone's description was plausible, but he had no firm count and for that matter neither did Hanks. But then Proctor wouldn't ask for five thousand Indians if he did not know they were there. Unless the note was a fake, he brooded. He would need to speak with Sergeant Stamp again.

"All these women and children are my responsibility," Hull said. "I'm not just a general, I'm their governor, their protector, and I have to ensure their safety. The actual number of Indians doesn't matter. The point is there are thousands out there and more still coming."

"You know, come to think of it, I didn't see any Indians moving south when we departed," Hanks blurted out.

Another cannon shot echoed around the fort, and Jackson felt the ground shake as a twelve-pound steel ball bounced with a thud on the parade square and hurtled through Hull's open door. Lieutenant Porter

Hanks half turned to see it the very moment before the ball split through his stomach, cutting him in half. His blood and organs sprayed the room, the lower torso still standing there as if wondering what to do without its head. It rocked backward briefly, then tilted forward and fell to the ground. Jackson's muscles tensed in shock, leaving him unable to move an inch.

"Oh God," Stone cried in disgust, stroking his face clean of Hanks's innards.

"Did that actually happen?" Hull asked, wiping a string of intestines from his own forehead.

Hull's obvious distress broke through Jackson's shock. "Let's go outside, sir. I'm afraid it did happen." He raised Hull from his chair, gripping him under each arm. "I'll have someone clean this up, sir."

Hull's eyes were still unfocused, his white hair stiff in a tangled mass. Blood and guts smeared the top half of his uniform, while the bottom, half shielded by the desk, looked as pristine as ever.

"Stone, this meeting is over," Jackson said over his shoulder. People were scurrying throughout the fort, carrying belongings and even children on their backs.

"Captain Jackson, may I have the key to the warehouse now? I've done all you asked." Stone seized his pistols from the table and gave the shocked sentry an animal growl.

"I'll see you at dawn tomorrow. I've got a few questions for you, Stone. And I'll be busy, so don't be late." Jackson staggered away, supporting Hull with one arm while picking bits of Porter Hanks from the general's uniform with his other hand.

Stone kicked at the dirt and brushed some fragments of flesh off his shoulder. In the tension, he unconsciously pulled at his collar so that he could take a deep breath. He reminded himself that all he had to do was wait one more night, just one more night. *Stay calm.*

"I'm better off than that useless Hanks … loses the fort, the island, and then gets himself cut in half … talk about a bad couple of weeks." Stone laughed to himself. A cannon roared in the distance and he instinctively crouched, waiting for the ball to strike. Nothing came.

"Don't be an idiot. Now I'm getting jumpy," he said. "No, I just have to be patient … back at first light, and all will be well." He wiped his hands together, ending in a slap. Success was near, and so was the freedom to do as he pleased. He needed to pay a visit to the miller now and make some arrangements. That would give him something to take his mind off thoughts of death.

Paxinos dragged himself into the Shawnee camp located southwest of Fort Detroit. The red ball of the sun had sunk in the west, and it was time to eat. Warriors in small groups sat cross-legged around scattered fires. At the crest of a small rise, Tecumseh sat by himself, poking a staff into the glowing center of his fire. He smiled as Paxinos approached.

"It's no fun running all day. The Long Knives must think there are thousands of us," Paxinos said. For most of the day, with a hundred other warriors, he had kept darting past a break in the forest at the top of a hill. Once past the break, they ran down the hill and up the other side, to run past the same gap again. "I hope your trick's worked on Colonel Findlay," he added. He brushed beads of sweat off his forehead with the back of his hand.

"You must sit down and eat … a gift from the Wyandot." Tecumseh threw Paxinos a roasted leg of wild turkey. "Listen, they chant to the Great Spirit for a victory tomorrow." He tilted his head in the direction of the drums.

"Will the Great Spirit give us a such a victory?" Paxinos bit into the turkey meat and then reached for a water bucket before drinking from a large ladle.

Tecumseh studied his young apprentice. He had grown into a good man, but a future with no land meant that he would inevitably starve. The battle tomorrow would decide much, and it was hard for him to think of anything else.

"The Great Spirit listens to our songs but does not interfere in the affairs of men. We must make our plans for battle, and it is we who must make the victory, not the Great Spirit."

"Is that why you forbid liquor drinking tonight?"

Tecumseh nodded. "And I have let the Long Knives know that if they surrender tomorrow, no prisoners taken will be harmed by our people."

"If we don't need the Great Spirit, why do we sing?" Paxinos persisted.

Tecumseh laughed. "From the time you could speak words, you have had so many questions." But it was a question Tecumseh had often asked himself. "I do not have all the answers you seek, so you must think about it yourself, but I can tell you that there are things much greater than any one man." Darkness had descended and in the mid-August summer, the heavens glittered with warm stars. Tecumseh waved his arm at the sky. "When we sing to the Great Spirit, it reminds us of something that is greater than ourselves ... our community, the love for our tribe and family, and respect for our mother earth, which sustains us."

Paxinos was looking puzzled. He took another bite of turkey, then with his free hand threw another log into the fire. "Are you going away after the battle?" He raised the ladle of water again to his lips.

The sound of the war drum sounded louder as more warriors sauntered back into the camp to finish their day.

"We must stop the chiefs from selling our land, and for this reason I will travel again. The tribes must join together so we will be stronger. We need space: the land between the Redcoats and the Long Knives." He kicked at the untouched end of a log so it landed back in the flames. "This is why we must stay in the center of this great burning fire with the British."

Tecumseh looked at Paxinos for some sign of understanding, but he saw none. He was convinced that few natives understood the future, and too many lived only for today, taking their present freedom for granted. Only a handful of chiefs had any plan for the threats that surrounded their people. "I must rest now to be ready for the battle tomorrow. More warriors cross the river tonight, and at dawn the British general brings his soldiers across in many boats. You will stay at my side during the fight." Tecumseh lay back on his giant black bearskin and closed his eyes. "Finish your food and sleep too."

Paxinos had not understood Tecumseh's entire lesson; in fact, he rarely did. He needed time to think about the man's words and work them into his own ideas. The tension in air had made him lose his appetite. He put a last maple log in the middle of the fire, then rested his head back on his blanket, gazing up at the crowded heaven. The Great Spirit surely had to notice him from such an immense sky. Paxinos determined that just in case Tecumseh was wrong, he would himself talk to the Great Spirit, in silence, and ask for guidance in tomorrow's battle.

"Still worrying about your bloody furs, Stone?" Captain Jackson asked. He stood without his jacket in the doorway of the officers' quarters but did not invite Stone inside.

In the bare morning light, Stone had bullied his way past the gate's guard by using the names of Hull and Jackson freely. During the night, he had turned again and again in his bed so that by morning he'd slept just a few hours, yet his excitement at escaping Detroit was evident on his owlish face. There was a fresh smell to the morning air, a new day for a new beginning.

"You said to be here at dawn, so here I am—the first thing on your agenda, sir. I started out in the bloody dark just to arrive on time."

Jackson reached into his breast pocket and pulled out a key. "Beyond the last farm, there are six warehouses built close together. Your furs are in the largest building, set well back from the river but closest to the mill, at the end of Trappers Alley."

He paused before handing over the key, and Stone watched him roll it between his fingertips. "I'm happy to be rid of you, Stone, but I still have a few questions."

Stone's body went rigid, and he could feel his heart start to pound.

"When you left Fort Mackinac, who did you leave the furs with?"

Stone stared at his feet. He had worked with Wagg, and Wagg had worked with the British, on the guarantee that the furs would be released once victory was at hand.

"There's an annoying little shit named Hicks, who never shuts up … works for Westlake Trading out of New York, so it seemed safe to give him the furs." Stone adjusted the pistols in his belt and then gave the belt a tug, securing it one notch tighter.

"You aren't working with the British again, are you, Stone?"

"Me and the goddamn British? Not bloody likely. They'll hang me if I'm caught."

"And Jonathan Westlake, what do you know of him?" Jackson still had the key in his hand, and Stone kept his eye on it.

"I've told you, he killed my brother, so I'll kill him if I get the slightest chance." He stroked the handles of his pistols. He would not leave without that key.

"That might be more difficult than you think." Jackson pulled on his jacket. "And he was at Mackinac too."

"So I'm told, but I never saw him there. If I had, I'd have killed him on the spot." Stone knew that if he kept to his story, there was no way that Jackson could know that he and Wagg had worked with the British at Mackinac, but his heart was beating in his ears.

Jackson stood in the dawn light, thinking. "Strange that Richard Westlake sent you and Wagg, and this fellow Hicks, and then risked his only son to collect the furs. There's more to this story ..." Jackson shook his head.

A young soldier in uniform ran up in front of Jackson and saluted. "General Hull's compliments, sir. He needs you immediately." After delivering his message, the man saluted again, about-faced, and marched away.

"Don't let me ever catch you working with the enemy. Now, get your furs and be on your way." Jackson finally threw Stone the key.

Stone snatched it out of the air. "You are a man of your word, Captain. Thank you, sir." He grinned and put the key in his trouser pocket, then gave a mock salute to indicate goodbye. He at last had the furs and now all he needed was his money, and then no one could ever touch him again. And maybe, just maybe, he'd take the girl too.

On the north edge of town, the last farm along the river belonged to the Robichaud family. Tired of his five daughters being harassed by soldiers, Monsieur Robichaud had moved his entire family back to Lower Canada, intending to wait out the war. Danny Lapointe had already told Westlake of his disappointment, for there was one daughter, the middle one, to whom he had become attached. With a broad smile, he described her face and her body. He had planned to eventually catch up with the Robichauds when he made his way to Montreal; that was his plan, but events seemed to always get in the way.

The Lapointe family settled into their substitute farmhouse, finding it not perfect but better than sleeping outside. Food and blankets were another matter, and for that Westlake and Lapointe had returned to what was left of his family home.

"So we wait three seconds after the blast, to give the cannon shot time to safely clear the house, and then run inside. I get the blankets and you get the food, and don't forget the cooked chicken, if there is anything left of it." Lapointe eyed the blown wall as Westlake nodded in agreement.

The cannon shot whizzed far overhead: Uncle George must have found his range, Westlake guessed. He darted into the house, snatched up what food he could carry, and ran out again.

"Did you get the *poulet*?" Lapointe asked, his arms full of folded blankets.

"Let's go. I got the chicken and more." Westlake started running. By the time they got back to the Robichaud farm, the sky had brightened considerably, and they were both out of breath. They walked the rest of the way up from the river. A few hundred yards to the north, Westlake spotted the mill by the river and several large buildings across the road. The wind blew out of the north, and from the smell he guessed that at least one of those warehouses was full of furs and a few carcasses.

"A big stink, eh? That's why I never liked this end of town. Those bloody carcasses smell like hell whenever the wind blows the wrong way." Lapointe continued to struggle uphill with all the blankets. A few paces from the door Westlake froze, staring back at the northern roadway leading to the mill. In a determined procession toward the warehouses, he could see Bill Wagg, Carson Stone, and Mary Collins. They paused at one large warehouse door, fumbling with a lock before proceeding inside.

Westlake ran into the house, dropped the food on the kitchen table, and snatched up a musket. He looked in on Parrish, but found his friend fast asleep and decided that with his splitting headache, Parrish would be of little help. Racing toward the front door, he loaded the musket on the run.

"What the hell are you doing?" Lapointe asked from behind his stack of blankets.

"Do you remember that owl-faced guy who rode away after they killed Ned?"

Lapointe nodded.

"He and Bill Wagg have just gone into that warehouse, and they have Mary Collins with them. I have to go after them."

Lapointe grabbed Westlake by the arm. "Are you sure this is what you want? Those guys would rather see you dead."

"I watched Ned die because of Stone. They have Mary with them, and Stone is a traitor who must answer for what he did. Is that enough for you?" Westlake charged out the door.

"Wait for me," Lapointe yelled after him, but Westlake was already running.

A mound of beaver carcasses, stripped of their skins and left to rot in the humid air, forced Stone to cover his nose with a white handkerchief. He heard Mary gag, but as she turned away, he squeezed her arm and pulled her up beside him. A large squat building, the warehouse was dark except for the light penetrating through the open door.

"You've certainly done your job, Stone." Furs were stacked to the ceiling and Wagg grinned, stepping closer to lean against a bundle.

"It's time to pay up now. There are Indians everywhere and the British are getting too damn close."

"You're not getting nervous?" Wagg said with a laugh. He placed his musket on a shoulder-high stack of pelts and reached under his shirt to unbutton a pouch that he kept tied to his waist. From this, Stone watched him count off a number of sterling notes and then hand them over.

"Where's the rest? The payment for my men?"

"Your men are dead, so you don't have to pay them," Wagg replied.

"I don't have time for this, Wagg. You got all the furs, now I want all my pay," Stone shouted angrily, his hands now balled into fists.

"I don't pay dead men—not a chance."

"Give him the money," Mary pleaded.

"Are you in league with him after all I've done for you?" Wagg shook his head, which set his jowls wobbling.

"Don't be ridiculous." Mary tried to keep her voice level but could not stop it from sounding shaky. "Just give him the money and we can go. There's more money to come on delivery of the furs."

Wagg reached toward his money belt but then lunged for his musket. Stone remained calm and deliberately drew one of his pistols with one hand. Mary stared in disbelief as he cocked the lever and fired just as Wagg turned round with his musket. The single ball ripped through Wagg's chest and into his heart. The musket fell from his grasp, his knees buckled, and his head struck the dirt floor hard.

Mary screamed and pulled her arm free of Stone's grasp. She rushed to her stepfather and lifted his head, but it lolled to one side in her arms. "You animal, he's dead." She sobbed, unable to hold back the tears.

Stone put the smoking pistol back in his belt, took out a knife, and cut Wagg's money belt free. All the money and the furs were now his. He looked down at Mary, her breasts heaving in despair, and decided that he wanted her too.

"Get up. We have to go. I gave him every chance. I'm the good guy here." He reached down, slid his long fingers under one arm, and lifted her up and away from Wagg's body. "Don't you see, I've won. I have everything now, and there's a boat waiting just across the road. The miller and I made a deal, so let's go. You can't stay here anyway."

As Mary turned back to her stepfather, Stone pulled her roughly through the door. Once outside, he slipped the padlock back in place and snapped it shut. He looked up at the blue sky and smiled to himself.

"You'll never get through the water patrols," Mary warned. "They're inspecting everything that moves."

"They're guarding for craft moving south, past Sandwich and Fort Amherstburg. But we're heading north, back into Lake Huron, where no one's watching." He guided her across the road toward the mill. "You see, I have it all figured out." He spread his fingers, batting his hooded eyelids.

"Not quite, Mr. Stone."

Stone tensed and swiveled his head back to the road. He knew that voice and his stomach clenched. "You again? Why can't you ever go away?" Stone thrust the girl between himself and Westlake. "You killed my brother, but I'll let it go. I've no quarrel with you now."

"Jonathan!" Mary cried. "He's murdered Bill."

Stone jerked her backward up a few steps and through the mill's open front door. Inside, the two great millstones ground together, creaking round. The grinding swoosh of grain even muffled the splash of the water wheel revolving in the river's current outside. The whole building vibrated as the wooden gears in the basement drove the millstones above.

From behind the wheel post came a smiling Jacques Tremblay, covered in flour dust.

"Where's my damn canoe?" Stone demanded.

"Well, *bonjour*, Monsieur Stone." The instant he saw Stone's face, Tremblay's smiled faded; something was wrong. "Your canoe is loaded with supplies just like you paid for, Mr. Stone. It's twenty paces up the river, to the north of this building—precisely as you instructed."

Stone's face was taut and angry. He pulled Mary in front of him and watched the front door. He then drew his second pistol and pointed it straight upward.

Tremblay made a run for the door. "I've been repairing the floor above the water wheel so the back door's open," he advised before vanishing out through the front door. "I'm not returning."

Westlake saw the miller come blundering toward him, flour puffing above his head with each step. An August sun lit up the doorway and a few yards inside, but otherwise the interior of the mill was dark.

Lapointe hailed him from behind. "Hey, Johnny, how can I help?"

"I'm going in. Stone's killed Wagg, but he still has Mary." Westlake gestured toward the side of the building. "Go down by the riverbank and make sure he doesn't escape. Shoot him if you must."

Lapointe looked him in the eyes, nodded, and without saying a word crept around the corner of the wall. Westlake inhaled deeply, put the butt of the musket to his shoulder ready to fire, then stepped through the doorway. Out of the sunlight, his eyes took time to adjust to the gloom, but he could see well enough by the time Stone spoke up from right behind the wheelpost.

"That's far enough, Westlake. You can't just let things be, can you? Always bloody well sticking your nose in." Stone had raised his voice to be heard over the vibrating wooden floor. "Stand still and drop that musket."

"Never." The musket pointed straight at Stone's side of the post.

"Are you quite sure of that? Don't you want your furs?" Stone moved slightly to one side of the wheel. "You can have them all if you just let us leave."

"Who told you that we were leaving York back in February? It was someone at the garrison," Westlake shouted back.

"Go to hell, Westlake. I'm not giving up my informants to you. Your last chance now. You can have the furs and go—or you can die. Which will it be?"

"You couldn't load up all those furs even if you wanted to, and the British Army is only a mile away. You're finished, a traitor to your country, a dead man."

Stone slipped out from behind the wheelpost. As the miller had warned, the back door was open to the water wheel, and the light shining through made Stone a clear target —except for the risk of hitting Mary. Stone had his left arm tight around Mary's neck and in his right was the pistol jammed against Mary's head.

"Be careful, it might go off." Westlake could see that the girl's eyes were wide with fright and her chin trembled just as it had on the first day he met her.

"Jonathan, just shoot him," she cried. "I don't care if you hit me. I'd rather be dead than stay with this monster."

"Shut up, you little fool. Nobody's listening to you." Stone pulled his arm tighter around her neck and she gagged. "Now put down that musket," he bellowed.

The grinding wheels made it difficult to hear, but Westlake knew what Stone wanted. The terror on Mary's face and watching her slowly strangle was too much to bear. He had no choice here and his only hope was that Lapointe would finish off Stone when he tried to escape. Westlake raised his left hand and with his right lowered his musket to the ground. He knew what was coming next. He was about to die.

"You stupid bastard." Stone lowered the pistol from Mary's head, turning it directly on Westlake. Less than ten paces apart, and he couldn't miss. Stone relaxed his grip ever so slightly on Mary's throat and pointed to fire.

"No," she screamed and with all her strength drove her clenched fist backward into Stone's groin just as he fired. Across the river, a cannon erupted, and its roar echoed through the cavernous mill along with Stone's pistol shot.

Westlake was rolling to his right in anticipation, but he still felt the burn of the pistol ball clip the flesh of his bicep. He winced, knowing he was lucky to be alive. The sharp pain of Mary's punch had jerked Stone's arm just enough to save his life.

Westlake jumped to his feet. Although Stone still had her in a loose grasp, Mary had turned to face him. Westlake watched her shove him backward.

Bracing both feet on the floor, she rammed her head into Stone's chest. Caught off balance, he stumbled out the back door and began to drop through the gap in the floor above the waterwheel. Mary tried to break free of his grasp, but Stone dropped the pistol and grabbed on to her arm. His only hope of saving himself now was to hold fast to his captive.

Westlake charged across the floor and took hold of Mary's shoulders with both hands. Stone's weight was pulling her toward the gap.

Westlake's hands slid to her waist and she doubled over. While the wheel now pulled down at his feet, Stone gripped the rim of the gap with one hand and held on to Mary's left wrist with the other.

Mary swung her right arm backward to grasp anything firm. Her hand slapped against Westlake's hip, feeling Ned's knife. Time seemed to slow as Westlake watched her small hand slide the knife from its sheath, then stab it down hard into Stone's forearm.

"That's for Bill," she hissed, but the first slash did little to lessen Stone's grip on her except to put terror in his eyes.

"And this is for me and your little favor." She slashed a second time, stabbing right through to the bone of Stone's forearm. He released his grip on her arm and she instantly stamped down hard with her heel on his fingers that held to the ledge.

Stone was dragged away by the rotating wheel and with his legs entangled soon plunged under the water. Some moments later, he broke the surface again with the upswing of the wheel, now moaning and gasping for air. Relentlessly, the mechanism hauled him upward, legs first, toward the millrace feeding water to turn the wheel. Between the floor beams of the millrace and the wheel itself there were only three inches of space.

As his legs were compressed into this gap, Stone began to scream. His hips and torso followed, but the screaming had stopped even before the wheel seemed to briefly pause. The giant gears in the mill's basement continued churning, the torque unrelenting, as Stone's head passed into the gap. By now the water course was gushing red with his blood.

"Hey, Johnny. *Comment ça va?*" Lapointe yelled up from the riverbank to the open door, where Westlake stood beside Mary. "Your uncle is at it again. Do you think he could hit us here?" He laughed and scanned the bloody wheel. "I see you got the bastard. You keep killing everybody who offends you, eh."

Westlake waved and drew Mary back from the wheel, holding her close. She was shaking as he took the knife from her hand. He kissed her forehead and spoke softly in her ear, "We're okay—you saved me."

He broke into a broad smile. When she lifted her face, he kissed her on the lips and looked into her dark eyes. "So many miles to find you."

"I knew you would come," she sobbed in his arms, and he felt her body quiver. "One day, I knew you would come."

23

......

MAJOR GENERAL ISAAC BROCK stood tall in the center of the boat, observing his flotilla push off, all oars out. With no wind and not a single cloud in the sky, the rising sun cast long shadows across the hundreds of the soldiers wearing red coats and white cross-belts. It seemed so peaceful at first, this invasion of the United States, until upstream, in front of the Baby residence, a cannon cracked out and then another. "That's more like it," Brock said to himself. He slipped off his wide hat and used it to wave back to the other boats, "C'mon, up and at 'em."

The stage was set for August 16, 1812.

In the water, the dozens of boats straining on oars were carrying three hundred and thirty regulars and four hundred militia. Brock studied a grassy hill over on the American side of the river but saw no sign of opposition. At the crest of the hill, the sole figure of Tecumseh, mounted on a white Mustang, studied the armada. Brock turned to glance back at the boats pulling for the far shore, filled with Redcoats sitting upright in anticipation. Tecumseh would be pleased with this impressive sight, and that pleased Brock too. He allowed himself a brief grin.

Relieved the troops would not have to fight their way ashore, he let out a long whistle wondering where the enemy had gone — an answer he assumed he would receive in minutes.

Brock's boat slid into shore at Spring Wells. No sooner had the other men disembarked than Paxinos rode bareback into view, carrying a feathered spear in his right hand. From either side of his nose, as far as his ears, his face was painted with two menacing black stripes. Brock listened as he shouted to them from the top of a low hill.

"I am sent by Tecumseh to tell you there is a large body of Detroit soldiers—at least three hundred—three miles to the south of your landing." He raised his spear, pumping his arm, and galloped away.

A simple but effective warning, thought Brock.

"Colonel Proctor, if you please, form the men in column—and double the normal space between them." Brock saw Proctor frown so he explained. "We must look greater in number than we are. And since we now have an enemy force behind us as well as in front, we march on Fort Detroit immediately."

"Sir." Proctor saluted.

"And Mr. Proctor, double the militia rearguard. I don't want any nasty surprises arriving from behind."

To Brock's left were at least six hundred Indians thrashing their way through the cornfields. Additionally, he had brought along his artillery of three six-pounders and three three-pounders. Not much, he knew, but enough to breach the twelve-foot-high wooden palisade surrounding the fort. Another obstacle was the eleven-foot-high, twelve-foot-thick parapet, backed by a six-foot-deep ditch that also measured twelve feet across. Brock took a deep breath. It would be hot work but a determined force could get across.

In the river floated the familiar sight of the *Queen Charlotte* and the *Hunter*, with their guns out. The two ships would keep the invading force safe for at least the length of the river road. Brock mounted his horse and rode to the front of the column, where Ensign Robert Simpson rode in the lead with newly appointed Quartermaster Nichol.

"Quartermaster, did you distribute those old uniforms to the militia?" Brock asked.

"I had Ensign Simpson help me, sir," Nichol replied. "You'll now look three hundred men stronger. The uniforms may be threadbare, but from a distance the militia will appear as much like regulars as the real thing." Colonel Nichol turned his head and squinted back at the winding column. "Can you tell the difference, sir? They're toward the rear."

Brock wheeled his horse around to inspect. "They look fine. Good show to the both of you." He touched the tip of his hat in salute. "I'm afraid that today our game is bluff as much as anything else."

Simpson grinned at the compliment; if only his father could see him now, riding at the head of the invasion column with a major general.

He was a real soldier. They had turned off the river road and were marching directly on Fort Detroit, Brock slightly in the lead.

"With the fort in view, sir, do you not think the officers should lead their companies forward?" Nichol asked. "Especially in light of those long twenty-four pounders sticking out of the fort's wall. In two shakes of a lamb's tail they could clean us off this road, sir."

The closer they got to the fort, the tighter Simpson gripped the leather reins of his horse. At any second, he expected the long guns to belch fire, sending canisters ripping through their packed column, starting with himself. His horse sensed his tension and stepped sideways into Colonel Nichol. Nichol grimaced and shot Simpson a frown.

"A few moments more, Colonel Nichol," Brock replied. "I want the enemy to get a good look at us—to fear us and see that we do not fear them. And I'll never ask the men to go somewhere that I wouldn't lead them."

The column gradually wound its way off the river road, toward Fort Detroit and its massive gates. From across the river, a cannon ball screamed overhead, and Simpson involuntarily ducked. He smiled nervously at Nichol, who ignored him. Captain Moore had obviously found his range again, for the ball crashed inside the fort and exploded. Simpson wondered what they were thinking on the other side of that palisade.

General Hull paced the floor of his office and spit. He didn't seem to care if he missed his tobacco bucket entirely, with brown spittle staining the floor. Captain Jackson turned away from the sight but had noticed that with each ball crashing in, Hull's body hunched tighter and smaller. The general had withdrawn his forces from outside the walls so that the fort's three acres were now jammed with anxious men awaiting orders.

"The artillery is asking if they can open fire on the approaching column. What are your orders, sir?" Jackson asked.

"You don't fire on men that you are asking for a truce. I need time to think. Have we heard from Cass and McArthur?"

Jackson shook his head. This request for a truce made his stomach churn. The thought of possible surrender, and the humiliation that came with it, was unthinkable only hours before. Another mortar blast screamed over the parapet and smashed into a storage shed not far from Hull's office. After the explosion sent splinters flying, Jackson walked to the doorway to look. Outside, he saw two men lying on the ground: one was unconscious and missing an arm while the other frantically pulled at his eyes in a futile attempt to remove the splinters.

Cass and McArthur had been gone two days now, and no one had yet heard a word of their progress. They had recently done everything in their power to undermine Hull, even circulating a petition to have him placed under arrest. Although Jackson was happy they were gone, he wished their troops were still in place. Inside the fort now were eleven hundred effective fighting men, not including the shaky Michigan militia. Cass and McArthur had taken with them three hundred and fifty of the best troops, leaving the fort outnumbered by the enemy.

As Hull explained the situation, they were already facing more than a thousand regulars and militia plus fifteen hundred Indians with perhaps as many as five thousand more on the way. Brock's cannons would soon reduce the palisade to matchsticks, the regulars would storm the breach, and then the Indians would finish off every man, woman, and child in the fort and the town. Hull had wished for cannons when he was outside Fort Amherstburg; now the situation was reversed but with the enemy possessing the cannons. Jackson heard a jarring thump outside, followed by the inevitable explosion. He watched Hull shudder once again. More screams and moans followed. The longer they held out here, the more explosions they would be forced to endure.

A knock at the door signaled a courier bringing them a note. Jackson closed the door and offered it to Hull, but he was waved away.

"Read it to me," Hull said.

"There will be no three-day truce, sir. Brock has given you only three hours."

There was no one now for Hull to lean on. Lieutenant Colonel Miller remained bedridden with the ague and the remaining high-ranking officer, Colonel Findlay, was part of the conspiracy. Another explosion shook the general's office and Jackson laid the note on Hull's desk.

"If you have orders for me, I would act on them now, sir. Otherwise, I would like to return to the south wall and face the British column." Jackson opened the door to leave as a young soldier appeared.

"I have been asked to report to you that part of the Michigan militia has been captured outside the north wall, sir. The rest are threatening to lay down their arms." The boy saluted, and Jackson returned the gesture.

"When was this, soldier?" Jackson asked.

"I ran fast—just moments ago. And, sir, Indians have already entered the north part of the town."

"You may go." Jackson saluted again, and the boy ran off just as another ball exploded amid the ruins of the storage shed. Jackson watched to see the lad struck down by the blast, and then rise, brush himself off, and run on his way.

"You may go to your wall, Captain Jackson. But take my tablecloth with you, and hang it from the top." Hull pointed to the white linen cloth covering his dining table.

"Surrender? Surely not, sir?"

"We're outnumbered here more than two to one. The enemy has cannons, which he can rain down on us at his will." Hull's face was ashen. "We can't reach Cass and McArthur, damn their skins. With our supplies dwindling, it's only a matter of time before we must give up."

"May I suggest that we use that time to resist? Cass and McArthur may yet turn up, sir?"

Hull shook his head as a further explosion rocked the building and both men crouched instinctively. Jackson straightened up, brushing at the folds of his jacket. Hull spit again, only this time he did not even try to reach the spittoon. He passed a hand through his white hair, brushing it back to some semblance of order.

"Cass and McArthur have shown themselves to be unreliable, and the Michigan militia is about to desert. If we surrender now at least we can save the women and children," Hull argued. "Tecumseh and Brock have given us their words that prisoners won't be molested. I believe them."

"But, sir, surrender? Can you get someone else to hang up the cloth, sir?"

"You're a good soldier, Captain Jackson. I won't let this reflect on you in any way. I'll take full blame myself."

"Sir," Jackson pleaded.

"Hang it now. That's an order."

By the time Westlake and Lapointe returned to the Robichaud farm with Mary, Parrish was awake and had eaten. He explained that his head still ached, but he was ready for the day. Westlake recounted to him what had happened at the mill, and Parrish visibly slumped over the kitchen table, disappointed in missing a chance to break Stone's neck.

"It was Ned's knife," Westlake explained. "It cut him to the bone."

Parrish nodded as if to say, "At least that's something."

When Stone's battered carcass had floated free of the great wheel, on its third pass under the water, Westlake had jumped to rescue Wagg's money pouch. Inside he found one hundred pounds sterling, a small fortune. At the table, he divided that in two and gave each half to Mary and Lapointe.

"I'm giving you the portion meant for Stone and his men," he said to Lapointe. "To help rebuild your house. I'm sorry." Westlake shoved the notes directly in Lapointe's pocket before his friend could argue.

The balance, still in the pouch, he handed to Mary.

"Wagg earned it. My father will be happy that he secured the furs so this money is rightfully yours." Mary began to protest, but Westlake forced it into her hand. "And I'm sure there will be more to come with the furs all safely in hand." She finally took the belt and strapped it around her slim waist.

"Say, Johnny, you noticed that the cannons have stopped?" Lapointe opened the door only to be pushed back inside by six Shawnee warriors, their heads shaved and painted red. Westlake instantly recognized the leader as Kawika, looking stern-faced and hostile. There were more Indians hooting outside.

He jumped up to place himself between Lapointe and Kawika. The Indian raised his tomahawk to strike, but Westlake did not flinch. Instead, he repeated what Paxinos had told him to say, "I am Jonathan Westlake, friend of Tecumseh and Paxinos. Leave us."

There was little room to move with warriors crowding into the kitchen. Kawika hesitated with his tomahawk still raised. Westlake prayed that Paxinos had spoken to him of their friendship.

"You will not stop us," Kawika snarled. "We must eat and drink."

"You'll not do so here, nor must you touch the damaged farmhouse farther along the shore." Westlake heard the click of Parrish's musket.

The warrior kept the tomahawk raised as Westlake continued staring him in the face. He suspected Kawika was imagining Tecumseh's wrath if he disobeyed his commands. Finally he lowered the weapon and raised the palm of his left hand. The rest of the warriors backed out of the house, following him.

"*Mon Dieu*, that was close, Johnny," Lapointe said. "That guy is scary."

"Stay inside, all of you." Westlake handed Marcel Lapointe his musket. "You should be safe now. If the Indians have got inside the town walls, and the cannons have stopped firing, it means the fort must have fallen."

"I won't be long, Mary." She stepped forward and he embraced her. "Parrish, you're with me."

"I'm not missing this either." Danny snatched up his musket and followed them out the door.

Brock and Tecumseh rode into Fort Detroit in tandem, at the head of the column. In the brightness of the day, even at a distance, Westlake could pick out the major general in his full dress uniform, with gold epaulettes and cocked hat. Dressed in buckskins and sitting proud in his saddle, Tecumseh rode with Paxinos walking beside him. Behind this first group rode Proctor, Nelles, and Nichol. Westlake caught up with Paxinos and slapped him on the back. He stared up at Tecumseh to see the warrior chief looking self-assured, though holding back a grin.

"I understand the advance guard ran into some trouble." Brock turned to Proctor.

"A small skirmish, yes. I'm afraid we rushed our fences somewhat, sir," Proctor replied. "They were not quite ready to surrender before we arrived, but all is settled now."

The British column passed without incident through the main gates. In the center of the parade square, the last of the U.S. Army of the Northwest were stacking their muskets, and when some men began weeping, Brock looked away so as not to add to their shame.

"Get that thing down, and up with the Union Jack," Proctor ordered.

"Captain Nelles, where is the guardhouse?" Brock asked.

Tecumseh and Paxinos broke off to find the storehouse while Westlake fell back beside Nelles. Parrish and Lapointe stumbled in a few seconds afterward.

"I can show you the guardhouse, sir," Westlake suggested, "since Parrish and I lived there for a few days."

Nelles pointed forward and Westlake jogged a few steps.

"Well, well, it's Mr. Westlake." Brock peered down from his horse. "I should've known that you'd show up. You and Parrish had orders to stay with your uncle at the battery. Problems with discipline, have we?"

"My orders were to stay with Mr. Westlake, sir." As soon as the words were out of his mouth, Parrish knew he had spoken out of turn. Through all the meetings and all the talk, Parrish had remained safe by keeping quiet, just like he and Ned had originally planned. Now he'd drawn attention to himself by opening his mouth.

"And you, Mr. Parrish, you look a disgrace." The clothes Parrish wore were still covered in the mud from his fall at the riverbank.

"Yes, sir. A proper disgrace I am, sir." Parrish grinned and stared at the ground.

"Danny Lapointe was with us at Fort Mackinac," Westlake said. "My uncle's cannons were shooting directly over the Lapointe farm. I had to warn them."

"And the Captain did the expected. He blew up my house. Without Johnny's warning, my family would be dead," Lapointe added.

"This is Danny Lapointe, sir," Westlake said.

"Thanks for your assistance at Michilimackinac, Mr. Lapointe. I'm grateful." Brock reached down and clasped his hand.

"And I'm sorry about your house, Lapointe. Not as good a shot as I used to be." Moore had limped unnoticed through the gates behind them. "But I'll help your family rebuild. On that, you have my word." He gave Lapointe his hand.

"By heaven, I've got half of Elizabeth's family in Fort Detroit. Your mother would have my head for it, if she knew." Brock laughed. "Did you find your informant, Mr. Westlake?"

"Unfortunately, Stone died before we could make him tell us, but he didn't deny that his man was someone inside York garrison, sir."

"Did you kill him, Mr. Westlake?" Brock asked.

"He shot at me first, sir." Westlake avoided the question, preferring to leave out Mary's part of the story. "You might say that Mr. Stone was put through the mill." He grinned, watching for Lapointe's reaction.

"Your jokes are so awful," his friend grimaced.

They had now reached the guardhouse, where a single American sentry stood at attention, not sure what to do in such august company. He remained still except for his eyes, which floated from officer to officer in turn.

"You are relieved, soldier," Proctor ordered. "Keys." He held out his hand as the startled sentry began to fumble. Before Brock dismounted, Parrish stepped forward and accepted the guard's musket. Proctor unlocked the front door and stood to one side, to give Brock the pleasure of opening it.

The reek of urine wafting through the doorway reminded Westlake of his time spent in this same prison. He glanced back at Parrish, remembering that the last time they were here had been with Ned. His heart quickened at the thought and he stepped back from the door, choosing instead to simply peer inside.

"Good to see you again, Sergeant Stamp. You were not mistreated, were you?" Brock asked. He took the keys from Proctor and opened the cell door.

"No, sir. Thank you for getting me out. Everything went as planned,

I can see." Stamp stepped back and pointed to a figure hunched in the corner. "There's your man from the Canard bridge, sir."

"John Dean, my name's General Isaac Brock. It's an honor to serve in the same army with you. I've come to take you home." Brock offered his hand, and Dean struggled to stand up with his broken arm still in a sling. They stepped outside into the light.

"Thank you, sir." Dean squinted in the sharp sunshine. "I've been listening to the shelling, praying it didn't hit the guardhouse," he confessed with a smile.

Proctor stepped forward and shook Dean's hand too. "I'm Colonel Proctor ... a brave thing you and Hancock did at that bridge. One for the history books, I think." This was as amiable as Westlake had ever seen Proctor behave.

Dean nodded a thank you, but he was thinking about his friend James Hancock, who had died of his wounds in the same action at the Canard River Bridge. He looked away so that his moistened eyes would not betray his emotions. When he raised his head again, his face broke into a broad grin. "Jonathan Westlake, good to see you ... and the Captain too, like old times, eh?" He waved at Parrish, and Moore circled his arm around Dean's shoulders.

Proctor shook his head and asked, "You know this man, Westlake?"

"Of course, sir," Dean replied. "I hope to enter the fur trade myself one day."

Nichols had approached during the celebration. "The list of captured supplies you wanted, sir." He handed several pages to Brock. "Apparently, there *are* more goods at the River Raison. And as you ordered, they are included in the surrender documents, sir."

"Gunpowder, forty-five barrels. Thirty-nine cannons with shot. Plus two thousand five hundred muskets." The excitement in Brock's voice rose with each item. "By God, now we can wage war. No more militiamen with pitchforks: they'll have real weapons."

His elation soon had Westlake grinning along with the others.

Brock turned the page. The Provincial Marine had captured numerous small craft on the river, and most importantly a brig called the *Adams*. Lake Erie would thus be in his hands for some time to come.

Brock was smiling, and everyone was watching him. "This is excellent, gentlemen."

"The balance, sir, of the supplies at the River Raison." Nelles handed him another page.

The list contained the goods that Hull had been trying to bring into the fort for weeks, supplies for his entire army: three hundred head of cattle and more than a hundred pack animals carrying provisions, tools, and other stores. Brock could barely speak as he now proclaimed that the victory had secured the future of Upper Canada, at least for the time being.

Another voice from Westlake's past spoke up behind him. "I am sorry to interrupt, but General Hull is ill and would appreciate a visit when you have time, sir." Westlake turned to see a short, well-turned-out man come to attention and offer him a sharp salute.

"Of course." Brock returned the salute, "Take us to him."

"Perhaps I should introduce you, sir," Westlake said. "This is Captain Daniel Jackson of the U.S. 4th Infantry."

Proctor frowned, glancing at Captain Moore.

Brock reached out and shook Jackson's hand. Westlake continued, "I promised to introduce you to him one day."

"Got your furs, Mr. Westlake? You look a sight warmer today than the last time I saw you." Jackson grinned.

"And you're now at the wrong end of the cannon," Westlake replied.

Jackson ignored the comment and continued. "From your back I remembered where I first saw you … at Prophet's Town, carrying an Indian child."

"Out of the clutches of Sergeant Harris and his village-burning bastards."

"Perhaps not the finest day for the 4th Infantry," Jackson conceded.

"They're all dead," Westlake said in anger. "Trimble, Haggard, Porter, and even your rotten Sergeant Harris, all dead. And your friends Wagg and Stone have also been dispatched to whatever hell awaits them."

Jackson turned ashen. Stunned by the change in events, he had nothing else to say.

Brock broke the tension. "Captain Nelles, make ready to leave. After my visit with General Hull, our work here is done." Jackson turned to lead Brock and Nichols away.

Sergeant Stamp supported Dean under his good arm as they made their way to the fort's gates, where Ensign Simpson eagerly awaited Stamp's story about the fake note detailing Indian hordes descending from Fort Mackinac and then his intentional capture. Westlake watched them and he suspected the ensign would be writing lots of stories home to England.

"I should get home now, Johnny. See you there soon." Lapointe jogged off.

Nelles gave Westlake's sleeve a tug. Once they were away from the crowd, he said quietly, "General Brock has expressed a desire that you accompany us, for what purpose I can't say." He looked back toward Parrish, who was lumbering along behind them. "And I guess he'd better come too. Did you yourself kill all those men you mentioned?"

Westlake recalled the image of Mary stabbing through Stone's flesh and then realized there would have to be one more guest traveling back to Maple Hill. He remembered Harris shooting Porter in the stomach, which reminded him of knifing Trimble and slicing Haggard's throat, and finally killing Harris himself. It was like reliving a nightmare, then he felt an arm around his shoulders.

"Westlake, are you alright?" Nelles said. "You've gone rather pale,"

"No, I didn't kill all of them, sir, but I do feel a little shaky."

"When we started this campaign, you said that you wanted to make a difference somehow. So how do you feel today?"

"It's been a lot of miles—several thousand, I suppose. Paxinos, Lapointe, Parrish, and I, all of us *have* made a difference. I've learned from the general himself that we here in the Canadas must fight for our own interests; no one else is going to do it for us."

"Then you've come a long way." Nelles sighed. "You've certainly made your mark with General Brock."

The group of officers soon went their separate ways, leaving Proctor and Moore standing alone outside the guardhouse. "Every time we meet someone new, they already seem to know your nephew. Just how is that, George? What's the bloody secret? Who the hell is he?" Proctor brushed a mosquito away from his ear.

Moore shook his head, reflecting how not a man was lost in the taking of Detroit. What a victory. He glanced up at the blue August sky and sighed. Colonel Henry Proctor, being now in charge of the entire Old Northwest and its lakes, would have to be told the truth.

"Henry, I've known you a long time and I consider you my friend, but sometimes you can be bloody thick. My nephew, Jonathan Westlake, is Brock's agent."

HISTORICAL NOTE

THE EVENTS AT TIPPECANOE, Fort Mackinac, and Fort Detroit happened much as described. Chapter 2 opens with natives burning down a settler's home on disputed land and finishes with Governor Harrison burning down the Indian settlement Prophet's Town in retaliation. Although the casualties at Tippecanoe were much in native favor, Harrison rode the myth of his victory all the way to the presidency on the slogan "Tippecanoe and Tyler too." Years later, Harrison was still being asked why his camp had not dug trenches, or built any defensive breastworks. His reply remained that he never had the implements to do so, though it seems hard to believe this was the case. The regular army blamed the militia for many things, so I have the fictional Sergeant Harris and his boys convince the militia to ditch their tools. Tecumseh never forgave the American army for what it did to his home, and many historians today feel that the real opening of the War of 1812 was the Battle of Tippecanoe fought in that cold drizzle of November 1811.

In late February 1812, four months before war was declared, Brock sent a secret courier named Francis Rheaume to find Chief Robert Dickson, a Scotsman who had become a Sioux chieftain. Brock knew that he could not win a war without the natives on side and that the only way they might join him was if he won an early victory. It was critical, therefore, that Dickson take his warriors to assist Captain Roberts in the capture of Fort Mackinac. However, history records that Dickson was already moving north when Rheaume caught up with him. This circumstance was the inspiration for *Brock's Agent* and for the creation of Jonathan Westlake, our fictional protagonist. Would Brock let the opening of the war depend on just one courier? Surely he would have sent a backup courier, in case Rheaume did not survive the journey. In fact, Rheaume was captured and strip-searched at Fort Dearborn [Chicago]. There he stood on Brock's note, hidden in his boot, much the same as Westlake imitated.

The attack on Fort Mackinac was an incredible feat of determination, dragging that cannon up the three-mile hill, through the bush, in the dark. While there are minor variations in the numbers, it cannot be denied that fur traders and natives played a large part alongside the assaulting forces. One can still visit Fort St. Joseph and Fort Mackinac today, so try walking from the landing beach up through the center of the island, to the very spot where Roberts's cannon loomed over the fort. Lieutenant Hanks clearly made the right decision in surrendering to the British, and thus prevented a massacre. Like many other events in the War of 1812, the reader may find it hard to believe that the American government failed to tell Hanks that war had already been declared.

This failure to communicate led to another disaster, and that was the capture of the schooner *Cuyahoga* with all of Hull's personal papers on board. Imagine his disbelief when at two o'clock in the morning a dispatch arrives to tell him that war had been declared two weeks previously, but that the war department entrusted his war notice to the post office for delivery. By the time Hull knows he's in a war, the *Cuyahoga* has already sailed and it's too late.

The Battle of Brownstown Creek, where Tecumseh put chase to a superior force almost ten times his numbers, is surely one of the greatest victories for the Indians during the entire war. For the British, it was imperative that Hull should not resupply Fort Detroit, and Tecumseh carried out his task to perfection. At Brownstown, again Hull lost all his secret papers to the enemy.

Near the beginning of the war, the one bright moment for the U.S. 4th Infantry occurred at the Battle of Maguaga, where Lieutenant Colonel Miller defeated a combined British force of regulars, militia, and natives under the commands of Major Adam Muir and Tecumseh. Miller's problem was lack of follow-through due to his illness, the miserable weather, and an excess of caution. In the end, after winning the battle, the American army retreated to Fort Detroit while their vital supplies remained at the Raison River.

There was not much Brock did not know about Hull's strengths and weaknesses by the time the fall of Detroit took place on August 16. There were few casualties on either side, and Brock played his game of bluff to ensure victory. Tecumseh's ruse of having warriors pass by the same gap in the forest, only to return and run past again, is a true story. Also true is that the unfortunate Lieutenant Hanks was cut in half by a bouncing cannon ball, thus spraying him around the room. An excellent popular history of the time can be found in Pierre Berton's *The Invasion of Canada* and I recommend reading it.

Brock's opening moves, even before the war began, secured Upper Canada for the duration of 1812. He seized thousands of square miles of territory and, more important, re-equipped his army, militia, and navy. He showed the civilian populace and a timid British government that if Upper Canadians were to act in their own interest, the province could be defended. Also, at least for the war's duration, the fur trade was back under Canadian control.

Nothing can compare, however, to the fact of bringing the natives on side with these early victories. To the British advantage, the tribes evened out the numbers somewhat and also terrified the Americans they fought. What many consider to be Canada's war of independence could not have been won without them.

With respect to Brock's love life, as far as I can find, there is only correspondence with his brother that speaks of a girlfriend. While he loved to read and dance, there is no record of an affair with any married woman. In life, he remained a bachelor until his death.

While Brock and Tecumseh are revered today, Hull's name is not held in high esteem. American historians have given him a less than favorable review. It should be remembered that he was saddled with a disorganized war department in Washington and a poisonous bunch of subordinate officers. If you go Fort Amherstburg today, renamed Fort Malden, it is easy to imagine the failure of any forces attacking without cannon. Hull was therefore right to delay his attack.

It is a wonderful treat to stand at the fort's gates, where Brock once stood. Grosse Ile, the island in the middle of the river, appears in basically the same condition today as when he viewed it. What were his thoughts when he looked across to Grosse Ile? To invade or not invade? The gamble was enormous.

Of Fort Detroit's surrender, it is difficult to say for sure that Hull could have prevailed against Brock's cannon and native allies. My guess is that Hull saved Detroit from a massacre of historical proportions, yet he faced a court martial whose presiding judge, Major General Dearborn, was the same man who had failed to launch his diversionary attack on Niagara as promised. Hull was convicted of cowardice and sentenced to be shot, only to be subsequently pardoned by the president.

Generally speaking, except for Brock's and Hull's high commands, most combatants on both sides in *Brock's Agent* are fictional, including Captain Nelles and Captain Jackson. Of course, Jonathan Westlake, Paxinos, Parrish, Lapointe, and their families are fictional characters too, as well as Wagg, Mary, Hicks, and Stone.

The War of 1812, while being an interesting sideshow to the contemporary struggle with Napoleon, was of paramount importance to North American interests. Canadian fur traders wanted to maintain their business, the natives wanted a buffer state, and British North America, one day to be Canada, was fighting for its survival as an independent entity. Of course, the Americans wanted to crush all three. To say that everyone would be surprised at the war's outcome is an understatement.

As for Westlake and Parrish, you can be sure they will journey again into the heart of the United States.

Readers can post a note on my website at www.tomtaylor.ca, where I will try to answer any of your questions.